# Snowflake's Inn

# Snowflake's Inn

BRYN BYRNES

HOMER PASS
ROMANCE
BOOK ONE

Bryn Byrnes Author
P.O. Box 30303
Acushnet, MA  02743
info@brynbyrnes.com

Visit our website at www.brynbyrnes.com

Cover design/art manipulation: Lynn Andreozzi
Stock photography and art by Bintang69/Shutterstock, Creative Travel Projects/ Shutterstock, PeopleImages/Shutterstock, CO Leong/Shutterstock, Tijana87/ iStock by Getty Images, lakalla/depositphotos, and sayanna/depositphotos
Interior design: David Wood

Paperback ISBN 979-8-9997590-1-6
eBook ISBN 979-8-9997590-2-3

First Addition November 2025

Where to begin? Snowflake's Inn began as a NaNoWriMo project in November 2023. I originally intended it as a light-hearted Christmas rom-com, you know, the kind you see on that greeting card channel. But as I continued to write, my characters had much more to say and much more complex histories to untangle before I could give them the happy ending they deserved.

I've noticed many authors now include playlists for readers to enjoy while reading. Songs that inspired them while they wrote, or simply songs they enjoyed that fit the overall mood of their book. I am not creative in that way usually, but I would be remiss if I did not acknowledge the motivation I received from a couple of songs, Visiting Hours by Ed Sheeran and I Am Not Okay by Jellyroll. IFYKYK.

These characters wormed their way into my heart and stuck with me through long periods of writer's block and self-doubt. Amber, Hunter, and all the rest of the folks from Homer Pass; thank you, we made it! I hope you love these people as much as I do. I can't wait to get started on the next romance brewing in Homer Pass.

Until then, take care of them for me, would you please?

**Disclaimer:** Snowflake's Inn is a full-length, standalone novel. And while it does tick all the boxes you would expect; spicy, Christmas, small-town, single-dad, second-chance romance with a guaranteed HEA, it also contains deep emotional themes that will pull at the heartstrings. This story has a depth beyond a simple holiday read.

**Content Warning:** Be advised that this novel is for mature audiences and deals with sensitive subjects including infidelity, miscarriage and death of a spouse. Reader discretion is advised.

# Also by Bryn Byrnes

## A Supreme Kind of Love

A Supreme Kind of Love is the debut novel by author Bryn Byrnes. A contemporary romance about lawyers falling in love and then struggling to make all work while pursuing their careers. It's steamy, sweet, heart wrenching, frustrating, and you might even find a chuckle along the way. There's nothing quite like falling in love at Christmas time, but can that love survive all the fireworks on the way to the Fourth of July?

Alexis Chambers is an enigma begging to be solved. Cooly proficient in all that she does and singularly driven to succeed. She hides behind business suits purposely designed to obscure her beauty. Ever the ice princess, she keeps everyone at arm's length. Love was no longer a consideration for Alexis Chambers, not a part of the plan. It was an inconvenience that should be avoided.

Jake Douglas is a dangerous man, dangerous for Alexis, that is. Dark, penetrating eyes that will peer into the depth of your soul if you let them. After being betrayed by his first true love, no women are part of his plan.

He is also way off limits. He's her biggest obstacle to making her way to the top of the corporate ladder and she's already engaged. He is not part of her plan.

A broken engagement. A bottle of wine. Blazing hot sexual chemistry. Plans just might have to change.

Paperback https://www.amazon.com/dp/B0BPVFZMVM
eBook https://www.amazon.com/dp/B0BNWL2QGB

# Contents

*Love does not begin and end the way we seem to think it does. Love is a battle, love is a war; love is growing up.*

James Baldwin

# Prologue

## Amber

I hate winter. The charcoal gray skies that warn of miserable weather to come. The bitter icy winds that cut you to the core and make you believe you'll never get warm again. Every time I see a snowflake, I want to run for home.

## Six years ago

I stared down at the white plastic stick in my hands. Two pink lines stared back at me.

I continued to stare. There continued to be two pink lines.

I was pregnant.

Tears of joy fell, and I knew I was grinning like a hyena. My cheeks hurt; I was smiling so wide. A shuddering breath escaped my lungs as an immense feeling of relief filled every pore in my body.

We were finally going to be "a proper family," as Lance liked to call it. When nothing happened after the first year and a half, we did all the tests, and they all came back saying everything seemed fine. Everyone told us we just needed to relax and enjoy the process. More than one medical professional told us that stress gets in the way of success.

And I'd definitely felt the stress. I blamed myself for the failure even though everyone kept telling me it wasn't my fault. Except for Lance. He blamed me. At first it was subtle, loosen up and have fun, he'd say, like that was our key to success. Maybe if he'd made it fun, I would have. I didn't marry him because of our intense sexual chemistry.

Our sex life had never been particularly enjoyable. Lance was what I'd call a lazy lover. Also known as selfish. If you asked him, things were just fine. He always finished, usually at a pace that was similar to the hundred-meter dash. His best trait was his recovery. The man could be ready to go again faster than anyone I've ever been with. Even at thirty, he could be almost instantaneously hard again. The problem was I rarely got to experience this talent, certainly not for my benefit. The man might have given me one orgasm, without my help, in the entire six plus years we were together.

None of that had ever really mattered to me. I loved Lance because he was dependable. His yes was always a yes, and no was a no. He was meticulous, deliberating all options before making a decision. It was a perfect match. I hated impulsive behavior. Great sex was not high on my list of must-haves.

To say he was financially stable was a laughable understatement. While I certainly didn't marry him for his money, it was a pleasant change not to have to worry about whether the bills would all be paid at the end of the month. Markedly different from my childhood. Though his family didn't exactly welcome me with open arms, he had defended me and forced them to accept me. It made me feel like I was truly the one he wanted. He chose me. He was loyal to me, and I was loyal to him.

A wave of nausea washed over me, and I dropped the test strip onto the vanity and fell to my knees in front of the toilet. This had been my spot at least twice a morning for the previous two weeks, though I wasn't sure the twist of my insides resulted from morning sickness and not the result of the potent emotions that flooded my brain and gut.

Fortunately, the churning in my stomach passed without me puking my guts out. I pulled myself up and turned around to sit on the toilet. It was the most convenient seat available while I tried to sort through the bevy of thoughts that raced through my mind.

Things between us had shifted in the last year. Lance had been more distant, and our sex life had devolved into a duty and a chore. He made even less effort in meeting my needs, and the little things he used to do, like bring me flowers, and make sure we had a date night once a week, disappeared entirely.

Romance, affection, it wasn't even a suggestion. I needed to do my duty. It wasn't about fun. It wasn't about intimacy. It was responsibility. I was to lie down, spread my legs or bend over so he could "give me an injection" before he headed to work. I had finally been successfully inoculated. At least I had eight positive pregnancy tests to base my assumption on.

Maybe, just maybe, he'd return to the charming man I fell in love with. The one that made me feel valued and appreciated.

I loved my job as a teacher. Making a difference in kid's lives was far more important to me than making money. Fortunately, Lance's family's wealth made it much more workable for me than if I had to make it on my own. Some people might say I was his trophy wife. I suppose I just accepted the role. He never complained about my minimal contribution to the family finances. All the women in our friend group were busy climbing the corporate ladder, chasing seven-figure salaries, or 'stay-at-home moms', volunteering at charities. Lance never seemed to mind I didn't fit into those boxes. Well, not until recently.

With a deep breath and a slow exhale, I pushed away all the stress and rejection I was probably just imagining. I'd worked on this in therapy before. The counselor suggested it had something to do with blaming myself for my father abandoning us. Perhaps I wasn't completely free of the ghosts from my past after all.

This was a jubilant occasion. Something we'd both wanted for so long, and I had to believe that I'd get my husband back once he heard the news.

We would begin planning for the joyful arrival of our first child and the start of the family we've both longed for. I wouldn't be the disappointment I felt like. This deserved a celebration.

And that's what we'd have.

Lance had shared when he left that morning that he'd be working late. Recently, he'd been doing that more and more. I could call the office and ask him not to stay late. Making him a romantic dinner to share the news could work, but he'd probably press me for answers on why I wanted him home. And if I didn't give him an answer, he might not come at all, and if he did, he'd likely be upset I'd forced him to change his plans.

When we first got together, I dropped by all the time to surprise him, and it usually ended up with me naked. It was one of the few adventurous parts of our sex life. I didn't think he would mind my dropping by the office to share this news and rekindle that spark. It had been a couple of years, so I was sure he'd truly be surprised. Maybe he'll see that the spontaneity he thinks I've lost still lives.

With happiness and excitement I hadn't felt in a long time, I searched through my drawers and found his favorite lingerie. A deep blue corset and panty set with matching garters and stockings. I paired it with a pair of peep-toe stilettos; Lord knows I wouldn't be wearing five-inch heels much until after the pregnancy.

I wrapped myself in my long wool coat and put a scarf around my neck for extra warmth. I tucked one of the positive test sticks into a coat pocket. I couldn't wait to see his expression when I handed it to him.

I made a quick stop at the grocery store and picked up a bottle of sparkling grape juice. Even though I knew a taste of champagne wouldn't be the end of the world, I didn't want to make excuses on the very first day I knew I was going to be a mom.

At that time of night, parking wasn't a problem, and I found a spot right in front of the building. I locked up my SUV and pushed through the revolving door that led to the lobby of Tabor Tower, the headquarters of Lance's family's real estate empire. Their company stood for the epitome of wealth and luxury, and they were ruthless once they set their sights on something.

They'd bought whole towns, forcing out families that had lived there for generations just to level it and build an exclusive getaway for the uber-wealthy. Ski resorts, unrivaled championship golf courses, seaside retreats, gated communities. You name it, they'd done it. Frankly, their methods and their lack of conscience made me sick, but I had no control over it. My only hope was someday, when my bastard of a father-in-law stepped down, maybe I could convince Lance to be the man I knew he could be.

Herb, the night security guard, who I think has worked here a hundred years, smiled up at me from behind the reception desk. "Good evening, Mrs. Tabor. Is Mr. Tabor expecting you? It's been quite a while since I've seen you here at this time of night."

"It has, Herb, and I've missed you. Lance isn't expecting me, but I've got some big news. I'd like it to be a surprise." I waved the bottle of grape juice disguised in a paper bag so he could see it, to make my point.

His brows rose, and his smile widened. "Well, whatever it is, congratulations, and I'll pretend I didn't see you."

"Thank you, Herb. I really appreciate it."

"Any time. Any time," he said, waving me on with a broad smile and a sparkle in his eyes.

I tapped my foot nervously as the elevator made its way to the top floor. I knew it was just me, but it seemed to take forever. Finally, after the longest ride of my life, the doors slid open to the top floor and the executive suites of the Tabor Group Properties.

Lance's office was down to the left, just a few steps away from the exorbitantly large office suite that belonged to his father. His great-grandfather started the company nearly at the same time Denver was founded. It was a much more modest firm then, dealing in local land deals, grazing rights for ranchers and the occasional mining claim.

Lance's father made it what it was now. An icon of conspicuous consumption and cutthroat practices.

The only space still lit was Lance's office and reception area. His office door was closed, and the privacy glass was activated, something I'd never seen him do before, but perhaps he had an important meeting that afternoon and had just forgotten to switch it back. Oddly, his assistant, Gina, was still there too as her purse sat in her chair and her coat was slung over the back of it.

The ball of anxiety in my stomach was right back where it had been a few hours before. Nothing about those circumstances felt right. My instinct told me to turn around and leave, but my mind disregarded the warning. There was no way I would leave any room for doubt.

I had never questioned whether Lance was being honest with me. I didn't think I had a reason to. If my instincts were right, that wouldn't be the case anymore. My mind was jumping to conclusions. And if I was right, the life I thought I was living was going to be a lie.

I hesitated, putting my ear to the door. I knew that was pointless. The office was soundproof, so none of their dealings could be overheard by anyone who didn't need to know. They even swept their offices regularly for listening devices like they were the freaking CIA.

When I put my hand on the doorknob. I wasn't surprised to find it locked. Lance would never be so careless as to be accidentally discovered. What I'm sure he wasn't counting on was my showing up and having a keycard. He probably didn't even remember giving me one, but way back, when I was a regular late-night visitor, he gave me one and I still had it tucked safely in my purse. I was very glad I had decided not to leave it in the car.

My hands were shaking as I rooted around trying to find the damn thing. After what seemed like an eternity, I finally found it. With a deep steadying breath, I placed it over the sensor above the handle. With a beep, beep and a flash of light, I heard the click of the lock disengaging. I pushed open the door.

I was assaulted with a view of my husband's bare ass at the end of his desk and a pair of stocking-clad legs waving in the air over his shoulders.

My head spun, and all I could hear was the erratic pounding of my heart in my chest. One quivering hand covered my gaping mouth; the other protectively covered my stomach. A million thoughts collided with one another as my mind fought to process the manifestation of my worst nightmare.

That was my husband. That was my spot at the end of the desk. Those were supposed to be my stocking-clad legs.

How dare she?

How dare he?

They were so caught up in their carnality that they didn't even notice me until I screamed.

I didn't recognize the sounds that came from my mouth. They may or may not have been words, but in my mind, I was spewing a string of expletives the likes of which I had never uttered before. I knew for a fact that it was the first time I'd ever called someone the "C" word, and I'll give you a hint; it wasn't directed at Gina, though I had a few choice words for her too.

Lance had the gall to stand there and stare at me with an utterly blank expression. He didn't show the slightest hint of remorse or guilt. More like dispassionate disinterest.

That was the knife twisting in my chest. The thing that sent me completely over the edge. He didn't care about me at all. I felt the bile rise in my throat, and somehow, I was lucid enough to refuse to give them the satisfaction of seeing me break.

Rage was the only option.

I don't remember deciding to hurl the bottle in his direction, but I recall his look of terror as it tumbled end over end at his head with surprising velocity. It was by sheer bad luck that he ducked at the last second, and it flew past his ear. A split second later, with a mighty crash, it slammed into the huge plate-glass window behind him. It cracked into a spiderweb of a million pieces spiraling out from where the now shattered bottle had hit.

It was then that Gina screamed, and Lance called me something to the tune of psycho bitch, but I can't be sure because I was already turning away and heading for the elevators. I don't know if he tried to come after me, but I do know I was surprisingly fast running down the hall in my five-inch heels.

I do know that when the window shattered, a bevy of alarms sounded in the building, and I had to run down fourteen flights of stairs. I didn't keep my heels on for that. I do know that I've never seen a greater look of concern from a man than I received from Herb when I burst from the fire stairs and ran across the lobby.

"What's the matter, Amber?" he yelled, and for reasons I'm still uncertain of, I stopped and answered him.

"My husband is a cheating asshole who was up there fucking his secretary." I whipped open my coat, exposing the very scant corset set I had on underneath to a man who was probably dangerously old to be seeing something like that.

I am truly thankful he didn't go into cardiac arrest. Though the fire department was pulling up to the building at that very moment, he probably would have received prompt medical attention if he'd needed it.

"He could have had this, but he decided he'd rather have that mousy little slut Gina. I'm sorry, Herb. I might have broken a window when I threw the bottle of sparkling grape juice at his head. You can charge it to his account."

With that, I turned and continued across the lobby, leaving a gob smacked Herb behind, and passing the Denver FD on their way in.

I made it to my car and leaned my head against the door. Up to that point, I hadn't shed a tear. I had been too damn mad, but now the gravity of my circumstances hit me like that fucking bottle should have hit Lance.

I was pregnant. I was about to get divorced. I was going to be a single mother and back to a life of living on the edge, if not completely consumed by poverty. What in fucking hell was I going to do?

I reached into my coat pocket and pulled out my car keys. I realized the test stick I was going to show Lance was gone. It must have fallen out at some point, but I didn't care. I was going to have a good cry, but I wouldn't do it sitting in front of this building. Besides, I wasn't entirely sure I wasn't going to get arrested for what happened to that window, and there was no way in hell I was getting a mug shot taken in what I was wearing.

I made it home through the tears and packed a bag. I probably should have gone to a hotel for the night, but I had one friend I could rely on. And it would probably be best if I weren't alone. Patty would know what to do, and through tear-clouded vision I made my way in a trance, through the streets of Denver until I found myself knocking on her door.

The confusion on her face when she opened the door transitioned quickly to a smirk as she looked me up and down. It was then that I realized I hadn't changed, and my coat was unbuttoned.

"Amber," she greeted me, clearly surprised, but seemingly pleased to see me. "You know I'm always happy to see you, but if you've shown up at my door at midnight to seduce me, I'm really sorry. You know I only like the D. I mean we did have that one night in college, but there was a lot of alcohol involved…"

I tried to laugh, because that was my Patty. We were always there to pick each other up when things got bad. And she could always make me laugh, but all I could manage was a half-snort that came out as a giant snot bubble before body-wracking sobs overtook me again.

"Oh, honey," she said, wrapping me in her arms. She pulled me through the door and looked down, noticing the suitcase I was rolling behind me. Her lips pressed together into a thin line, and her brow furrowed. She took the case from my hand and set it against the wall before guiding me into her living room.

The room was so homey and lived-in compared to my sterile white mausoleum of a house. She led me over to an overstuffed armchair in a mauve and cerulean patterned fabric that I loved.

"Are you okay for a minute?" she asked. I nodded and moved my lips into what I hoped looked at least a bit like a smile. From her scrunched forehead and frown, I gathered I hadn't succeeded. "Okay," she said on a heavy sigh. "I'll be right back."

A few minutes later she returned carrying a pair of leggings, an oversized sweatshirt, a bottle of wine, two glasses and a pint of ice cream with a spoon sticking out of the top. "Now," she said, thrusting the clothes at me. "First you change, and then you can tell me all about it."

"Thanks," I mumbled, taking the clothes. I slipped off my coat and pulled the sweatshirt over the corset. At this point, I couldn't be bothered to take it off. I peeled off the stockings before pulling on the leggings and sinking back down onto the chair.

It took all I had to shut the waterworks down long enough to speak. "I'm so sorry for dumping my shit life on your lap."

"Stop," Patty said abruptly. "Don't you dare. You've always been there for me when I needed you. How many times in college did I land on your doorstep in the middle of the night?"

I shrugged. It had been a few times. I didn't keep track. Obviously.

"It was a lot." She locked me in her stare. "I've never admitted this to you before, but more than once I was ready to end it all. To just give up. I didn't want to go on anymore, and every time, every time, Amber, you picked me up. I am here today because you were there for me. I will always be there for you. You're my ride or die, and don't you ever doubt that. Ever."

"Okay," I muttered weakly.

She poured the wine and thrust a glass into my hand. "Based on your attire, I'm going to assume that seducing Lance didn't go exactly as you planned tonight.?"

I shook my head and looked longingly at the glass in my hand. I wanted to chug it down in a single gulp, but I had more than just myself to think about. "That's more or less half of it."

"Oh," she said, her voice rising along with one of her perfectly sculpted eyebrows. "What's the other half?"

"I'm pregnant." And before she could maul me with congratulatory hugs I did not want, I told every gory detail of what had happened to my life over the last six hours.

When I had finished, she sat in silence. I watched as her jaw flexed, and her fingers dug into the arm of the chair she was sitting in with enough force that they turned white with the pressure. "That fucking little…" She exhaled and poured herself more wine and took a large gulp. "Okay." She paused. "Hmm." Another longer pause as I watched her struggle for control. "So, what do you want to do?"

"Other than cut off his dick?" I asked, not entirely joking. "I don't know."

She choked on the mouthful of wine she'd just taken, and then wiped the dribble with her sleeve. "Oh, we are definitely going to hurt him, but only financially and emotionally. As tempting as it is, we can't go full-on Lorena Bobbitt. He's not worth the jail time. We're going to bleed him dry with child support. That's for sure, but what can we do that will hurt him the most?"

"No," I said, my stomach clenching into a knot. "I will not tell him about the baby. No way. He wants a family more than anything, and if he finds out, he'll gaslight me until I take him back. I don't trust myself right now not to let him back into my life. You know how charming he can be when he wants something."

The foot that hung over her crossed legs rotated in a rapid series of figure eights, and her fingers tapped out a furious beat on the arm of the chair. I could tell she was fighting back saying what she wanted to. An uneasy quiet lingered between us. "Fine. I won't push you on the child support." She hesitated for a moment. "For now." Her brows drew together in an impressive glare. "But there's got to be something we can do to punish him."

I thought for a moment, and the only thing I could think of was our house. He had chosen it, and it was his pride and joy. It had never truly felt like a home to me, but I knew if I could get it, it would drive him crazy. He hated losing. "I'll fight for the house," I said. I didn't really want it, but it was the best I could come up with.

"Good," Patty said, leaning back in her chair. "You can stay here tonight, but tomorrow morning we're going back home, and we'll have the locks changed by noon. If you're going to fight for it, you have to be there. And I'll be right beside you every fucking step of the way."

Just the thought of fighting Lance made me nauseous all over again. But I knew she was right. I would do this. I didn't have a choice.

# 1

# A Perfect Metaphor

## Amber

The view beyond my windshield was ominous. The clouds were so dark they were virtually black. They looked a lot more threatening than the 'flurries up to an inch' the meteorologist had predicted on the morning news. I knew that the weather was often different in the mountains than it was in Denver, but what lay ahead, that looked extreme.

I felt the tension build between my eyes and pinched the bridge of my nose. This was not what I needed today. I'd psyched myself up before I left. I needed this sale. I was going to get this sale. Those positive vibes had lasted about ten minutes.

Then, my mother called.

Every year. Several times a year. For the past five years, we have had the same discussion. *Why don't you just fly down to Florida? Families should be together for the holidays. I worry about you all alone.*

I should have just recorded the call and played it back. It would have saved her the time and energy it took to guilt-trip me, because that's exactly what it was.

I felt guilty; I couldn't just hop on a plane and go see my mother. She was my rock for the first twenty-five years of my life. Never more than a short drive away. Then, ten years ago, she and her husband retired to Florida. It was a choice, of course. They didn't have to move, but he suffered from severe arthritis and needed to be somewhere warm. I didn't resent her moving. I don't know, maybe I did just a little, but what I resented more was that at thirty-five I was still failing at being a financially independent adult.

The home I'd fought tooth and nail for in my divorce cost me more than the twenty-six-hundred-dollar mortgage payment. I was convinced that the stress and Lance's vitriol during the drawn-out legal process played a large part in losing my baby. I couldn't lose the house. I'd already lost enough, and the commission on the ten-million-dollar home I was showing today would not only make ends meet but give me a little cushion.

I ended the call with a promise to call tomorrow on Thanksgiving Day and to go to Orlando for Christmas, keeping my fingers crossed I could afford it.

It was only two in the afternoon when I pulled up in front of the home. The snow was intensifying, falling much heavier than the predicted flurries. The dark gray skies and swirling winds were a perfect metaphor for the tempest of stress I felt inside.

My mood was completely different when I left Denver in the morning. I was confident this showing would result in a sale. The home was exactly what my client had been searching for. Five bedrooms, virtually ski on and off from the backyard and zero through traffic in the neighborhood. The asking price was high, but they were prepared to make a full-price offer on the spot, which I was sure would be accepted. The house had been on the market for a year, and my connection with the listing realtor said they hadn't received an offer within five hundred thousand dollars of the asking price.

I greeted my client's the McKinnons, at the end of the driveway. As we were walking up the front walk, another family was leaving, having just seen the home. Not just another family but my ex-husband, Lance, and his new, very pregnant wife and child.

"What are you doing here?" Lance snapped as he spotted me coming toward him through the shin-deep flurries.

"I have a showing," I answered with all the professionalism I could muster. What I wanted to say was, none of your fucking business, you cheating asshole but - you know, not a good look to be the bitter ex-wife in front of clients. I also wanted to add a snarky comment about him spending daddy's money because he never earned a nickel on his own. The whole time we were together, it was all trust fund and getting success handed to him just because of his family name.

A humorless laugh escaped from his mouth in a cloud of steam into the frigid air. "That's right. I heard something about you trying to sell real estate. I didn't believe it, actually. How did the principled Amber Scott ever give up teaching inner-city kids for a career that might actually bring financial success? But then again, from what I hear, you're not much of an agent. I guess it's a good thing you never agreed to come to work for my family when you had the chance. You've always thought sales was beneath you."

I froze in place, stunned into stiffness by his hateful words. You'd think I was the one who had been caught cheating, ruining the family he claimed he wanted. Ironically, the woman standing next to him was bouncing a toddler with another one obviously due at any second. He'd gotten what he wanted anyway. Where the hell was karma?

Maybe I was lucky. He didn't look like he was a very attentive father. He couldn't be bothered to carry his daughter and give his very pregnant wife a break. I was snapped out of my momentary statuesque behavior by the clearing of a throat. "Perhaps we should get inside out of the snow and get this showing over before the weather gets any worse," Mr. McKinnon suggested.

"Oh… oh, of course," I stuttered, desperately trying to compose myself. I motioned them toward the door. Just as we passed Lance and his new family, he turned toward the listing agent, who was standing on the porch to greet us.

"Let the sellers know I'll have an offer sheet for them by the end of the day. I'm texting my lawyer as soon as I get in the car with the details."

My stomach sank and shriveled into a ball the size of an orange. I could only hope his offer was below asking and we still had a shot.

"Can I tell them what the offer is?" the agent asked.

Lance's mouth tipped up into a smile I knew well as his fuck you smile, and it was aimed directly at me. "Tell them eleven five, but we want this home, so if other offers come in, we want the option to revise. Am I making myself clear?"

"Yes, Mr. Tabor." The man could hardly contain his excitement. "Thank you."

Lance didn't even acknowledge the thanks. But that was just him. I would have been excited too if I were that realtor, but I wasn't. This wasn't the first time I'd ended up on the wrong side of a bidding war. The orange ball expanded into a watermelon-sized lump of stress, which turned into nausea as I realized I'd wasted fifty dollars' worth of gas driving out here for nothing. I knew I was fucked, and the commission I so desperately needed was lost. The next few moments confirmed it.

"Did that couple just offer eleven and a half million?" Mr. McKinnon asked.

I nodded as the listing agent verbalized confirmation. "More than a million over the asking price," he added just to pour salt in my already gaping wound.

The McKinnons turned toward me and began walking away from the stoop. "I was willing to go full asking price, Amber, because we liked the looks of this place and it checks all the boxes. You assured us we wouldn't end up in a bidding war because no one had come close to the asking price. It seems like you've wasted our time or maybe should have been a little more aggressive in getting us a showing because now we're late and I have no desire to waste any more time looking at a home I have no interest in buying."

"I'm so sorry, Mr. McKinnon. There are two new listings I can send you that just came on the market today." I did my best to disguise the pleading in my heart from leaking into my voice.

"Fine, but make sure they're still available before you do." His irritation was obvious, and I doubted I would be their realtor much longer.

With that, they brushed past me and disappeared into the snow, which had become so intense that my car at the end of the walkway was nearly invisible.

"Sorry about that," the agent offered as he locked the front door to the home. "That took me completely by surprise. Mr. Tabor didn't seem at all interested and kept commenting as we went through that he wouldn't even consider a full-price offer. In fact, before he and his wife walked out the door, he made it sound like they wouldn't be making an offer at all."

"That fucking asshole." I grumbled, apparently not just to myself. I've never thought of murdering anyone before, but at the moment if I had a gun I wouldn't have been able to stop myself from putting a bullet right between Lance's cheating, beady little eyes.

"Sounds like you've got a history with him."

I gifted the guy with a very unladylike snort. "You could say that. He's my ex-husband, and the bimbo he was with was the secretary I caught him fucking on his desk."

His open-mouthed expression summed it up perfectly, and I didn't wait around for more small talk as I turned and walked back to my now snow-covered car.

I rummaged through my back seat, which was a cluttered mess of files and whatnot, in search of my snow brush, but it was nowhere to be found.

The stinging in my eyes has nothing to do with the icy wind cutting through the valley. Running into Lance today hurt way more than it should. That was a blow I was not ready for. That slut was standing where I was supposed to be.

It had been over four years since our divorce was final. Over four years since I had seen his face. With Patty standing by me every step of the way, I had found the strength to fight for the house. I won, but being in that house all alone only served as a daily reminder of everything I'd lost. Seeing him here today with his new family made that loss only more vivid, more real.

A sob rocked my body, followed by a shiver, reminding me I was standing in the middle of the road in a blizzard. I pulled my canvas bag out of the backseat, and shut the door before sliding behind the wheel. Fortunately, I'd thought to bring a warm change of clothes. My professional-looking silk blouse and dress slacks were necessary for the showing but not what you wanted to be driving around the mountains wearing in the middle of a snowstorm. If I broke down, I'd freeze in a New York minute.

I pressed the heels of my hands against my eyes to push the tears still threatening to fall back where they belonged. My head throbbed, and I had a pain in the center of my chest. The ragged edges of my still-broken heart made their presence known again.

I thought I was over it. I thought I'd moved on.

Bastard. Why did he still affect me like that?

And at the rate the snow was falling, there would be a foot or more of it by the time I hit the highway back to Denver. I turned the key in the ignition. There was a brief whine as it fought to start in the cold. The engine revved to life, and I cranked the defroster up to high. I blew on my icy blue fingers while I waited for the heat to come up.

I wriggled out of my long wool dress coat, tossing it in the back. Slipping off my blouse, I folded it neatly before slipping on the turtleneck and heavy wool ski sweater I'd brought to change into. Normally, I would never dream of changing in my car, but it was covered with snow, so if I couldn't see out, I was confident no one could see in.

Next, I slipped out of my dress slacks, pulled on nice thick wool socks and lined leggings before lacing up my winter pac boots. They were heavy and clunky to drive in, but they were warm, and that's what mattered most to me. Betsy, my twelve-year-old SUV with nearly three hundred thousand miles on it, had her quirks. For instance, if the defogger was on, the heat on the floor was not. Today, a clear windshield was far more important than toasty toes.

When the fog on the inside of the windshield finally began to clear, I turned on the wipers. They screeched back and forth, leaving a thin layer of ice behind. After a few more minutes, the window cleared enough for me to start on my way home. Reaching over to the passenger seat, I pulled my CD folio out and shoved one in the deck. Betsy was far too old for Bluetooth or satellite radio, even if I could have afforded it.

One good thing about this snow, at least I'd have to focus on driving and wouldn't end up letting my thoughts wander. Two hours in a car was a long time to be alone with your thoughts. To be alone with the image of your ex-husband and his new wife; that would just be adding insult to injury, and I was sure the bastard had just spent eleven and a half million dollars just to spite me.

Was he still that mad at me for keeping the house? Surely sour grapes over losing a house in a divorce didn't warrant spending over twenty times that on another one just to deprive me of a commission? Why did Lance hate me so much? I just couldn't understand.

I put Betsy into drive and crept my way out of the exclusive neighborhood at the base of the resort. Already the snow had changed the landscape enough that I was having a hard time recognizing the landmarks I had made a note of on my way in here. And despite my best efforts to focus on my driving, images of the life Lance and I shared kept dancing in my vision.

# 2

# *Plowed*

## *Amber*

I wiped the tears from my eyes. Despite knowing I needed to focus on my driving, seeing Lance again had brought back all the hurt and regret I'd thought I'd moved past. The memories came uninvited, and I didn't know how long I was lost to them. It was a miracle I hadn't driven off the road with how distracted I'd been.

The snow got heavier and deeper, and Betsy's all-wheel drive had trouble keeping pace. My wipers were losing the battle; there were barely eighteen inches of clear windshield. If I could have found a place to pull over for the night, I would have, but the road was desolate, and, worse than that, I didn't see a familiar landmark the entire drive. The fact that I hadn't been paying attention, lost to memory as I had been, didn't help.

I chanced a quick check of the dashboard clock and realized that I'd been on the road for nearly an hour. I should have seen signs for I-70 by that point, as well as much more in the way of civilization. The bare minimum the state could have done was send out a damn plow.

The road was also much curvier than I remembered on my way there. It was not a night to get lost. It could have been fatal. As if on cue, I saw a hazy amber glow flashing up ahead. I sent up a quick prayer that it was a plow; at least I wouldn't have to deal with a foot of snow on the road.

My CD skipped. I reached up and gave the dashboard a good hard smack.

My world spun.

The rear hatch was in front of me, and I was facing where I had just been.

Then I was facing toward nine o'clock, and a steep mountain cliff filled my blurred vision. I yanked the wheel hard to the left. It did nothing.

I yanked the wheel in the other direction, and now I saw nothing but a swirling wall of snow as the slope of the mountain dropped away from me and into the abyss of what must be the valley below.

*Holy Shit.*

*I'm.*

*Going.*

*To die.*

Another half-turn had me looking back up the mountain face. With a thud and a thunk, I came to a jolting halt.

I could hear my heart thundering as my blood rushed to my head. The adrenaline rush had me thinking I had a mouthful of rusty nails. My fingers were still locked in a death grip around the steering wheel, and I took a much-needed breath.

It took a few seconds to believe that I'd actually stopped spinning. I chanced a quick look in the rearview mirror. My rear end was facing down the mountain, which meant I was on the wrong side of the road. I didn't think I was in danger of slipping backwards down the mountain, but my hood was sticking out into the oncoming lane of traffic. Before I had time to blink my eyes, the world disappeared in a tidal wave of yellow flashing snow. There was an ungodly crash of metal on metal. A microsecond later I was enveloped in an explosion of pillows.

Now I was facing the direction I had just come from. At least that's the direction I thought I was facing because after what happened I wasn't entirely sure I was still alive.

The sound of air brakes and the squeal of a heavy truck braking to an abrupt halt eased my fears of death but didn't help with my general sense of befuddlement. As the airbags deflated, I looked out my windshield to find an ocean of snow.

I was startled out of my stupor by an urgent rapping on my window. A large round face wearing a green hat with some kind of elk on it, covered in several days' worth of whiskers, and a stub of a cigar tightly gripped in the corner of its mouth stared back at me through the ice and fog on the glass.

"Are you okay?" The muffled, gravelly voice shouted.

I tried to roll down the window, but it didn't budge.

"Are you okay?" The voice repeated with slightly more urgency.

I nodded and then regained enough awareness to push open my door, requiring much more force than it should have. "Yes." I blinked at the stout figure of a man standing next to my car. "At least I think so." The icy wind and snow scratched at my face, and I shivered. "What… what happened?"

"I was going to ask you the same thing." The round little man replied with a tone of irritation that didn't sit very well with the very confused me.

"I don't know. I was driving, then I was spinning, and then you hit me." I took a deep breath to ground myself. "It all just happened so fast."

"Hmph" was all that came out of his mouth. From the sound of it, a mix of frustration and irritation. "Why on earth were you driving out here on a night like this?"

I didn't really want to get into that with a total stranger, but I couldn't exactly walk away and ignore him. "I was trying to get home. I had a meeting in Breckenridge, and the TV said this was just supposed to be flurries."

A wry smile crossed his face. "Wish I could get paid to be wrong. You must not have listened today then. I guess it turned into some kind of bomb cyclone. Supposed to snow like a bastard until tomorrow afternoon now, maybe four feet up here, they say. Where's home, hen? You might want to call 'em and tell 'em you're gonna be late."

"Denver. I'll be fine, thanks." Hen! who the hell…

"Denver? What in God's name are you doing here? Not only are you stuck in a snowbank, but you're headin' in the wrong direction."

"Trying to get to I- 70 that's what." I was done with this guy. I mean, I knew it wasn't his fault he plowed me into the side of the road, but I was tired, more than a little hungry at that point, and I wanted to get home and hide under my covers. It had been one of the worst days of my life, and I just wanted it over. "Just how far from the highway am I?"

The wry smile that had been on his face disappeared and was replaced by I wasn't sure what, maybe pity. "Lady, you're miles from Breckenridge, and in the wrong direction. You went south when you should have gone north."

My mouth must have gaped, and I snapped it shut, chewing on what he had just told me. I couldn't hold back anymore, and as much as I hated to be that woman, tears fell down my face, the freezing wind making them scrape my cheeks like shards of frigid glass. "What am I going to do?"

I was talking to myself and didn't realize I had actually spoken out loud.

He took a step backward and looked toward the front of my car. Shaking his head, "Well, you're not going anywhere in this thing. Even if I tried to pull you back onto the road, and that would break about a hundred rules, your front end is in terrible shape."

With that revelation, my eyes went wide, and one glance toward the hood of my car caused my tears to flow again.

He cleared his throat and tossed the cigar stub into the woods behind us. "Grab your things and get in the truck. I'll take you into town. There's a nice inn there, and you can get a hot drink and hopefully a bed for the night, maybe a bite to eat too."

"What about my car?" Unable to hide the desperation I was feeling.

"There's only one wrecker for miles, mine, and as I'm busy plowing, it's going to have to stay right there until tomorrow at the earliest. Don't worry, I'll mark it on my GPS so I'll know where to dig."

"Dig?!" Dogs could hear me a mile away; my pitch was so high.

"Don't worry, you're not the first, and you won't be the last. But get your things and let's go. It's freezing out here. I've got a job to do, and the county doesn't much like riders, but I'll be damned if I'm going to let you walk five miles into town in a blizzard like this. We'd be looking for your frozen dead body until spring." He smiled; likely that was his best attempt at comforting someone. It fell woefully short, but food, a hot drink and a bed to hide in sounded like the most I could hope for. I reached into the back and grabbed the canvas bag with my clothes and briefcase and waded through the snowbank.

"Thank you." I croaked through my emotionally choked throat.

"Don't you mention it. Just basic human decency. My mother would haunt me from her grave if I left you stranded." His eyes sparkled with mischief as he spoke. I couldn't help but offer a weak smile in return.

It wasn't until he was helping me up into the cab of the large dump truck with two huge plow blades affixed to winches in front that I noticed just what he was wearing. He had on a military surplus parka with fur around the hood. A neon yellow t-shirt that was more than well-worn and didn't quite cover his large and likely well-earned beer belly, a pair of black basketball shorts that fell just below his knees meeting the top of his fir-brimmed pack boots. He didn't have a white beard and red suit, but the phrase, a right jolly old elf, seemed appropriate.

He pulled himself into the cab. And gave me that same impish smile. He released the hand brake and jerked the truck into motion. "There's a turnaround just up ahead. We'll swing around there, and I'll have you warm and tucked in, in no time."

He might not look like the stereotypical white knight, but he certainly came to the rescue of this damsel in distress. Looking over at him, I repeated myself. "Thank you." I hoped he knew how much I meant it.

# 3

# *Welcome Holmes*

## *Hunter*

Tossing my phone onto the counter, I turned and walked out of the kitchen toward the front desk. I needed the business badly but didn't have the time to deal with a new guest at the moment. "Snow," I yelled, walking down the short hall toward the front desk.

"Dad, stop calling me that!" A glaring pair of sapphire-blue eyes that were darkening in anger by the second stared back at me. So much like her mother, I could hardly stand it. Her wavy blonde hair was tied up in a high ponytail, and her arms were crossed with a hip jutting to one side, which was the same as her mother did any time I said something stupidly male. I couldn't help the wide smile on my face, which caused her brow to furrow even more deeply.

"I'm so, so sorry I keep forgetting you're too mature for a pet name anymore."

"What do you want?" Her tone got the dad single cocked eyebrow. She might be a sassy sixteen-year-old, but she didn't give me attitude. She was still a little scared of her old man. "Sorry," she added, dripping with snark.

Okay, maybe not that scared.

"Leo just texted me, and apparently he's bringing in a stranded motorist. Do me a favor and shovel off the front steps. I've got to get these pies in the oven for tomorrow."

"DAD," she said in a tone that suggested I was asking her for a vital organ.

"Elizabeth." I let that hang for a moment, eyebrow still cocked.

"Fine," she said with a huff and requisite roll of the eyes.

God help me. How many more years did I have to suffer through adolescent girl attitudes?

"Thank you."

She turned and headed for the coat rack with every ounce of attitude she could muster.

Honestly, I couldn't blame her. It was a miserable night out. The blizzard was still raging. The little mountain village of Homer Pass was accustomed to such storms, but they were rarely easy. What choice did we have? We weren't bears and couldn't just hide in our caves until spring.

For my family, though, winter was a chance to stay afloat. This little inn barely broke even throughout the year, but if we had a good ski season, with lots of snow, maybe, just maybe, we'd survive one more year. One more year to keep Jenn's dream alive and food on her daughters' table.

I turned and faced the family photos that lined the shelf behind the reception desk. Placing two fingers to my lips, I kissed them and then gently pressed them to the photo of my wife and three daughters, all four of them smiling with the same golden blonde hair and sapphire blue eyes. *Help me Jenn. Show me the way. Give me some kind of sign that it will be alright.*

Walking back into the kitchen and looking at the total chaos, I heaved a deep sigh. Thank God my father taught me how to cook. I was not one of those dads who fed his kids mac and cheese from a box every night. Tomorrow there would be apple and pumpkin pie, fresh rolls and a turkey with all the fixings.

I gave the pumpkin filling a quick stir, ready to pour it into the pie shells when my phone rang again. My sister Janine's name came up on the screen. I wiped my hands on the front of my apron because that's what aprons were for and then pressed the button to put her on speaker.

"Grand Central Station," I said.

"It's snowing sideways out there and piling higher by the second. You can't possibly be that busy," she laughed. "No one is going to just happen to be driving to Homer Pass in a storm like this, and Snow told me you only had three reservations tonight."

"As a matter of fact, we have a guest on the way even as we speak."

"Seriously?" she asked. "Anyone out right now is either brave or crazy."

"This one might just be unlucky. Leo called, and I guess he found her stranded in a snowbank about five miles up the Breckenridge road."

"Wow. Maybe she was unlucky to end up in a snowbank, but I'd say she's pretty lucky Leo found her."

"True," I agreed. "As much as I'd love to chat about the weather, I've got three pies sitting on the counter in front of me that need to get into the oven for dinner tomorrow. Why did you call?" I know I sounded short with her, but I really didn't have time for a cozy catch-up.

"Rude," she drawled out. "I see you're as warm and fuzzy as ever."

"Janine," I snapped but stopped myself from going any further. I was trying to get back to the cheerful person I used to be. It was just so damn hard.

"I was just calling to find out what time dinner was tomorrow."

"Two o'clock. Just like always."

She laughed. "You're such a creature of habit. We tease Henry about holding to tradition, but you're nearly as bad."

My jaw clenched, and I sat the bowl of pie filling down on the counter with a little more force than I should have. Our older brother, Henry, was a sore subject for me. Mostly because he blamed me. The problem was I had never figured out what for. "We don't tease Henry about anything because he hasn't shown his face around here in three years. I haven't spoken to him in ten."

I could hear Janine's heavy sigh as if she were standing next to me. "I know, Hunter. I can't help it. I miss our brother. Maybe someday he'll come back."

"Maybe," I said, because despite everything I missed him too. "But if he does, he'd better have a long apology planned, otherwise I want nothing to do with him."

We were silent for a long time. My mind drifted back to my relationship with Henry, trying to find when the brother I looked up to changed into an angry, selfish ass.

## *Hunter—Age 10*

Are you okay?" I asked Henry. He was sitting all by himself at the end of the dugout bench.

The other kids were piling in behind me after we'd all done our pregame warm-ups. We were all excited. I was anyway. It was the biggest game I'd ever played in. If we won tonight, we'd be in first place with only two games left in the season. We would be junior baseball champs, and Principal Miller would call our names out during the morning announcements, and we'd get extra dessert for a week. It would also mean I was better at something than Josh Souza, my best friend.

That never happened.

He was the starting pitcher for the other team tonight. Maybe I'd even get a hit against him if I was lucky enough to go in as a sub later in the game. I'd end up in the outfield. That was okay. I really liked second base, but that was Henry's position. But the outfield was alright. I just wanted a chance to play. That would be so cool.

Henry just looked up at me and then back down at his cleats. It kinda looked like he'd been crying. He must have hurt himself cuz he was our best player. We really needed him tonight.

I sat down next to him and nudged his shoulder. "What's wrong, Henry?"

He threw his glove against the wall and spat out a mouthful of sunflower seeds on my cleats. "Leave me alone, Hunter. Just leave me alone."

"Hey," I yelled. "Why'd you do that? What did I do wrong?"

"Nothing, Hunter. Nothing at all. You never do anything wrong. Not according to Dad, and now I guess Coach thinks so too."

"I do plenty wrong. I get into trouble all the time. You know I do. And what's coach got to do with anything?"

"He benched me," he said, pounding his fist into the wooden bench, close enough to my leg that it made me flinch. "The biggest game ever, and I'm sitting out. I'm the best player on the team, and you know it. Everybody knows it, but that doesn't matter because he says I don't try hard enough. Effort counts more than talent, he says. I guess it must because you're starting at second tonight, not me, and you suck. We're going to lose tonight, and it will all be your fault."

He might as well have hit me with that fist because it sure felt like he did. He was my big brother, and we'd always been a team. He was never mean to me. Until now. It sucked. It really sucked.

I might not be as good as him, but I knew I didn't suck, and I did try. Really hard. "Screw you. Sit there and act like a baby if you want, but they don't let babies play baseball." I got up and walked to the other end of the bench. I didn't believe him anyway. There was no way I was starting tonight. I was one of the youngest players on the team.

"Hunter."

"Yeah, Coach," I answered. My heart was suddenly in my throat. He walked up to me, his smile reaching his eyes. Well, at least he wasn't mad. My heart dropped back to its normal spot, but it was still pounding much louder than normal in my ears.

He put his hand on my shoulder and gave it a squeeze. "You're starting at second base tonight and batting eighth."

"I am?" I said, unable to disguise the sound of disbelief in my voice. I shot a quick look toward Henry, but he was still studying his feet.

"You are. You've been trying hard in practice. You've earned the chance."

"Thanks, Coach."

He gave my shoulder one last squeeze. "Go take the field. Play hard but, most of all, have fun."

I nodded and swallowed hard before picking up my glove and running onto the field with my teammates. I looked back one last time toward Henry, hoping he'd at least give me a thumbs up, but he wasn't looking.

It was a good game, but we were losing by one run in the bottom of the sixth inning; the last in youth baseball. I was up fifth, which meant that if I got to bat, we could win the game. Surely the coach would substitute Henry for me in that case.

Our first batter grounded out to second. The second batter reached base when the shortstop dropped the ball. The third batter walked. So we had the tying and winning runs on base. I was ready for that tap on the shoulder telling me I was out of the game. I was ready to wish Henry good luck, but the tap never came. I was on deck. My whole freaking body was shaking. Please. Please. Please don't let this game be up to me.

The fourth batter grounded the ball down the first-base line and was tagged out. The tying run was now at third base, and the winning run was on second base. The coach *had* to pinch-hit for me. But he didn't. I could barely breathe as I walked to the batter's box.

Josh was still pitching, and whenever we played in pickup games, I usually struck out against him. The first two pitches were fastballs. I swung and missed the first one and fouled the second one straight back. Just like usual. His last pitch to me was always a curveball. He'd throw it. I'd duck because I was scared it was going to hit me in the ear. Then I'd watch it go over the middle of the plate into the catcher's mitt for strike three. I watched the ball leave his hand. I knew it was a curveball. I just knew.

Don't duck.

It won't hit you.

Don't duck.

Crap, my arms felt heavy. I tried to swing, but my arms felt like they were frozen solid. Oh, God. I was going to strike out. We were going to lose. It was going to be my fault. The ball curved away from my ear and toward the middle of the plate. I felt like I was trying to run through neck-deep water when finally my arms thrust out, off my shoulder. The ball was just inches away from the catcher's mitt and strike three when the very end of the barrel of my bat made contact with the ball. My eyes went wide as the ball sailed down the first-base line, over the head of the first baseman, and into right field just a foot on the fair side of the foul line.

By the time I hit first base, my teammates were screaming their lungs out. I turned and watched as the winning run crossed home plate. The fact that we had won the game hadn't fully registered in my brain when I was mobbed by my team. I was at the bottom of the world's best pig pile ever.

When I finally crawled out from under my very excited team, I noticed one of them was missing. I scanned the field but couldn't find Henry. I spotted a blur in the parking lot. He was pedaling away as if nothing had ever happened. He didn't spare us so much as a glance over his shoulder.

## Hunter - Present

"Is there anything you need me to bring?" Janine's voice snapped me back to the present.

"Huh? Um." I stuttered, shaking off the cobwebs of the past. "Just you and your urchins."

"Sounds good, big brother," she said with a laugh. "Get those pies in the oven, you slacker."

All I could do was shake my head. She was such a pain in my ass some-times, but what else are little sisters for? "Goodbye, pain. See you tomor-row."

"Goodbye, ass. Love you," she laughed.

I ended the call and finished pouring the filling and getting the pies into the oven. I set the timer and went over to the sink to clean up. I scratched the end of my nose, likely adding a smudge of pumpkin to my already messy appearance.

Before I could finish the cleanup, I heard Snow call to me from the lobby.

It was always something.

It wasn't easy raising three girls and keeping a business from failing, but I was doing it, somehow, some way, and maybe someday it would get easier, but if it didn't, so what. I could do it. I had to do it.

# 4

# My Knight in Shining Armor?

## Amber

Iwasn't like most of my fellow Denver denizens; I didn't jump for joy at the sign of the first snowflake. I never much cared one way or the other about winter. I used to live for Thanksgiving and Christmas and all the potential that Valentine's Day held for romance, but other than that, I was quite content to plod my way through until the warmer weather came again. That said, I rather enjoyed my first ride in a plow. The stout little man behind the wheel seemed to enjoy it as well. If the smile that was pasted to his face the entire way back into town was any indication.

As he guided the plow onto what I had to assume was the main street, I was greeted by the most picturesque mountain village I had ever seen. Streetlights wrapped in garland for the holiday season with a halo of white from the streetlamps shining through the snow tugged at my heart, and, for a moment, the ball of stress that had my insides strangled, relaxed.

I felt like I'd just stepped into a snow-globe. It was beautiful. The little mom and pop stores, all decorated for Christmas. One shop on the corner had a lit tree and an animated Mr. and Mrs. Claus giving a magical life to an otherwise deserted downtown. It made me forget all my troubles and, for an instant, step back to the wonder I used to feel as a little kid. Santa Claus and Christmas cookies, ribbons and bows and mistletoe.

The plow slowed and took a U-turn into a circular drive in front of an inn that looked like it had been a bulwark against storms like this for over a century. It was small by today's standards but so beautiful, even in the middle of a blizzard. A wide porch ran the entire front of the building, with second-floor windows peeking out above the sloped roof. It couldn't have very many rooms, and I hoped that there would be one left for me.

My would-be knight in shining armor pulled the plow to a stop and hopped out of the cab almost before it ceased moving forward. My door jerked open, and a whoosh of frigid air brought me back to reality. His meaty hand reached up to help me out of the cab. A gentlemanly gesture I truly appreciated. He helped me up the stairs, which, surprisingly, looked as though they had just been cleared and salted, and then opened the heavy oak front door. It was decorated with a beautiful balsam wreath, garnished with holly and a red and green plaid ribbon.

The warmth of the inn hit me as soon as I crossed the threshold, and I don't believe it had anything to do with the central heating system. The dark paneling and wide oak floorboards showed loving maintenance and were likely original to the building. Instantly the aroma of fresh baked goods wrapped around me, apples, cinnamon, pumpkin and nutmeg. This little inn in the middle of nowhere smelled like home. I felt like I was home.

My escort's booming voice snapped me out of my moment. "Hey there, Snow…" The girl perched on a stool behind the front desk peered over her phone and eyed him narrowly. He cleared his throat mid-sentence. "Sorry. Elizabeth, is your dad around?"

The girl's expression softened when she looked at me and graced me with a smile. It was one of those expressions you see when someone recognizes you after not having seen you in years. It was nice, but a little odd all the same. "Dad," she bellowed in the modulated way that teens do when yelling for their parental units, and I couldn't suppress a smile. This was certainly a family operation.

I was not prepared for what happened next. Emerging down the hall to the left of the reception desk was a man. Dear God, what a man.

Easily over six feet and broad shoulders that seemed to me at the moment nearly as wide as he was tall. He wore a red patterned flannel shirt with his sleeves rolled up, exposing sinuous, muscled forearms. Covering his clothes was an apron that was plastered in flour along with, based on the delectable smells I was greeted with, the remnants of apple and pumpkin pie filling smeared from top to bottom. His chiseled jawline and high cheekbones would have been the envy of any classical Italian marble bust. There was a smudge of flour on his cheek, and my tongue darted across my lips, hinting that it was quite interested in tasting this delicious-looking cross between a lumberjack and the Pillsbury Doughboy.

"What is it, Elizabeth? Is the…" He paused, noticing me standing there before coughing. "Is the, ah, credit card um, credit machine acting up again?" He asked, tripping over his words.

Elizabeth glanced at him until he made eye contact with her. She sighed and licked her thumb, cleaning the tip of her father's nose. "Honestly, Dad," she huffed. "It's like I'm your mother sometimes." She nodded in my direction. "Our new guest is here."

He turned to face me. His profile had already caused an acute reaction in me that my core had not felt in five years, but when his eyes locked with mine, I damn near melted into a puddle right there. Just like Frosty in the greenhouse. His deep brown eyes were like pools of warm melted chocolate, darkening by the moment. His lips parted slightly, and his tongue licked them as if he were about to devour a particularly tasty meal. I sunk my teeth into my bottom lip, and the thought crossed my mind that I would like that meal to be me.

"Found this stray on the side of the road halfway up the mountain." The plow driver said, breaking the moment. "Thought maybe you could help her out with a place to stay for a couple of nights." I could hear the mirth in the man's voice so much so that I almost missed 'a couple of nights'.

I could see his Adam's apple bob as he swallowed, maybe I wasn't the only one feeling something. "Does the lady have a name, Leo?" he asked. His body shifted as he spoke as if his clothes didn't fit quite right, though he looked damn good to me.

"Um," my rescuer stuttered. "Never thought to ask."

"Amber Scott," I said. "Thank you again for your help."

He opened his mouth to say something but paused before continuing, "Leo McPherson, second cousin to Hunter Holmes, proprietor of this very inn." He half whispered in my direction, "figured I should let you know of the family connection, ethics and all, not that there's more than one other option in town," Leo added with a smile and wink.

"Thanks, Leo, we'll take good care of her," the girl's voice brought my attention back toward the front desk and the very perfect specimen of masculinity standing behind his lovely daughter. "Just two nights, Amber?"

I opened my mouth to reply that I was hoping for only one, but Leo answered for me. "Oh, it will be more than that. That car isn't coming out of the snowbank before tomorrow afternoon, and then who knows what shape it's in. The bearing hub is snapped, left front panel is trashed, radiator was pissing fluid, so that's toast, and I haven't even tried to look under the hood and see what else is busted up. It'll take at least a couple of days to get the parts, probably more with it bein' a holiday weekend and all."

I looked back at him, and whatever warmth had filled me since walking through the door was gone. It felt like all the color had drained from my face. I shivered again with the cold.

He gave me a shrug of his shoulders and a sympathetic smile. "Wish I could say something different, but…"

"We'll make her comfortable for as long as she needs it, Leo." Hunter's deep baritone voice startled me, and I turned before seeing Leo give him a nod and turn to the door.

"Let's see what other treasures I can find on the mountain tonight." He said to himself as he closed the door behind him.

"He's good people." Hunter smiled at me, one dimple peeking out from his oh so handsome face. My body was back to liquid heat. God, what was this? I'm far too young for menopause. "Good thing he found you. Nothing good ever comes from getting stuck halfway up the mountain on a night like tonight."

I tried to speak, but the heat of Hunter's gaze stole my voice. I could see a smirk sneaking over Elizabeth's face as she looked back and forth between me and her father. And then her expression went blank, like she was looking at something way off in the distance.

"It's her," she mumbled before seemingly snapping out of a trance, earning her an odd look from her father.

"What did you say?" Hunter asked.

She collected herself and exhaled. "Nothing, Dad. I'll tell you later." She met my eyes with an expression I couldn't quite identify. "You're actually in luck because we have a room available for as long as you need it."

Her words brought my focus off the apron-clad lumberjack and back to the situation at hand. Ensuring a place to stay for the night. "Thank you. I hope I won't need it for too long. I need to get back home to Denver. I must have been distracted and made a wrong turn, and then the snow was so heavy… I don't know, just a bad day that hopefully a nice hot bath will cure." Suddenly I realized I had nothing more than basic makeup with me as far as toiletries and only the clothes I'd changed out of earlier. "I don't suppose there's a convenience store within walking distance. I don't have anything with me."

The girl rolled her eyes in very typical teenage fashion. "Not in Homer Pass after six and never on a holiday. I think I can find a spare toothbrush and stuff for you though."

I gave her a smile. "Thank you. I truly appreciate your kindness."

"And I'm sure you'll love the bath supplies in the room. I chose them myself." There was such pride in her words it was impossible not to smile.

I sighed, relieved that there was actually a tub. "I can't wait to try them. You have no idea what kind of day I had."

She laughed, "Well, from what I've heard, it sounds like it's been a regular suck-fest."

"Elizabeth! Language." Hunter's stern voice did little more than garner another eye roll. Yes, that was something I could already tell she was adept at.

"Book her for a week Elizabeth, with this much snow, we might get an early rush of ski traffic this weekend. No sense in taking chances."

A week? My gut twisted with anxiety. I didn't know how much a room here was, but it had to be pricey. Quaint and home cooking came with a cost. Not to mention there was no way I could miss work for an entire week. I had to sell something soon, or commission or no, the agency would let me go. Real estate might be in a boom, but I certainly was not. "Oh, there's no way I'll be here that long. I have to get back to work by Monday." I said. I pressed a smile onto my face and did my best to look confident. The look I got back from two sets of eyes did nothing to boost that confidence, however. "How much per night, by the way?"

"It's $389 a night plus tax," Elizabeth said.

"Don't worry about that right now," Hunter added. "The last thing you need is another unexpected expense. From the way Leo sounded, your car is going to need a lot of work to get it running again. Let's see how long you have to stay and then we can figure something out."

"Thank you, but I'll pay for what I have to. If the room is half as cozy as this space right here, I'll be quite happy. Maybe a couple of days unplugged in the mountains is just what I need."

"Denver's a big city and all, and maybe that's what you're used to. But up here we take care of people when they're in a tough spot because sooner or later they're going to take care of you," Hunter said.

I opened my mouth to argue, but his look left no room for discussion. Just when I'd given up on all forms of human goodness, I'd literally crashed into Homer's Pass and in just over an hour and a half come to realize not every man in the world was going to screw me over. "Thank you. I'm sure we can work something out."

"Good." His smile broadened and, God help me, a second dimple blossomed. "Sn… Elizabeth, will you get Amber registered? I'll go back and throw a flame under the beef barley soup and heat some rolls. It's not the Ritz room service, but it's homemade and what was for dinner tonight. I hope you'll like it."

"Please don't go to any trouble."

"It's no trouble at all, and don't tell me you're not hungry; I can see it in your eyes."

He smiled, and I just felt like he genuinely cared about me and wasn't just being polite because this was a business.

I wasn't used to strangers exhibiting kindness. It took me a moment, but I finally agreed. "Thank you. That sounds wonderful."

Hunter turned and headed back toward what I assumed was the kitchen. "Don't you dare tell him I said so, but it is delicious." Elizabeth whispered conspiratorially, like she'd just admitted she'd snuck out the second-floor window and taken the family car for a joyride. "My dad's a great cook. Even Amy eats everything he makes, and she's impossibly fussy." Her eyes rolled again. She must have read the question in my eyes. "She is my youngest sister. She's six, and Megan's ten."

Despite everything that had gone wrong today, the kindness I'd experienced in the last fifteen minutes made me believe maybe things would turn out okay. It made no sense. Maybe I wasn't thinking right. My reaction toward Hunter certainly didn't make sense. My body reacted to his in a way I never had before. Wanting a man that way seconds after meeting him was borderline crazy. I was being stupid. Because lusting over a man with a wife and three daughters was not a very smart thing to do.

# 5

# Room 108

## Amber

T here, that should do it." Elizabeth said as she handed me back my license and credit card. "I'll send up a pot of hot water and our selection of teas with your dinner. Don't worry, we have Scottish Breakfast Tea," she said, smiling.

"That would be just perfect. A nice hot cup of tea sounds marvelous right now. But how on earth did you know Scottish Breakfast was my favorite?"

"Intuition, I guess," she said with a shrug. I found her expression a tad unsettling, like she knew something I didn't. I brushed it off as my over-extended brain being just too tired to function properly. "I bet a nice cup of tea would be good with that bath you want too."

I chuckled; she was a very intuitive young lady. She hadn't told me her age when she told me about her sisters, but I'd guess maybe fifteen or sixteen. She was still in the awkward stage. I remember it all too well. "Thank you; you're very kind and very good at your job."

Her shoulders tipped just a tad further back, and her smile widened. "Here's your room key. Number 108 is just up the stairs and on the right at the end of the hall. We have three other couples staying with us right now, but they're at the opposite end. You shouldn't be disturbed."

Elizabeth walked away toward the double French doors at the end of the hall on her right. I guessed it was the dining room. It was then that I took notice of the family photos displayed behind the front desk. School pictures, candid shots of the girls, some new, some obviously from when they were newborn, and a photo of a stunning tall blonde woman with the three girls in front of her. The sunlight streamed through the mist from a waterfall in the background. They were all decked out in hiking clothes and wore ear-to-ear smiles. It was definitely a happy family on a sunny day.

From the size of the girls, the picture had to be at least three or four years old. Still, this was a family business and one run by an obviously close and happy family. I thought it a little funny that I hadn't seen or heard the girls' mother, but maybe she was putting the youngest to bed or taking care of other hotel business.

Shrugging that thought off, I grudgingly accepted she had landed one of the few good men in the world. I would never be that fortunate because taking that kind of chance was not an option. Fool me once…

Picking up my meager belongings, I headed up the wide staircase on the other side of the lobby. The time-scarred treads creaked under my feet. Far from disconcerting, I warmed to the charm of a building that held many memories, had seen so many years and so many travelers. I loved old hotels so much more than the cookie-cutter national hotel chains.

I unlocked my room and flicked on the lights. It was one of the most charming rooms I had ever been in. It had a very feminine feel to it, a woman's touch. The king-sized brass and white enamel bed was covered in a fluffy floral comforter and begged me to crawl into it and dream away the last twelve hours, the last five years.

There were two pastel print wing chairs with an end table and a tiffany style lamp. It made me wish I had a library's worth of books to curl up under a throw and read for hours. I set my briefcase and canvas bag in one of them and peeked into the bathroom. My heart stopped; there sat a huge claw-foot soaking tub.

On the back of the door were two white fluffy robes, and I knew exactly what I was doing as soon as I finished my dinner. Arrayed on a shelf next to the tub was a beautiful assortment of bath sundries. I walked over and inspected them more closely. Unscrewing the cap, I inhaled a heavenly blend of lavender and chamomile. Miss Elizabeth had exquisite taste, and I would have to make a point of praising her tomorrow when I saw her. I wondered if her mother had helped, but the way she spoke, it made me think it was all her.

I padded back into the main room and pulled off my Sorels. At least I hadn't been stuck in the snow in heels. Looking over my shoulder and out the window, I could see the storm raging harder than before. Leo apparently wasn't being funny when he said he was logging the location of my SUV into the GPS so he could find it again. Four feet of snow looked like a conservative estimate. With a shiver that was purely psychological, I pulled the drapes shut and noticed the gas fireplace in the corner of the room. If I was stuck in the mountains in a blizzard, at least I had been fortunate enough to drop into a cozy inn in which to weather the storm.

Just then there was a knock at the door, and I made my way over and opened it to the scrumptious smell of homemade soup and hot, out of the oven rolls. As promised, there was a large carafe of hot water and a box full of every kind of tea imaginable on the tray. A smiling Hunter was holding it, and his dark brown eyes were holding me speechless and apparently immobile as well.

"Hi," a cherub-like voice spoke from the direction of Hunter's left hip. "I'm Amy. Snow told me that a beautiful lady checked in and Daddy was bringing her dinner, so I decided to help."

I pried myself from the intensity of Hunter's gaze to look down and see a miniature copy of Elizabeth. "Hello, Amy." I said, grinning because it was impossible not to grin looking at that adorable child. "I'm Amber."

"Snow was right; she is beautiful."

I could feel my cheeks warming and couldn't help but notice Hunter had gained a little color too. "Who is Snow, honey?" I asked, assuming it was the family cat or her doll.

"My big sister!" she said with the insinuation that I might be the stupidest person in the world.

"Amy, watch your tone. Miss Scott doesn't know that." He looked apologetically at me. "That's Elizabeth's nickname. Amy is the only one who can still use it without getting the death stare and a whole lot of attitude."

I smiled and nodded at him. "I'm sorry Amy I'll have to remember that, but I think I should still call her Elizabeth if that's okay with you."

"Okay." She nodded, nonplussed and waltzed into my room like she owned the place. Come to think of it, she did in a way.

I stood at the doorway, taking all of this in, and then realized I still hadn't either made way for Hunter to come in with the tray or made any effort to take it from him. "God, please come in. Just set it on the bureau."

"I'm sorry I didn't realize that she'd put you in this room, or I would have opened the dining room for you. Most of the other rooms have a table or a desk you could eat at."

I waved him off. "Oh, don't worry. You've already gone to way too much trouble for me. I'll just curl up in one of these darling chairs and enjoy my soup in front of the fireplace. This room is beautiful. Your daughter chose perfectly."

"I'll tell her you like it. She'll be very pleased. She's a natural at inn-keeping. She's going to do very well someday."

"I can tell you and your wife have trained her very well." There was just a hint of something that changed in Hunter's expression, like I'd said something wrong.

"My mommy's…"

"Amy Marie." Hunter cut her off with a firm tone. "Miss Amber has had a very long day and doesn't need any more chatter. Let's leave her to eat her dinner in peace while it's still hot. Come on." Without another word, the little girl took her father's hand and walked to the door with him. "You can just leave the tray in the hall. We'll come by and pick it up later. If you need anything else, just call the front desk. I'm usually up until at least eleven." He started to pull the door shut behind him. "Oh, and Elizabeth is searching for a toothbrush for you. She should be up in a few minutes."

"Thank you again. You've been very kind." The door was shut almost before I'd finished speaking.

I sat down in the comfy chair and tucked my feet up under me. I picked up the bowl of steaming broth and took a careful bite. It was wonderful. I took another, and it melted in my mouth. How could something taste so good? I wondered if that tall, strong, handsome man had kisses that would taste wonderful too.

My body reacted to him in ways that it hadn't to anyone in maybe ten years. Since my divorce, I'd been on a handful of dates, been asked out many more times than that, but none of those men made me feel this way. I don't think Lance ever made me feel this way. This just wasn't fair.

Why did the man who finally broke through and made me think all hope wasn't lost have to be married with three daughters? Why did this man, who was so out of reach, do that to me?

The other side of my brain kicked in to answer, because he's taken silly. You can't have him, so it's safe to want him. If he weren't married and you'd felt like this, you would have turned and run out that door, trudging through waist-deep snow naked in high heels if you had to. Not stopping until you made it to Denver or froze to death.

As usual, she made perfect sense. Of course, I'd want a man I couldn't have; he couldn't hurt me; he couldn't cheat on me; he couldn't cheat like my father did to my mother before he left us never to come back.

Damn it, why can't there be a good man for me? And why does my body seem to think Hunter is a good idea when he's not?

# 6

# Peanut

## Hunter

Walking down the hall, away from Amber's room, I let out a long breath that I'd probably been holding since I first caught sight of her. Thank God for Amy, or I would have found some excuse to stay and talk. She looked like she could really use a friend, and for the first time in three years I had the overwhelming urge to be that friend and a lot more.

Her brown eyes were flecked with yellow, and they glowed in the low light from the fireplace. I could have stared into them and gotten lost. It's like my body demanded that it come into contact with her. It took all my strength not to brush up against her when I stepped past her with the tray.

I must have seemed rude. I'll have to apologize, but I just had to get the hell out of there. Especially with my little shadow here, I looked down at the bobbing mop of golden hair skipping along beside me.

"Thank you for helping me, Peanut. You're getting to be a very big girl."

"Thank you, Daddy. I like helping. I know Mommy wants all us girls to help you."

Amy was so young. She must be getting that from seeing Snow work so hard. I reached down and gave her hair a tousle, which got me the giggle I was hoping for.

"Daddy. Stop mussing up my hair. Now you're going to have to brush it before you tuck me in."

"Of course I will, Peanut."

We made our way to the top of the stairs and creaked our way down. I made a mental note to see how much it would cost to install a carpet runner. More than I could afford, of course, but maybe that would lessen the creaking on the stairs. More than one guest has given it the side-eye on the way up. Not everyone appreciates the charm of an old building, the creaks and groans a building this old can't help but make.

"Daddy?"

"Yes, Peanut?"

"I know Elizabeth really doesn't like to be called Snow anymore, but please don't stop calling me Peanut, okay? I really like it. I know it means you love me."

"Whether or not I call you Peanut, I will always love you." She was the most sensitive of my three girls, and we seemed to have conversations like this at least once a week. It never stopped warming my heart, even in my darkest of days.

We took another three steps down the stairs before she looked up at me with the most serious and inquisitive of stares. "You love me even when you call me Amy Marie?"

"Yes, even when I call you Amy Marie."

She stopped on the stairs and wrapped her little arms around my thighs. "I love you so much, Daddy. I really want you to be happy."

I bent down and picked her up, hugging her as tight as I could without crushing her. "I love you too, Peanut. And I am happy. How could I not be happy when I have you and your sisters?"

She gave me an extra squeeze, and I carried her to the bottom of the stairs before setting her down. We walked hand in hand down the hall to the back of the inn, where I had put the addition on for our private family quarters.

Just as we pushed through the door that separated the inn from the addition, Elizabeth rushed by with a toothbrush and what looked like one of my T-shirts. Before I could ask what she was doing, Amy hit me with another barrage. "Do you think Amber is pretty? I think she's very pretty and nice too. I like the way she smiles. I think she really wanted a hug. She said she had a bad day. You should have given her a hug, Daddy, like you do for me when I have a bad day."

I was not about to admit to my six-year-old that I thought Amber was more than just pretty. I wasn't even going to admit that to myself. "I hadn't really noticed." I lied, hoping first, she wouldn't notice and second, there wasn't some sort of special level of hell for fathers that lied to their six-year-old daughters.

"Really, Daddy?"

Ya, she was onto me, but in for a penny… "Really."

"Well, I haven't ever seen you smile at a lady like that before, and she was smiling at you too. You know what, Daddy?"

I was petrified to ask. Amy was incredibly observant and brutally honest. I had no choice. "What, Peanut?"

"I think she likes you too."

"That's nice, sweetheart. Enough talk." Yes, this was going nowhere good. Time to make a subject change. "It's way past time to get you into bed. Now get changed, hop into bed and I'll be back in a minute to read to you."

"Okay, Daddy." She disappeared down the hall to her room.

A few minutes later, I tucked my daughter into bed and read her a story. When I thought she had drifted off to sleep, I leaned over, kissed the top of her blonde wavy hair that was so much like her mother's and whispered, "I love you. Good night, Peanut."

A very sleepy little voice said half into her pillow. "You should go up and read Miss Amber a bedtime story. I bet she'd like some cuddles too."

I slipped out of her room, flicking on the Elsa night-light, and pulling the door shut behind me. With all the guests that have come and gone through our family's inn, never once has she said something like that before. I could only shake my head.

First, my oldest daughter put Amber in the room that was my wife's favorite. It had been our room when we first bought the inn; it was the room Elizabeth was born in on a very snowy night, just like tonight. If Elizabeth had anything to say about it, it was always the last room we filled. Tonight, there were thirty other rooms available, but she gave Amber that room. Now my youngest was suggesting I go up and tuck her in. Ms. Amber Scott must have some kind of magic about her.

Magic that made my heart beat faster the moment I laid eyes on her. Magic that made me want to wrap my arms around her the second I set down the tray in her room. Magic that was drawing me to go up to that room right now just to see if she was okay. Just to see if she needed anything else.

There was a certain melancholy about her that made me want to protect her. I haven't felt that way for anyone in a long time, not since…, not anyone except my girls.

I collapsed into the leather recliner in our darkened family room. Finally, a moment of peace. It had been a busy, busy day. I looked across at the mantel and could see my wedding portrait. I was embarrassed. I shouldn't be feeling this way for anyone but her. It was always supposed to be you, Jenn. Only you. It's not my place to protect Amber from whatever is troubling her.

Who was I kidding? I couldn't protect anyone. Not my mother dying of cancer when I was seventeen. Not my father from drinking himself to death from loneliness after she died, not my sister from her abusive ex-husband and not Jenn, especially not Jenn.

The ever-present flaming ball of angst pulsed in the center of my chest. The girls, God somehow, someway I will protect them. I pressed the heels of my hands against my stinging eyes. I would not cry. Crying didn't do anyone any good. I didn't have time to protect anyone else. Besides, in the end I always fail. Always.

# 7

# Barbie Heaven & Hell

## *Amber*

I was half-way through the most delicious soup I had ever had when there was a light rap on my door. I hated to stop eating, and I hated more to have to pry myself out of a nice warm chair in front of a nice warm fire. Grudgingly, I set the soup down on the end table and padded my way to the door. I was greeted by a smiling Elizabeth.

"I found you a toothbrush and some toothpaste. And I brought you one of Dad's t-shirts to sleep in. I figured if you didn't pack a toothbrush, you probably didn't have pj's either."

"Thank you so much." It was very thoughtful of her, but I couldn't help but wonder why she wouldn't ask her mother to borrow a nightgown if that's what she had in mind. Judging from the photo, we couldn't be too far off in size. She was certainly taller than my five-six, and I had a few more pounds but still… "Your mom and dad aren't going to mind me borrowing your father's clothes?"

The smile slowly faded from her face, and I wished I had just kept my mouth shut and accepted her kindness without question. She shrugged her shoulders. "Dad will never notice, and I'm sure he wouldn't mind if he did. My mom's…" she swallowed hard, "my mom was killed in a car accident three years ago last September. I was going to get one of her nightgowns," she peered up at me from under long, beautiful lashes, "but then it just felt kinda creepy."

My heart sank to the bottom of my stomach. I felt like a total fool. Despite having only just met her, I pulled her close for a hug. "God, I'm so sorry, Elizabeth. What you did was very thoughtful. I'm sure your mother would be proud of having such a kind daughter." I was surprised that she returned the hug but very pleased. I whispered down at her, "I promise not to tell your dad you raided his closet for me. It can be our little secret."

She pulled back from the hug, and a small smile hit her lips. "Thanks. I'd like that." She turned and started to close the door behind her. She turned and opened her mouth to speak before hesitating a beat. "Good night." And closed the door.

I wondered what she really wanted to say until I finally drifted off to sleep, comfy and warm and happier than I had been in a long, long time. It broke my heart to think of those three girls without a mom under such tragic circumstances, but I felt a lot better about the warm feeling I had inside any time I looked at their father. I felt even better about how he had looked at me.

I awoke the next morning buried under the warm, fluffy comforter and clean, crisp sheets. I slept like a baby for the first time in ages. Only the knowledge that the fireplace was keeping my little hideaway nice and toasty coaxed me out from under my cocoon. I slid out of bed and walked over to the window, pulling back the drapes to discover no change in the weather. I groaned. It was still snowing sideways and piling up higher and higher, definitely four feet plus. I was going to be here for a while.

There was a knock on the door, and I headed toward it before realizing I was in nothing but Hunter's T-shirt. I made a quick detour to the bathroom and wrapped myself in one of the luxuriously thick white robes.

I pulled open the door to find a smiling Elizabeth. She greeted me with a bright, "Good morning," holding a tray of scrambled eggs, a Belgian waffle topped with whipped cream and strawberries, toast with a selection of what looked like homemade preserves, two rashers of bacon and two sausage links.

"That smells delicious. I didn't realize how hungry I was." My stomach rumbled in agreement. "But you didn't have to bring this up. I could have come down to the dining room."

"It was no trouble. We had only three other parties last night, and they're all visiting family in town for Thanksgiving. Leo made sure their way was plowed before they left. Homer Pass is a really small town. Even if they had to walk, they probably could have made it to where they were going."

"Still, I feel bad for imposing," I said. I've always felt guilty when someone went out of their way for me.

"Really, I wanted to. Besides, it's no fun eating all by yourself in a big empty dining room." She stood there for a moment, as if she were waiting for something. "I brought both coffee and hot water for tea. I didn't know what you liked."

"Did you make this all yourself?"

She nodded, grinning from ear to ear. "Dad's busy with dinner, so I offered to help."

I took a bite of the waffle, and it just melted in my mouth, the real maple syrup smooth and sweet on my tongue. "Elizabeth, this is wonderful. You're very thoughtful."

She shrugged her shoulders, trying to be a nonchalant teen, but I could tell she was thrilled I was enjoying the special breakfast. "Well, breakfast comes with the room, and I couldn't have you miss out." She looked over my shoulder out the window. Shaking her head, "No one's going to make it out here from Denver today. Looks like you're kinda stuck with us after all."

The genuine sound of concern in her voice touched me. She might have plenty of teen attitude, but she had a kind, caring heart. I gave her a half-smile. "Well, there's really no one to come get me, anyway. I guess I'm stuck regardless."

Her eyes widened, obviously not expecting what I said. "No husband or boyfriend?" I could almost see the flood of thoughts behind her eyes before she added, "or girlfriend?"

I couldn't help but laugh. "No, Elizabeth, no husband or boyfriend. Just me. My mother lives in Florida. Hopefully, the snow will stop, and my car will be fixed before she can fly in and rescue me." That reminded me I should probably call her and let her know my situation. Prepare her for the possibility that she'd once again have to dip into her retirement fund and bail out her failure of a daughter from a financial catastrophe. My gut was already telling me insurance would fall far short of what I would have to spend to fix Betsy.

"That really sucks." She put her hand over her mouth. "Please don't tell my dad I said that. He hates when I don't talk like a lady."

I held her shoulders and looked her in the eyes. "Elizabeth, I promise you that our conversations will always be between just you and me." A look of relief washed over her, and I was glad I could give her that. I didn't know why, because I was only going to be in her life for a hot minute, but I felt in my gut it was important to say. "Besides, you are right; it does suck, and there isn't really a nicer way to put it."

She grinned, "Thanks." She took a few steps toward the door. "Thanksgiving dinner is at two." She started to pull the door closed behind her and then stopped. "Dad doesn't make us dress up or anything, so don't worry, okay?"

"Oh." I hadn't really thought about that. I figured I'd have to find a place in town to eat. "I didn't realize that dinner was part of your room package."

She cocked her head to the side and raised her eyebrow. "It's not, but you've got to eat, right?"

"I'm not going to intrude on your family dinner."

She just kept smiling and shrugged. "The thing with small towns is everybody's family. Or at least they act like they are," she laughed. "Dinner's at two. Don't be late." And she shut the door before I argued further.

I finished my delectable breakfast, washed up and put on the outfit I had arrived in yesterday. I only had two choices. It was that or the slacks and blouse I wore to my showing. I could wear that for dinner if there wasn't a place in town I could go so I didn't intrude.

Not wanting to be more of an inconvenience to them, I wandered down the stairs with my breakfast dishes. I already felt more like a guest in their home than at their inn. No one was at the front desk, but I could hear voices in the kitchen, so I headed in that direction.

I walked through the swinging door to the sight and sound of organized chaos. Hunter and the girls were busy at work. Hunter was basting the turkey while Elizabeth was shaping dough onto a baking sheet for rolls. Megan, the only one of the Holmes girls who I had yet to officially meet, had her head down focused on peeling potatoes. Little Miss Amy was in the far corner on a stool, carrying on an animated conversation with her Barbie dolls.

They didn't notice me standing there. Without my permission, my mind considered how I might fit into this slice of domesticity. My heart swelled at the sight of this man and his three daughters making a holiday dinner together. A memory that I knew would stick with the girls all their lives. While some men would retreat after a loss like that, he stood strong and was there for his girls. He could give them twice the love and protection if that's what he had to do.

There was that stinging in my eyes again. It reminded me I could watch them, appreciate all they have, but I would never be a part of a scene like this. Fate had shown me I wasn't meant for a life like this, yet I still yearned for it. I thought I had taken the first step on the journey the day I said 'I do,' but Lance took that from me. I didn't think I could ever give anyone the chance to hurt me that way again.

I cleared my throat. "Where would you like me to put this?"

Hunter looked up, startled, and almost dropped the half-cooked bird onto the floor. Fortunately, he recovered and safely slid it back into the oven. "You didn't have to bring that down. You should have just left it in the hall."

I waved him off. "Well, I didn't. Where should I put it?"

He cocked his eyebrow, and I could tell there was something he wanted to say but stopped himself. "Just drop it here." He pointed to the stainless-steel prep table in front of him.

Megan looked up from her potatoes, the intense concentration on her face giving way to an enormous grin. "Hi Amber, I'm Megan." She cast a quick glance in Elizabeth's direction, and the two exchanged a look the way only sisters can.

Something inside me said they were up to something. "Hi Megan. It's nice to meet you."

"I would shake your hand, but," she held up a half-peeled potato in explanation.

"That's okay." I said. I couldn't help but think how well Hunter had done with his girls. They seemed happy, content and adored. You could never know from looking at them they'd suffered such a terrible loss. Hunter seemed like he was holding together pretty well too.

I was snapped out of the morbid rabbit hole I was heading down by Hunter's soft, deep voice. "Don't worry. Leo will get your car out as soon as he can and get right to work on it. You won't be stuck here forever."

I started to correct him but quickly covered myself. "I'm sure he will. It just doesn't look like the storm is letting up soon." I wasn't worried about being stuck there at all. At that moment, I rather liked the idea of being stuck, and that scared the crap out of me. "I was wondering where I could go to grab dinner tonight. If you could, maybe recommend a good restaurant."

Hunter appraised me with a bemused smile, the one that you give a young child who has uttered something so innocent and sweet that you can't bear to tell them that the cruel world will crush that dream the first chance it gets. After falling under his scrutiny for a few moments, he answered, "You'll be joining us. Didn't Elizabeth tell you?"

"She did, but I've already imposed enough. I can't plop myself in the middle of your family dinner."

"You're not crashing our dinner. You're our guest." His tone left little room for discussion and disagreement. He'd done that to me before, and I would usually bristle at being told what I was going to do. I'd had quite enough of that from Lance. Somehow from him, it was an invitation that I simply couldn't say no to.

"Please, I don't want to be a bother."

With a heavy sigh, his shoulders slumped. "This isn't Denver, Amber. Your only option is Leo's gas station for a candy bar or a bag of stale potato chips. If that's what you want, be quick. If he bothered to open at all today, he'll be closed by noon."

There was really no escaping this unless I intended to starve myself.

"Please, Amber," Elizabeth caught my eye with such a look that it melted me.

"Yeah, Amber," Megan added, "we really want you to."

Amy's cherub-like voice startled me. Somehow, she'd managed to sneak up next to me and tugged on my sweater. "Don't you like us?"

Well, hell, didn't I just feel like a total ingrate? Bending down and hoisting her solid little body into my arms. "Of course I like you." Rubbing her nose with mine in an Eskimo kiss just to prove the point. "How could anyone not like you?" Giggles erupted as I tickled her belly.

The smile on Hunter's face as he looked at the two of us reached straight inside me and turned the heat to boiling. He could take it outside and melt the nearly four feet of snow that blanketed the town. "So what can I do to help? If I'm going to stay, I've got to earn my keep."

"Just grab a book from our library and curl up in front of the fire with a cup of tea. The girls and I have it all under control."

I cocked my head and lifted an eyebrow, but it had zero effect on the man.

Amy cupped my face with her chubby little hands to bring my attention back to her. "You could play Barbies with me. I've got a dream house and a camper and a bug and," she took a deep breath, "and a pool with a slide and all sorts of cool stuff. Wanna see?"

I took a quick peek in Hunter's direction. I didn't want to overstep any boundaries, but his expression was even more welcoming than before. "Sure, honey, I'd love to play Barbies with you."

She squirmed down out of my arms and grabbed my hand, pulling me toward a door on the opposite side of the kitchen from where I'd come in.

Amy led me through the door and into a large family room that was exactly what I would expect Hunter to have. It was earth tones and exposed beams. One wall was dominated by picture windows that looked out over the mountains, just visible through the still-falling snow. Another featured a large fieldstone fireplace with a huge flatscreen TV over the mantel. The furniture was overstuffed leather, worn enough to look comfortable but obviously high quality. I could easily picture myself curled up in front of that fire in one of the armchairs, lost in a good book on a snowy day like today.

Her determination to get me to her room didn't let me linger in that vision too long. That was probably a good thing for me. We walked down the hall to the right of the fireplace and into her room.

It was impossible for me not to smile. Amy's room was the epitome of a princess's paradise. The walls were painted in a soft pink with rainbow and unicorn decals. There was a large shelving unit filled with stuffed animals and, in the center, a full-size white canopy bed. Fairy lights lined the ceiling, and in one corner were more Barbies and paraphernalia than I'd ever seen in one place. Toy stores included. She had everything she said and so much more.

We sat crisscross on her bedroom floor for more than an hour with those dolls. She provided all the inspiration and dialogue. Most of her fantasy world was centered on Ken and Barbie, daddy and mommy. She couldn't have been much older than three when her mom died. She likely remembered her mother only because of the stories other people told her. It was only natural that this little girl wanted that kind of life, and I lifted a silent prayer toward whoever or whatever was in heaven to give it to her.

A single tear escaped from the corner of my eye. I brushed it away quickly. Just like the thought that had caused it to spill out. I hoped she would have it because I knew I never would.

Tired of the dolls, she scooted, unprompted, into my lap, and snuggled into me as tight as she could. Instinctively, I stroked her hair, and she burrowed herself deeper into my chest. Unable to fight it any longer, I gave in to my own fantasy. Of having my own little girl to love. To play with and teach her how to navigate her way through life. I missed teaching. Maybe it didn't have the income potential that real estate did, but at least I felt better about myself. For a few hours a day, I got to be the person who helped young minds grow.

"That suits you."

I jumped, lost in my brief fantasy. I hadn't heard Hunter coming down the hall. His muscular frame filled the door, and a warm smile brought out the dimples that were so terribly lethal to my heart. I smiled and kissed the top of Amy's head. "She's just so sweet that it's impossible not to want to hug her. I think she might be ready for a nap."

"Nope," her little voice floated up from my chest, "I just ready for cuddles. You smell really nice. Come here and smell her daddy."

I couldn't help but laugh at her innocence. I stole a quick glance at Hunter, and I swear I saw him twitch in my direction. If he came within an arm's length of me right now, I don't think I could control myself anymore. He wasn't playing fair, all the hunky handsomeness a girl could ever dream of and dad of the year to three perfect children.

I knew this could never be mine, but at that moment, it felt like it could. It felt like I wanted it to be, and from his expression, he seemed like he might want it too.

# 8

## Tickle Me Too

### Hunter

It had been over an hour since Amy had dragged Amber down the hall to play with her dolls, talking her usual mile a minute about whatever was on her mind. Her cute little mouth never seemed to stop moving. Whatever was running through her precocious little head was streaming past her lips. She had zero filter, which occasionally caused awkward moments. I recalled an incident when she was three where she informed the lady checking us out at the grocery store that her mother had strictly forbidden chili as a menu option in our home because "daddy stinks when we eats it."

I was quite surprised to hear no sound at all coming from her room as I walked down the hall to rescue Amber from her torrential stream of chatter. For half a second, I envisioned little Amy gagged with a sock in her mouth, and tied up in the corner because Amber couldn't handle the constant talking anymore. What I hadn't expected at all was to see my daughter curled up in Amber's lap like a content kitten in a blanket. Amber stroked her soft blonde waves mindlessly as she gently rocked her back and forth.

As adorable as Amy is, she wasn't one to just warm to anyone; quite the opposite. Since we lost her mother, there were only two people she sought out, Elizabeth and me. She could spout blood from a vein, and she would push past anyone but the two of us to find comfort. My sister tried and tried to step in and fill the hole that losing Jenn made in us all. Amy has had none of it, and yet this woman, who had landed at our inn less than twenty-four hours before had somehow broken down a wall that no one had breached.

Maybe there really was something about Amber Scott that was special. I knew my reaction to her was immediate and powerful. I married the only person I'd ever felt that way about before. Even then, I didn't re-member reacting as strongly the first time I laid eyes on Jenn. Yet in a few brief hours, Amber had won the heart of my youngest, made some kind of connection with my oldest, and the middle child seemed predisposed to accept her based on the unusually warm greeting she received in the kitchen, and me? Well, I was thinking about things I hadn't thought about in a long time. A very long time. Thinking about them so much that when Amy softly cooed that I should come over and smell Amber, I actually had to grab hold of the door frame because my body started moving toward her before my brain could stop it.

"I don't think Amber would appreciate it if I came over there and start-ed sniffing around like a dog." The smile on Amber's face and in her eyes insinuated maybe she wouldn't mind if I came a little closer to her, which was all the encouragement Hunter junior needed to snap to attention. Hopefully, with my hands in my pockets, it won't be obvious, but now I'm stuck standing here in this doorway, unable to move or I'd definitely be giving myself away.

"Maybe I'll let him have a little sniff later, Peanut. Would that be okay?" Amber interjected, leaving me wondering if she was serious.

Amy shifted slightly to look up at Amber. "How did you know that's what Daddy calls me?"

Amber shrugged her shoulders. "I didn't, but he must call you that because you're so cute and he wants to eat you all up." At that point, she tickled Amy, and the giggle-fest began.

"Daddy, come tickle me too," she squeaked out between bursts of unbridled joy.

I was a vigorous man and could resist many temptations, but when your six-year-old asked to be tickled, there was just no reason to resist. Those requests will be a distant memory far too soon. I pounced through the door and began my merciless assault. We continued until she was laughing so hard that I was afraid she might stop breathing.

I leaned back with my hands on my knees as Amber did the same. She lost her balance slightly and pressed into my shoulder. Without a thought, I placed my arm around her back and rested my face on the top of her head. My daughter was right; she did smell good, very good. The soft scent of lavender and something else I couldn't name became my new favorite aroma. So good that I had the overwhelming urge to cup her face and pull her lips to mine and discover if she tasted just as good as she smelled.

It was in that split second I realized just what I had done, but before I could ease myself away from Amber and avoid a really, really awkward moment, Amy jumped up from the floor and hugged us both. With her head wedged underneath ours, her little arms pulled us closer together. I wanted badly to glance sideways to gauge Amber's reaction. I just couldn't bring myself to do it because if it was negative, it would ruin the hope that ran through me. Hope that I hadn't felt since the day that I lost my wife and my unborn son in one dreadful instant.

"Are you okay, Daddy?"

A concerned child's voice snapped me back to the present. Along with a soft hand giving my arm a squeeze and a gentle thumb brushing something wet from my cheek. Amber was a fitting name because her concerned brown eyes with flicks of gold burned like hot coals into mine. She must have felt the intense heat between us, too. Her eyes fluttered shut, and long, delicate eyelashes spread over her cheeks.

"Of course, Peanut," but I wasn't looking at my daughter. I was looking at a beautiful woman who had just wiped the only tear I had shed in years from my face. I have raged, God how I raged. I have brooded and sulked and been an absolute asshole to everyone in my life except my daughters since that September afternoon just over three years ago, but I have never shed a tear until this moment. "I'm sorry," I whispered to Amber.

With a quick flick of her head, she dismissed it.

"How about you clean up your Barbies and we let Amber have a bit of a break before dinner?"

"But, Daddy," Amy whined.

"No buts. It was very nice of Amber to spend so much time with you, but I think she deserves some time to herself, don't you?"

"Okay, Daddy," she replied with less than adequate enthusiasm.

I pushed myself off the floor and then reached down with my hand to help Amber to her feet. She laced her fingers in mine, and I pulled her toward me. There was this urge deep inside to pull her close and not let go, but my mind shoved that feeling aside. Jenn's memory was still so strong. Wanting Amber didn't feel right. She looked up into my eyes, and we stood, inches apart, for longer than was necessary.

I cleared my throat and croaked out a "thank you" past all the emotions that were stuck there.

She just shook her head and put her hand on Amy's head. "Thank you for inviting me to play with you, Amy. I had a really nice time."

Amy spun around, grinning from ear to ear. "Thank you, Amber. I had so much fun. Can we play later?"

Amber started to answer, but I cut her off. "We'll have to see. Right now, finish cleaning up and then get ready for dinner."

"Okay."

I made my way out the door, and Amber followed, walking down the short hall and through the family room. "We'll be eating in the dining room. My sister and her kids will join us, and maybe Leo too if he isn't still behind the wheel of a plow. That boy loves to push snow around." I couldn't help but laugh. Kids love to go sledding; Leo loves to plow.

"See, I knew I'd be intruding. I'll just come down for leftovers later when everyone leaves."

Likely a little more forcefully than I intended, I put a hand on her arm and turned her to face me. "No guest in my home is going to be all alone on a holiday like Thanksgiving." I placed a hand much more gently on her other arm. "The girls would be really disappointed if you didn't come down."

"I would be too." I could feel her body soften at my words, and my chest ached to pull her closer. I was not a man easily scared, and I was terrified. So, I did what every cowardly man would do in that situation, attempted humor. "Besides, you more than earned your dinner after an hour in Barbie hell." I said with a chuckle.

A soft smile played at the corner of her lips, and she peered up at me from under those beautiful, sexy lashes again. "To me, that was Barbie heaven." She rocked up on her tiptoes and kissed my cheek. I wanted to leap for joy. "I wouldn't want to disappoint the girls." She turned and started down the hall, and I swear she swayed that way just to torture me. "I'll see you in an hour," she said, looking back over her shoulder.

*9*

# Family Thanksgiving

## *Hunter*

Hustling around the kitchen trying my best not to spill more than half of everything on the floor, I piled bowls high with mashed potatoes and green beans, frozen from our first garden this summer. I carefully set out the platter of roasted acorn squash wedges. As quickly as I had the serving dishes full, Megan and Elizabeth would whisk them out to the table.

Their mother would be… was so proud of them. I knew she was looking down on them, looking down on me.

I could hear my sister's laughter coming from the family room, likely from a long story Amy was regaling her with.

This felt like the holidays. This felt like home. This was the first time…

The ding of the oven alarm let me know the rolls were ready to come out was a fortuitous interruption. I didn't need to obsess about losing Jenn. I needed to be thankful for what I had, my girls, my sister, my niece and nephew and, if I was being honest with myself, for the most recent guest at the Snowflake Inn. Somehow, in the few scant hours she'd been here, she became a part of this family. The girls took to her like bees to honey, especially Amy. And there was that guilty feeling gnawing in the pit of my stomach for hoping that her car was so damaged that she'd have to stay long enough to realize that she didn't want to leave.

As if the mere thought of her conjured her into existence, she walked into the kitchen from the dining room. I froze, paying no attention at all to the heat that was searing into me through the too-thin oven mitts from the pan of rolls I was holding. The heat was nothing compared to what the rest of my body was feeling. She wore a cream-colored silk blouse that fell gracefully over her delicious curves. Buttoned modestly down the front, but enough to reveal a hint of her generous cleavage. Her charcoal gray wool dress slacks hugged her womanly hips and shapely legs. On most women, this would be merely simple conservative business attire. On Amber, it was as sexy as the laciest lingerie I could imagine, and I've got a damn good imagination.

An amused smile filled her face, and she nodded toward the pan I was holding. "Want some help with those?" She strode towards me, and I was embarrassed to admit that my eyes dropped to the gentle bounce of her breasts under their silky covering. I felt a low rumble of lust in my throat and coughed, hoping that hid the obvious excitement I felt at her presence. "The girls said they had it under control, but I wanted to help."

"Um, sure," I stuttered, uncommonly flustered. I dropped the tray of rolls on the prep table, finally realizing that I'd likely just burned my hand. "There should be a basket in that cabinet over there. Liners are in the drawer below."

She walked to the cabinet. She had to be aware of how my eyes followed her, but she didn't let on. The rear view was every bit as tempting as the front as she stood on tiptoes to reach the cabinet shelf with the baskets. Setting the chosen one on the counter, she took a napkin from the drawer below and lined the basket. Her hand smoothed the fabric to mold into the basket. My mind wandered, imagining how those delicate fingers would feel smoothing the fabric of my shirt over my chest. How she would look gazing up at me as she straightened my tie. With her hands running over my shoulders, raising herself on her toes to meet my lips as I tilted forward, our mouths met tenderly. The way her long, beautiful lashes would flutter shut as she lost herself in our embrace.

Fuck. Shit. Damn.

In seconds, I had turned the simple act of meal prep into some sort of erotic fantasy. What the hell was wrong with me? I didn't have those thoughts. I didn't want those thoughts. Not anymore. I didn't think I even owned a damn tie. I couldn't do this. I couldn't feel that way. She'd be gone as soon as her car was fixed. She'd be gone, and I'd be alone again. Me and my girls. That's all I needed. That's all I wanted. That's more than I deserved to have.

# *Amber*

I could sense Hunter's gaze as it scanned my body as I walked toward him with the basket for the rolls. Our eyes locked for the few steps it took for me to reach the other side of the prep table. He cleared his throat, but his voice still crackled on the first few syllables. "You look," he paused, "very nice, Amber. Elizabeth should have told you we don't bother dressing up for dinner."

I felt the heat rise on my cheeks. He wanted to say beautiful but caught himself. It had been a long time since I had heard that, and I was going to accept it even if it was edited. "Thank you. She did, but my wardrobe selection is severely limited. I wanted a change from my yoga pants and sweater." I took the hot rolls from the pan and put them in the basket. Hunter's eyes never left me. When he reached down to grab a roll and help, he got my hand instead. It lingered a beat longer than necessary. I didn't mind.

"You look pretty nice yourself." I gave him my best flirty smile. "There's something about a man in an apron." I hadn't really meant to mention the apron out loud. But, oh God, if an apron could be hot, Hunter nailed it. His flannel shirt stretched over his broad chest and hugged his biceps, half hidden under the apron. I let my mind stray and considered Hunter in just the apron. And my core rejoiced at the diversion.

I've spent a lot of time over the past five years pushing men away. It made me feel good that I hadn't lost the ability to lure them in, at least the one man I was considering giving up my no-contact policy for.

"Thanks, um. I'd better check on the turkey." He turned and stepped toward the bank of commercial ovens. His movements were stiff, and I smiled at the prospect of the reason being that something else was stiff too.

"I'll just take these out to the table."

"Great. The bird's ready, so we can eat anytime now."

I walked back out to the dining room carrying two baskets of mouth-watering rolls. My stomach rumbled in agreement with my nose. Elizabeth and Megan were locked in a deep conversation that abruptly stopped with my arrival. I cocked an eyebrow at the guilty smiles that greeted me. "Your dad says the turkey is done, so we're about ready to eat."

"Okay," the two chirped in unison.

"Just what are you two up to? You look like you just got caught with your hand in the cookie jar."

"Oh, nothing." Elizabeth replied, regaining control of her expression. "Meg, go get Aunt Janine and let her know dinner's ready."

I continued to eye Elizabeth suspiciously, trying to divine exactly what she and her sister were up to, but she gave nothing away. Placing the rolls on the large table set for a big family meal, I appraised what might still need to be done. "Elizabeth, is there anything we're missing?"

"I don't think so. Just the turkey and dad doesn't let anyone near that except him."

Moments later, the quiet was shattered by the arrival of Aunt Janine, her two children, both seemed between Elizabeth and Meg's age, and the ever chatty Amy.

"Aunt Janine, this is Amber." Elizabeth introduced me to the woman who could be no one other than Hunter's sister. Tall at nearly six feet herself, she had deep brown eyes and chestnut hair. The same amiable smile and a hint of the same weariness that Hunter wore when he thought no one was looking.

"It's very nice to meet you. So, you're the one Leo tried to plow down the mountain."

I chuckled. "Oh, I don't think it was entirely his fault. I spun out, and he was just right there. He didn't have much choice."

"Well, I'm very glad you weren't hurt, and welcome to our family. I feel like I already know you," she laughed. "Amy couldn't stop talking about how much fun she had playing with you this morning."

"She's a wonderful child. So smart and so loving."

Janine smiled. "She has enough love for all of us."

As if on cue, I felt a warm hug around my legs. Instinctively, I reached down and hugged her head to my side. "Sit next to me, Amber?"

Before I could answer that I'd love to, Elizabeth interrupted, "Amber is sitting here, Amy," pointing at the chair just to the right of the head of the table. "You know that."

Amy looked up at me; a disappointed frown formed. "Sorry, Snow, I forgot," she told her sister in a stage whisper, like it was supposed to be some big dark secret.

"You can sit on the other side of her, if Aunt Janine doesn't mind," Elizabeth added.

Janine nodded, and Amy's face transformed back into her customary cheery grin.

I caught Janine sneaking a sideways glance at Elizabeth and me. I suddenly felt like I was in the middle of some kind of plot. She interrupted my protest. "These are my two, James and Karen." I received a polite hello from them. Karen was a little taller than James, but otherwise they were the male and female versions of the same person.

"Are they…"

"Twins? Yes," Janine cut me off. "God knows what sin I committed to deserve that." She laughed, and the twins rolled their eyes. Not the first time they had heard that joke. "I wouldn't trade them for the world, but the last three months of pregnancy…"

I laughed, "I can't even imagine."

I took a moment to look around the large hotel dining room as Janine settled the twins. I hadn't taken the time this morning when I'd brought down my tray. It was truly an impressive space and hinted at the elegance this hotel had when it was first built.

It took up the entire west side of the hotel. The ends and the outside wall were made up entirely of large picture windows offering views down the main street of the picturesque town at one end and a panoramic scene of the Rocky Mountains at the other. I could only imagine how majestic they would seem when not obscured by clouds and snow.

The wall against the main building was painted a soft yellow, adding warmth and brightness even on a snowy day like today. The molding and columns that supported the domed ceiling were white and clean. Two enormous crystal chandeliers hung in the center of the room.

Two fireplaces were spaced evenly along the wall and boasted huge mirrors over the mantels, making the grand space look even larger. The room could easily be set up to serve over two hundred people. The family table had been created by pushing three smaller tables together, at the south end closest to the kitchen.

I turned to Janine, putting a hand on her shoulder. "This is such a beautiful room. Grander than the rest of the inn, which is so homey and quaint but not at all out of place."

She nodded and smiled. "You should have seen it when Hunter first bought it." She shook her head, obviously picturing it in her mind. "It was covered in dirt and dust. Half the windows were broken or had rotting sashes. The floor buckled in spots, and one chandelier was in pieces on the ground."

"I can't imagine the work it took to bring it back. Now it looks like something right out of the Gilded Age."

"It does, doesn't it?" Janine agreed. "And you're right; it took a lot of work."

"Have you guys ever thought about promoting it as a wedding venue? I can imagine it's beautiful in the summer and fall and a great way to fill rooms when it's not ski season."

A small frown formed on Janine's face, which she pushed away with some effort. I soon discovered that I'd inadvertently said something triggering. "You're right," she said. "It is a beautiful space, and I'm sure Hunter would be successful if he marketed it that way, but I think it might be a little hard for him."

I swallowed, unsure if I should ask but couldn't contain my curiosity. "Why?"

She scanned the room, and a sad smile appeared. She folded her arms across her chest and focused on the far end of the room. "Right over there," she nodded at the north end, "is where Hunter and Jenn took their vows. She had always dreamed of getting married in this room. So, when they bought the inn, that was the goal. Like when they'd finally finished everything, they could celebrate completing the rehab by getting married."

It was easy to tell that this was a bittersweet memory she was sharing with me, and I was truly moved that she felt comfortable enough with me to do it. I placed my hand over my heart. A strange mix of emotions flooded my chest. The sympathy that had me fighting back tears made total sense, but the twist in my gut that signaled the appearance of the green monster of jealousy had me wondering just what the hell was wrong with me.

"Except, Jenn was pregnant with Elizabeth, and they moved up the timetable a little bit." Her smile was more relaxed now, and she chuckled. "Hunter and his best friend Josh worked practically around the clock to get things done in time for the wedding, but it was impossible. Every time they thought they'd turned the corner, there was another rotted joist or faulty set of wiring discovered."

"That must have been so frustrating for him," I said. "And cost a fortune."

"It was, and it did. But that's what you get when you try to revive a building that's over a hundred years old," she agreed. "In the end, they finished the south half of the room and just covered the north end with gauzy fabric and fairy lights. Everyone ooed and aahed at how romantic it was. We had a good laugh knowing the real reason was there were still holes in the wall and cracked windows."

"I bet it was still beautiful," I said. "It must have been a memorable day for everyone."

She exhaled a loud belly laugh. "Oh, Amber, you have no idea."

"Oh, Lord. What happened? Please tell me she didn't go into labor in the middle of the ceremony."

"Nothing that dramatic," Janine said. "She was only four months along when they got married." She took me by the arm and led me further into the room and away from the kids, who were still setting things on the table. "Actually, it was the night before at the rehearsal that everything hit the fan. Hunter asked our older brother Henry to be his best man."

I had noticed an extra seat at the table. "Will he be here today too?" I asked.

Janine snorted a laugh. "God, no. And you're about to hear one of the many reasons why." She paused, collecting herself. "Anyway, Henry has always acted like the world owed him anything he wanted, and if Hunter had it, he wanted it even more. That included Jenn. When they first started dating in high school, Henry asked her to homecoming."

"You're kidding me." I couldn't believe what I was hearing. How could someone's own brother act that way?

"Nope. He told her he was the older brother and would be the successful one. It was honestly kind of sad. He said some stupid stuff when they first bought the inn, and there have been other things along the way, but what ended it between Hunter and Henry was the wedding."

"Henry showed up for the rehearsal drunk," she continued, "and spouted some crazy ideas about going into a partnership deal with some developers in Denver. Turning the inn into a thousand-dollar a night spa hotel and using the land from our family's mining claim to convert Homer Pass into an ultra-luxury ski resort. Told Jenn he loved her and he was the one that really shared her vision for the inn, Hunter was just weighing her down."

I couldn't help my sharp intake of breath.

"I know, right?" Janine said. "As you can guess, Jenn outright dismissed him, and Hunter punched him so hard he broke two fingers and Henry lost a tooth. We didn't see or hear from him again until ten years later at Jenn's funeral."

All I could do was shake my head in disbelief.

"Even then, he hadn't changed. The only reason he came back was to get Hunter to sell to him. Fortunately, the sheriff and I saw him first and kicked him out before Henry could get close enough to Hunter to do any damage. Hunter was so crazy with grief, God knows what would have happened. Henry hasn't come back since."

"I'm so sorry you went through all that," I said, meaning it with all my heart. This family had been through so much, and yet they still could show me kindness. It made me appreciate Hunter even more. And Janine had an air about her. I struggled to trust people, but I knew I could trust Janine. I didn't know how or why, but I just did.

Hunter pushed through the swinging door from the kitchen with the biggest turkey I had ever seen. "Okay, everyone. Time to eat," Hunter said, putting everyone into motion toward the table.

Everybody found their seats, and I made my way to sit next to Hunter under the watchful gaze of his daughters, all beaming with excitement. As I sat, I caught an exchange between Hunter and Elizabeth, a questioning eyebrow, received shrugged shoulders with an impish smile. The grin that slowly washed across Hunter's face had me squirming to get comfortable. My lady bits aflutter.

We fell into an easy rhythm. Hunter served the turkey, and side dishes were passed in a dance of reaches and waves. Conversation jumped from topic to topic, children laughed and no one had to urge anyone to eat their veggies. I could never remember feeling so at home. I was at home with people who, twenty-four hours ago, I didn't even know existed.

The meal was absolutely delectable, especially the rolls Elizabeth and Hunter had made from scratch. It just wasn't fair that a man that good-looking was so talented in the kitchen. My mind wandered, imagining that he might have skills suitable for other rooms, as I reached for my third roll. Instead of latching onto an orb of starchy deliciousness, my fingers tangled around a rather large, strong hand.

I froze. My eyes traced the length of the arm attached to the hand until I looked into the face of the man I'd just been fantasizing about. Those damn dark brown eyes warmed me straight through to my core. His smile slowly widened as I failed to remove my hand from his. Lord, it was getting hot in here. It wasn't until after an extended pause and a raised brow I regained control of my faculties enough to release his hand.

Better late than never, I quickly withdrew my hand and placed it in my lap. I exhaled slowly and looked everywhere but in the man's direction to my right. I spied Megan whispering in Elizabeth's ear, both of them staring knowingly in my direction.

"Don't you want a roll, Amber?" Megan asked around a giggle.

Elizabeth elbowed her in the side and glared at her. I tried to eavesdrop on what they were whispering but was suddenly distracted by the deep voice next to me. "Yeah, Amber, don't you want a roll?"

"No, thank you. I'm fine," I croaked, sounding just like a prepubescent boy.

"Don't be a jerk, brother," Janine said from the other end of the table.

"Who, me?" he mouthed, pointing to his chest and widening his eyes so he looked like some kind of deranged owl.

"Why are you being a jerk, Daddy?" Amy asked, totally unaware of the exchange between her father and me. Thank God.

"I'm not, Peanut. Your aunt's just being a pain like usual," Hunter said.

Janine was opening her mouth to reply when Elizabeth, thankfully, refocused the conversation. "Isn't it time for us all to say what we're thankful for, Dad?"

"That's a wonderful idea," Janine said as she grabbed a bottle of wine and topped off her glass.

Hunter did the same for me before taking care of his own. "I'll start," he said. "I'm thankful for my daughters. The best daughters a dad could ask for."

We went around the table, each taking a turn. The twins both said they were thankful for their mother. Meg said she was thankful for books, which got a laugh from everyone, which she seemed genuinely confused by. Elizabeth said she was thankful for the early season snow, impressing me with her focus on the family business.

Janine was next. "I'm thankful for family." She paused and looked at each person at the table, finally landing on me. "The one we're born into, but more importantly, the one we choose." Her smile was warm, and she raised her glass toward me in salute.

I swallowed back the lump in my throat. Surely, she didn't mean to include me in her family, but it certainly felt that way in that moment. Fortunately, Hunter prompted Amy to go, which gave me a moment to collect myself.

"I'm thankful for Miss Amber." Amy's words hit me right in my already vulnerable heart. "She's the nicest. And she's really pretty too," she finished, nodding her head for emphasis.

"Thank you, sweetheart," I said and gave her a big hug.

"It's your turn," Amy said. "What are you thankful for?" Her big blue eyes looked up at me as if what I was about to say was the most interesting and important thing she would ever hear.

Usually, this kind of thing made me feel awkward and uncomfortable. Having met these people only a day before should have made it especially so. But it wasn't. It was so obvious to me I didn't even have to give it a moment's thought. "I'm thankful for all of you," I said, looking directly at Amy. "When I arrived at this inn last evening, I thought I was having one of the worst days of my life. But you all have been so kind and made me feel so much more than welcome. The love that this family has shown me, a complete stranger, is overwhelming." I paused and took a deep breath to steady myself. "Thank you."

I felt a hand on my arm and a gentle squeeze, and I was drawn back into the warm embrace of his gaze. "You're welcome," he said. I sunk my teeth into my bottom lips and my body leaned toward his. He turned my arm so my palm was facing up, and I was sure he was going to take my hand in his. I was going to let him. It didn't matter that everyone was looking at us. I didn't know that for certain. My attention was entirely on Hunter, but why wouldn't they be looking at us? He was the most interesting thing in the world.

Suddenly, there was something warm in my hand.

"Have another roll, Amber," he said with a chuckle. "No leftovers. Right, girls?"

With that, the spell was broken. And the organized chaos of a family meal resumed.

There was one empty seat at the table. Leo hadn't made dinner. The storm was winding down, little more than scattered flurries at this point. Just over four feet of snow was piled high outside the windows. A flicker of fear crossed my mind, wondering how in the world he could ever get my poor Betsy out from under all that snow if he could even find her at all. My concern must have shown on my face because I felt a large hand cover my knee halfway up my thigh and a gentle squeeze. I looked to my left to see molten chocolate-colored eyes boring into me and a hint of a reassuring smile. Maybe he wouldn't find my car, and I'd have to gaze into that sea of chocolate until spring. There would definitely be worse things that could happen to me.

# 10

# Good News, Bad News

## Hunter

**M**y girls had a strict rotation of who got to sit next to me at dinner. They agreed on it themselves and never, ever varied. Each had their turn, but today Amber was there, and I knew without a doubt it had been by unanimous consent. I had to admit, it felt right.

Her smile, her laugh and lively conversation seamlessly blended with the chaos that was my family. She and Janine hit it off like they had known each other all of their lives.

It was a shame that Leo hadn't been able to make dinner, but I promised him a large plate of leftovers. I knew he would be by before the day was out to collect.

It had been three Thanksgivings, three Christmases and many more gatherings since I heard this much talk and laughter around our family table. I took a glance to my left and saw a bright smile and twinkling eyes, and I knew the reason.

My girls and the twins cleared the table to prepare for the smorgasbord of desserts still to come. I was more than ready to pull out the sweatpants and claim the big leather couch in the family room for a well-deserved nap, even if I said so myself. But I knew my family and the pie and apple spice cake were just as important as the turkey to our celebration. My father used to say that a good meal is never complete until you eat something sweet. My girls and my sister had inherited that particular family gene. At least we had dessert in the family room.

I pulled Megan close as she cleared my plate and gave her a big kiss on her forehead. Whispering in her ear. "You're getting so grown up and responsible. Your mother would want you to know how proud we are."

I could see a trace of sadness in her eyes that quickly passed, replaced by a smile and a kiss on my cheek. "I know," she whispered back, "there's something else she'd want too." And she side-eyed Amber before she took my dirty dishes and hurried into the kitchen.

Her words shocked me. Megan rarely expressed an opinion; she just went with the flow. And while alluding to something else her mother would want might seem vague to most, it was exceedingly direct for her. Maybe it wasn't just me falling under Amber's spell. I just wasn't sure if they were just so desperate for a mother figure in their life that they were jumping at the first opportunity that had come along. Or had everyone else in the family seen just how special she was too?

I was full to the brim with turkey and fixings. I truly felt as if I was going to explode. "I think it's time to adjourn to the family room to watch some football."

Amber stood up and stepped back from her chair, hesitating a moment before taking a deep breath. "Thank you all so much for inviting me to your family dinner. I don't remember ever having a more delicious meal or better company."

Janine looked at her with one eyebrow raised. Another family gene inherited. "Well, we're not done yet. There are desserts and at least two more bottles of wine that need drinking, and if this man-child crashes like he usually does, us girls can have a nice juicy talk."

Amber smiled. "Thank you so much, Janine, but I think Hunter and his girls have seen far too much of me already. I've got to be the most bothersome guest they've ever had at the inn."

My sister and I both blurted out contradictions at the same time, effectively making it impossible to understand. "Don't be silly, Amber. There's a nice big fire and wine," Janine insisted.

I could see Amber's resolve falter. "You all make it very hard to resist."

"Of course we do." Janine said without a hint of embarrassment.

"Mom, it's stopped snowing. Can we go out back sledding?" Karen asked, with James nodding right behind her.

Megan piped in, "Ya, Daddy, can we?"

We exchanged a quick glance before I answered for both of us. "Sure. I don't see why not. Remember your helmets and, Elizabeth, you and Megan, make sure Amy isn't left out. You two get caught up with your cousins and forget she exists."

"We will take care of her, Dad," Megan agreed.

There was a mutual yell of excitement as the kids hurried to finish clearing the table and get outside while there was still light.

"That should keep them occupied until way after sunset," Janine said, then grabbed the wine from the table and motioned for Amber to follow. Apparently, what I did was no longer of any concern to my little sister.

"It should and then we'll have to hang them all by the fire to thaw out." I laughed. I was happy that they were going to have the same type of fun that Janine and I enjoyed and happy that we would have some peace, at least for a little while. I felt guilty for wishing that it was just Amber and me sharing the wine, but it was certainly safer that way.

We made our way out of the dining room, through the kitchen and back into our living quarters and into the family room. Amber and Janine laid claim to the big leather sofa, so I accepted my place in the recliner after throwing a couple of logs on the fire to bring it back to life. I clicked on the big-screen TV over the mantel and leaned back in my chair.

Amber handed me a refilled glass of wine and clinked hers to it. "To new friends."

I nodded and smiled. Somewhere inside, a little voice chirped that we should be more than just friends. I was both terrified and enamored of the thought. She was a mix of melancholy and spunk I couldn't figure out. Maybe that's what made her so alluring. It was more than just her physical beauty that had me enthralled.

Ignoring the television, I spent the rest of my conscious moments admiring how the firelight danced over Amber's olive complexion, the way there were the cutest little lines at the corner of her eyes when she smiled or laughed at something my sister said. Taking in her grace and warmth and ease. How she unintentionally teased me with just a little better view of her ample cleavage when she leaned forward to pick up her glass and how I wanted to press my lips against her soft, warm skin and trace gentle kisses over every inch of her amazing body.

The next thing I knew, I was snapped out of a dream of doing exactly that by Leo's booming voice. "Thank God I came when I did, ladies. Apparently, this old man can't stay awake long enough to entertain two such beautiful women. I could never sleep when women such as yourselves were in the same room."

I grunted at him. "Keep that up and I'll find a stray dog to give your dinner to."

He laughed, not knowing I was serious, well not really, but I could be.

"Is that any way to greet a man who comes bearing good news? Well, mostly good news."

"Oh?" I asked, wondering what the hell he was talking about.

He nodded and turned to face Amber. "So, we not only found your car, but I grabbed a half-dozen guys and dug her out. We were able to get her on a flatbed and back to the garage. She's thawing out in the bay even as we speak."

"Oh, thank you, Leo. I'm so sorry you missed dinner because of that." Amber's genuine thanks and regret warmed my heart.

"Well, don't thank me yet. She's going to need quite a bit of work to get her roadworthy again. Looks like both front bearing hubs are snapped, and I didn't do more than a quick glance in the engine well. It looks okay other than the radiator, but I'll have to run her for a while to know for sure. Then there's the bodywork. I'll have to farm that out, but there's a really good collision guy down in Fairplay. He owes me a favor or three so I can get you to the front of the line."

I could see Amber deflating a little more with each word and sat up in the chair so I could ease my way over to support her.

"Anyway, I'll take a better look in the morning and order the parts I need. With any luck, they'll be in by Monday or Tuesday, and we can get you back on the road."

"Monday or Tuesday?" Amber asked, her voice high-pitched and concerned.

"I am sorry, but it's a holiday weekend, and wherever I can find that's open isn't going to get the parts up the mountain until then." I sat next to her on the arm of the sofa and put what I hoped would be a reassuring hand on her shoulder.

"I'm sorry, Leo. I don't mean to sound ungrateful. I just don't know what I'm going to do. Please call me and let me know what you think it's going to cost." She ran her fingers through her hair before looking back up at him, with a look I hadn't seen since my teammates in youth baseball when we were losing twenty-five to nothing.

Leo waved his hand in dismissal. "Don't you worry a bit about the cost. I already called the county supervisor and let him know he'd be getting a bill. Told him I swiped you when you were parked along the side of the road. Which is pretty much the truth. He doesn't have to know you hadn't intended to park there."

"That's kind of you, Leo, but I can't let you take the blame. If anything, I'm at fault. I was the one who lost control and spun out. I don't want you to lose your job or have your insurance take a hit."

"Amber, I've been driving plow for over twenty years and I've never so much as taken out a mailbox. They're not going to fire me for that, and even if they were inclined to, there aren't enough drivers, especially up here. It's not going to cost me a cent other than time, and we're done talking about it." He leveled a look at her that might be comical if you didn't know the stout little man, but Amber apparently understood he wouldn't be convinced otherwise.

She forced a smile. "Okay, Leo, I won't argue. Please know how grateful I am."

## Amber

I did my best to keep smiling, even though all I wanted to do was cry. Not having to make up the difference from insurance to repair my car was a relief, but a week here was going to cost me more than I could afford. Even if Hunter gave me a fifty percent discount, which was much more than I expected, six nights here would be over a thousand dollars. And I needed something to wear. At the very least, I needed clean underwear and a couple of tops. This was so not in my budget.

I'd have to figure something out. I didn't want to beg from my mother. She would help without a second thought, but, argh; I was such a failure. A muscular hand rubbed circles on my back. My body leaned into Hunter. There was no denying how much I needed support in the moment, and I couldn't help how good it felt.

"What is it, Amber?" Janine asked. She took my hand and wrapped it in both of hers. "I can see the worry written all over your face."

I looked up and met her concerned gaze. I found it hard to concentrate. Hunter's comforting was more than distracting and disturbingly arousing despite how stressed I was. "There's so much more than the car to worry about." There was a temptation to word vomit everything that had gone through my mind in the last minute, but I was not a needy, whiny person.

"Like what?" Hunter asked from behind me.

"Like clean underwear for starters," I snorted a frustrated laugh before realizing I just said that in front of Hunter. "Oh, God. I can't believe I just said that out loud." I buried my face in my hands. "And who knows how work is going to react to my being unavailable for a week? It's not a busy time, but still. I'm already struggling when everyone else in the office is making record numbers."

Janine patted my hand and met my gaze. "Baby, I have been where you are more times than I can count. This family and everyone in this town have had my back every single time."

I didn't doubt her sincerity, and I so wanted to believe they could help, but I just didn't see how. "Thank you, Janine. You all have been so kind to me. This has been the best Thanksgiving I've had since my mom moved to Florida ten years ago, but…"

"But nothing," Janine cut me off. "You obviously noticed the twins' father was not at the table today."

I nodded, even though I knew I didn't need to.

"He was and probably still is a drunk and an abuser. As soon as we were married, he moved us two hours away. I'd spent the first nineteen years of my life here in Homer Pass. All my family and friends were here. I now know that's exactly what abusers do. They isolate you, cut you off from all support."

Her words rang true. Lance hadn't moved me hours away from home, but he'd certainly surrounded us with his friends. The only one of my friends I kept was Patty, and that was probably because she wouldn't let me drift away.

"I don't know how many times I ran back here, seven, maybe eight times…"

Hunter cleared his throat and started to speak. Janine leveled him with a glare that could have stopped a freight train dead at full throttle. "Sounds about right," he said, running his hand over his chin and looking at her from under his brows with a sheepish look I found worryingly adorable.

Janine nodded and continued. "Every time I showed up at Hunter's door, he took me in. I didn't have to say a word more than I wanted. He and Jenn were just there to do whatever I needed."

My eyes stung listening to what this woman went through, but she didn't need my tears. She was trying to tell me something, but I still wasn't making the connection. I wasn't running from abuse; I had a busted-up car.

"And then he'd come here, sweet-talk me into believing it would be different next time, and I'd go back, just like the stupid kid I was." She sighed. "Until the last time."

"I showed up here at the inn. My left eye was swollen shut. I had three broken ribs and a split lip." Her fingers traced her top lip absentmindedly, and I noticed a half-inch scar, just beneath her nose. "The twins were wailing in the back seat. Had been for the entire drive here. James had a welt on his scalp where his father had hit him when he tried to keep his father from kicking me again. I had exactly one kitchen trash bag worth of clothes and toiletries for the three of us. It's all I dared to take the time to grab. My husband once he thought he'd taught me the lesson I needed, he went to the store to get cigarettes and more beer. I had at most fifteen minutes to run."

"Jesus Christ, Janine." I reached over and took her hands in mine. "Thank God you got out."

She swallowed and took a deep breath. "Thank God and thank Hunter and Homer Pass." I could hear the tremor in her voice, and her eyes watered with unshed tears. "Hunter got us settled in a room. Jenn got the doctor to get us patched up, and within two hours, there were clothes in the lobby and anything else I might need. I had three jobs as soon as I could work, even though nobody really needed help. I promise you I would have had a place to stay too if I didn't have the inn."

I nodded and returned her smile. I admired the hell out of this woman. Not only had she survived hell, but in sharing her story, she didn't once sound sorry for herself. She sounded grateful for the help she received and proud of her family and community.

"Do you mind my asking what happened to him? Did you press charges?" I asked.

"The sheriff advised her not to," Leo said, smiling with a sparkle in his eye that led me to believe there was a story behind that. I looked at Janine but didn't ask for an explanation. I already felt she had shared so much of her past. I was flattered by her trust in me. It was something I struggled so hard to do.

She looked at me with a smirk and shrugged. "I don't really know what happened to him. I was in bed for a few days. All I know is that Hunter, Leo, and Josh Souza were missing from before dawn the day after I came back and didn't return until nearly midnight."

"We went fishing," Hunter said. The smile on his face told me it was total bullshit. "Never seen the salmon bite the way they did that day. We easily caught twenty or thirty each. Isn't that right, Leo?"

"True story," Leo said, his expression leaving no doubt in my mind that it wasn't.

"Then why did I never see a single one of them?" Janine asked.

"Bear," Leo answered without missing a beat. "Big ol' grizzly it was. Came charging out of the woods, knocked us down, and stole our creels before disappearing back the way he come from. Darn lucky we're alive, I'd say."

"Darn lucky," Hunter echoed, still grinning like a loon.

"There hasn't been a grizzly bear in Colorado since long before any of us were born," Janine said. "If you're going to lie, at least do it with facts."

"How does that even make sense?" Leo asked.

Janine waved a hand in his direction in dismissal. She gripped my hands, bringing my focus back to her. "Whatever happened, my divorce sailed through, he waived parental rights, and I haven't heard from him in nearly four years. After a bit of time, I got the money back he had embezzled from me."

I squeezed her hand back. "I'm so glad everything worked out for you and you had such a wonderful support system." I sighed. "But what I'm going through is nowhere near the same as the hell you went through."

Janine looked me square in the eye. "It doesn't matter that it's not the same. You're in a tough spot, right?"

I nodded. There was a lump of emotion in my throat, making it hard for me to swallow.

"And I'm willing to bet there's more to your story we don't even know the half of."

I nodded again. My eyes stung as I fought to hold back tears.

"Amber, I'm going to help you because I can; end of story. You're with us now, and we will not let you down. I run the general mercantile, and I will be here at eight-thirty sharp tomorrow morning, and we'll have you wardrobed right down to your pretty little lacies before noon. If you pay me a dollar a month for the rest of your life, then that's what you do. I mean, what girl can resist that kind of shopping spree? And don't worry, it's not all Carhart and granny panties."

I couldn't help the smile that filled my face. Janine's confidence and friendship were impossible to resist. "Thank you," I said, feeling like that was woefully inadequate to express the gratitude I felt. "This is all so overwhelming. You have all been so kind. I feel like getting plowed into a snowbank might have been one of the best things that has ever happened to me. You have made me feel like one of the family. Thank you." Janine wrapped me in a hug that felt good. It felt like what I had dreamed a sister's hug might feel like.

# 11

# Getting to Know You

## Amber

I swear my heart stopped beating when Leo told me it would be five days before he could get the parts to fix Besty. It didn't escape me that he hadn't said how long it would take to fix her after he got the parts. I wanted to argue with him about the bill. The accident was my fault, but I couldn't afford that kind of pride. And Janine, I didn't even know where to start with her. We'd met all of three hours before, and it was like we'd been best friends since childhood. I've lived in Denver all my life, and there was only one person there I could say the same about, my best and only real friend, Patty.

Hunter, with his hand on my shoulder, was such a distraction. It felt so right. It was a shame that it couldn't be. I had to go back to my job. He had enough on his plate without me, and even if he was interested in something, he needed a woman who could be a mother to those beautiful girls. I wouldn't even know where to begin. How could I ever measure up to the girls' mother? I couldn't risk having my heart broken again.

The kids came bursting through the door covered from head to toe in snow and laughing, snapping me out of my thoughts.

"All of you, don't you dare leave the tiled area with anything with snow on it. I don't care if you're naked." Hunter barked, getting up and walking toward the happy gaggle dripping in the entryway. I immediately missed his touch.

"Don't be gross, Dad," Megan whined an indignant retort.

"I'm not being gross. I'm being serious. Everything wet and snowy on the floor and then go put on something warm and dry. When you're done, you can sit by the fire and have some hot cocoa."

"Yay. I love cocoa." Amy cheered.

Janine placed a hand on my knee. "I guess that's my cue to head to the kitchen. Would you like to come help?"

I doubted she needed my help, but it felt nice to be included. "Sure, lead the way."

We got up and headed into the kitchen. She put a large saucepan on the range and poured a mix of milk and half and half into it before putting it on a low flame. "I think the cocoa powder is in that cabinet there. I'll grab the chocolate over here."

I retrieved the cocoa and then searched the cupboard for mugs. It only took a moment to find them, and I grabbed five, setting them on the counter next to the stove. My mind swam with everything that had happened in the last day and a half. But most of all, I was trying to make sense of Hunter Holmes.

Before Lance, I'd certainly been impulsive once in a while. Not that taking the walk of shame was a regular occurrence for me in college, but it happened. And I felt no shame at all in scratching that itch. Maybe it was just because I'd not experienced so much as a tickle in ten years that I felt so off. It was just that this felt so different. This feeling was way more than an itch. How could it feel so natural and so wrong at the same time? Actually, it didn't feel wrong at all; it felt damn dangerous.

I continued to stand there, lost in my own little world, mindlessly arranging and rearranging the mugs.

As Janine was slowly whisking the melting chocolate, she glanced over at me and gave me a long look.

Feeling the weight of her gaze, I asked, "What?"

She opened her mouth and then closed it again, looking back down at the cocoa. Peeking back up at me, "I know we've just met, but somehow it already seems like I've known you for years."

"Funny, I was thinking the same thing just before the thundering masses descended on us," I said.

She laughed and then took a deep breath. "I know the car trouble and an unplanned vacation you can't afford are weighing on you. And I know it's really none of my business, but is there something more?"

I hesitated; there was a whole lot more, but despite feeling like I'd known her for years…

"I'm sorry. I'm way overstepping." She shook her head as if she were upset with herself, which tugged at me. I had no doubt she was asking because she genuinely cared. "Would you mind handing me the mugs? I don't want the milk to scorch if I stop stirring."

"Of course, I'm supposed to be here to help, right?" I added with a laugh and handed her the first mug. It was my turn to take a deep breath. "You're right, Janine, there is a lot more, actually."

"If you want to talk, I promise I'm a nonjudgmental ear." It was a weak but honest smile. "Does it have to do with Hunter?"

I sighed. "I thought I was doing a better job of hiding it."

"Hiding what? That you two keep looking at each other and there's obviously some kind of connection there."

I laughed. "That obvious, huh?"

She pushed the cocoa off the heat and faced me, smiling. "Amber, a blind man could see it." She started pouring the thick brown liquid into the mugs. "Clearly from a mile away. I know he's my brother and I'm totally biased, but he's a damn good man."

"I know he is Janine. I just don't think I can do it."

"Do what? Take a chance and see what happens?"

"I think we both know it has to be more than a 'what the hell let's see where this goes' with Hunter. If, and I'm not saying I'm even really considering it, but if things didn't work out, I'd feel even more terrible because of the girls."

"Children are very resilient, Amber, but I think you know that."

"I do, but why chance adding one more loss to their lives?"

She smiled. "Because you could also be a wonderful addition, and I think you know that too. There's more, but I'm guessing you're still trying to figure it out, so I won't continue to intrude." She smiled and nodded toward the steaming mugs of cocoa. "Let's get these out to our freezing kids."

I smiled. I couldn't deny that I very much liked the sound of *our kids*, and that scared me even more.

As we pushed our way out the door, mugs in hand, she whispered in my ear, "Just don't think we're done talking about this."

That thought had never crossed my mind.

The kids had changed and were sitting in a semicircle in front of the hearth. A board game had appeared, and there was much discussion about how much of the colorful money they each got to start and who got to pick their game token first last time. All debate stopped as Janine and I distributed the mugs of chocolaty deliciousness. In just seconds, there were five smiling children with brown mustaches.

"Where's your mug, Amber?" Amy's blue eyes searched mine.

"I don't have one Peanut, but I do have a glass of wine over there." I answered. She had such a sweet spirit it was impossible not to adore her.

"Wine's yucky. You can share my cocoa if you want."

I knelt down and kissed the top of her head. "That is very kind of you, Amy." I took a sip because somehow I knew that would make her happy. And went back to my place on the couch. Hunter had returned to his recliner, and I would be a bold-faced liar if I said I wasn't disappointed. Get a grip. Either you need to be strong and stick to your plan or give in to the Hunter temptation and suffer the consequences. Stop flipping back and forth like a fish out of water before you drive yourself crazier than you already are.

Leo had taken up residence in a winged-back chair and had lost himself in whatever football game was on. I knew it wasn't my family, and I knew I would only be in these people's lives for days, but I felt at home here, with them. I took a sip of my wine and lost myself in watching the kids play their game. I could see the expression on Janine's face from the corner of my eye; it's like she knew exactly what I was thinking.

Three long tones that had me thinking there was a test of the emergency broadcast system went off, though they came from the kitchen and not the TV. Everyone in the room except for Amy and the twins, turned in Hunter's direction. Once the tones stopped, there was a garbled voice that I couldn't quite make out, but I saw Hunter let out a long breath and run his hands over his face and back through his hair. "Shit." He muttered and rose to his feet. He hurried down toward the bedrooms and reappeared carrying his turnout gear. Leo had also gotten out of his chair. Hunter quickly kissed the girls, promising to be back as soon as he could. The two men walked briskly out the door without another word. Elizabeth and Janine exchanged worried looks, and then Janine placed a hand on my knee and gave it a squeeze.

It took a second for everything to register in my brain. The t-shirt I wore to sleep in, Hunter's t-shirt, had a crest and the words Homer Pass Volunteer Fire Rescue. Hunter was a firefighter. I mean, how could he not be?

What concerned me more than the thought of Hunter rushing into a burning building, and that definitely had me nervous, were the expressions of worry on Janine and Elizabeth. I arched an eyebrow in Janine's direction, and she pasted a smile on her face, but it hid absolutely nothing. She nodded toward the kitchen, and we quietly left the children to play in front of the fireplace.

As soon as the door closed between us, I turned to her. A dozen questions buzzed through my head, but I already felt I was intruding into their family's business. I forced myself to wait quietly until she was ready to speak.

She looked down at the floor and put her hands behind her head. She took a deep breath and let it out. When she looked up at me again, I could see the tears welling in her eyes. "I feel like this is something that is Hunter's to share and not mine, but if I know my brother, he'll keep it all bottled up inside. If anything happens between you two…"

"Don't say anything you feel you shouldn't." I cut her off. "We can leave it at being worried about a loved one who does a dangerous job."

She sighed again. "No, I know Hunter will try to protect you from his demons, feels he has no right to burden you with them and he needs someone that isn't me." She sat herself up on the stainless-steel prep table and tapped the space beside her. I joined her.

"You know the girls' mother is dead," Janine said, meeting my gaze. "Do you know how she died?"

I nodded. "Elizabeth told me it was a car accident."

She tried to speak, but emotion clogged her throat. She took another breath and wiped away a tear that had escaped her eye. "It was. I don't think the girls know the full story; maybe Elizabeth does, but I'd be surprised if she did." She took another deep breath. "We were going to have a big family dinner that night. Jenn's sister had just moved back to town with her wife, so they were coming. Leo and Josh were going to be there. I was here with the kids. It was a few months after I finally escaped my ex. It was going to be a big thing. Anyway, Hunter was supposed to go get some things for the party, but he was just finishing the remodel of the last two rooms on the third floor, and Jenn convinced him to stay and finish and she would go."

I already knew where this was going, and my eyes clouded with liquid emotion. I put my hand over my mouth, and Janine nodded. "A log hauler was coming down the mountain and lost its brakes. The driver did everything he could. He swerved to miss her sitting at the stop sign, but the sharp turn put too much stress on the tie-downs and the load broke loose. She was crushed under fifty tons of logs." She wiped more tears from her face. "She died instantly."

"Oh, my god Janine, that's horrible, and he blames himself for letting her go?"

She nodded. "The worst part was that those same three tones you just heard sounded that morning, and Hunter was the first firefighter on the scene."

I tried to speak, but nothing would come out.

"I thought for a while we were going to lose them both that day. It took five men to get him off the pile of logs on top of her car. He broke a state trooper's nose. They had to give him a shot to sedate him."

"How can he even still do that job? I could never move past that."

"It took him two years, Amber. Even hearing a siren would cause him to tense up and break into a cold sweat. He didn't exactly take it out on us, but he wasn't much fun to be around. The only place he was ever the old Hunter was around the girls. As far as I know, he never once said a cross word to them, even when they could have used a good scolding." She smiled, trying to lighten the mood.

"The end of last August, he finally went back. Said he needed to force himself to move forward. He could never be the same, but he could be whole, and he said he had to do his best for his girls. Leo and I kept a close eye on him, especially for the first couple of calls, but he did okay. Better than I could have."

"Why do I feel like there's a but coming?"

"But on the first weekend of October there was a terrible house fire. Mutual aid from four different towns, and it took them the better part of a day to put out all the hot spots. The house was a total loss and nothing more than a pile of rubble. It was Jenn's sister's home."

"Please tell me she didn't die, and he blames himself for that too."

"No, she didn't die," Janine said, but her tone suggested that there was more.

"Oh, thank God," I said, exhaling a relieved sigh.

"Her wife did."

I raised a hand to cover my mouth. Just how much tragedy could this family endure?

"The two of them were supposed to go away for the weekend, but Janet ended up going on her own. It wasn't uncommon. Janet's in corporate marketing, always jetting off to somewhere, and Madison would never leave her pottery studio if she had a choice."

Janine pinched the bridge of her nose and exhaled before continuing. "Hunter called Janet as soon as he could, but she never picked up. She didn't know her house was gone, and so was her wife, until late the next day when she finally called Hunter back."

"The house was fully involved when they got there. There was no way to save her, even if they had known she was inside."

"Please tell me she doesn't blame him for her dying?"

Janine just nodded her head. "It was an ugly, ugly scene. She was inconsolable, totally out of her mind with grief. Called him a coward and selfish for not trying to rush into the flames to save her. Then she moved on and told him if he hadn't been so selfish and made Jenn do what he was supposed to, her sister would still be alive. It's been two months, and no one has heard or seen a thing from her since."

"Did he let her guilt him into feeling responsible for Madison's death?"

"No, but it resurrected the guilt he'd managed to get past about Jenn. He was pretty much right back where he started, but he didn't leave the department."

"That poor man. He doesn't deserve that."

"No, he doesn't." She put her arm around me and gave me a big hug. "It means a lot to hear you say that." She looked at me for a moment, and her expression softened. "I hope you take this in the positive way it's meant."

"What?" I asked, feeling apprehensive about what she was about to say.

Her smile was warm, and she held me closer. "I haven't seen Hunter as happy and comfortable as I have today since before the accident. And I'm not the only one who's seen it. Elizabeth called me last night, said that Leo had brought you here and the moment he saw you, it was like her father was back from wherever he's been."

"Janine, really…"

"Hush. I'm not saying that to put pressure on you. I'm just saying that I'm glad to see him at least a little closer to the old Hunter and that if you had even the smallest part in making that happen and you and I never see each other after this week I'll owe you a debt for the rest of my life."

"Well, I don't believe I had a thing to do with his improved mood, and even if I did, you owe me nothing. But I do hope that we can become friends regardless of what happens."

"You can count on that." We hugged, and I had to admit I didn't want to let her go. "Now let's get back out there before all hell breaks loose."

# 12

# Kiss Away the Bad Dreams

## *Amber*

Janine and I returned to find a happy but loud game of Monopoly. We shared small talk, and she told me about the small town of Homer Pass and most of its nine-hundred and something residents. Everyone knew everyone's business, but no one was ever left in want. We made plans to meet for breakfast before she took me shopping in the morning. She might be disappointed because there was no way I would let her spot me hundreds of dollars for a new wardrobe. I would get the essentials and suffer through having to rinse out a few things if my stay was extended for more than a few days.

I could tell she was anxiously waiting for Hunter to come back, but as it neared nine, there were some cranky, overtired children in need of their beds. I convinced her I didn't mind staying down in the living room, and being near the girls until he comes home. My room was lovely, and the gas fireplace made it very cozy, but who could complain about a roaring wood fire and a comfy sofa to curl up and read a book on? She finally conceded when I took her number and promised to text her an update on her brother.

I got the girls to bed, though Megan was more than capable of doing everything on her own. It surprised me she seemed to like me tucking her in. I knew Elizabeth was buried on her phone in her room, and Amy got me to read two stories before she finally fell asleep curled into my shoulder. I allowed myself the guilty pleasure of snuggling her just a little longer than necessary. It was going to be very hard to leave her behind in a few days. In just over twenty-four hours, they had all found a permanent place in my heart.

Easing myself off of Amy's bed, I crept out into the library area just off the lobby and found a well-worn paperback to spend the rest of my evening with. The last thing I should have read in my state was a romance novel, but I couldn't resist.

I was already halfway through the book when the antique hat-shaped mahogany mantel clock chimed eleven. Hunter quietly made his way in through the back door.

He stealthily dropped his gear in the entryway. He was grumbling something to himself about the fire not being properly banked for the night when he saw me curled up on the couch. He jumped, startled. "Christ, you scared me."

"I'm sorry. I guess I should have said hello."

"I wasn't expecting you to be here. You didn't have to stay here to watch the girls. Elizabeth has watched them while I was out on a call plenty of times before."

"Well, I guess I'll just go up to my room then."

"No, no. That's not what I meant," he said, scrubbing his hands over his face and back through his tousled hair. "I'm sorry if I sounded upset."

I couldn't help but smile at the way he was stumbling over himself, worried that he might have offended me. "Not at all, Hunter. I'm sure you're tired and want to go to bed."

"Please stay a little bit. I am exhausted, but there's no way I'd be able to sleep yet."

His eyes were dark, as were the circles under them. Still, I could see the longing for companionship in them. "If you want me to, sure. Is everything alright?"

"I'm fine. Just a little keyed up. It takes a while to get the adrenaline I get from going on a call out of my system."

"Okay." I really didn't know what to say or do. I didn't know this man, but my heart ached for him. I wanted to be a comfort to him as well as to keep my promise to Janine. "It's just that Janine mentioned…" I paused, noticing his brows narrowing and jaw clenching. "Never mind."

"What did she mention?" He asked in a slow, measured tone.

I couldn't lie to him. I didn't want to. Throwing Janine under the bus wasn't ideal, but I didn't think she'd mind. "She told me what happened. With Jenn. With your sister-in-law."

"She shouldn't have troubled you with that." His words were sharp.

I stood up and closed the distance between us. I placed my palms on his chest. I could feel the cut of his muscle just below the fabric of his shirt, and my mind swam with a thousand thoughts, nearly pushing what I had meant to say out of my mind. I must have noticeably hesitated in my distraction because he raised his eyebrow just slightly in anticipation and encouragement. "She didn't trouble me with anything. The only reason she said something is that she loves you and wants to make sure you're okay."

I caught the briefest flick of his gaze toward my hands, still pressed against his chest. I flinched, knowing it was too intimate a gesture for me to do to him. But my body refused to obey my mind, which was urgently telling my hands to retreat. And then his hands were on top of mine and his eyes locked with mine. My body was in complete overload and my lady bits were…, well they were doing what lady bits do when it has been eons since there was even a hint of interest in my life and now suddenly I'm in a state of never been this interested before in my life and didn't know it was even possible for a body to react this way.

"Is this an entirely altruistic gesture on your part, Amber, or do you care if I'm okay too?"

I swear to God my legs were shaking. My lips parted, but no sound passed through. My eyes darted from his, down to where his hands covered mine, and then back. Over and over and over. Then, just as my inability to form sound was becoming painfully obvious, his hand closed softly around mine, and he brought it to his lips, lips now smiling at me, and he kissed the palm of my hand.

"What are you doing, Hunter?" All I could muster was a whisper.

"You didn't answer my question, Amber; do you care too?"

My mouth was drier than Death Valley at noon in August. "I was concerned." I croaked out. My teeth worried my bottom lip, and I looked down, too afraid to see his reaction.

He let go of my hand, but before I could pine for its absence, he cupped my cheek and gently lifted my gaze to meet his. "I will always come home to my girls, Amber."

They were simple enough words with a plain meaning. But there was no doubt in my mind he meant much more than that he would always come home to his children. He was telling me he would always come home to me too.

The Amber I was before I landed here a little over twenty-four hours ago would have bristled at the insinuation that I was 'his girl' to come home to. I wasn't and wouldn't be possessed by anyone. But damn my foolish heart for beating faster at his words. And damn my head for not stepping in and correcting my heart.

He inched closer to me, and my body, entirely without my permission, inched closer to him. I could feel the heat radiating between us. How could a man this powerful be so gentle? His head tilted to the side and leaned down. I mirrored him, and our bodies pressed softly together. My lips parted. This was really going to happen. I was actually going to kiss a man for the first time in years. I wanted to kiss a man for the first time in years. I could feel his breath on my lips, and my eyes fluttered closed.

"Daddy, I had a bad dream."

In a millisecond, we were six feet apart, and my heart was pounding so hard I thought it was going to break my ribs.

"Huh? Um… What, Peanut? You had a bad dream?" Hunter was fumbling for words and nearly tripped; he was so addled as he moved toward the tearful Amy.

"Were you and Amber kissing?"

"No, Peanut."

"You looked just like the boy and girl do in Snow's kissing movies."

"What do you mean, we looked like we were kissing?" The realization of what she said washed over him. "What kind of kissing movies? And why were either of you watching movies like that?"

"You were really close, just like they are, and then Amber closed her eyes like the girls always do."

"We weren't kissing Amy. We definitely did not kiss," Hunter said as he scooped Amy into his arms. "And what kind of movies have you and Snow been watching?"

"Just the Hallmark Channel, Daddy."

He sighed a deep heartfelt sigh of a man who has to deal with three daughters with no backup. "Why are you out of bed?"

"I told you I had a bad dream, silly."

"Oh, right. Do you want to tell me about it?"

She wiggled in his arms, resting her head up under his chin. There was a large part of me that was still humming with excitement at our not-a-kiss that wanted to be cuddled up in his arms too. "No, Daddy, I'm okay now."

"That's good, Peanut." He cast a glance at me and smiled. "Let's go tuck you into bed, then."

"Can Amber come too?"

"We don't need to bother her with that."

"Please," Amy begged. Drawn out the way little kids do while they still believe there's magic in that word and that there is a Santa Claus.

If ever a man gave a woman a dear God help me look, it was the one I got from Hunter. If Amy's request for my presence to tuck her in hadn't completely melted my heart, that look surely finished the job. "Of course. I'll come and help tuck you in."

We walked down the hall to her room. Her chubby cherub arms were wrapped around Hunter's neck, and one eye peeked over the top of his shoulder just to make sure I was still with them.

I pulled back her covers as Hunter lowered her softly onto the bed. We tucked the comforter in around her. He brushed her bangs back off her forehead and gave her a kiss. "That should chase all those nasty bad dreams away." He gave her another before stepping back. "Sweet dreams, Peanut. I'll see you in the morning."

We took a step toward the door. "You're not going to kiss me, Amber?" Her blue eyes, dark with only the night light for illumination. "To make really sure I don't have bad dreams."

I stepped back and placed one on her forehead, the same as her father. "Sweet dreams."

I turned and walked out the door past Hunter, who was watching his daughter with such love and kindness I ached inside. Just as he turned to leave, "Daddy?"

"What is it, Amy?"

"Make sure you kiss Amber goodnight too, so she doesn't have bad dreams."

I put my hand over my mouth to keep the giggle from escaping and to hide the smile from Hunter.

"Go to sleep, Amy." He turned and heaved an exasperated sigh. "And stop talking about kissing," he mumbled as he walked down the hall.

I couldn't hold it back anymore. My laugh escaped as an unladylike snort, which got me an arched eyebrow, but even he couldn't contain his smile.

I decided I had better go back up to my room before someone else caught me and Hunter almost kissing, or worse, almost doing something else. "Are you feeling better now?" I asked.

"Much, thank you."

"I think Amy gets all the credit for that. I didn't do much of anything to help."

His grin morphed into a smoldering promise; this fireman was doing the exact opposite of putting my fire out. "You did a great deal more than you know, Amber."

How does he make my body respond that way with just his voice? Fight? Flight? Freeze? Flight, please, and the first available. "Um, well, I guess I should head up. It's getting late, and apparently, I have to have breakfast with your sister before she convinces me to go into an obscene amount of debt and buy a new wardrobe."

"Yeah… of course… I didn't realize it was this late." He stood there like a kid on his first date, without a clue what to do. There was no question that Hunter was a model quality, handsome man, but this big hulk of a guy, bashful? My panties were disintegrating as I stood there. "Should I set a wake-up call for you? We've got one of those automated systems."

"Thanks. I'm good. I've got my phone," I answered.

"Okay then, um, goodnight, I guess."

"Goodnight." I took two steps before his hand was on my arm, turning me, and two lips crashed into mine. I tipped my head back and parted my lips, and my world spun out of control. Somehow, my hands found their way into his wavy locks. His tongue darted between my lips and took my mouth as a willing prisoner. I felt his hands slide lower down my back, pressing our bodies together. And I think he may have forgotten to take a flashlight out of his pocket because there was something pressing against me that couldn't have been all him. Could it?

Our kiss broke, and I leaned back, still uncertain of where I was or why. "To make sure you don't have bad dreams." Mister Bashful was long gone, and the heat in his molten chocolate eyes was more than I had experienced in my life.

"Ah, um, thanks. I, ah, better…" I aimlessly waved my hand in the direction I thought my room was.

His hands slipped off my shoulders, and a shiver coursed through me in their absence. He nodded, and I feebly stepped toward the door. I could somehow put one foot in front of the other until I reached the base of the stairs.

I put my hand on the newel post and rested my forehead on top of it. One, two, three deep breaths. Bad dreams? Dreams of a hot, hunky innkeeper named Hunter kissing me, definitely. Dreams of the same man running his hands up and down my bare skin, likely. Dreams of that man's naked body entangled with mine doing all sorts of naughty, wonderful things together, possibly. Bad dreams? That all depended on your perspective. Falling for Hunter Holmes could be a very bad thing. I had a sinking feeling I was going to find out, even if I didn't think I wanted to.

# *Hunter*

I watched as Amber disappeared out the door toward the lobby. I had the overwhelming urge to follow her and continue what we'd just started. My heart was still thundering in my chest, and I could still taste her on my lips. A hint of wine. A hint of hot cocoa and something magical that made me want to keep kissing her and never stop.

I shouldn't feel this way.

But I did.

When Amy blocked my first attempt, I took it as a sign from the cosmos that the attraction I'd felt toward Amber since she crossed the threshold yesterday evening needed to be tamed. I breathed a sigh of relief as I carried Amy down the hallway to her room, thinking she'd saved me from a terrible mistake. But then the six-year-old matchmaker told me I had to kiss Amber goodnight to keep the nightmares away, and the thought of kissing her was right back in my head.

Now I had even more thoughts in my head. None of them pure.

I scrubbed my fingers through my hair and let out a ragged breath. I needed a long, cold shower. What I wanted was exactly the opposite.

With another sigh, I turned and walked toward my room, briefly stopping outside Amy's door. The slow, even sounds of her breath comforted me. I was a dad. I had responsibilities. And I didn't have time for distractions. Time didn't really matter. I wanted Amber, whether or not it made sense.

A cold shower it was.

# Shop 'til You Drop

## Amber

Sleep did not come easily last night. My mind raced with a million conflicting thoughts and emotions; the most prevalent was that I hadn't wanted that kiss to end.

When my phone alarm went off at seven, it felt like I'd just dropped off to sleep. I was very tempted to hurl it out the window and into a massive snowbank. But that just reminded me of the trouble I seemed to get myself into with snowbanks.

I crawled out of bed and padded sleepily to the bathroom. The woman who stared back at me from the mirror looked the worse for wear. My dark caramel hair was tousled wildly. It made me look like we did much more than kiss. Perhaps my dreams slipped into the possible phase. Too bad I didn't remember the dream.

Not only was there over four feet of fresh snow outside, but the local temp on my phone said it was in the low teens. So, washing this mess without having time for a blow dry was not in the cards. I raked my brush through it and whipped it up in a loose bun before stepping under the stream of steaming hot water. What I wouldn't give for a showerhead like this at home.

The shower restored my body enough that I felt human, and when I got out of the bathroom, I found a pot of hot coffee waiting on my bureau. God, I hoped it was Elizabeth that did the delivery. The thought of Hunter being that close to my naked body was too much to comprehend this early.

Back into the yoga pants and sweater. At least choosing an outfit was easy. And I could change into something different after I got back, hopefully with a little left in my bank account.

I made my way down the stairs and brought my long wool coat up around my neck, bracing for what was likely going to be a brisk walk to where I was meeting Janine for breakfast before our shopping spree. "Amber." Elizabeth called out to me from behind the front desk.

I turned to see her waving a cream-colored Scandinavian knit hat and matching mittens at me. "I got these last Christmas from a great-aunt I've never met. They're not very stylish, but they're warm. You have to put something on, or you'll get frostbite today."

"Thank you, Elizabeth, that's very kind of you."

She smiled back, and there was something more to it than being pleased with my gratitude. I turned and walked toward the front door. Then I realized if we had almost been caught kissing by Amy, what if Elizabeth had seen us? There was no denying the kiss goodnight was a kiss. My toes were still tingling. I looked back over my shoulder, and she was still watching me with the same smile.

Yup, she knew something.

I returned her smile as best I could and stepped through the door into the winter wonderland outside. I walked down the steps and onto the walkway in front of the inn. Taking a right at the end of the drive, I walked down the main street until I spotted the Bighorn Diner up ahead.

Before I made it to the front door, Janine came out holding a large paper bag and juggling a tray of four coffees. "Oh good," she said, giving me a hug without spilling a coffee. A feat I could never manage. "Change of plans. We're going to have to go straight to the shop. My assistant, Carly, called, and she's still on her way back from her parents. She told me the roads are still pretty bad in spots."

I looked up and down the main street. It only dawned on me then that there was almost no evidence of the blizzard. The road was wet but virtually bare of snow, and the sidewalks were clear. Only knee-high snowbanks lined the edge. "What happened to all the snow here?" I asked.

Janine laughed. "We only have a half-mile of downtown to plow and a big snow blower. It all goes in the back of a dump truck and gets hauled out. Leo pays special attention to our town roads, and when you live up here, you learn pretty quickly how to handle the snow."

At the end of the block, we came to a stop in front of a darling storefront. It was the same one I saw on my drive into town with Leo. Mr. and Mrs. Claus were still doing their animated dance next to a beautifully decorated tree. "This is your store?"

"It is." Her pride in it was evident in her broad smile.

"I remember thinking how cute your window display was when Leo drove me past on Wednesday."

She handed me the tray of coffees and unlocked the double front doors. "Come on in, and I'll show you around," she said, holding the door open. The bells above it tinkled to announce our arrival.

We set our breakfast down on the cash-wrap counter. I waited there as she slipped into the back room to turn on the lights. I scanned the space, which was larger than it appeared from the outside. The front of the store was all women's wear. And I could already tell I was going to have a hard time sticking to my budget.

"What do you think?" Janine asked.

"It's awesome," I said, hoping how impressed I was showed in my tone. "I can't wait to look around."

Her smile showed me how much she appreciated my enthusiasm. "How about we have breakfast first? I think breakfast sandwiches are best when they're hot," she said, pulling one of the aforementioned treats from the bag and handing it to me.

I peeled back the wax paper to reveal a lovely soft bagel, egg, cheese and bacon creation. My stomach rumbled at the delectable aroma, and sunk my teeth into the yummy sandwich. "Mm. God. This is fantastic," I said. Moaning at how unreasonably good it tasted.

"I know. They're sooo good," she said after swallowing down her own bite. "I swear they add something secret to make it addictive," she added with a laugh. "It must be in the butter because there's nothing else I can think of."

We finished our breakfast, and then she gave me a quick tour of the store. There was a lovely mix of functional and stylish clothing. Intimates were at the back of the space next to a large staircase leading to the second floor.

To the left of the staircase was a cased opening with a sign that said 'Man Cave', indicating the entrance to her menswear department. She led us up the stairs. They looked new but had a classic Victorian style; wide treads at the base led to a landing halfway up where the stairs split and doubled back on either side of the lower section. I trailed my fingertips over the polished dark oak railing, admiring the excellent craftsmanship.

The second floor featured her home goods department. She had a lovely mix of modern farmhouse, rustic, and southwestern style accessories. The kitchenware section made me vow to come back and stock up on all the gadgets I craved but didn't really need. Just as soon as I could afford it.

"What a great place to work," I said. "Is this one of the jobs you were telling me about yesterday?"

"Yes, and no. The Robertsons owned this place forever and brought me in a couple of days a week. It was a perfect fit. I never realized how much I loved shopkeeping. Honestly, at that point, I didn't know much about who I really was because I'd spent so long being who my ex made me. Anyway," she continued, obviously not wanting to deal with those memories, "they were way past wanting to retire. So after about six months, they offered to sell me the business, and I jumped on it without a second thought."

"Wow," I said, genuinely happy for her. "It couldn't have been easy finding financing."

She paused for a moment as we headed back down to the first floor. I realized that my last comment might have come across as prying. I didn't mean it that way, and I tried to correct myself. "I'm sorry, Janine. I'm not trying to be nosy. I'm not asking for details. It's just that I know how hard it is for regular people to just go to a bank and get a business loan. It's like they only want to loan you money if you don't need it."

She placed a reassuring hand on my arm. "Don't worry. I know you're not prying. And you're right; it wouldn't have been easy." She left it hanging there like there was more, but she didn't want to share. That was fine. It was her business, and I certainly empathized with the desire for privacy.

We continued back to the front of the store, placing our empty coffee cups on the counter. "Do you remember how I told you my ex had embezzled from me?" I nodded. "Well, our ancestors founded this town around a silver mine. It's been closed for a long time, but Henry, Hunter and I have a comfortable trust fund. One that will let us live an upper middle-class life and never have to work."

"In my ignorance, I'd let my ex take control of my portion, and I was very lucky he hadn't spent it all. He spent a lot, but I got a pretty good chunk back, and that's what I used to buy this place."

"I'm so glad you could get that money back," I said. "It's kind of a silver lining. You ended up tucking money away without knowing it."

Janine laughed. "I'd never thought of it that way, but you're right. The trust was also what allowed Hunter to rehab the inn. For the first couple of years, he tried to do it with just our annual disbursement, but it was going to take millions to do the whole hotel. When Jenn got pregnant, he had to admit he couldn't do it bit by bit and survive."

"We have a firm that manages the trust much like you would have for your 401K. After Hunter tried and failed to get a mortgage through traditional banks, they came up with the idea that the trust could get the mortgage and then Hunter could pay back the trust. Honestly, it was a risky move given how vindictive Henry is, but the three of us all have equal votes on how the trust is managed. It would take some extensive legal wrangling for Henry to override us, and he can't afford those kinds of lawyers."

"It also allowed me to do a complete remodel here. When I first started, it was old and dusty. Everything was on those old round hanging racks or shelves along the wall. The men's and women's clothes were all mixed, and there weren't any home goods. It was only one floor, and you couldn't have paid me to walk up those stairs they were so rickety."

"You really have done an amazing job. This place looks like it belongs in a high-end resort town, but still fits perfectly with the small-town character of Homer Pass. Hopefully, you get enough traffic here to pay the mortgage."

"Thank you," Janine said. "It really means a lot to me you think that because it's exactly what I was aiming for. And I'm good financially. Between locals happy they don't have to drive over an hour to shop, and the tourists, I'm debt free. I could pay the loan from the trust back early. It's tight, but at least I don't have the same worries Hunter does."

"Well, you nailed it," I said, smiling and genuinely happy for this woman.

"Thanks, now let's get down to the business we came here for," Janine said with a mischievous smile.

I was unsuccessful in completely containing Janine's enthusiasm for providing me with a new wardrobe. I more than met my needs for the week I was going to be here. Nor would she hear a word of protest I made when she only rang a three-hundred-dollar charge through on my credit card. She didn't give me the chance to do more than glance at the price tags, but from what I saw, that charge wouldn't cover what I had in the bag.

I hated the thought of being a charity case, but she dissuaded me of that idea and replaced it with a sneaking suspicion that she was dolling me up to impress Hunter. That type of help was much more palatable to me. And there's no way it should have been.

The clue to this little theory of mine was that when I joked with her, I was surprised she wasn't trying to get me into a bunch of silky lingerie. Her reply was that the long flannel nightgown I had picked out would be much more impactful on Hunter's libido than any lacy something, something ever could. I almost put it back on the rack.

I walked back to the inn, two shopping bags full to the brim, to find a disheveled Elizabeth, hands raking stressfully through her blonde hair, nearly shouting into a phone, "Thank you for calling the Snowflake Inn. Please hold."

"Thank you for calling the Snowflake Inn. Please hold."

"Thank you for calling the Snowflake Inn. Please hold. What? You have been holding? I'm sorry. How can I help you? A room for this weekend? Yes, we have three left. I'm sorry; room one-oh-eight is taken. No, I'm sorry, I can't switch the reservation. We already have a guest checked into that room."

I tried to get her attention and tell her to give them that room. I waved my hands and mouthed 'move me'. Even though I loved that little room, I owed this family so much already I'd be willing to sleep on the couch. She simply shook me off.

"I'm sorry then," she said, not hiding the irritation in her voice. "Yes, perhaps another time."

She looked up at me and breathed heavily, raising her bangs in the breeze it generated. "It's a madhouse. It started just after you left. First rate calls and then I guess there's not a room left in Breckenridge, so now all the ski bums will pay anything just to get up here and ski the powder. We've only got three rooms left, and I haven't even started on prepping them."

"How can I help?"

She shook her head no and picked up one of the calls on hold. I raised an eyebrow at her and let her know there was no way I would not pitch in. After hanging up, there were now two rooms left.

"What do you need me to do, Elizabeth, and don't you dare say nothing."

"God, Amber, I don't know. I don't have time to show you the reservation system. Meg's trying to get the rooms ready. Towels, toiletries and things like that. At least the beds are made up. Tomorrow is going to be a disaster 'cuz Dad's never gotten around to hiring people for the season yet. He scrambled to the grocery store because we've got nothing here for food and we'll have a full dining room tonight." She took a deep breath and let it out slowly. "I don't know. Can you cook a big pot of some kind of soup, maybe? Bake some rolls. The recipe should still be on the counter."

"I think I can manage that just fine." I looked down in the bags I was holding, realizing that there was nothing in there that said cooking in a commercial kitchen. "Do you think maybe you could grab another one of your dad's t-shirts for me to use?" pulling a forest green print sweater out of the bag and showing it to her, "I don't think this would actually be very practical in there."

She gave me a huge grin. "Dad's going to lo... I mean, you're going to look great in that. I'll get one in a minute as soon as I finish these calls."

"Thanks, I'll be right back down. I just want to put on some clean clothes." I turned and hustled up the stairs. I changed as quickly as I could, pulling on a new pair of leggings and slipping on the comfy pair of flats Janine had convinced me to buy stating I couldn't shlep around the hotel in boots all the time and headed back down to the front desk.

Halfway back down the stairs that it dawned on me I had agreed to cook for God knows how many people. The inn had thirty-six rooms, which meant at least sixty people, and I wasn't sure if they opened the dining room to the public. I was a decent cook, and the thought of being set free in that spacious commercial kitchen excited me, but the biggest meal I ever prepared was for eight. Something told me that today was going to be a whole different animal.

I approached the desk, and Elizabeth gave me a weak smile. "We're officially full, and the phone is still ringing off the hook." She reached under the counter and handed me a shirt. Not the T-shirt I was expecting, but a navy blue polo with a big snowflake on the left breast. "This will fit you much better than one of dad's tees, and if you're going to work, you might as well get the free uniform that comes with it."

"Thank you. I will wear it with pride."

She offered me a satisfied smile. "You might want to wear an apron though, just in case. We might need you to wait tables tonight. I've tried a few people in town who sometimes help us in a pinch, but no one's answering. They're probably all doing hand to hand combat to get the doorbuster deals down the mountain."

It had completely slipped my mind that today was Black Friday. The only people I had to buy for were my mom, Walter and Patty. Online, a couple of clicks and no crowds. "So, just how many servings of soup should I be making?"

She thought for a second. "Enough for forty to fifty, I think should be enough. I'm pretty sure there are about twenty servings of chowder in the freezer you can throw in the warmer. Check what's in the racks for makings. You might have to make smaller batches of different soups. I hope Dad gets back soon or he'll be stressed trying to get everything prepped."

"Okay, well, I'd better get cracking. I'll try not to pester you with questions about where everything is."

She slipped off her perch behind the desk, walked out, and gave me a hug. "Thank you. Dad's going to be pissed because you're a guest, but God, we need you, Amber. You have no idea."

I hugged her back, but it struck me that she might not just be talking about the help I was offering in the kitchen.

# 14

# Unexpected Help

## Hunter

I walked into the kitchen with a box of what would eventually be to-night's dinner menu at the inn, to see a frantic Amber in an apron covered from head to toe with who knows whatever it was she was concocting. It seemed like an awful lot for a late lunch. A beat passed before it clicked that she shouldn't be making her own lunch anyway. She was a guest here, not part of the family. I couldn't afford to contemplate why I liked the concept of her as part of us. I was so far behind in prep I had no idea how I'd have dinner for sixty ready in four hours.

Amber was so intent on what she was doing she didn't notice me. Her brow was knit together as she focused on the binder spread open on the prep table. Her wavy brown hair was doing its best to escape the loose bun. There was a particularly troublesome strand that hung directly in her line of sight. After several attempts to blow it out of the way, she reached up and tucked it behind her delicate ear. My fingers twitched as my mind longed for it to be my hand tucking the wayward strand away before kiss-ing her ear.

Finally snapping back to my senses, I cleared my throat and placed the box of groceries on the counter. "Oh, hey." She smiled at me with a warmth that had my mind right back to thinking about kisses.

"Looks like quite a lunch you're fixing yourself. You must have worked up quite an appetite shopping this morning."

"Haha, funny man. I'll have you know that there are two pots of soup on the stove, and I'm putting the finishing touches on the third. The dough for the rolls should be rising nicely by now and be ready for the oven shortly. If you managed to find vegetables for a salad, I could prep those for you too. Which means all you have to worry about is the entrée."

"Amber." The husky way her name tumbled from my lips was both a prayer and a desire. I was at a loss for words. Not only was I now back on schedule, but ahead of it. "That's, um, that's wonderful. I can't thank you enough, but you're supposed to be a guest at our inn, not the sous chef."

"You're welcome. I came back to find an overwhelmed Elizabeth at the front desk and couldn't bear to see a sixteen-year-old have a nervous breakdown."

I shook my head because I knew exactly what my poor daughter must have gone through. I felt guilty for leaving her all alone, but I had no choice. I knew she and Janine thought I was just procrastinating about hiring staff, but they didn't know how tight things were financially. The inn was not breaking even, and every new employee meant dipping into what should have been the girls' college trust funds. I just couldn't do it. Jenn was the brains behind this, and I struggled to make intelligent choices in running the business. I was failing in my part of keeping her dream alive.

"I know it was crazy when I left at nine. The tough thing about living in a town this size is the lack of commercial supply sources. The local IGA just doesn't have much to choose from when I have to buy in volume. At least Tom, the butcher there, helps by doing the prep for me. I think he likes it. It's a change from grinding hamburger all day."

She laughed and stepped back from the prep table to investigate the boxes I set down. "Where are the veggies for the salad?"

"You don't have to do that. You've already done so much."

"Don't be stubborn." She reached across the narrow table and grabbed my jacket, pulling me closer. She leaned up on tiptoes and kissed my cheek. "Maybe you can thank me in some special way later."

Even if I didn't see the twinkle of mischief in her eyes, my mind was already coming up with several plans. As she turned to go back to work, I admired the view. Even though the shirt she was wearing covered half of her full, round bottom, I had seen it before and knew without a doubt it would feel heavenly to cup it in my hands, to use that grasp to pull her close and kiss her. To hold on as our bodies, pressed together as we… My faded jeans were suddenly uncomfortably tight. I shook my head. "Salad stuff is still in the truck." I turned to walk back out and get the rest and added more to myself than Amber. "You can count on it."

"Count on what?" She yelled after me.

I turned and smiled, giving her a wink. "Me thanking you later."

She just smiled and went back to what she was working on. Though I caught her peeking at me from under her long lashes. There was more color on her cheeks than usual, but the kitchen was hot and she was working very hard. I didn't want to read too much into it, but I was certainly hoping that the prospect of some one-on-one time later excited her as much as it excited me.

I finished unloading the groceries for the weekend and went about getting ready to serve a full inn's worth of guests. We would have more than a full dining room tonight with all the skiers flocking to be here for the weekend. Saturday night would be busy, but less crowded. A lot of the ski bums sought pizza joints or restaurants that featured après-ski entertainment. By Sunday night, we would be back to a quiet, little, mostly vacant inn in a sleepy little town. That would give me a chance to hire some help. The long-range forecast called for a snowy and cold December, just what the Snowflake Inn needed to get its head back above water.

Amber and I spent the next two hours working in silent companionship. Despite the pressure to be ready for the dinner rush, I felt more at ease than I had in a long time. It was nice to have someone with me in the kitchen, even if we weren't having deep conversations. It was nice to have Amber there. Even in the big kitchen, sometimes we got in each other's way. And I'd be lying if I didn't get closer to her than was necessary to do what I had to do. There was just something about her that made me want to be close to her, something more than my building desire for her.

By four o'clock I was ready for the evening to come, and I could finally take a relaxed breath since early in the morning. I leaned back against the counter and poured myself a fresh cup of coffee. Amber stepped over and did the same, leaning in close but not quite touching me. "Wow, that was a lot of work, but I think we're ready." It felt nice to hear her say we. "What's next?"

I was just about to tell her she was free to go when my stomach grumbled loudly. I could certainly use the help, but I felt I had already more than imposed on a woman that was technically one of my guests at the inn, though she was feeling more a part of the family with each passing minute.

I could feel my cheeks warm with embarrassment. "Excuse me. I never got to eat lunch."

She patted my stomach. "I can tell. What can I fix for you? Would you like to taste test my soup before serving it to your guests?"

"Well, to be honest, I already snuck a taste when you weren't looking, but I would love a bowl of that chicken noodle. I think it might be the best soup I've ever tasted."

The smile that spread over her face made me feel warm all over, I mean all over. She turned to get me a bowl and handed it to me with a hunk of baguette; we pulled up two stools and sat while I tried to focus on eating instead of on Amber. Having her so close was becoming more and more distracting. I had to admit it was getting harder to remember that she would be gone within a week. As far as I was concerned, she was right where she belonged, but then I really didn't have a say in that. "This soup really is terrific. I thought you said you didn't have any experience."

"Thank you. I think this is the first time anyone has ever complimented me on my cooking."

"I can't believe that."

She just shrugged her shoulders. "I've mostly just cooked for myself. My ex was never complimentary about much to anyone, and he would never let me entertain at the house. He preferred to go out to fancy restaurants and show off how trendy he was to our friends."

I had an overwhelming urge to pull her into me and hold her. To tell her I would never treat her so poorly and would be proud to entertain with her. I chickened out, not wanting to scare her off, and gave her a gentle squeeze on the leg. "Well, I would be happy to eat whatever you decided to make for me."

She was still smiling, but there was something more behind the smile, just a hint of sadness, maybe. "Well, thank you again. But you didn't an-swer my question. What's next?"

"Nothing really, I guess, until we serve at six. Janine said she was com-ing to help with that, and one of the girls who works for her is going to help too. I've got to double-check and make sure that Megan got all the rooms ready, and I want to give Snow a break at the front desk before the check-in rush starts. You've already done so much I'd hate to ask any more of you."

"You're not asking, I'm offering. What am I going to do, go up to my room and read? I couldn't, knowing you were all here working so hard, and I owe you so much."

"Amber, you owe me nothing. You were in a predicament, and we did what we could to help. It's what humans do for other humans, at least that's what they should be doing."

Her eyes met mine, and I couldn't pull my gaze away. I saw the whole wonderful world behind those brown eyes and the yellow specks that looked like sparks, sparks that were lighting me on fire. "Give me something to do, Hunter, please."

There was no way I could refuse her, and the fact that I couldn't fathom having her more than a few feet away from me ever again wouldn't have allowed it if I could. "If you want to help me in the kitchen, that would be great. But I have to warn you, I can sound a little cranky when things get busy. Janine says I don't ask for things; I bark for them. If you promise not to take my tone personally, I could certainly use an extra pair of hands."

"I promise not to take it personally, and if you say something really stupid, I'll just tell Janine." She gave me a wink, but I was wondering just how she knew that would be such an incentive to stay civil. Janine can be a royal pain when I do something stupid. "In the meantime, how about I take care of giving Elizabeth a break? I'm sure she can show me how to answer the phone, and I'm perfectly capable of taking messages."

"Perfect. If you don't mind, take her a bowl of the soup too. I bet she hasn't bothered with eating all day."

She gave me a salute and in a flash was out the door with food for my daughter. I gave myself a moment to collect my thoughts. It seemed that whenever Amber was around, I had trouble focusing on anything else. Tonight was going to be our busiest night at the inn in over three years. I needed to go back through my mental checklist. We needed good reviews so that maybe, just maybe, we could keep up the momentum.

# 15

# *You Said What?*

## *Amber*

As I opened the door to the lobby, the din of multiple conversations hit me at once. Hunter and I hadn't heard a thing in the kitchen, but I'm finding myself increasingly unable to focus on anything but him when he's within twenty feet of me. Rounding the corner, I found Elizabeth looking more frazzled and rushed than she did when I came back from shopping. I didn't think that was possible. Guests looking to check in were five deep in line, and one couple looked particularly perturbed.

I quickly set the food on the counter and pulled the apron from around my neck. "What do you need me to do?" I whispered into Elizabeth's ear. She jumped, so intent on what she was doing she hadn't noticed me step behind her.

"God! I don't know, take their dinner times down after I check them in. There are ten tables of four; figure an hour and fifteen minutes for each table."

"Got it." I placed a hand on her shoulder and gave it a gentle squeeze. "You're doing great."

She managed to give me a small smile and then went right back to processing the guests in front of her. The steady stream of people continued to arrive until all but two of the reservations we had, I mean *they* had, for the weekend were checked in and dinner reservations were made. Looking at the sheet, we wouldn't be done serving dinner until after ten tonight. My feet were already telling me they were ready to be done for the day, but they'd just have to suck it up. I had big plans for a nice soak in my large tub and a glass or two of wine when all of this was done.

It was already quarter to six, and I looked at the now stone-cold bowl of soup I had brought out for Elizabeth. "Have you eaten anything at all today?" She pointed to the shelf at her knee level, which contained several empty soda cans and a crumpled-up bag of Doritos. "That's it? You must be starving."

"I don't care. I hit half of the major food groups. All I'm missing are chocolate and ice cream." She gave me a weak smile, but my raised eyebrow showed I was having none of it.

"Go back and tell your dad what you want for dinner. I'll bring it out for you, and it better be good and healthy or I'll pick something that is, understand?"

She looked me up and down and then smiled. "Yes, Mom," she said, drawing out the mom with all the attitude of the teenager she was, but dutifully headed to the kitchen as I'd asked.

For the briefest of moments, I let myself soak in how nice it had felt to have someone call me Mom. Even if it wasn't true and delivered with an attitude, I knew she didn't really mean it. I was brought out of my little daydream by a clearing throat.

"Excuse me," an attractive woman I would guess was in her early forties stood in front of me at the counter.

"Hi, I'm sorry."

"No need to apologize. I can tell it's been a busy day for you folks, and I've got a daughter the same age. I have to fight to bite my tongue when she gives me attitude over simple things. She's doing a great job, though, so efficient and businesslike for a young woman. You and your husband have done a wonderful job raising her."

"I'm…, she's…, um, …, thank you." Best just to let it go, I thought. "That's very kind. I'll be sure to tell her father. How can I help you?"

"I was wondering if it would be possible to get an extra set of bath towels sent up. I know I'm not going to resist that tub tonight, and we'll be heading to the slopes early in the morning. I don't want to bother you during the breakfast rush."

Damn, I hadn't thought about that. Maybe just a quick bath. "Certainly. What room are you in?"

"We're in room 212."

"Perfect. I'll take care of that for you."

"Thank you so much. If the food is half as good as everything else here, we'll be back to see you a lot. I just love these old hotels, so much nicer than the indistinguishable lodging up in Breckenridge. And this is obviously family-owned and operated. I'd much rather support small businesses."

"That's very kind. I'll be sure to check on you at dinner and see how we're doing."

She smiled and turned away just as Janine came bursting through the front door, carrying a shopping bag in one hand and Amy holding her other. "Hey you," she called out, far cheerier than a woman who had worked all day and was about to spend another four-plus hours on her feet waiting tables should be.

"Amber," Amy squealed excitedly, letting go of her aunt's hand and rushing behind the desk to give me a hug.

"Where have you been all day?" I asked Amy.

"At my friend's. Daddy takes me there sometimes when he knows the inn is going to be busy. He doesn't want me to be bored."

"Isn't that fun?" I said.

She nodded. "Want to go play Barbies with me?" she asked, eyes full of hope.

It killed me to disappoint her, but apparently, I was part of the busy inn too. At least for tonight. "I'm sorry, sweetheart, I'm helping Daddy tonight. Maybe tomorrow?"

"Okay," she answered, nonplussed. "I'm going to go see if Meg wants to then." She took off around the corner and through the door into the family addition.

I shook my head and looked up at Janine.

"Look at you fitting right in and all decked out in your very own official Snowflake Inn shirt."

I almost forgot I had one on. "Elizabeth figured I should look official even if I was just volunteering."

She walked behind the counter and dropped the bag, pulling me in for a hug and a big wet kiss on the cheek. "We'll get you to be an official part of this family one way or the other. Now give me your room key and I'll run this up really quick before I have to start serving."

"What is this?" I asked, looking suspiciously at the bag. "I already have everything I bought."

Janine shook her head. "Nope. I realized you forgot a couple of things, so I took care of that."

"Janine," I sing-songed. I didn't know what to say; I felt so overwhelmed with her generosity.

"Just give me your key. I know you're going to love it." Her smile was wide and genuine, and there was a sparkle in her eyes that made me think she enjoyed doing this just as much as I appreciated it.

"You don't need to do that. Elizabeth should be back out in a second, and I can do it before I go back to the kitchen."

"He's got you cooking tonight?"

"He does. Well, helping him anyway. I imagine I'll just be serving the sides and putting up the plates. Where's your help? Hunter said you were bringing someone with you."

"Oh, I imagine Carly's going in through the kitchen to make sure Hunter sees her. Poor girl has it bad for him, but he's never been the least bit interested in her."

My stomach tightened as those words left Janine's mouth. The thought of someone hitting on Hunter was not the least bit appealing to me, and I shouldn't give a damn. I had no right to care. He'd only kissed me once, and it hadn't even been hinted at the entire time in the kitchen together. I think we both knew it couldn't go any further.

Janine raised an eyebrow and tilted her head to the side. I wasn't going to face the questions I knew were coming. "You know what, just stay here for a minute and I'll take the bag up. I need to use the bathroom, anyway."

"Go for it, girl."

I grabbed the bag and noticed a red cashmere sweater that I had tried on and loved but passed on because it was far more expensive than I could afford. "Janine," I said, drawing it out in an accusatory tone. I did my best to level a critical glare, but based on the smile that spread across her face, I failed at being very intimidating.

She shrugged her shoulders. "I just added a couple of things. A girl needs choices after all. You never know what might pop up." She wiggled her eyebrows suggestively and was not apologetic in the least. I shook my head. There was no sense in arguing with her, and neither of us had time for that with dinner to serve in less than fifteen minutes. I couldn't deny it made me feel very warm inside. I'd never had a sister to have my back. It was nice, even if it was only for just a few days.

When I finally got to breathe and looked at my watch, it was nine-fifty-two. I brushed my hands on my apron and then rested them on my hips. Somehow, Hunter and I had prepared and served seventy-two meals in the space of a little over three hours. That might not be much for a place like Applebee's, but for two in the kitchen and two servers, I was impressed. I looked up to see Hunter running his hands through his hair and surveying the disaster area of a kitchen. There were dirty pots and pans, dishes piled high, and trash bags stacked at the door. We might not have to cook anything more, but there was still plenty of work to do.

He caught me staring at him and smiled. "I look that bad, do I?"

I could feel the heat rise on my face. "I was just thinking you look pretty hot, honestly." My god did those words just come out of my mouth? Exhausted me, doesn't have a very good filter.

His smile broadened, and, holy moly, he might even be blushing. "I could say the same for you. You were a rock star tonight, Amber. Are you sure you've never worked in a kitchen before?"

"My only restaurant experience is about fifteen minutes of being a bad waitress."

"Maybe you weren't a very good waitress, but I couldn't have done this tonight without you." He closed the distance between us and pulled me into a hug. A big, strong, warm bear hug that my body just melted into. He smelled so damn good, pine and cinnamon and a little bit of everything he'd cooked tonight. That last part triggered a growl in my stomach that I'm sure was registered by the United States Geological Survey as a four on the Richter scale. I wanted to die of embarrassment, but in his brawny arms wouldn't be a terrible place to go.

Damn him, I was not supposed to be feeling these things. He kissed the top of my head, and I hugged him tighter. He cleared his throat and loosened the hug. "What would you like to eat? I know Janine will want nothing more than soup if we have any left, and I'm not sure what Carly will want, but let me fix something for you. I know you're hungry. I can hear it."

At that moment, Carly came into the kitchen carrying a tray of dirty dishes. She froze where she was. Her eyes widened as she stared at Hunter and me. Despite knowing I should break our embrace and maybe even feel a bit of embarrassment at being caught in a compromising position, I held on just a little bit tighter.

Carly's eyes flicked between Hunter and me, and I stared right back. That little possessive voice inside of me shouting 'mine'. After a moment, she bit her bottom lip and her shoulders sagged. It could have been the weight of the heavy tray she was holding, but I saw it as an admission of defeat. 'That's right, bitch,' the voice said. 'Mine, and don't you forget it'. Only he really wasn't. And I didn't have any right to claim him. It wasn't fair to stand in the way of Hunter finding someone who could be with him long term. That little voice didn't care.

"Just three more parties finishing up their dinners," she said, continuing on toward the sink.

"Great," Hunter said. "Thanks so much for helping tonight, Carly. I really appreciate it."

"No problem," she said, not looking up from what she was doing. "I don't mind."

I could hear the disappointment in her voice, and I felt guilty for our little nonverbal exchange.

"What would you like for dinner?" he asked her.

"I'm good, thanks," she said, finally turning to face us again. We had broken our embrace, but I still stood closer to him than was necessary. Maybe I didn't feel *that* guilty.

"Are you sure? The T-bones look great. Tom cut them just the right thickness."

"No thank you," she said, offering him a smile that had my little green monster snapping back to attention. "I've been stealing rolls all night and now I just want to go home, take a hot shower and go to bed."

She really was a beautiful woman, looking at her objectively. Which wasn't at all easy to do. Long blonde hair pulled back in a neat ponytail. Her blue eyes were a darker sapphire hue than the girls'. She was a couple of inches taller than me and slender. Much closer to what Jenn looked like, I guess, from looking at the pictures from behind the front desk. She was younger, maybe late twenties, but despite that, probably much more his type than I was.

"Okay," Hunter said. "You can go now if you want."

"Thanks, but I'll help finish up. Your sister is dragging. She's had a long day too." With that, she pushed her way through the door and back into the dining room.

I peered up from under my eyelashes to see his dark brown eyes staring down at me. All thoughts of food were gone, but there certainly was a different hunger I felt. He cocked an eyebrow. I hoped to hell he wasn't reading my mind. "How about you?" he asked me. "Can I tempt you with one of these steaks?"

A steak sounded delicious, but at this hour, if I ate anything that heavy, it would go nowhere but straight to my hips and stomach fat. "The soup's fine, really. I think there's enough minestrone left. The beef barley was gone pretty quickly. We have tons of dishes to do. I'll get started on that."

A very weary-looking Elizabeth pushed through the kitchen door that led from their private quarters. "Amy's sound asleep and Meg's in bed watching TV." She scanned the kitchen, taking in all the cleanup that still had to be done, and shook her head. "Dad, you have got to hire some people. What if this were next week, and I was in school on Friday? You would have been totally screwed, and we'd have a lot of very unsatisfied customers."

"I know I do. I'll post an ad online tomorrow, I promise."

"You don't have to. I already did that about fifteen minutes ago."

"Elizabeth!" His voice was raised, and I could tell the fatigue and stress of the day was setting in. I gently gave his arm a squeeze, and he took a deep breath. "I'm sorry, honey, thank you. I just worry about expenses, you know?"

"I know, Dad, but we already had five couples that reserved for next weekend too. I guess they're predicting two more storms next week, so we're getting a great start to ski season." Hunter motioned to her, and she stepped into his arms for a hug that melted my heart. "Oh," she said, and she pulled back from her father. "One woman who made reservations asked me to give this to you, Amber." She pulled a folded note from her pocket. "She actually made reservations for every weekend through the end of January, two adjoining rooms." She side-eyed her dad; what for I wasn't sure until she continued. "She said to give it to my mom." She was still smiling, but I could tell there was some pain behind her eyes. "I almost corrected her, but then I remembered I had called you Mom when she was walking up to the desk earlier."

"You said that?" The expression on Hunter's face was unreadable. A little confusion, a little sadness, maybe?

"I had just told her to come back and tell you what she wanted for dinner. She was living on soda and chips all day. She gave me some good-natured sass to let me know I was being a pain in her teenage rear."

She smiled and stuck her tongue out at me, and Hunter leveled a parental stare at her that would have had me quaking in my shoes. Elizabeth simply gave him the same treatment. I couldn't help but laugh, causing Hunter to turn his brooding stare in my direction. Yup, I was quaking, but not from fear.

"Aren't you going to read it? Tell us what it says." Elizabeth was bouncing on her toes in anticipation.

"Elizabeth, Amber does not have to read you a letter that was addressed to her. It's none of our business."

"But it's about the inn, Dad. I know it is."

"Did you read it already, Snow?"

"Don't call me Snow, Dad! And no, I didn't read it. I'm not rude, you know."

Fearing this had the potential of going downhill quickly, I was just as excited to read it as she was to hear it. "Of course I'll read it to you both." I carefully unfolded the letter to see a neatly composed handwritten letter in flowing script. I couldn't remember the last time I had read something that wasn't an email or text. I cleared my throat and began to read it aloud:

> *Dear Amber,*
>
> *Please forgive my familiarity, but your darling daughter gave me your name. First, let me thank you so much for your family's hospitality. As I said earlier, it's so nice to stay in a place like this. My husband and I feel welcomed as if we were guests in your home, not a hotel. Thank you also for your prompt response to my request for additional towels. I was barely back in the room when your younger daughter delivered them, along with additional bath products. I'm sure I will enjoy them.*
>
> *Dinner was marvelous and again, just like home, not some nevue cuisine that is more trendy than edible. I could see you and your husband hard at work in the kitchen, and I can tell you that your efforts and love for this place and your children easily explain your success.*
>
> *I know we spoke about teenagers and their attitudes before, but in all seriousness, you must be so proud of all your girls, especially Elizabeth. She is a hard worker and so mature. She shared with me the story of how you came to purchase your dream and that she was born right here in the inn during a blizzard, which is how she got her nickname, and the inn got its name. She seemed very proud that you named it after her and that although she doesn't always like being called Snowflake anymore, she still smiles when she sees the sign out front. You should really put that on your marketing materials. I'm sure it would resonate with many people.*
>
> *As I promised, I have made reservations every weekend for the rest of the ski season. I look forward to seeing much more of you and your darling family in the coming months.*
>
> *Warmly,*
> *Rebeca Small*

I smiled at Elizabeth and then at Hunter. He was already hugging her and kissing the top of her head. She was absolutely beaming with happiness. "I didn't know you were born here at the inn."

Hunter smiled at the memory. "In a storm worse than the one that blew you to our doorstep. She was delivered by Leo and one of the other firefighters. The doctor finally arrived by snowcat about fifteen minutes after she arrived. We actually debated about calling her Snowflake for her legal name but decided that we were neither hippies nor Hollywood celebrities, so we couldn't do that to her."

I laughed. "She would hate you all her life if you did."

"I would, and then I'd change my name the day I turned eighteen."

"No, you wouldn't, and you know it. That name comes from a whole lot of love, and don't you ever forget it, little girl."

"I'm not a little girl."

Hunter smiled wistfully. "No, you're not, but you'll always be my little girl." He hugged her again and then turned her to face the door. "Now go get some sleep. We've got breakfast to serve in seven hours."

I groaned at the thought, but she gave a very polite "yes, Dad. Goodnight Dad. Goodnight, Amber, I mean, Mom," she said, the teasing sarcasm obvious in her voice. She peeked over her shoulder and gave me a wide grin with a twinkle of mischief in her eye.

"Goodnight, Elizabeth."

We both watched her go out the door, and I don't think I could have been any prouder of her if she was my daughter, and the look in Hunter's eyes told me he was, indeed, very proud of his daughter.

Once the door closed behind her, Hunter turned and looked at me, and I felt the heat in his gaze. I looked down at the beautiful, heartfelt letter in my hand, and a pang of guilt washed over me. It wasn't meant as a deception, but I wondered how Mrs. Rebeca Small was going to feel when she found out that I wasn't the girl's mother. "I, um… I'm sorry. I guess I should have corrected her on the spot. I hope this doesn't make things awkward. I mean, she might get offended, and you'll lose a good customer."

"Don't…" Hunter stopped himself, mouth open. It closed, and a smile spread across his face. "Well, we can't have a dissatisfied customer, can we?"

I just stared blankly back, not knowing what to say. "No. That wouldn't be ideal, but maybe she'll understand. She seems very nice."

Hunter's expression turned serious. "Nope, can't chance it. She was probably one of those customers who would rake us over the coals. Post bad reviews everywhere just because we offended her."

"Hunter, I think that's just a little ..."

"You're just going to have to be here every Friday and Saturday night until spring." He couldn't hold his expression any longer and broke into a smile.

I swatted his shoulder. I still had my doubts. I had a life to go back to in Denver, well, a half-life anyway, but I would not wreck this moment we were having. "Is that so? I'm supposed to rearrange my life just to cover for a little white lie?"

"Lying's a sin, Amber. This is your penance."

I swatted his shoulder harder this time, and he caught my hand in his. His big, strong, warm hand. He brought it to his lips and kissed my palm and held it there. I sighed. Tendrils of electricity shot through every nerve in my body, and I wasn't sure how much longer I could stand on my own. I inched closer to him because my body needed to be nearer just to survive. "Why do I not think lying is the sin I should be most concerned about right now?" I breathed.

His hand that wasn't holding mine cupped the back of my head and pulled me closer. I leaned up on my toes and tilted my head. My lips parted just as he met mine and pressed tight. His fingers curled around mine, and he pressed them to his chest. I could feel the thump, thump, thump of his heart beating. My hand fisted his shirt as he pulled me tighter. His tongue snaked through my parted lips and claimed me. The need I had for him was like nothing I had ever experienced. Not with Lance, not with anyone. All I wanted at that moment was for him to swipe away everything on the prep bench and to take me right there in the kitchen. I would have gladly surrendered my body to him at that moment.

"It's no damn wonder the food was so slow coming out of the kitchen tonight, if this is what you two have been doing."

Buckets of figurative ice water crashed over us, and we jumped three feet apart at the sound of Janine's voice. Hunter knocked a stack of baking sheets to the floor with such a mighty crash that I was sure that the girls would be snapped from a sound sleep and come running in to see what had happened.

"Jesus Christ, sis, don't you, like, know how to knock or something?"

"Knock before coming into a kitchen I'm working in? I'd tell you two to get a room, but I know you already have one." She did that wiggling thing with her eyebrows again. "Why don't you go somewhere private and finish what you've started, and Carly and I will finish cleaning up?"

I wanted to hide in one of the cabinets. I haven't felt so embarrassed in like years, high school freshman year with that freckled-faced boy, whatever his name was, playing spin the bottle when his parents came downstairs and caught us.

"I was just saying thank you for all her help tonight. We can all do the cleanup."

Janine simply put her hands on her hips and raised a brow.

"What?" Hunter asked, feigning ignorance. Rather unconvincingly, I thought. Who's sinning now, wise guy?

She looked at Hunter, then she looked at me and then back at Hunter. "You are adults. You have nothing to be embarrassed about and nothing to hide. Anyone with two eyes can see there's something between you. Even little Amy can see it, and she's too young to know what *it* is."

"She does not." I couldn't hide the fact that just the thought of her seeing the lust in my eyes mortified me.

Janine threw her arms into the air. "I give up. Let's get this place cleaned up so I can leave, and you two can pretend that nobody knows what you're up to."

"We aren't up to anything, Janine," Hunter said in a tone that made it clear he didn't want to talk about him and me anymore.

"I may be your baby sister, and it may have been a long time since I've gotten any too but I know a kiss," she dropped her voice low for emphasis, "when I see one and that was one hell of a kiss."

"Can we please, God, just clean up and stop talking about kissing?" Hunter replied.

That sounded like a lovely idea, and I turned and started collecting things and heading toward the sinks.

Fortunately, all talk of kissing stopped, and the four of us got everything washed and put away in less than forty-five minutes. Carly said goodbye and let herself out the back door. I expected more of an attitude from her based on what Janine had told me earlier, but she was quite pleasant. Either she had accepted defeat or hid her disappointment very well.

Janine gave her brother a kiss and a hug and then did the same to me. "Enjoy yourself," she whispered in my ear as she hugged me. I wanted to protest but knew I could never to it with a straight face. As she was walking out, she yelled back over her shoulder, "If I were you, big brother, I'd take the show up to Amber's room. I wouldn't want the girls to be getting any kind of extra education." The door shut behind her before either of us could respond.

Hunter smiled at me, but then something changed behind his eyes. It's like he left me for a moment and went somewhere else in his mind, and it didn't seem like a happy place.

I stepped toward him and placed my palms flat on his deliciously broad chest. "Is everything okay? It seems like something's bothering you."

He looked down at me. I could still see the desire in his eyes, but it was different. There was sadness in him. He had the same look when he was talking about his sister-in-law dying in the fire. "Nothing's wrong. I guess I'm just tired. You must be exhausted. It's been a hell of a day." His smile was back, but not as bright as before. "Thank you again. We never could have done this without you."

I leaned in and kissed him on the cheek. "Um, well, maybe you can thank me properly."

"I really think I should."

"Mm hmm," I kissed him again. This time he turned and kissed me back once again, taking my breath away. Once I caught my breath, I ran my thumb over his stubble cheek, thinking of how that would feel on the soft skin between my legs. I couldn't deny what I was feeling any longer and, for the first time in years, I didn't feel I wanted to. "Janine's probably right. Why don't we grab a bottle of wine and go up to my room? I think the girls will be okay for a little while."

His expression changed again, and he put his hands over mine and let out a long, slow breath. I knew what was coming. "I don't think we should, Amber. I can't, I mean I thought I could and God I want to, but I just can't."

I felt like a total fool for putting myself out there and getting shot down. Everything leaked out of me like a balloon with a pinhole. I could feel the stinging in my eyes, and I'll be damned if I let him see me like that. "Of course. It's fine. I just thought. Um, I'm going to go up now. I guess I'll see you in the morning. Breakfast starts at six, right?"

"Amber, I'm sorry; it's not you, it's me. I'm just…"

"Hunter, it's fine. I get it, really, I do." I cut him off. I was not about to be rejected. Not again. This would be my choice. "We had a moment, so let's not make it awkward now. I'll be down at six to help with breakfast."

"Don't worry about breakfast, sleep in. Please, you've already done so much."

I shrugged my shoulders. I would not force myself on him. "Okay.

Goodnight." I turned and headed to the door as quickly as I could without running, hoping I could make it before the tears fell.

"Amber, please don't be upset."

I kept walking. The tears fell. I didn't make it, but he couldn't see them. No man was going to see me hurt again.

# 16

# The Wisdom of Snow

## Hunter

I watched Amber walk out the door of the kitchen, and I wanted to run after her. I knew I had hurt her. She felt rejected, and it had nothing to do with her. It was all on me.

When Janine suggested we go to her room, I knew she was right. I didn't want to wake the girls or place Amber in an embarrassing situation if one of them got up in the middle of the night. Nor could I see Amber having to sneak out at the crack of dawn to head back to her room. We were both past the walk of shame stage of our lives. Plus, there was nothing to be ashamed of.

I knew without question that once I got that woman into my bed, I would never want her to leave. But I couldn't. Something inside me slid right back to Jenn. I felt like she was standing there looking over my shoulder. I guess it's best we found that out in the kitchen and not when I first walked into that room. That would have only made it worse.

I walked back into the residence, but I was still angry with myself. I banked the fire and switched off the lights. "DAMN IT" my fist slammed against the wall, denting the wallboard. "Fuck," I muttered under my breath, shaking my hand, which was now throbbing with pain.

"That's two bucks for the swear jar, Dad." Elizabeth's smug words did not sit well.

"What are you still doing up?" I barked.

"Geez, Dad, I thought you were done taking out your frustration on the people that love you. Guess you've just expanded it to us now."

I felt like total shit. I was mad at myself, and no one else. "I'm sorry. You're right, you didn't deserve that."

"Thank you. Did you bark at Amber too? Is that why she's not here with you? Because if you did, you'd better go apologize."

"Elizabeth, first I didn't bark at Amber and second, why would she be here with me? Her room is upstairs in the hotel."

Elizabeth put her hands on her hips and leveled me with an are you kidding me stare that would have made her mother proud. "What's got you upset, Dad?"

"Nothing."

"Dad."

"Nothing."

"You haven't punched anything in months. You've been happy for the past two days like I haven't seen you in a long time, and I think it's got something to do with Amber, so why aren't you at least smooching on the couch? Did you say something dumb to her?"

The intent look in her eyes let me know that even pulling the dad card was going to be useless. "Not exactly dumb."

Elizabeth had the teenage eye-rolling thing down pat, and she executed a particularly effective one. "Go apologize, Dad."

"It's not like that, Elizabeth. I did nothing that needs an apology, not precisely anyway."

"What did you do?"

"I'm not telling you."

"Well, you must have done something worse than trying to kiss her. You've already done that anyway." She said with a sigh. I wasn't going to lie to her, but I certainly wasn't going to confirm it either. "Really, Dad. Go apologize."

"Elizabeth, I think you're forgetting who the adult is and who the teenager is. What I did is between Amber and me, and that's the end of it. Now, is there something that has you up or did you just decide to harass me because neither of us has had enough aggravation for one day?"

"I heard you slamming around out here and figured you were upset about something, so I came out to check, just in time to see you try to put your fist through the wall."

"I'm sorry I disturbed you. Really, I am. Everything will be okay in the morning. Let's go to bed. Six is going to come early."

"Dad, for real. Go work out whatever it is with Amber. You'll never sleep if you don't, and I don't want to have to walk around on eggshells for another two years, avoiding angry dad because you blew it with a really great woman."

"Fine, I'll go talk to her, but tell me something. Why are you so eager to get me and Amber together? Doesn't it seem just a little disloyal to your mom?"

She stepped closer and wrapped her arms around my waist. "I love you, Dad. And so does Mom and we both want you to be happy. You're too young to cut yourself off from life out of some misguided loyalty to Mom. She didn't want that. None of us do. And I have this feeling about Amber, this really good feeling."

"Don't tell me it is more of that Lakota seeing the future stuff."

"Dad, you know it's real, and it's not seeing the future, just a sort of heightened intuition. I know Mom had visions sometimes, but I just kinda know things once in a while."

"I don't know if it's real."

"Then how is it that two weeks before she died in that accident, she made you promise that if she died, you'd remarry? Made you promise you wouldn't waste your life mourning her? Why is it she sat me down and told me to make sure you kept your promise? That's what I'm doing, Dad, just making sure you keep your promise to Mom. It's honoring her, not betraying her memory. Maybe Amber isn't the one, but I know the way you two look at each other; she could be. And I happen to like her. I like her a lot, Dad. We all do."

This was an argument I would never win, and with a sixteen-year-old, nonetheless. I know Jenn always claimed to be able to sense things, and she attributed it to her Native American blood. Her great-great grand-mother had been a Lakota medicine woman, or something like it. It always tickled me that my blonde-haired, blue-eyed wife clung so closely to her Native American ancestry, but she was right more often than she wasn't. I just figured it was hormones. "Fine, I'll go talk to her. She's probably already asleep."

"Trust me, whatever you did upset her. She's not sleeping."

I kissed her on the top of her head. "I really am very proud of you, but you're growing up way too fast."

"I know, but I'll always be your little girl." She jumped up and kissed my cheek. "Promise you'll talk to her."

"Go to bed." She gave me a look. "I'm going right now. Now go to bed."

She turned and walked back down the hall to her bedroom. I heard the door click shut and let out a sigh. Elizabeth was right. I needed to go talk to Amber. I was torn up inside because I knew she felt rejected. I just had to figure out what I was going to say. Knowing I'd obsess about it all night and never do it, I grabbed a bottle from the wine rack and two glasses, and headed for the lobby stairs.

I trudged up the stairs, still trying to find the right words to say. It wasn't until I rapped on her door that I concluded that I just had to tell her the truth. She had a right to know all the crap I was lugging around inside. She could decide if she really wanted anything to do with all the baggage I had and my three girls to boot.

# 17

# Explanations

## Amber

I held myself together, shedding only a few tears, until I closed my door behind me and flopped onto the bed. How could I have allowed myself to get my hopes up? He still loves his wife. How could he not when he sees three miniatures of her every day? I know he feels something for me. He couldn't kiss me like that and not. And oh my God, I hate myself for allowing myself to feel something for him, but I do. Somehow, I'll get through the next few days. I'll find a way to keep my feelings in check and help for the sake of the girls and Janine. I owe her so much.

I searched through the bags and pulled out the flannel nightgown. Maybe a little soak in the tub. I don't have wine, but just the heat may help me relax enough to quiet the voices in my head and get some sleep. I padded my way into the bath and opened the faucets. Steam was rising, and I poured in one of Elizabeth's lovely bath salts. I looked in the mirror and saw my tear-stained face. Yup, another piece chipped off of a much-shattered heart. I peeled off my clothes, dropping them in a heap, and spread out the bathmat. I'd get through this. I'd only known the man for two days, a week of recovery tops, and I'd be good to go. A little white lie to yourself isn't so bad now and again.

I was startled by three loud raps on my door. "Who is it?"

"It's Hunter."

"What do you want?"

"I want to talk."

"It's late, and I was just getting into the bath."

"Please, Amber."

"It's not a good idea, Hunter."

"Please let me in."

"I'm naked." There was a long pause. Maybe he'd given up. The knot between my shoulders eased just a fraction, but the disappointment in my heart ratcheted up twice as much.

"Then put something on if you have to."

There was a gravelly edge in his voice that sent shivers through my body. "Can't this wait?"

"Amber."

I could sense his frustration. My heart desperately wanted to hear his words, but my head knew it was an exceptionally bad and potentially fatal idea. "We can talk through the door."

"Amber, I have wine, and if that's not sufficient incentive, I'm going to go down to the desk and get the passkey."

I was about to threaten to slide the privacy lock in place before I noticed there wasn't one. Is that even legal? "Fine. Give me a minute." I looked at the bags and wondered how long it would take me to put everything on, but that still wouldn't be enough to make me feel protected. Layers of clothes couldn't protect my brittle heart. I finally decided that a robe would just have to do.

I opened the door to see a very repentant Hunter holding a bottle of wine and two glasses. "Come in before you wake up the entire floor."

"Thank you." He set the glasses on my dresser and opened the bottle. "I wanted to apologize for the way I acted before."

"You already did, and I told you it's fine. I understand."

He poured a glass and handed it to me before pouring one for himself. He scanned the room, saw the bags I had piled on the chairs, and let out a sigh. He stepped over and cleared the chairs, motioning for me to join him. "You can't understand because you don't know the whole story."

"You still love your wife, and you grieve for her. I understand. And I respect you for it. I'm not going to deny the chemistry I feel with you, and I'm sure that you feel something for me, too, but that's okay. I totally get that you can't do anything that you're not ready for. See, I do know, so all I wish is that you didn't kiss me like you kissed me because then I wouldn't know what I'm missing," I said rambling on because I was nervous and that's what I do when I'm nervous. Ramble on.

He ran his hand through his hair, giving it a tug before letting go and sighing. "I appreciate your magnanimity, I do, but there's more to it than that. So, are you going to let me explain?"

"Fine. I'm sorry. I guess," I said, easing down onto a chair and studying my toenails.

He took a sip of his wine and let out another breath. "You've got part of it right. Jenn still weighs on my mind, and you're the very first woman that I've kissed. I mean, really kissed since she died. Part of it is, it doesn't seem right to me. I get to love again while she turns to dirt. She was always a better person than me. It seems disloyal to me to care for a woman that isn't the girls' mother. And I don't want them to feel like having someone else in their life would be unfaithful to her."

He was struggling, and I could see the sincerity in his eyes. I could feel his hurt, and somehow, though it didn't hurt me any less, I wasn't mad at him like I was before, damn it. I put a hand on his knee. "I told you I understood Hunter. Please don't beat yourself up."

He looked over at me and smiled. "Tonight, I was ready to try to move past it all. You're so beautiful, Amber. Inside and out, I could never repay you for all that you've done for my family. We were taking water over the side bad today, and this whole thing would have sunk us tonight. It really would have, but that's not why I have feelings for you."

"Anyway, I'm way off track. I was all set to try it and see where you and I could lead until Janine mentioned coming up to this room. Amber, this is the room Jenn and I lived in for the first three years we owned the inn. It's where we lived until the addition was built, and it's the room that Elizabeth was born in. I was scared that if I was in here alone with you and we were kissing like we were kissing in the kitchen, I would see too many ghosts and send you the wrong message. I ended up doing it in the kitchen anyway."

"And if we ended up in your bedroom, wouldn't there be ghosts there too?"

Hunter just shook his head. "This was Jenn's room. All the fabrics, the furniture, the color scheme. This was her, not a bit of me. I've put away a lot of her things downstairs, repainted the bedroom, just so there weren't constant reminders, but here it's like she could walk through the door any second." He stared out into space for a moment, and I could tell he was remembering but also collecting his thoughts. I gave him his moment. He looked at me and smiled. "When we needed a few minutes away from the girls after they were asleep, we would sneak up to this room for some privacy. I don't think Janine knew that, or she wouldn't have suggested us coming up here." The smile faded, and he took a long sip from his glass.

"It was one of those short escapes that she sat in the same chair you're in right now and held my hands and made me promise her that if anything ever happened to her, I wouldn't spend the rest of my life moping. That

I deserved love, and the girls needed to know what it was like to have a whole family. So, they could learn from watching." A tear trailed down his cheek. "The moment I looked up and saw you standing in my lobby Wednesday afternoon, covered in snow and looking so forlorn, that was the first time that I thought about keeping that promise. It was such an easy promise to make. I never dreamed anything would happen to her. She was healthy as an ox, and I was the one who ran into burning buildings. She was upset I didn't take her more seriously, but I just blamed it on hormones. She was always emotional when she was pregnant."

"You're probably right, Hunter; it might have been just hormones. Was it when she was pregnant with Amy? That was at least three years before the accident. That would be an awfully long time to be a premonition, don't you think? It's got to be a normal thing to think about when you have children. Haven't you ever wanted to make sure they were cared for if something happened to you?"

He shook his head slowly. "I think about that all the time. I know Janine would step in and they'd never want for anything, but it's always there. I've nearly given up firefighting a dozen times because every call I go on, it's right there." He took another deep breath. "The thing is, Amber, that she sat there and made me make that promise three days before she died. Then I guess because I didn't give her enough confidence, she sat Elizabeth down and told her she needed to help me keep that promise."

"That's an awful lot to put on a ten…" I stopped mid-sentence. The realization of what Hunter just told me finally clicked into place. "You mean to say she was pregnant when she was killed… Oh my god Hunter. Oh, my God." I was out of my chair before I finished my words. I wrapped my arms around him and kissed his creased forehead. The robe had half come open, and I could feel his face on my bare breast, but I couldn't have cared less. I could feel the wetness of his tears, and in that moment, I would have given or done anything to ease his pain. My hands traced through his thick, wavy hair.

He pulled back and looked up into my eyes, and the tears were streaming down both of our faces. He swallowed hard. "She was on her way to pick up the supplies for our reveal. We planned to share the news with everyone that night. She was four months along, and we hadn't said anything sooner because it was when Janine was going through all that crap with her ex. She had been staying with us and seemed to be getting back on her feet, coming out of the darkness, and we thought it was time to share some good news." He poured himself more wine and took a long drink. "No one knew she was pregnant, Amber. Not the girls, not Janine. No one. I thought Leo might have known. He was the one who removed her body from the wreck, but if he did, he's never said a thing. It was hard enough for the girls to lose their mother. I couldn't bear to have them know they'd lost the baby brother they'd always wanted."

He shuddered, and tears flowed freely down his face. I pulled him close to my chest and just held him in silence, kissing the top of his head. We stayed that way for a long while until he cleared his throat. "Thank you, Amber. Thank you for listening to me. I'm sorry I burdened you with this, but honestly, I feel like I can actually breathe for the first time since she died."

I couldn't think of words to say. I tried, but nothing seemed adequate. Without thinking, I cupped his chin in my hand and placed a soft kiss on his lips, a sweet, salty, tear-stained kiss. "Now I understand Hunter, truly I do."

"Thank you. I know you do." His strong, calloused hand cupped my face, his thumb traced my cheek, and then he slid that hand behind my ear and pulled me to his lips. Our mouths met and slowly, gently kissed, then stronger and stronger until every ounce of emotion, all the hurt and all the desire that was built up inside both of us exploded into that kiss. Our need to connect with another human fulfilled in one kiss manifested, and the only thing I wanted or needed in the world was to hold that man, that beautiful broken man, in my arms. To feel his body against mine and let him know I would help him bear the weight if he'd let me.

"Amber, I have no right to ask this of you, but give me a chance. I know it's not fair to you. There will be moments like tonight when Jenn's ghost haunts me, but what I feel for you isn't something I've ever come close to feeling with anyone except her, and I want to try. I want to be the man you need me to be. Will you at least give me a chance?"

His dark brown eyes searched mine for the answer, and the need that they communicated had me forgetting all semblance of reason and logic. I lived in Denver, two hours away in good weather, and he was halfway up the Rocky Mountains, and it was the beginning of bloody winter. He had three girls, and I had no clue how to be a mother, and I wasn't supposed to have anything to do with a man ever again. But I found my head nodding and couldn't help my mouth from forming a smile. "Yes, Hunter, I will give us a chance."

We kissed more, and I wanted him so badly it hurt, but I would not put that kind of pressure on him right now, especially in this room. "Maybe I should ask Elizabeth to move my room once the guests leave on Sunday."

He shook his head. "No. You love this room, and I need to face things. I know Jenn isn't the one that's haunting me. It's all the things I do to myself. The only way I'm ever going to be the man you deserve is if things like being in this room don't bring me to my knees in grief. Somehow, I have to remember her with fondness and love and still be able to live." He smiled and kissed me so firmly I was sure our lips would be swollen in the morning. "I've always known that I have to keep living because of the girls. You have shown me now that I still want to live for myself, too."

That might have been the most wonderful thing anyone has ever said to me. If I wasn't careful, I might just fall in love.

# 18

# Wake Up

## Amber

Iwoke to the sound of a strange alarm and a large hand cupping my breast. It was still dark outside, and my body rebelled at the idea that it was time to get up. The large body attached to the hand groaned and stirred, depriving me of the warmth that I had quickly become accustomed to.

"Fuck" was all that large body uttered that was discernible.

I rolled over and grabbed his phone off the nightstand, silencing the alarm. The large hand tried to pull me back toward him. My body wanted to comply, but I knew it would be all too easy for me to drift back off into blissful sleep, which would mean we would have several hungry and upset guests who didn't get breakfast before heading to the slopes. It might also mean that his daughters would realize that he had spent the night in my room, and while nothing really happened, I didn't want them to get that impression, not after only knowing Hunter for a couple of days. It might also mean I could control myself as well as I had last night and just hold the man and do nothing more. "Come on, sleepyhead, we've got breakfast to make and guests to feed."

"Just another five minutes."

"Nope, it's five fifteen, and you don't want Elizabeth waking up to find you not there."

"There is no chance that Elizabeth will wake before noon left on her own. I will need dynamite to wake her to help with breakfast as it is."

"Let the poor girl get some sleep. I'm going to help you with breakfast, anyway. You told me last night you could handle it on your own."

"How about we forget about that part of last night and focus on the fact that I haven't slept that well in a very long time? Thank you." He pulled me closer for a kiss. "Now give me five minutes. I'll go down and put a sign that says, the cook died and be back before my side of the bed gets cold.”

I hadn't seen the sparkle of mischief in his eyes before and had to admit that it was doing some delightful things to my insides. “As tempting as that idea is.” I kissed his forehead. “We both know you can't do that. Now go downstairs and change. I'm going to take a quick shower, and I'll meet you in the kitchen in fifteen minutes, and please, please, please have coffee ready or I take no responsibility for anything I do or say.”

“Okay, boss,” he grumbled. “You're no fun at all.”

I quickly straddled his prone body, making note of a pretty impressive morning wood that was pressed against me through the covers. “I'll have you know I am a lot of fun. And if you're a very good boy today, you might just find out how much fun I am. But right now, you have a job to do, and I intend to help you do it, not keep you from it.” I leaned forward and kissed him, not at all caring that the flannel nightgown I had thrown on before we snuggled last night hung away from my body and he could have a full view of my breasts if he looked. From the growl that escaped from deep down his throat, I guessed he had made the choice I had hoped he would. I slid out of the bed and made my way to the bathroom to start the shower.

“I'm going to hold you to that promise.”

“I hope you do,” I said seductively as I closed the bathroom door behind me.

“Hmph,” I heard just before I heard the door close to the room.

# 19

# Memories

## Hunter

There was absolutely no rational reason for a smile as wide as the one I was wearing when I left Amber's room at five-eighteen in the morning. Nobody smiles at that hour.

I wasn't exaggerating; I hadn't slept that well since before Jenn died. It was rare that I'd sleep for more than a couple of hours before waking and tossing and turning for an hour. Rinse, wash, repeat.

I struggled to walk straight as I descended the stairs, not out of fatigue but because of the teasing Amber had done before she left me high and dry and disappeared into the bathroom. I was painfully hard at the moment, and it had little to do with morning wood. And a whole lot to do with the view I had down her nightgown and the way she'd ground into me when she straddled me before getting up. From the smirk on her face, she knew exactly what she was doing.

As soon as I was awake enough, I was going to come up with a plan to make her pay for that.

I quickly checked on my girls, all sleeping like the angels they were, before hopping into the shower. I sighed as the hot water washed over my tired body. Doubt crept back into my mind. A maelstrom of emotions swirled in my brain.

Desire for Amber warred with loyalty to Jenn. The pure coming of age love I still felt for Jenn compared to the appreciation for Amber's strength and genuine empathy. Knowledge of all I'd had and lost with Jenn versus the potential for a future I wasn't sure I deserved with Amber. All of this set against the responsibility I had for my daughters and the burden of keeping this inn going and someday, maybe, finally bringing it all the way back to its former glory. I still had a way to go, but I was a long way from where I started.

# *17 years ago*

Ileaned against the truck, looking up into the clear July sky at four stories of peeling paint, loose clapboards and God knows how many leaks in the roof. My head hurt. My back ached. And my hands flexed in stiffness, and I hadn't even swung a hammer in anger yet.

Jenn was squeezing my arm, vibrating with excitement, enthusiasm, and pure joy that I just couldn't ignore. It's what made me love her so damn much, and it was that love that kept me from ever telling her no.

She was the reason I was standing here looking up at the decrepit Homer Pass Hotel wondering just what in the living hell I was thinking. The old relic had been standing here empty for at least ten years, probably more. I recall timidly going inside the thing as a little kid, maybe six or seven, grasping my father's hand like my life depended on it. I was sure the place was haunted.

We were visiting my great-granduncle, something or other, who had valiantly been keeping the old place open. God only knows why. I'm sure it had once been a stately fixture on the only road through Homer Pass. A mining town built around the silver mine my great-great-grandfather Homer (hence Homer Pass) had founded in the early 1860s. He was Homer Holmes and the likely reason every damn male in my family had a name beginning with the letter 'H'. A trend Jenn and I had no intention of carrying on. Kids were a long way away, though. We weren't even married, and we had a hotel to renovate.

My brother Henry, on the other hand, deliriously bound to family traditions, would no doubt continue. He was enough of an asshole to name the poor lad Horacio or Hubert. I would have to make it up to the kid by being the cool uncle. Challenge accepted. I loved kids.

The pain in the ass in question was only a few feet from my right, swinging his legs while sitting on the gate to his pickup bed stuffing a sandwich into his mouth. "You're wasting your money, Hunt. Money we could use to bring the mine back to life. There are millions in silver down there. You know it, and I know it."

"Oh, for fuck's sake, Henry." I groaned. He was a goddamn broken record, convinced we could get rich sinking our trust funds into a hole in the ground that hadn't broken even in fifty years. "We've been through this a hundred times. If you want to make a tourist attraction out of it, go ahead. Josh and I both told you we'd help you build the visitor center. But the Homer Pass Mining Corporation is done. Dad shut it down forty years ago for a reason."

"You're only saying that because Jenn's leading you around by your dick."

Jenn's grasp on my arm tightened, keeping me from swinging at his arrogant face and breaking his nose. Again. Henry Holmes was my older brother in chronological age only. He had tried to date my fiance even after we started dating in high school and felt that because he was the oldest son, he should have first pick of whatever the fuck he wanted. He liked to think our family was still king shit in this town, but the fact was, it had been a long time since the mine that started this little community had been the primary employer or even made money.

My father had left Henry the control of the family mine with the stipulation that Janine and I each receive fifteen percent of the profit generated from whatever he did with it. There was no value to the mining claim, but he had sixty-five hundred acres to play with.

All three of us had an equal share of the family trust and an equal say on what would be done to manage it. Fortunately, Janine and I agreed and left management of the fund's investments in the hands of professionals. We were quite satisfied with the one-hundred- fifty-thousand-dollar disbursement that hit our bank account on the first of March every year.

That disbursement was how I could stand here today, deed in hand for the Homer Pass Hotel. So here I was, standing in front of a building that the love of my life had dreamed of returning to its glory since we were in junior high. I was pretty sure no one alive could remember its glory days.

The Homer Pass Hotel might never have been more than a very basic roadside inn with marginal food and uncomfortable beds, only occupied because in the days before automobiles and paved roads there was nothing else available within a day's worth of travel. Supposedly, Teddy Roosevelt once stayed here whilst he was on his famous wanderings, but that was a local legend I strongly doubted was based on fact. I figured it was much more likely that if he saw the place at all, he took one look and said, 'Fuck no, I'll sleep in a tent'.

"Don't let his jealousy get to you, Hunter." Jenn whispered in my ear. "Besides, even if he's right, you know you love what I do to that dick while I'm leading you around by it."

That woman knew exactly what to say to distract me from my jackass brother's foolishness. Distract me from anything, really. I smiled down at her and kissed her firmly. I couldn't help it.

"Just remember, big guy. I promised to fuck you in every room in that hotel, and I always keep my promises."

I snorted out a laugh and shook my head. She swatted my arm and pouted at me. "Don't laugh at me." She stepped back and crossed her arms. "I have every intention of keeping that promise."

I stepped toward her, drew her back into my arms and kissed the tip of her button nose. "And I have every intention of holding you to it. I just hope we don't die when we crash through the rotting floorboards. You know we sometimes get a little too vigorous about it. By the way, how's that bruise on your ass?"

"Hunter Holmes, you're a jerk and a real killjoy," she complained, cheeks flaming while she pushed out of my arms and stormed up the rickety steps before struggling to pry open the warped entry door.

I was just about to follow her carefully up onto the porch that was valiantly trying to remain attached to the front of the old building when my friend Josh pulled up in his work van.

He hopped out and surveyed the building with a look of concern I understood all too well. "So, you really did it? It's all yours?"

I nodded with a rueful smile. "Every last rotting board, rusty nail and leaky pipe." I had paid thirty-five thousand dollars in back taxes and took ownership from the town. I'm pretty sure the town clerk was skipping all the way to the bank because it would have cost the town a hell of a lot more to tear it down.

"Well then, let's get to it."

The man was my best and oldest friend. He'd been two years ahead of me in high school, but we were nearly inseparable. And when he went into business for himself, I was more than happy to swing a hammer right next to him. In the years that Jenn and I were away at college, Josh had established himself as a custom home builder and had four crews working on multimillion-dollar vacation homes from Breckenridge to Buena Vista. At twenty-six, he had a wife, a kid and a multi-million-dollar business. At twenty-four, I had a fiancé, and a condemned building? I wouldn't trade my life with his for the world.

I looked back over my shoulder at Henry, still sitting on his tailgate, as Josh and I climbed the steps up onto the porch. "You coming?"

"You're fucking joking, right? If you want to piss your inheritance away to make her happy with no chance of getting that money back, have at it. I want nothing to do with this mess."

"Come on, Henry. We're family."

"Yeah, we are, and yet that doesn't seem to mean fuck-all to you."

"What the hell does that mean?"

Henry slid off the gate and slammed it shut, shaking the truck with the force. "It means you chose her dreams and not your own flesh and blood."

"Henry," I called after him, but he'd already climbed into the cab. I didn't bother to say anything else. He wouldn't have heard me anyway as the diesel engine roared to life. All I could do was shake my head. He was more stubborn than all of us, and that was saying something, but he'd come around. At least, I hoped he would.

"What the hell crawled up his ass?" Josh asked, slapping me on the back.

"What hasn't? He's pissed at me because I won't consider investing in his scheme to turn the old mine into an eyesore of a pit mine on the vague hope there's more silver to be found on the family claim. He's pissed at Jenn because she chose me over him, and he expects the world to fall at his feet and is amazed and pissed when it doesn't."

Thankfully, Josh had the good sense to drop it as we followed Jenn inside once she'd pried the massive oak and glass door open. Josh let out a long, low whistle. He was right. Even covered in dust and with more than a hint of mold, the old lobby was still impressive. Jenn had the vision and dreams to bring this place back to life, and while I shared her dream and vision, I also knew just how much work… and money it was going to take to make her dream a reality.

As if reading my mind, Josh elbowed me. "I can see the potential of this place, but just so you know, it's going to take a hell of a lot more than what you have in the bank to bring it back to life."

I knew that, but I tried not to think about it. I guessed I had to. "How much do you think?" I asked, certain that I didn't want to hear his answer.

"Fuck, I don't know, man," he said with an ominous groan. "Somewhere between five and ten million. If the bones are good, maybe less, but if we have to replace floor joists and bearing walls…" He left that statement unsaid because I already knew the answer, a lot more money than I could ever get.

I was going to do this a little at a time if I could. I'd spend what I had and then get to the rest as we made money from the rooms we had finished. I thought we could do this one floor at a time. If not, I was going to have to get a mortgage, and I doubted there was a bank in the world that would loan me, a twenty-three-year-old kid with no business experience, millions of dollars.

Jenn turned to me and wrapped her arms around my neck, pulling me in for a kiss. "Thank you." She smiled, pulling back. "I know this isn't your dream, but thank you for doing this for me."

"Your dream is my dream, babe. Always has been. Always will be."

With any luck, and a few feet of snow to entice guests to go skiing, we'd make enough money. Josh and I had to get the first-floor common areas and the sixteen second-floor rooms done by winter. Then we could figure out what to do from there. There were sixteen rooms on the third floor and fourteen on the fourth. We had a lot of work to do before the Homer Pass Hotel would be fully functional again. We should probably start by finding a better name for the old dump. Something that didn't conjure up visions of a Stephen King movie.

## Present

"Fuck." I shut the shower off and grabbed my towel from the rack. I didn't know how long I'd been lost in that memory, but even a minute was time I didn't have to spare.

I walked into my bedroom, still dripping, and searched for the clock on my nightstand. Five-thirty-five. Shit, not as bad as I thought, but still not good. I was rushing to get dressed and wasn't as quiet as I normally would be.

Reasonably certain I was fully dressed, I hurried out of my room and almost ran over Snow, coming out of hers. "What time is it? Why didn't you wake me up?" she groaned.

I had to stifle a laugh. Her hair was a tangled mess, and I wasn't entirely sure she knew she was standing and talking to me. "Go back to bed." I leaned down and kissed the top of the rat's nest of blonde waves. "Amber's going to help with breakfast so you can sleep in."

A smile ticked at the corners of her mouth. "I knew I saw that, and it wasn't a dream," she said, turning back into her room. "I think I already love her," she mumbled as she disappeared into the dark.

All I could do was shake my head at her delirious ramblings, seeing stuff and already loving Amber. I quickened my pace toward the kitchen, bursting through the door and turning on the lights just as Amber entered from the other side. Our eyes met, and the swirl of emotions was back in full force. Somehow, someway, I was going to have to find a way to rationalize my building feelings for Amber and my everlasting commitment toward Jenn.

## 20

# Chili

### Amber

Complimentary breakfast was served at the inn from six to nine, though virtually all the guests were heading for the ski slopes, and those that had eaten breakfast with us were gone by half past seven. Hunter and I had handled it together seamlessly as though we had been doing it together for years. He cooked, and I brought the steamy trays of eggs and still-sizzling bacon to the dining room and cleared the tables. Some guests passed on their requests for dinner reservations, and others noted they wouldn't be joining us for dinner. I made some notes for Elizabeth about requests for towels and such and generally enjoyed the feeling of belonging that it gave me. It slipped my mind temporarily that I would only be here for a few more days, at least in this capacity.

I had told Hunter that I would give him a chance, but the more I thought of it, the more ludicrous it seemed. Committing to a long-distance relationship after only three days was well beyond anything I had ever done or ever would consider. Still, my heart told me not to be so narrow-minded. I would have to think about how this could succeed.

When we were done serving breakfast, Hunter pulled me in for a hug and a kiss I didn't realize I had been dying for. Leaning back from the kiss, he slid his hands through his hair; I learned he did this quite a bit when thinking. "What's on your mind, big guy?" I ran my hand over his chest, wishing there wasn't a thick apron, a flannel shirt and a tee shirt between my palm and his rippling muscles.

"Just contemplating what to do for a dinner menu, honestly." He drew my hand to his lips, softly kissing my palm. "By your count, we should have about thirty for dinner tonight, and after a day of skiing, they usually like comfort food a lot more than chops and steaks."

"Sounds reasonable. I know I would."

"Do you know how to make chili?"

I smiled. I did in fact make a pretty mean chili. "You mean to tell me that a firefighter can't make chili?"

"Oh, I can make chili, but they'd all be looking for something to put the flames out that were in their mouths, and I refuse to lower my chili standards."

"And who's saying that they wouldn't be doing the same for mine?"

He pulled me closer and kissed me. "Because you're far too kind to use as many ghost peppers as I do." He gave me another soft kiss, effectively ending any thought I had about rebuttal and placing other thoughts in my mind. "If you would start the chili, I'll head to the market and pick up supplies for a couple of large lasagnas and some sliced roast beef and turkey and we can do open-faced sandwiches. That should make it simple enough for tonight."

"You're the boss."

He smiled, and there was a twinkle in his eye that told me he had plenty of ideas about how he'd like to boss me around; none of them had to do with this kitchen. "Glad to know you realize that." I swatted his shoulder. "While I'm gone, I want you to think about something for me, okay?"

"Okay?" There was no hiding the questioning uncertainty in my voice.

"You told me you'd give me a chance."

"I did."

He continued to smile, but his eyes were asking me not to interrupt him. "Well, that means that hopefully you'll be here quite a bit because I can't run this place from Denver." I nodded just to let him know I was following him. "I'd like to hire you as the first seasonal employee. We can work out the details, but you would keep your room, and I'd pay you."

"Hunter, I have a …"

"Just think about it. I don't expect you to drop your career, but maybe you could just be here on the weekends. We can talk about it when I get back. Just think about it, please. We can figure something out that works for you."

I sighed. I couldn't see a way that it could, but I guess I could mull it over for a couple of hours. At least he wouldn't feel like I was dismissing the idea because I wasn't interested. I was. I just couldn't see how it could possibly work. I almost always had showings on weekends. "I'll think about it."

"Thank you." He kissed me again. "Now, I'm going to go to the store so this can all get prepped and hopefully we can have a little time for our-selves this afternoon."

I pulled myself up against his body. "That's something I definitely like the sound of."

A soft rumble was washing through his chest, and he was about to pull me in for yet another kiss when three sleepy girls came ambling into the kitchen. "Good morning, Dad, Amber." Elizabeth forced a smile.

"I'm hungry." Amy stated firmly.

"Me too," Megan grunted more than spoke.

"Good morning, girls," Hunter said, being purposely obnoxiously cheerful. "Elizabeth can fix you guys breakfast. I have to head to the mar-ket."

I could see Elizabeth's frustration and felt bad that so much responsi-bility was heaped on this girl. "I'll make them breakfast; you go." I turned Hunter toward the door with a gentle nudge.

He gave me a shy smile, whispered thanks and ruffled Amy's hair af-fectionately as he made his way to the door. Before he made it out, three tones sounded, and Hunter muttered a curse. "So much for grocery shop-ping," he grumbled. "Duty calls. I'll see you later, girls." And he trotted out the door.

The girls' breakfast was made and served, and a large pot of chili was on the stove simmering as I made my way back up to my room. It was nearly eleven, and I felt like I'd been up forever. I wanted to get my new wardrobe sorted and put away. I'd have to check my email and see if I had any messages. There was nothing yesterday when I checked, but I knew I had to connect with the handful of clients I had. Maybe by the end of next week I'd have a vehicle and be able to show homes again. Hunter would be back soon, I assumed, and if not, perhaps I'd be able to get in a catnap.

As I put my things neatly into the dresser, I found the extra things that Janine had seen fit to include. Most notable were several impractical sets of bras and panties that were very nice but designed to be removed once discovered by a special someone. Someone Janine had in mind, and she wasn't being very subtle about it. It made me smile. There was also an exquisite Christmas sweater, not one of the ugly ones you would wear for an office gag day, with a note pinned to it.

> *We have a family tradition of dressing up on Christmas Eve. I'm*
> *hoping you'll have a chance to wear this with us.*
>
> *Love J.*

I held it close to my chest. I didn't see how I could, but honestly, I hoped so too.

Clothing safely put away, I pulled out my laptop and dutifully went through the couple of dozen emails I had. Sending replies and searching through a handful of listings that had been forwarded to me by clients to get more information on. I grabbed my phone from the nightstand, where I had left it yesterday afternoon. I'd been so consumed with helping at the inn, I'd never thought of checking it. I had three missed calls yesterday from the McKinnons that started this whole adventure and then a series of calls from my office starting at seven forty-five this morning and continuing every fifteen minutes until after ten. The icon at the top of the screen showed multiple voicemails, so I swiped it to check them. My stomach balled tightly. I didn't have a good feeling about this.

The office was technically closed for the holiday weekend, but beyond not working on Thanksgiving Day, most of the agents still checked in with clients or made an occasional showing. I would have to let them know that their worst-performing agent would be unavailable for the better part of a week.

My voicemails started with three from the McKinnons informing me they had first found another place to look at, and then, that they would no longer be needing my services because they had found an agent that would return calls promptly. It wasn't a surprise. I'd known this was coming since the disaster in Breckenridge Wednesday afternoon.

Those were followed by a string of calls from my boss who at first was upset to hear I had lost a client that was ready to spend a solid seven figures on a home, moving on to being irate that I hadn't returned his call within minutes during a day that I wasn't even technically supposed to be working. The very last one where his temper was once again under control but regretted to inform me I no longer had a position with his agency. He suggested was for the best as my heart was obviously not in being a real estate agent.

I clicked delete on all the messages and sank back into my chair. My first feeling was relief. I hated the job; I hated the pressure and backstabbing and, honestly, a big part of me was glad that the decision had been made for me. The relief was short-lived as the realization of the mortgage and other bills that needed to be paid flooded me with panic. I had no savings to fall back on. I would lose the house I had fought for, and Lance would get his last and best laugh at my expense. The bile rose in my throat, and I resisted the urge to scream at the top of my lungs. Why had the universe done this to me? I had no car. My family was hundreds of miles away, and soon I wouldn't have a place to live.

I don't know how long I stared out the window at the gray sky and snowflakes that were lazily falling. A sharp rap on my door snapped me out of my mire of despair. I thought about ignoring it for a moment but realized that it could only be Hunter, one of the girls or Janine, all of whom would know that I was in there because where the hell else could I be?

I pushed myself out of the chair with all the energy I had and then some. I opened the door to find Hunter smiling with a bouquet and a tray of tea and snacks. He met my eyes, and his smile instantly morphed into concern. "What's wrong?"

I just waved my hand in the air, realizing that when I thought about talking that there was far too much emotion in my chest to speak.

"That's not really an answer, Amber. Is there something wrong with your mother?"

I shook my head, not ready to speak the truth out loud.

He set the tray on the dresser and pulled me into his chest. His arms wrapped around me and gave me a kiss. I guess he knew enough not to say he was sorry, or maybe he just didn't know what to say, but all he did was hold me. Tightly. His muscular, large, powerful arms and the warmth from his body soothed my fear. I had no idea what the hell I was going to do but by nothing more than the strength and the warmth of his body I had a sense that it was going to be alright because Hunter was there and he wouldn't allow it to be any other way.

# 21

# Inside and Out

## Hunter

I thought I'd seen her look of hopelessness when she walked in my door from the blizzard on Wednesday afternoon. I had the overwhelming urge to wrap my arms around her then and let her know I would make everything alright, but of course then I didn't even know her name. Today I had that advantage, but I didn't know what the problem was. My instinct upon seeing that expression was that there was a problem with her family, and the only family I knew of was her mother. She said that wasn't the case.

I didn't know what was wrong, only that something was, and it wasn't something small. I held her there, with the door to the hallway wide open, for a long time. She didn't seem to want to let go, and I had no problem holding her for as long as she wanted. The longer she held me, the more I wanted and fought to tamp down those less than honorable urges. As much as I desired her, now was certainly not the time. Eventually, she loosened her grip, and I pulled back just enough to shut the door and give us some privacy.

No sooner had I turned back toward her than she pulled me back into a hug. "Thank you." She spoke into my chest.

"Do you want to talk about it?"

She shook her head. "Not yet." She squeezed me a little tighter. "Just hold me for a minute?"

My answer was to slowly run my fingers through her soft wavy hair as I had done so many times with my daughters when only actions were needed to show comfort. She nuzzled into my chest and gave a contented moan.

"Nobody has done that for me since I was a little girl." She broke our hug and kissed me quickly on the cheek. "Thank you for bringing tea.

That was very thoughtful."

I forced a smile and poured us each a cup. She sank into a chair, and I noticed she'd put her things away. A sense of contentment hit me without warning. I liked very much the idea that she was prepared to stay. Of course, she didn't have much choice in the near term. Her car wouldn't be repaired for several more days, but I allowed myself to believe that she'd be here longer if only I could play my cards right.

We sat there in companionable silence for a while before Amber sighed and set her tea on the end table between the chairs. "So, what did you have in mind when you asked me to work for you?"

I hadn't been expecting that question. I don't know that I was expecting anything, but as much as I wanted her to stay and work by my side, I knew she had her career and would be happy if she could spend a day or two up here a week. "Um, I don't know." I stammered. It was obvious she'd caught me off guard. "It's obvious I need help everywhere. What would you like to do?"

Her shoulders dropped, and the smile I could tell she was already forcing disappeared. "Oh, I, um, thought you had something specific in mind." She looked down at the hands she was wringing together. "I guess, um, never mind, then."

I was on my knees in front of her in a flash. The confident, determined woman I had seen for the past three days was nowhere in sight. Something was truly weighing on her, and she clearly thought I had been asking her to stay offhand. "Amber, look at me."

She gave me a quick glance under her lashes but returned her gaze to her lap.

"Amber, please." Slowly, she met my eyes. "There is nothing I want more than to have you working here with me. Now please tell me what's bothering you."

She exhaled. "I can't stay. I just got a voicemail saying I was fired. I need to find a job that can pay my mortgage, and we both know you've got your own troubles to worry about. I can help you until my car's ready, and then I'm going to have to go home and get my life sorted out."

I didn't know where to start. She was right that I could never pay her enough to support whatever she was paying for a mortgage in Denver. I wished I could, though. "Your boss left a voicemail saying you were fired?"

An ironic smile tipped her lips. "Well, he left six messages before that, but yes. Apparently, it didn't matter that the office was closed. He felt I should have called him back within the forty-five minutes it took to leave the messages. In a small way, it's a relief. I hated that job, but I needed the money."

I clasped her hands and brought them to my mouth, gently kissing her knuckles. "We'll work something out."

I could see the silver tears welling in her eyes, but she fought them back, the corners of her mouth tipping up slightly. "Thank you. You're a kind man, and I haven't known very many of those." She pulled her hand from mine and ran it through my hair. I didn't want her to stop. "It's not; I'm not your problem. You really have more than enough to worry about without adding a mess like me to your list."

"I don't think you're a mess, Amber. And even if you are, I have a feeling you are more than worth whatever trouble you would add."

She laughed, though with little humor. "Oh, you really don't know me well, do you?"

I pulled her forward and pressed my lips to hers. Her lips parted and welcomed me in, putting aside the heaviness of the troubles she had. The kiss intensified, and I pulled her out of the chair and on top of me on the floor. When at last the kiss broke, our eyes met, and I brushed away the tear that trickled from the corner of her eye. "I want to know you, Amber. I want to know every inch of you, inside and out."

Our mouths crashed together again. Her loose-fitting sweater hung from her torso, and I could feel the warmth of her skin on my fingers as I grasped her waist. I traced my thumbs over the softness of her waist, and she moaned into our kiss.

I inched my hands higher up her body, and her kiss became more urgent. Her core ground against mine, and I could feel the heat of her arousal. My hands found her full, round breasts, and I kneaded them through the lacy bra she wore. Her nipples peaked against the thin fabric.

In unison, we pulled each other's tops off, and she reached behind her quickly discarding the bra before pressing herself against my chest. My hand cupped the back of her head as our tongues continued their frantic dance.

She pulled back from our kiss, lips swollen and deep pink. Her eyes were dark with passion, and her hands idly rubbed my chest.

She had perfect breasts. I gave myself a moment to fully appreciate them. I reached up, cupping one in each hand. They were firm, dark cherry nipples the size of silver dollars, and they puckered to hard points as my thumbs made lazy circles around them.

"There's a perfectly comfortable bed right there. How about we get off the hard floor?" she said.

I nodded, and she got up, pulling back the covers. In the back of my mind, I knew the girls would make their rounds doing up the rooms for the day, but I doubted they would bother with this one. I pulled myself to my feet, and she stepped forward, undoing my pants and letting them slide to my ankles. I stepped out of them before hooking my fingers under the band of her leggings and carefully pulled them down. She sat on the bed, and I pulled them the rest of the way off her shapely body. She scooted back onto the bed and smiled. I couldn't move. My eyes scanned her from head to toe and back again. I could feel my heart slamming against my ribs so hard I thought they might crack.

She reached out, breaking the trance I was in, and I took her hand as I climbed in beside her. My lips brushed her neck, and there was still a hint of maple syrup from this morning's waffles. She moaned into my kiss as I nipped behind her ears, and her hand snaked down the length of my body before firmly wrapping her fingers around my stiff shaft.

My whole body shuddered at her touch, and I knew I had to have her then. Normally I would want to build up to that; to give her pleasure before seeking my own, but I needed to be one with her more than I needed air. And in that instant, I felt a wave of panic crash into me. I hadn't planned this. I hadn't come prepared.

"Fuck," I groaned. "We can't, Amber. I didn't bring protection."

She smiled and placed a soft kiss on the tip of my nose. "It's okay. I'm on the pill and very clean. I haven't been with anyone for well over a year."

"Are you sure? I haven't been with anyone since Jenn, but we can…"

She shook her head and kissed me, rolling on top of me as she did. She rocked back, straddling me before grabbing my cock and easing me inside. She settled herself with a contented sigh and rolled her hips, moaning in satisfaction. She leaned forward and pressed her body against mine, her breasts spreading out against my chest. We settled into a comfortable rhythm. Our bodies moving as one.

Being inside her was like going to heaven. I had never been with a woman who was so ready for me without me doing anything. She was warm and slick and gripped me so tightly I thought I would explode at any moment. The soft moans she made with each thrust echoed my own.

I rolled us so that I was on top. Easing down her body, my mouth found her breast. My tongue traced her perfect nipple, then sucked it into my mouth.

"Fuck," she moaned, her hands held my head in place. Her hips raised, pressing her core against my belly. I could tell she needed us back together. She needed it all.

I needed it all too, but I knew I wouldn't last, and I wasn't close to ready for this to end. I couldn't help the doubt that leaked into my mind. We couldn't be sure of what our future held, and if this was the only time we could ever be together, it was going to last. Amber deserved more than a quickie. She deserved everything. And I was going to do my best to give it to her.

I gave her other breast the attention it deserved and eased further down her body, whispering kisses over her belly. I edged her legs apart with my shoulders. She spread herself for me in an offering I in no way deserved. My mouth covered her core, and my tongue traced a trail the length of her seam, finishing on her sensitive bundle of nerves.

She gasped as my tongue flicked back and forth over her clit. If I had any doubts about being out of practice, her enthusiastic response dissuaded me of any inadequacy. "God, Hunter," she whimpered. "The things you're doing to me." Slowly I slid two fingers inside and her back arched as I found that special spot inside.

"Jesus. Fuck. Yes," her cries became louder and more guttural. I should have worried that Snow or Meg could walk by, but I didn't. For just a few minutes, I focused on being Hunter and not Dad. Seconds later, it all became worth the risk as Amber's body quaked with a spasm that could only mean I had done well.

Her breath slowed, and a satisfied smile spread over her face. She cupped the back of my head and urged me up her body until her lips pressed against mine. She groaned into the kiss. "More," she said. "I need you inside me. Please, Hunter."

It was a request I couldn't have refused if I'd wanted to. I reached down and pressed the head of my cock against her entrance. My impatient girl rocked her hips, inching me inside. "Yes," we hissed in unison. Her legs wrapped around me, and her hands stayed locked behind my head, keeping us joined in a kiss that was so much more than a kiss.

I didn't hold back this time. Our bodies moved as one. It felt like we had been doing this forever. Like we were made to fit together like this. Two halves finally made a whole.

My body stiffened, and I felt my orgasm build from the soles of my feet.

"Come for me, Hunter," she said. Her words were both a plea and a command. Who was I to deny it?

"Fuck. Fuck. Fuck," I groaned, and I pulsed my release inside her.

As my orgasm faded, our eyes locked, and far beyond the physical connection we made, our souls fused, and I knew in that moment, Amber Scott was the only thing in the world that would ever satisfy me again.

We lay in silence for a long while. Her head on my shoulder. Her hand lazily drifted through the hair on my chest, and her leg draped across mine. There was a peace inside of me I hadn't felt in many years, long before Jenn's accident. We hadn't been having an easy time of it, and I know we were both hoping that our new child, our first son, would help pull us back together.

The peace was interrupted by an earthquake-level growl of my stomach, which was promptly answered by one from Amber's. We laughed, and I pulled her closer, kissing the top of her head, breathing in the clean fresh scent of her shampoo and burning it into my memory. "Maybe we should get up and make some lunch."

I groaned. I knew she was right.

"Come on. I should probably stop by the garage and see if Leo's made any progress with my car before we have to get started on dinner."

"I don't want this moment to end," I told her. Moments of peace like this were too rare.

She kissed my chest before peering up at me. "Me neither, but maybe if you're a good boy, we can do this again later when we don't have to get up."

"Hmm, personally, I don't care if I serve frozen lasagna tonight, but if it means we get to be like this later, then I suppose I could be convinced to do the right thing now."

She gave my chest a playful swat and swung her legs over the edge of the bed. I rolled to my side and watched her pick up her clothes and head toward the bathroom. She caught me watching and raised her brow questioning. I simply returned the same. She smiled and put a little extra sway in her walk.

I heard a muttered, "Oh my God," come from behind the bathroom door.

"Something wrong?"

"You've ruined my hair."

"Oh," I chuckled, "sorry." Though I was obviously not, and she didn't think so either.

She came back into the room, working her hair into a messy bun.

"Don't lie to me." She was smiling from ear to ear, so I could tell she was teasing. I pulled her close and kissed her gently on the lips.

"I'm not lying. I am sorry your hair is a mess, but I'm not the least bit sorry about why."

She kissed me back. "I'm not sorry either." She winked. "Now let's get going. We've got a lot to do and not much time to do it.

We walked into the kitchen to find that Elizabeth had already made lunch for her sisters. She looked up from her sandwich and eyed me with a knowing look. She was too damn mature for a sixteen-year-old and much more than I was comfortable with. That said, I wouldn't take the bait and have to lie to her face. "Meg, do you mind being on your own for a couple of hours so Elizabeth can have some time for herself?"

She sighed but gave me her patented "that's fine, Dad."

"Aunt Janine just texted me, Elizabeth. She's sending Carly over this afternoon to watch the front desk. Once she gets here, you can have the rest of the afternoon off. Just let me know what you're doing and where you are, okay?"

A huge grin filled Elizabeth's face, and it made me more convinced I had to hire more help. I knew the inn meant a lot to her, but I'd been putting way too much on her shoulders.

"Can Snow and me go sledding?" Amy asked, bouncing with excitement in her chair.

"I'm going to need your help with a couple of errands because I want Snow to have some time just for her. She's worked harder than all of us this weekend, and I think she deserves it, don't you?"

She huffed, but gave me a smile. "I guess so." A thought caught in her eyes. I knew it would come out of her mouth instantaneously. She was not one to hold anything back. "Can I pick us out a special dessert?"

"If you're a good girl at the market, yes."

"Yay!" she squirmed happily in her seat. "Can Amber come too?"

"I have to go check on my car at Leo's, honey."

"Oh," her previous excitement disappearing in disappointment.

"I'd be happy to stop there with you." I could sense a hesitation in her eyes and quickly added, "unless you'd like a little time by yourself."

"No, that's not it at all. I just don't want to impose on daddy-daughter time."

"But I want you to come, Amber," Amy pleaded.

She met my eyes and smiled. "Okay, Peanut, as long as Daddy doesn't mind."

"I would mind if you didn't come." I put emphasis on the second to last word to make sure she got my point clearly. Handing her the sandwich I'd just made, I shooed the girls along. "Now go get your coat, hat and mittens, Amy. We've got things to do."

"Okay, Daddy," she slid off her seat and ran into the living quarters. I said a prayer of thanks and hoped that she would be this cooperative for at least a few more years.

"I'll go up and get mine," Amber mumbled with a mouthful of sandwich and headed out.

The sense of peace I had in Amber's bed just minutes ago hadn't left. It had actually grown. I still felt like a whole person. With any luck, this feeling would last.

# 22

# *Opportunities*

## *Amber*

Hunter pulled his pickup to a stop outside the service bay door at Leo's garage. A thin layer of icy slush crunched beneath my boots as I made my way to the office door. A sense of dread filled me with what I was going to be told once inside. Leo had promised that the county would cover the cost of the repairs, so at least I didn't have the expense to worry about. What worried me was what if he found more damage or it took longer to fix than he expected. Every day here cost me money I didn't have. Even if I could work at the inn on weekends now, I still needed a full-time job to pay my mortgage.

Leo's rotund figure greeted me with a smile and a hug as soon as I shut the door behind me. "There's my favorite snow angel. Nice to see Hunter found his manners and didn't make you walk."

I'm embarrassed to admit that the first thing that came to mind was how I wished Hunter would find things that would make it hard for me to walk. The gravity of my present situation didn't let me hold on to those pleasant thoughts for long. "Oh, he's quite the gentleman." I smiled and gave Leo a conspiratorial wink.

"Yes, I am." Hunter's booming baritone filled the room. At the same time, a bolt of blonde-haired little girl underneath a pink pompommed hat raced between us and landed in an old office chair with a squeal of delight and a spin. "What's the latest on Amber's car?"

"I'm sorry, but no different from what I told you Thursday. I ordered the parts. They should be here by Tuesday."

"Yay, Amber gets to stay three whole more days," came the excited cry from Amy, still spinning back and forth in the chair behind the desk.

"More than that, kiddo. I still have to fix it once the parts arrive. Honestly, Amber, I'd tell your work you'll be out until next Monday. Enjoy your time here… and the company," he added with a not at all subtle nod in Hunter's direction.

The bell over the door jingled with the announcement that another customer had arrived. The man was a little shorter than Hunter but just as solidly built, and the thought crossed my mind that there must be something in the mountain air. If a girl was looking, she might have trouble choosing if this was what was on the menu up here. "Hunter Holmes, how the hell are you? It's been ages. You're never at the Moose Jaw on Fridays anymore."

"Ha, well, I can't enjoy my return to bachelor days quite like you. I've got three girls to worry about full time and an inn to run."

"It's true, you got the short end of that deal, but that doesn't mean you aren't entitled to guy time now and again." He slapped Hunter on the shoulder and gave it a squeeze. It was easy to see that this was the 'Josh' I'd already heard stories about as Hunter's best friend.

"And who is this lovely lady?" he asked, turning his attention to me. His bright white smile was charming, and I got the sense he was quite the flirt. I couldn't help the smile that hit my lips as Hunter slid a possessive arm around my waist. It made me feel a little less guilty about how I acted when Carly was near.

"This is Amber Scott. Amber, this is Josh Sousa, my oldest and best friend. And the best builder this side of Denver. He did most of the rehab work at the inn and the addition we live in."

"Nice to meet you," he said, pulling the glove off his hand and extending it. "Glad to see you finding friends again, Hunter. I guess you're getting out and about again after all," he added, turning to Hunter and flashing a smile that had obvious undertones.

"Nice to meet you, too. Getting out?" I asked, looking between the two to unearth the meaning.

Josh laughed. "Hunter would never leave the inn if it was up to him. I never have to call ahead. All I have to do is drive past the IGA and the hardware store. If his truck isn't there, then I know he's at the inn. I assume he must have ventured out to meet you. No guy is lucky enough to have a beautiful woman like you drop right in their lap."

Hunter shook his head but laughed at his friend's good-natured jibe. I wasn't going to offer that I landed on his doorstep, but Hunter did it for himself.

"First off, Sousa, that's not true. I go plenty of places, and second…" Hunter countered.

"And secondly?" Josh teased, interrupting him.

"And second, I met Amber at the inn."

A deep rumbling laugh escaped from Josh's chest. He bent over, shoulders shaking. "Only you, Holmes. Only you," he wheezed.

"What the he… heck," Hunter corrected himself with a quick look in Amy's direction, "do you mean by that, Sousa?"

Josh composed himself and suddenly seemed much more serious. "I mean that everyone who cares about you has been trying to get you back to yourself for a while now, and apparently the universe saw fit to force your hand."

I glanced quickly at Hunter, wondering how he was going to react. Josh was jumping to some conclusions I was feeling a little fidgety about. I doubted Hunter was any more comfortable. Things were still very new, and while this morning certainly put a different light on our relationship. There were still more questions than answers.

"Noone's forcing anything, Josh," Hunter said, a hint of defensiveness in his tone. "We just met." A lump formed in my throat as my mind braced to hear that I meant nothing to him. It certainly felt like a lot more than that earlier. "I like her." He paused. "A lot, but please don't read things into it and put so much pressure on us that things get ruined."

As Hunter spoke, he placed his hand in the small of my back. The nervous lump vanished in a flash, replaced by something much warmer and feistier.

Josh stepped back, smiling and raising his hands. "Let's not get froggy. All I'm saying is I have eyes. I know you and when you're being protective. Don't worry, no one's trying to steal your toys."

"Daddy doesn't have toys, Mr. Sousa." Amy added from her perch behind the desk. "Though he does play with my Barbies sometimes."

That caused a chuckle to spread through the room, and thankfully all discussion of what I was or was not to Hunter was quickly forgotten. Josh asked about Leo's availability to fix a truck, and we shared some small talk before I elbowed Hunter, reminding him we still had groceries to get and lasagna to make.

"Well, we'd better get going." Hunter spoke. "I've got hungry skiers to get ready for. Good to see you," Hunter said to Josh, clapping him on the shoulder.

"Good to see you too, man. You and Amber should join us at the Moose some night. It would be nice to catch up."

"It will probably just have to be Hunter." I cut in. Trying to save Hunter from having to explain my absence when I disappeared back to my real life. "I've got to get back to Denver and find a job, so I don't know how much I'll be around."

"You lost your job?" Leo asked.

I nodded. "I was just about to tell you when Josh came in."

"Good." Leo smiled and removed the ever-present cigar stub from his mouth.

"Good?" I squeaked.

"Yes. Good. You didn't like your job. You were putting yourself under way too much stress feeling like you had to sell a house or starve."

"You're a real estate agent?" Josh interjected.

I gave him a nod. "Used to be anyway."

"Hmm," he hummed, rubbing his jaw thoughtfully.

"You told me you used to be a teacher, right?" Leo continued, bringing my focus back to him.

"You've got an excellent memory because I don't remember saying that, but then all I remember about that ride in the plow was that my car was lost in a snowbank."

"Well, the town just posted a long-term substitute position, and I know Hunter needs help at the inn. Well, help for a lot of things, but let's focus on the inn for now."

My heart leaped at the idea of getting back into the classroom, and the thought of spending more time with Hunter at the inn certainly made things interesting. Still, I had a house in Denver, and that was a lot to assume after only a couple of days of knowing the man. This impulsiveness was so unlike the cool, careful me, I didn't recognize the thoughts going through my mind. "Wow, I guess I could think about it, but I doubt a substitute position is going to pay enough."

"I told you I hire you at the inn and maybe between the two, it could be enough." I looked up into Hunter's eyes, and it almost took my breath away. His dark eyes swam with promise and hope. No one had ever looked at me like that before. Just the thought that I could mean that much to him had my insides turning to mush.

"Wow, jeez, I don't know. There's a lot to think about there." I was so overwhelmed.

"Just think about it." Hunter's warm hand cupped my cheek as he met my eyes again. He brushed a whisper-light kiss across my lips, and it just wasn't fair that a man that strong could be so gentle too. I wanted to climb him like a tree right there in the office. Amy was right there, which is probably the only reason I could restrain myself.

"I will." I agreed. "Now let's get to the grocery store. It was nice to meet you, Josh," I said as I shook his hand. "I'm amazed at how everybody is so welcoming in this town. It's like having a family of hundreds."

Josh tilted his head back in a hearty laugh. "Oh, you have no idea, and it's not always a good thing. Just be warned. If you stay around long enough, everyone will know your business whether you want them to or not. And the less you want them to know, the more likely it is they'll know it."

We were in the grocery store parking lot before it sunk in that I had no way back to Denver for at least a week. Somehow, it didn't matter as much to me as it had a couple of hours ago. Nothing had really changed, and yet I had this unfamiliar sense of hope around me. I wasn't waiting for the other shoe to drop. I didn't know how, but somehow things would turn out okay, and the man sitting next to me would make sure it did. I had someone on my side.

# 23

# Mountain Man Monkey Sex

## *Amber*

My mind raced with a thousand contradictory thoughts the entire weekend. I pushed most of them aside and focused on helping Janine serve food to the host of skiers that crowded the inn every night and morning.

On Sunday afternoon, I had just settled into one of the comfy chairs in my room to read for a bit when there was a knock on my door accompanied by a chorus of giggles. I didn't have to guess who was on the other side; I just couldn't imagine what they wanted. I left them at lunch with the expectation that I would see them again at dinner.

I set my book down on the end table and uncoiled myself from the chair. Padding over to the door, and asked, "who's there" in a silly British accent, which caused more giggles.

"It's us," Amy answered in a tone that suggested she had missed my attempt at humor.

As soon as I opened the door, Amy tugged on my hand. "Let's go," she said with a sense of urgency that had me immediately confused.

"Calm down, Amy," Elizabeth said patiently. "Amber doesn't even know why we're here."

"We want you to come down and help decorate our Christmas tree," Meg supplied before I could ask.

"Yeah. Come help," Amy said, her head bobbing in agreement. "Daddy's waiting for us."

"You want me to help decorate your Christmas tree?" I asked, the surprise and uncertainty I was feeling clear in my voice. It warmed my heart that they'd want to include me in their family time, but insecurities around relationships made it hard for me to believe they'd want me there. I looked at each of the girls for confirmation and saw nothing but excitement.

"Dad wanted to come up and get you, but I told him we'd do it," Elizabeth said. "We couldn't risk him getting distracted and taking too long. We only have a couple of hours to do it before he has to start dinner service."

There was a glint in her eyes that made my cheeks heat. I added embarrassment to the jumble of emotions I felt. Desire for Hunter and following the impulses I felt for the first time in my life. Fear of opening my heart to being hurt again. The tug of being my normal responsible self and returning to Denver and doing what had to be done to make ends meet. The lack of trust I had for virtually everyone. And not least of which was the deep affection I had for the three girls standing there wanting to include me in their lives.

"Well, we certainly wouldn't want to have your dad distracted. That's for sure," I said, not looking at Elizabeth. "Let's go. Time's a wasting."

The girls escorted me into the family room, where Hunter already had a ten-foot live tree set in its stand in front of the large picture window that looked out over the rolling hill where the kids had gone sledding after Thanksgiving dinner. The view beyond, over the Rocky Mountains, looked like a framed Ansel Adams photo, only in color. And oh, what colors!

Laid out on the floor were storage totes with ornaments, lights, tinsel and garland. I suspected many of the ornaments had meaning to this family, and I wished I had meaning to someone other than my mother. I was happy to be here. To be included, but there was a part of me screaming that I was a pretender, this was just a pleasant diversion, but that when Christmas came, I would be by myself back in Denver. I hated it was so hard for me to believe that I could have good things.

Elizabeth eased beside me and handed me a cup of hot cocoa. "We're really happy you're here," she said, as she wrapped an arm around my waist. "Maybe it sounds crazy. I hope you don't think we're putting too much pressure on you. And if we are, we don't mean to. But I've got this feeling that you belong with us. It feels right." Before I could form a response, she slipped away, grabbing a string of lights and a stepladder and started draping the lights on the top of the tree.

Meg stepped up underneath, feeding the strand to her as she wrapped it around. Not to be left out, Amy grabbed an ornament and placed it on a bow that was as high as she could reach.

"Amy, wait." Meg snapped a little harshly. But before anyone could correct her, Meg apologized. "I'm sorry, Amy. Let Snow finish stringing the lights before we start with ornaments, okay? We don't want to break any."

Amy looked up at her, and I could tell she was fighting back emotions, but nodded and took the decoration down and came over to nestle against my legs.

I bent down and hugged her, and she snuggled closer to my chest. "It's okay, Peanut. You're just excited," I whispered into her hair and punctuated it with a kiss on the top of her head. It was then that I noticed the ornament she held in her hand. Hand-painted, it showed Gabriel and the shepherds with an inscription underneath. *Momma's Little Angel. Amy's First Christmas.*

I bit the inside of my cheek to keep from tearing up. Hunter's hand rested on my shoulder. It was impossible to miss the gratitude in his expression. "She always makes sure it's the first one on the tree," his soft words informed me.

I swallowed and covered his hand with mine. Words weren't needed to let him know I understood. Once Meg and Elizabeth were finished with the lights, I hefted Amy into my arms. "Let's put that up high where everyone can see it," I said, and stepped next to the tree.

Her smile went from ear to ear as she placed it about halfway up the tree. "Perfect," she declared before squirming out of my arms. The girls then all went to work placing a variety of ornaments. Some were homemade, and others, though store-bought, seemed like they had sentimental value, just like Amy's.

Hunter and the girls kept handing me decorations to put up, making sure I didn't sink into the background like my insecurity was encouraging me to do. He even made me help string the garland once all the ornaments were in place. The girls added the tinsel as the finishing touch, and we all stepped back to take in the now completely trimmed tree.

I stood there and soaked in the beautiful tree. Colored lights twinkled and sparkled off the tinsel and decorations, reflecting off the glass of the window behind. Beyond, brilliant fuchsias and purples of the sunset framed the picture, and I could have stood there lost in the beauty forever. Strong hands rested on my hips, and a large solid body pressed against my back.

"Thank you, Amber. It feels like Christmas for the first time in three years. Not a single tear was shed this year. You coming here, coming into our lives has meant so much."

I started to dismiss his comment, but Elizabeth interrupted us. "Oh,

God. I almost forgot. Don't move," she said, looking at me, and ran down the hall toward her bedroom.

I turned to Hunter with my brow furrowed and gave him a questioning look.

"Beats me," he said with a lift of his shoulders.

A moment later she returned, holding a small paper bag. "Amy, Meg and I walked down to the hardware store after lunch. We all have our own special things on the tree, and we wanted you to have one too." She handed me the bag, grinning, and Amy and Meg moved closer to watch me open it.

I reached into the bag and pulled out a small square box. Inside was an ornament shaped like an apple. I was about to question how they knew I had a thing for apples when I read *World's Best Teacher.* So many thoughts swirled through my mind it was nearly impossible to pick one to focus on. How did they know I used to be a teacher? Had Hunter told them about what Leo said?

"Can I help you put it up?" Amy asked, breaking me out of my thought spiral.

"Sure, sweetie," I said, taking it out of the box and picking her up. "How about if Meg points to where she thinks it should be?"

"Okay," Amy agreed, and I looked to Meg, whose smile was wide and eyes twinkled with delight.

"Right there," Meg said, pointing to a spot next to Amy's ornament. Ironically, it was about the only spot on the tree without a decoration hanging from it.

Elizabeth stepped up next to us and threaded a hanger through the loop in the decoration. "Meg's going to love having you," she said, shocking me to the point I almost dropped both Amy and the ornament. "I'm jealous I'm already in high school."

"What are you talking about, Snow?" Hunter asked, taking the words out of my mouth.

"Did you tell them about the substitute position?" I asked Hunter, finding my voice.

"No," he said, drawing the word out, still looking toward Elizabeth for her explanation.

"Just a hunch," she answered with all the confidence of someone with inside information. "I mean, it makes sense. Everyone knows we need a new teacher for fifth and sixth grade ELA. Amber needs a job. She used to be a teacher. We all want her here. It's two plus two simple, Dad."

The look he was giving her led me to believe that he didn't think it was simple at all. There was more to this that I didn't understand, but that discussion would have to wait. I'd barely started to think about what to do, and I didn't want the girls to set their hearts on something that was far from certain. Especially Amy.

"Thanks for helping us decorate the tree, Amber," Meg said before I could voice my doubts.

"Yeah, thanks, Amber," Amy parroted and kissed me on the cheek.

"Thank you. All of you," I said, returning Amy's kiss before hugging both Meg and Elizabeth. "This was fun."

The girls scattered off toward their rooms, and Hunter pulled me into a hug. "It was fun," he said. "But it was more than that. There was happiness here today. For the past few years, it's been really somber. Like something was missing. It's like hope is back in the season. We have hope."

What could I have said to that? I just leaned back against him. Hope. I could sense it somewhere but couldn't quite bring myself to believe it. If I let myself feel hope and it didn't come to pass, I'd be crushed.

I helped Hunter clean up the totes and put them away in the storage room off the back hallway. Then we made our way to the kitchen to prepare dinner for the hotel guests.

Dinner service was markedly less rushed than it had been the previous two nights. Only a handful of guests were staying Sunday night, and there were just twelve for dinner. I did little other than keep Hunter company and take care of the dishwashing. Hunter even took the time to visit with the guests as they ate.

One party was the Smalls. The woman who had written the complementary note and confused me as the girls' mother. I walked over at the tail end of the conversation to hear him explain that while I wasn't the girls' mother; I was a recent addition to the family and a welcome and important one. He hadn't seen me coming, so I had no doubt those were his honest feelings. Warmth filled me. Maybe I wasn't quite the outsider I thought I was. That warmth felt an awful lot like hope.

Mrs. Small smiled at me as I stepped next to Hunter, placing my hand on his shoulder. "Here's the woman we've been gossiping about," she said, before taking a sip of her coffee.

"I'm so sorry for the confusion. Please know…"

"Don't be silly," she cut me off. "I would take it as such a compliment if my stepdaughter treated me that way. You must be a very special woman to have formed that kind of bond with her. Teen girls are a very tough nut to crack," she laughed. "Trust me, I know."

I fought to find the words to thank her, but I didn't want to make things between Hunter and me out to be more than they were. Before I could, she continued.

"Hunter shared that your relationship is new. I hope you don't mind my butting in, but it's just so nice to see a family. A real family meshing well and working together. I know it's all new and you don't know what the future holds, but trust the kids. They know, and from what I've seen, those girls care about you. The battle's won, Amber. Just sit back and enjoy the victory."

I smiled and said the only thing that I could. "Thank you."

Hunter was busy getting the girls ready to go back to school the next day, so I excused myself and headed up to my room for a long soak in the bath. Impulsivity was never my thing. I wasn't someone who acted on my emotions. I thought things through. Did the prudent thing. I had come so close to telling Hunter I wanted him and the girls too. But I just couldn't force those words past my lips. It was all so fast. Just a few days. How could careful, cautious Amber just pick up and move to a small town hoping this relationship would work out?

Teaching was what I loved to do. The transition into real estate was a calculated decision. I was good with people; people seemed to trust me by default, so I should have been a natural salesperson. On paper, real estate sales was a smart move, but not one I liked. My trouble was I always felt I was being pushy when it came time to close the sale.

Marrying Lance was planned, analyzed and discussed too. And yet, despite all my planning, things turned out to be a total disaster.

Did I really have anything to lose by staying here and giving love a chance?

Was it worth it to give Lance a chance to laugh at my ultimate failure? In the beginning, he had tried to convince me the house would be a lot to afford on my own with just a teacher's salary. Looking back, he was probably being honest and trying to help, but I wasn't in a place to accept it. When I dug in and made it clear that keeping the house was a personal vendetta to me; that's when he turned nasty and condescending. And why do I even give a damn what he thinks?

I could stay at the inn. Hunter had already said that, and if I got the teaching job, and why shouldn't I, could there really be that many credentialed teachers in this little town at this time of year that aren't already teaching?

At least I could apply, see if I got it, what it paid and go from there. Hopefully, I could work something out at the inn and trade working weekends for a room and then keep my mortgage up with the teaching job. Maybe, just maybe, Betsy would last the winter, and then I could go from there. See if things worked out with Hunter and then put the house up for sale in the spring if they did. The market will be better then anyway.

I deserved this, and for once in my life I'd live for the moment because I wanted to, not because I was forced to make a change I didn't want.

I sat in the bath until the bubbles had disappeared, my fingers and toes resembled dried fruit, and gooseflesh covered my body. Only a shiver snapped me out of my head to make me realize it was time to get out. I realized I'd been ruminating so long I'd forgotten to shave, like I'd planned. It wasn't a regular part of my routine anymore, but I'd wanted to clean things up in case there was a repeat performance with Hunter. I was about to hit the hot water for a warm-up when my phone rang in the other room.

I'd left a voicemail updating my mother on everything and figured she was returning the call. I dried off quickly and slipped my flannel nightgown on over my head. Crossing to the nightstand, I picked up the phone to find a missed call and voicemail not from Mom, but from Patty, my closest friend back in Denver. We met in college and stayed close. She had helped me find the job in real estate through her industry connections. She'd taken on a larger role at the company she worked for a little over a year ago and only managed the occasional lunch or quick drink after work since then.

I didn't want to admit defeat and tell Patty I'd been let go, but I didn't want to put off one of the few people I could call a friend. There was a chance I could avoid telling her I was unemployed and stranded without a car in the mountains; so I returned the call.

"Amber! Thanks so much for getting right back to me. How are you?"

"Patty, hey. I'm doing good. How are you?"

"I'm great. And you sound good. I thought you'd be much more down after they let you go."

I sank down onto the bed. Maybe I should have listened to the voicemail first. "How did you know I'd been fired?"

"I'm still close with the girls in the office. We met for lunch this afternoon, and one of them asked about how you were doing. I was embarrassed to have to tell her we hadn't talked in a while. I'm sorry, Amber. I take it you didn't listen to the message I left."

I shook my head and then laughed, realizing Patty couldn't see me. "No, I just got out of the bath and saw the missed call. I was happy to hear from you. I'm sorry. I should have listened to it first. What's up?"

"Oh, honey, don't apologize. I'm happy you called back so quickly. I'm pretty sure I can get you a place at the firm I work for now. Any chance you can meet me on Tuesday morning at ten?"

I inhaled and then let out a slow breath. That was the last thing I'd expected. "God, Patty. Thank you. Unfortunately, I'm kind of snowed in up in the mountains without a car."

"Snowed in? How are you in the mountains without a car?"

On a heavy sigh, I gave her an abbreviated version of everything that had happened and how I was likely going to be without a car for at least another week.

"You poor thing. Getting plowed into a snowbank, having to spend Thanksgiving alone at a hotel and losing your job because of your asshole ex… you need some good luck."

She wasn't wrong that I had needed some good luck for a change, but getting stranded at this inn might actually turn out to be pretty lucky. I just didn't want to jinx it by speaking it out loud.

"Look. I've got a contract signing tomorrow morning, but I can head up there right after that and pick you up. I'm sure you can get your insurance to pay for a rental if the county is already taking responsibility for the accident, and we can pick that up for you so at least you don't have to lose your mind worrying about everything while stuck in some little backwoods hick town in the mountains."

The smart thing to do would be to take Patty up on her offer, but a wave of defensiveness washed over me about Homer Pass. She had it completely wrong. It might be small, but I'd felt more at home in the past few days than I had in a lifetime of living in the city. "The people here have been very nice. They're good people, and they've treated me like family. Believe it or not, Patty, I love it here."

"Really? I thought you were a city girl through and through, and you always complained about the winters."

I laughed. She wasn't wrong. "I'm not saying I'm overjoyed about snowbanks over my head, but at least I've felt welcomed, and it's made the mounds of white stuff much easier to handle." My responsible side told me to take up her generosity, but my heart wasn't on board. "It's a long drive, and there's a ton of snow up here. I don't want to impose."

"Don't be silly. You'll be perfect for this job. It's salaried, not commission-based, with a lot more customer service than sales. You'll be much happier and feel less pressure. The drive back will give us time to catch up. It's been too long. Do you think the inn you're at will give you a late checkout? I doubt I'll get there much before dinnertime."

I sucked in a sharp breath. Hunter and the girls, at least Amy, were excited to have me for the week. I realized I was going to have to explain to him I was going back to Denver? And the girls, Amy. My heart twisted into a knot at the thought, and that seemed absolutely foolish. I didn't even know they existed five days ago. "I think they'll be okay with it, especially when I'm coming back." I hoped that was true and not another lie I told myself.

"Why would you be going back, Amber?"

I looked up at the ceiling. How could it feel so automatic that I would come back? "Well, I'll have to pick up my car once it's fixed."

"Oh, right, of course. So, what's the name of this place?"

"The Snowflake Inn."

"Oh, God, Amber. Could they have a sillier name? That's just so cliché."

"There's a very sweet story behind it." I couldn't help the defensive edge that crept into my tone.

"Alright, don't get defensive."

"I'm not."

"You are." I heard the pause in Patty's voice. She was on to me. "Is there more to this story you're not telling me?"

"What do you mean?" I asked, doing my best to sound innocent. It didn't. I was a shit liar.

"There is! Amber Scott, you've met some hunky guy, and you're having hot mountain man monkey sex.? Is that why you sound less than enthusiastic about coming home?"

"I refuse to answer that." I knew my face was flaming with embarrassment. I was glad she wasn't there to see me. There would be no doubt in her mind then.

"Mm hmm. It's a long ride, sweetie, and you know how persuasive I can be."

I laughed and felt a warmth inside I'd been missing. I'd almost forgotten how good Patty made me feel. "We'll see." I hesitated because I figured there'd be no way I'd be able to hide my feelings toward Hunter in front of her, and even if I tried, he would make it impossible by just being…him. It was a long ride. I should at least buy her dinner. "We can eat at the inn before we head back. My treat. There's no place else in this town unless you want wings and burgers, but honestly, the food is so good here. Not fancy, just good old-fashioned home cooking."

"That sounds nice, Amber. Oh, honey, gotta go. I've got another call coming through. I'll see you tomorrow night."

She'd hung up before I said goodbye, but that was Patty; always on the go.

Monday morning dawned bright and cold. Hunter was out the door early, driving the girls to school, and he had some errands to run afterwards. Carly was covering the front desk until noon when a couple of college kids came in to service the rooms. All Hunter gave me for an explanation was that it was some kind of co-op deal he'd arranged with a community college hospitality program. They came four days a week.

He handed me a set of keys and told me I could use his truck if I wanted to go out. Given my recent driving record, it was a leap of faith I wasn't sure I deserved. It was way too cold for my liking, but the exercise of wandering around town would be good for me and much safer for Hunter's insurance rates. Everything was within a few blocks, so why not walk?

I stopped at the gas station first. I resisted the temptation of asking Leo for an update and snagged my sunglasses out of the car. The sun was shining brightly, and snow blindness is real.

I wandered along the main street, soaking in the feel of small-town life. It felt good. I slipped into the general store to say hi to Janine before walking to the other end of Main Street and Town Hall. The purpose of this walk was to apply for the long-term substitute position.

I assumed I would be handed an application to return later, so I was taken completely by surprise when the superintendent greeted me personally and interviewed me on the spot. There's something to be said for the lack of bureaucracy in a small town.

When the superintendent offered me the position pending the results of the background and reference checks; you could have knocked me over with a feather. The salary would be more than enough to pay my bills, provided Hunter let me stay at the inn in exchange for working there, at least for the time being. I might just be able to stay for a while without selling my house.

Just to be sure, I grabbed a copy of the local weekly newspaper, The Homer Pass Gazette, on my way back to the inn to check for rentals. I had promised the superintendent an answer by Friday, which was acceptable because they didn't need me to start until after the Christmas holiday break.

As it was well after noon by the time I finished at city hall, I checked out the Bighorn Diner before going back to the inn. I had to ask Hunter if he wanted me to pack my things so he could rent the room. We also had to figure out things for the coming weekend. So I couldn't take long.

It would also give me a chance to take in some locals and think about the best way to talk to Hunter about what I had in mind. The diamond pattern chrome front and large windows on the front of the building were classic Americana. I smiled at the quaintness of the downtown and thought how well this little eatery fit in with the overall atmosphere. True to its name, an enormous set of ram's horns were mounted on the sign over the double entry doors.

The tinkle of bells announced my entry as I stepped in out of the frigid air. Warmth and a cacophony of sounds surrounded me as I made my way to one of the empty red vinyl-covered stools at the counter. The din of a dozen conversations, the clanking of dishes being cleared from booths and the hiss of meat sizzling on the grill coming from the open kitchen welcomed me like a warm hug. I couldn't help but smile at how, without a single word, I felt welcome here. It was nothing like the sterile sameness of the chain restaurants that saturated every strip center and corner where I lived in Denver.

"Coffee, love?"

I looked up from stowing my mittens in my pockets to be met by a smiling waitress. The woman wore a red polo shirt with ram's horns and 'Emma' embroidered on the chest. "Please," I answered as I returned her smile.

Emma produced a cup and saucer from below the counter and a steaming pot of coffee, seemingly by magic. "There are hooks over there if you want to hang your coat up. Hector keeps this place subtropical. You'll melt if you keep that jacket on long enough to finish that coffee."

"Hector?" I asked.

"I'm sorry," she said, shaking her head and placing creamers in a pile next to the coffee. "Hector is the owner. I just assumed Janine would have given you the 411 on this town before letting you venture out into the wild."

"How do you know…"

"How do I know who you are?" She laughed. "Honey, this is Homer Pass, and half the town knew about you before Leo even deposited you at the Inn after plowing you into the snowbank. And let me tell you, the other half knew after your visit to the market yesterday."

All I could do was shake my head, I didn't believe I would merit the attention of half the town. "Surely you all have more important things to worry about than a stranded motorist."

"First off, this is a small town, and it's in our DNA to be nosy. Second, there's not much that goes on around here in winter. Hiking and hunting are done for the year, so all we have to do is hope this snow keeps up and Hunter and his girls get enough business to keep that inn going. Lord knows that man deserves a break. Hunter also happens to be the most eligible bachelor in a sixty-mile radius. Word spread pretty quickly about a mystery woman spotted with him and Amy in the produce aisle. Sheriff Nelson has half the single women in town on suicide watch."

I couldn't contain the belly laugh that escaped. "I went grocery shopping with the man, not shopping for wedding dresses."

"Oh, love, from what I hear, the looks he was giving you when you weren't looking melted the entire freezer aisle. The kids in town are going without tater tots and chicken nuggets for a week because of that little trip."

I could feel my cheeks flaming with embarrassment and just a little thrill if what Emma was telling me about how Hunter had been looking at me was true. Hoping to move the discussion away from my love life with a complete stranger, I asked, "So what's good? I haven't been lucky enough to eat at a diner in ages."

"Normally I'd say you can't go wrong with the open-faced turkey sandwich, but if you're like me, you're done with turkey for a bit, so I'd go with the Reuben. Honestly, everything's good here. Hector is a natural at comfort food."

"The Reuben sounds perfect, and I take it that Hector cooks too?"

Emma nodded. "Started as the dishwasher thirty years ago, worked his way up to line cook. When old man Thompson passed, he willed him the deed. We take care of our own here, always have; always will."

I smiled. "Seems to me you take care of others too."

"We do," she agreed, "but I get the feeling you're going to be one of us soon enough."

My stomach twisted with an unfamiliar warmth, and my heart tapped out a staccato beat in my chest. I'd never considered that I'd been a part of any community I'd ever been in, and for a complete stranger to suggest that I was a part of her community. It was a foreign feeling of belonging, but not unwelcome. It helped to calm my uneasiness about the conversation about the future I knew I'd have to have with Hunter later.

"I'm Emma, by the way." She extended her hand across the counter, smiling.

"Amber," I replied, taking the offered hand, "but I'm betting you already knew that."

She offered me a conspiratorial smile and a wink before turning away and placing my order on the carousel in the opening between the counter and the kitchen. "Order up," she bellowed.

I slid off the stool, walked over, and hung up my coat on the hooks lining the far wall. Smiles and nods from the diners greeted me from everyone I made eye contact with along the way. It felt a lot like I was being greeted by old friends, people I'd known all my life. Emma couldn't have been exaggerating; people seemed to know me already.

I'd barely settled back onto my stool and taken a sip of my coffee when I was ambushed with a bear hug. "Look at you mixing in with the locals." Now I really was with a friend. I swiveled and returned Janine's embrace.

"It seems like the thing to do, but honestly, I was just stopping for lunch."

Janine sat down on the stool next to me, which had been vacated by five other patrons shifting down the line to make space. Something that I would have never seen happen at home. Something that would have been met with complaints and eye rolls of annoyance if she'd been bold enough to ask. Emma had already placed a coffee down in front of Janine and called to her from the other end of the counter. "The usual?"

"You know it, girlfriend," she answered with a smile. Turning back to me, she dropped her voice. "Hector will give you grief for not finishing, but make sure you leave room for the pie. I swear, some days, I'd rather skip the meal and live off his pies. I don't know what he does, but they're addicting."

I smiled and patted my stomach. "I can't afford that kind of addiction. But I can't believe they're better than the ones Hunter made for Thanksgiving."

"I'll admit that Hunter's apple pie is delicious, but Hector's lemon meringue and banana cream are to die for," she whispered conspiratorially. "And with your figure, you've got a long way to go before you have anything to worry about. And if my knucklehead brother ever makes you think differently, you let me know and I'll take care of him, don't you worry."

I wasn't going to share that Hunter had made me feel more desired than any man I'd ever been with, but there was a part of me that couldn't understand why he would want me. My insecurities were never far from my mind.

"Hey," Janine nudged me out of my thoughts. "I've seen the way my brother looks at you. He knows just how perfect you are. Trust me on that. The man has it bad for you."

"We just met, Janine. I'm not going to pretend I'm not attracted to him or that I think he's not attracted to me." I paused, staring down at my coffee and wishing I didn't drink it black, so I'd have something to do to distract her from this conversation. Adding cream and sugar would buy me at least a few seconds to collect my thoughts. "But it's way too early to assume there's anything more than attraction."

Janine considered me, peering over her mug before taking a slow sip. "If you say so." She smiled as if she knew a secret that I didn't. "I understand being cautious with your heart. I certainly am, after what I've been through. Let's just promise each other we won't be so careful we miss what's right in front of us."

"I honestly don't think I'm missing anything. I'm just not going to jump to conclusions."

I was eternally grateful when our food arrived at that moment, effectively ending that discussion. The plate in front of me held perhaps the largest and most delicious-looking Reuben I'd ever seen. "Oh, my Lord, Janine. That's enough to feed an army." I wrapped my hands around the sandwich and attempted to open my mouth wide enough to take a bite but couldn't manage it. "I'm going to have to eat this with a fork."

Janine smiled and laughed, scooping a creamy spoonful of baked mac 'n' cheese. I noticed it was loaded with a kind of meat I couldn't identify. "Mm," she hummed, "so good."

"It looks scrumptious. What kind of meat is that?"

Janine shrugged. "Who knows? Hector's loaded mac 'n' cheese is a little different every time. Usually some kind of game. Today's tastes like it's probably venison. Other times it is more traditional ham or buffalo chicken. Here, have a bite."

She scooped up a portion and fed me like I was a toddler. A low moan escaped my throat that was just shy of orgasmic. "That's incredible. Sooo cheesy."

"That's the trick. Hector has this magical sauce, and he won't give up the recipe. I swear it doesn't matter what meat he puts in it. It could be a cat for all I care; I'd still eat it."

Order envy threatened to overtake me, but mine looked pretty good too. I cut into the gooey, cheesy, pastrami concoction and let out another moan of satisfaction. It was almost magical, rich and with just enough zing from the sauerkraut. "The food here might just be better than sex."

Janine barked out a laugh. "It's a definite foodgasm, but I wouldn't go telling Hunter that or he might take that as a challenge."

I snort-laughed the coffee I'd just taken a sip of half through my nose. I grabbed a napkin, choking with laughter. "That could have its benefits." I cupped my face in my hands the moment the words left my mouth. "I can't believe I just said that. God. He's your brother, for Pete's sake. I don't know what's gotten into me."

"From the blush on your face, I'd say Hunter, for one."

"Janine!" I slapped her on the shoulder. "Stop that."

"What?" Janine chuckled, feigning innocence.

All I could do was shake my head. "You're terrible. I'm not going to talk about my sex life, and certainly not with his sister."

"You mean to tell me you don't have girlfriends back in Denver that after a few glasses of wine, the lips get loose?"

I could feel my mood slipping. My smile faded from my face. "I lost most of my friends in the divorce. My only real friend there is Patty, but she's busy and, honestly, I haven't been on a date in nearly a year."

Janine sucked in a sharp breath of disbelief. Opened her mouth and closed it quickly. Exhaled, and then smiled. "Well, luckily you have me now."

I couldn't help myself. I leaned over and gave her a hug. "Thanks." I bit my bottom lip as I tried to hold back the emotion pushing to escape the corners of my eyes. I was so used to holding people at arm's length because eventually everyone always leaves, I couldn't understand how I could feel so close to everyone in this family, Janine, the girls and especially Hunter. I had to admit I was well past the point where I could walk away without a world of hurt. I'd better control myself, or I'd never survive when it ended. "It means so much to find a friend." I sat back in my seat, letting go of the hug. "But don't expect me to share the steamy details about Hunter with you. I don't think I could ever be comfortable with that."

Janine sighed and smiled. "Trust me, I don't need the steamy details about my brother, but I'm here if you need me. Just know that."

Emotion clogged my throat. All I could manage was to nod and go back to work on the deliciousness on my plate.

We finished our lunches in companionable conversation and hugged goodbye. Pushing open the heavy chrome and glass door, I braced myself against the cold and walked back to the inn. I still had to speak to Hunter about how this would work, and if he still wanted me back for the weekend. I wasn't at all sure he'd be happy I was leaving at all, but I needed to keep this potential job with Patty as an option. I needed to be smart and not let my heart get in the way.

# 24

# Promise You'll Come Back

## Amber

A bitter gust of wind hit me in the face as I turned the corner onto the drive up to the inn. I pulled my parka high around my shoulders and shivered, despite the warmth of the fur-lined hood. The calendar had just rolled over into December, and yet it seemed like winter was already well established here in Homer Pass.

I tipped my head back and was met with dark blue-gray clouds. Fuck. More snow. I could only hope it wouldn't be much because Patty and I were driving back to Denver tonight. The last thing I wanted was to end up in another snowbank. Then again, Patty was likely better prepared than I had been. There would be measurable tread on the tires of Patty's luxury SUV. She also had Bluetooth and GPS, less chance of getting lost or skipping CDs.

Opening the weighty oak and glass door leading into the main lobby, I was met with the smell of baking. That brought back the memory of the first time I walked into this lobby just a few short days ago. Only this time instead of pie I was met with the aroma of freshly baked bread, or maybe rolls. Whatever kind of deliciousness it was, it had my mouth watering despite having just finished lunch.

Hunter appeared through the swinging door that led to the kitchen wearing his moose apron, covered in flour and several other unidentifiable smudges. "Hey, you." A smile filled his face as he closed the distance between us. "I didn't realize you were out. When I saw the truck keys still on the hook, I thought maybe you were hiding in your room reading."

"Nope. Though that sounds like a great way to spend the rest of the afternoon." I unzipped my coat and unwrapped my scarf from around my neck. "The snow is so beautiful I just wish it didn't have to be so damn cold."

Hunter shook his head. "Yup, funny thing about the snow, it's always cold. A real mystery."

"Are you making fun of me?"

He replied with an immediate, "Never," that lacked any semblance of sincerity, and his twitching lips as he fought back a smile confirmed it. "So where have you been? Trying to acquaint yourself with the local charm?"

"Well, that was an added benefit. I had a few things in town I wanted to get done while you were out, and then I ran into Janine when I stopped at the Bighorn. It turned out not to be the quick bite I'd planned on."

Hunter laughed, "No. Meeting my sister ended all hope of quick. And don't you dare tell her I said that."

Those damn dimples were on full display on his cheeks, which sent a wave of thoughts that were a lot less than pure through my body. "Hmm, I think maybe you'll have to make it worth my while."

He closed what little distance that was left between us and leaned in for a kiss. Cupping my bottom, he pulled our bodies together. Our lips met, and I couldn't help but open myself to him. His tongue swept across mine, and he swallowed down the throaty moan I offered. He pulled back from the kiss but not before placing a light peck on the tip of my nose.

"As much as I'd like to continue this, I should get back to the baking. We've got guests coming this evening. I thought maybe it was them getting in early."

"How did you even know anyone was out here? I barely made a sound when I came in."

"There's a sensor on the door connected to an app on my phone. It's pretty annoying, actually, so I only activate it when I'm here alone and working on something."

"Any luck finding help?"

"No, but I was hoping maybe we could talk a little more about you working at the inn."

I swallowed the lump that formed in my throat. I knew we had to have this talk, but I hated the possibility that he wouldn't understand my need to weigh all the options.

"Yeah, we should probably do that." I said as I exhaled a long, slow breath. "Let me put my stuff in my room, and I'll meet you in the kitchen? I've got some news to tell you."

"News? Is any of it good?"

"I'll tell you when I get back down." I forced a smile and kissed him. "Patience."

"Not one of my best qualities," he said.

I couldn't help but smile. "I'm seeing that, but you'll just have to learn."

The smile faded from Hunter's and he shrugged his shoulders. "I'll do my best, but don't hold your breath."

I sucked in a gulp of air, popping out my cheeks and making bug eyes.

He laughed, shaking his head, giving me the response I was looking for. He pulled me in for another toe-curling kiss.

"Mm, nice," I said. It felt like whatever tenseness between us disappeared in that kiss.

"Yes," he hummed. "Go up and put your stuff away, and I'll take the bread out of the oven. We can sit in the family room, have a nice cup of coffee and sort things out. Janine is picking the girls up from school today, so we have plenty of time, and you can tell me your news."

"Okay. I'll see you in a few." I pressed a quick kiss on his lips and headed up to my room. He turned and went back to the kitchen.

Hunter was already waiting for me on the couch with a fresh pot of coffee on the coffee table. He stood up and wrapped me in his arms. "So, what's your big news?" He asked before pulling me down onto his lap.

"How am I supposed to concentrate on what we're talking about like this?"

"We could concentrate on other things first," he said. He pushed my hair over my shoulder and placed a whisper-light kiss on the perfect spot just below my ear. My body responded automatically, leaning into the contact.

"You're not playing fair," I groaned, making zero attempt to pull away.

"I know." I could feel his smile against my skin as he continued to kiss down my neck.

I heaved a sigh and squirmed off his lap. "As much as I would much rather do what you have in mind. We have things we need to talk about."

"Fine," he said with a huff I could tell was mostly a joke. "But we're going to visit this again after the girls go to bed."

I swallowed and looked down at my hands. I couldn't; I wouldn't lie to him, but I didn't want to start this discussion by saying I was heading back to Denver in a couple of hours. My gut told me he was going to take this as a rejection, and that's not what this was at all. My brain froze. I didn't know what to say.

"Hey," he said, lifting my chin with his finger until I met his gaze. "What's wrong? Am I coming on too strong? "

"God, no," I said, taking his hand and kissing his palm. "There's nothing I want more right now than to take you to bed and forget all about the world. The problem is we'd still have things to figure out." I took a deep breath and exhaled, steadying myself. "I kind of wanted to save this for last, but my friend Patty is on her way up here now to pick me up. I talked to her late last night, and she heard I got let go at the real estate agency. There's a job opening at the firm she works for. She thinks I might be good for it. I have an interview with them tomorrow morning." I hesitated for a moment to gauge his reaction, but his expression was unreadable. "It will also give me a chance to pick up a rental car until Leo is done with mine," I added.

"Oh," he said, sinking back into the corner of the couch.

Even though our legs were still touching, he felt too far away. It felt like there was suddenly a wall between us. "Hey," I said, taking hold of his leg and giving it a squeeze. "What's the matter?"

"Nothing," he said. His brow furrowed, and his smile failed to meet the panty-melting wattage I'd become accustomed to.

"Hunter Holmes, we might not have known each other very long, but I can tell that something is bothering you."

"It's nothing. Really." He hesitated for a moment, and his smile became a little less forced. "I don't adjust to change well, Amber. In my mind, I had you all to myself until at least next Monday." He let out a slow breath. "It's okay. I understand you need to work. And I know I can't offer the financial security you need with a job at the inn. I truly wish I could." He paused and ran his hand over his face before pinching the bridge of his nose. "In a few short days, you have become important to me. I enjoy having your pretty face around. Who knows how long it will take for you to get things sorted and come back. I'm going to miss you."

Warmth spread through my chest, and I felt really and truly wanted by this man. I shifted so my body hovered over his and pressed a kiss on his lips. A soft moan escaped his mouth, and the heat in my chest rose another ten degrees. "I'm going to miss you too. You might not like change, but I don't do well being spontaneous, especially with big decisions. Unless I check everything, including the job Patty is suggesting, I'll doubt whether I'm making the right choice. I'm not at all impulsive. I need to check all the boxes. Then I can make the right choice for me."

"What choice do you have, Amber? I was thinking you could help me in the kitchen. I'd have Elizabeth show you how the front desk works and just fill in where we need you. I could probably afford to pay you five hundred dollars a week, and of course you'd have the room at no cost and obviously food because you'd be eating with us as a family. If you want to, of course. But that's not what you need. You need what Patty's offering. I couldn't ask you to give that up. I want you, but I know wanting isn't always enough."

I could see the uncertainty still swimming in his gaze. He was scared I wouldn't come back, but that thought hadn't even crossed my mind. It was only a few days, but I already knew Hunter was someone I wanted to get to know better. He was the first man I felt like taking a risk on. "Even if the job at Patty's firm turns out to be right for me, I promise I'll be here every weekend for as long as you need me. For as long as you want me. Even if I don't take the job, I'll need to take care of my house. You know, pay bills and stuff."

"So you're planning on coming back, regardless?"

"I am. Besides, I have an offer here in town to consider too."

"What?" Hunter asked, his voice rising. "What are you talking about?"

I couldn't help the smile that filled my face until my cheeks hurt. "The main reason I went into town this morning was to check on the substitute position. Superintendent Miller offered me the job. See, I do have things to consider."

"You're kidding," he said, his broad smile matching mine. "That's awesome."

I nodded. "It's good. It's not a lot of money, but I think I could make it work. I just have to see all my options. That includes giving what Patty has serious consideration too." I took his hand and waited for him to meet my stare so he could see my sincerity. "This is more than just money. I need to consider everything, or it won't be fair to either of us. I don't want to second-guess myself."

"I can't ask for more than that," Hunter said, holding my gaze. "And I'll support whatever decision you make. I'm content knowing that you'll be back."

"I promise."

"Okay."

"I'll get back here just as soon as I can. I'll even keep you updated on what's going on."

"You better," he said, with a hint of mischief in his eyes. "I'd have to find a way to punish you if you didn't." He placed a finger on his chin as he pretended to think about it. "Oh, I have it. A good spanking should be threat enough to discourage unacceptable behavior."

I laughed. I loved his playful side. "Hmm, not exactly the disincentive you think it is for me."

His groan was the end of me. My core temperature was officially at internal combustion level.

# 25

# *Choices*

## *Amber*

Icould feel Patty stealing glances in my direction as we made our way out of Homer Pass. I continued to stare out the window, watching the snow-covered pines pass by. It was nearly nine o'clock by the time we'd finished dinner and said our goodbyes. I couldn't resist when Amy asked me to tuck her in and read her a bedtime story. Unfortunately, that gave my best friend time to interrogate Hunter. I'll have to be sure to apologize when I call him to tell him I'm home safe. Something he insisted I do, and notably something Lance never did. Not once in the six years we were together.

"Well?" Patty asked, like I knew what the question behind that obtuse word was.

I did actually, but playing dumb was my plan because I didn't know that I was confident in my answer. "Well, what?"

"Well, what's the thing between you and Hunter? And don't you dare say 'nothing'. I have eyes and ears, and this is not just mountain man monkey sex. I know you've been long overdue to scratch that itch for years, but there's more to this than what you led me to believe when we talked on the phone."

"You're the one that called it mountain man monkey sex, whatever the hell that means." I exhaled slowly, not really wanting to get into this right now. Mostly because I didn't have the answers yet for myself, let alone being able to explain it to Patty. But my friend would not let this go if I knew her at all, and maybe, just maybe, talking with her might give me another perspective to help me understand the strange emotions floating around in my gut. "I know this sounds crazy, but it sure feels like a lot more than just casual. It's stupid. It's not me. But when we talk, it's like we both feel so much in such a short time. If I had any common sense or a sense of self-preservation, I should not be letting myself feel the way I feel. And I certainly shouldn't be thinking about making plans that could lead me into a winter wonderland hellscape."

"Who are you? And what have you done with Amber, the careful, meticulous planner I've known for ten years?" She chanced a quick glance in my direction, a mischievous smile gracing her face.

"I know. Right? I should have lists and spreadsheets and an encyclopedia's worth of reasons why something this impulsive could ruin me forever."

"Honestly, honey, nothing is going to ruin you forever. You're way too strong for that, but I can't disagree that this seems impulsive, especially for you." Before I could reply, she continued. "I've got to say I haven't seen you look this content in years. Not even before the douche canoe did you dirty with that bimbo. I'm not saying I don't see you struggling to think this out and make a good choice, but there's something underneath I can't quite put a name to. Something a little bit like hope that tomorrow will not be an unmitigated shitshow."

"It seems that way to you? Because I'm pretty sure there is going to be shit aplenty tomorrow and the next day and the next." I had to ask because it certainly didn't feel that way to me.

"Ah. Mm. No. You expect a shitshow because you've been living one so long, but there's a glint in your eye that tells me you think there's at least a chance for fifty percent less shit in your future." I couldn't help the unladylike snort that escaped. She ignored it and continued. "And, be honest with me, getting your car is the least important reason you have for going back by Friday, isn't it?"

I bit my lip and nodded, and I knew she could see my head bobbing in agreement even in her peripheral vision. My gut churned with guilt. We hadn't been on the road for half an hour, and I already wanted to turn back. It really felt like I was heading away from home instead of heading toward it. All I had in Denver was a house. But as much as I was tempted to tell Patty to turn back, I felt like I at least owed it to both of us to interview for the job, and at worst I could get myself organized so I had everything I needed from my house.

"Well, out with it. Let me hear your reasons. Maybe it will help you feel better about this to say it out loud. At least you know I won't judge you and won't hesitate to tell you you're out of your mind if I think you're making a mistake."

I knew she was right, and I knew she was my best chance at an unbiased opinion. Actually, she wasn't unbiased; she was in my corner, ready to fight for me like nobody else in my life, except maybe my mom. And somehow my brain added Hunter to that list without my permission. We had more than an hour left to drive. I might as well take advantage of her undivided attention.

"It's going to sound crazy."

"No, it's not. And if it does, maybe we can figure out why," she said as she flashed me a smile before focusing back on the road. "Stop avoiding the topic."

"I'm not avoiding anything," even though I knew I probably was. "I'm just trying to get my thoughts into words." I sighed, bracing myself before leaping into the abyss. "Something about that little town just feels," I hesitated, "right," I finished, feeling like I'd finally found the word. "From the moment Leo pulled me out of the car, I've met more people that genuinely seemed to care about my well-being than I have all my life in Denver."

"Hunter and the girls took me in and gave me a place to stay when I was freaking out about how I was going to afford it. They run a business and honestly need every nickel of revenue they can get but wouldn't let me pay. Hunter's sister basically supplied a full wardrobe for me for the price of one outfit." I fought to explain to Patty just how good I felt. I was happy. I felt like somebody other than her accepted me with no expectation of something in return.

"I've spent the last five years, more than that really, fighting to catch a break. Trying to feel like I belong and find my place, and yet in that little town I've found a job teaching, and honestly, I've never felt more wanted. It was as if the superintendent was almost begging me to take the job. Hunter and his family could use my help with the inn. Even when I felt like I was more in the way than a benefit, they all made me feel appreciated, more than appreciated really. For the first time in forever, I feel good about myself. I feel like I'm making a difference instead of just taking up space."

I studied Patty's expression as I spoke. She could put up a professional front, but I knew her well enough to see beyond the business veneer. When I finished, I saw her neck ripple with swallowed-down emotion. Her left hand swiped something on her cheek. If I didn't know Patty to be someone opposed to mushy displays, I would swear she was fighting back tears. "Oh, honey, if I weren't driving right now, I would pull you into the biggest hug. I don't know anyone in this world who deserves all the good things more than you do. I'm so happy for you."

For a moment I waited. It seemed she wanted to say more. "But?"

"No buts. I'm truly happy for you."

"I believe you, but you definitely wanted to say something more. I know you too," I added with a chuckle because two can play this game of not letting each other get away with shit.

"How much do the girls have to do with your attraction to Hunter?"

Her question took me completely by surprise. "Why would the girls play into it?"

"I'm not trying to be a bitch, Amber."

"It never crossed my mind that you were, Patty," I answered, totally bewildered.

"Lance's betrayal took more from you than your marriage, Amber. I know how much you wanted a family, and when you lost that baby, you lost a lot more. I'm not saying this is what you're doing. I just want you to make sure you're sure that you're not attracted to Hunter because he comes with a ready-made family that you'll never be able to have for yourself. Like I said, I'm not trying to be a bitch and yuck on your yum, I just want to make sure that it's just a coincidence that the first man you've been interested in in five years comes with a pre-made family."

Yeah, that was a right cross to the jaw I didn't see coming. Leave it to Patty to cut through the crap and ask the uncomfortable but necessary question. After I found Lance that night in his office, the next couple of months were one long battle. Lance did all he could to make it seem like I was the one who was to blame, and under the stress and uncertainty, I crumbled under the weight of it all.

The only way I could think of to make him pay for what he'd done to me was to fight for the house. Money was the only thing that ever meant anything to him, and keeping the house cost him. I knew it was petty then, and it's still petty now. I needed at least one minor victory.

I knew there wasn't research that linked stress with miscarriage, but it certainly didn't help. I didn't tell him about the pregnancy because I didn't know what he'd do. I couldn't take the chance of losing custody because he had better lawyers. Then I lost the baby anyway.

I lost myself too.

I was so depressed and distraught it was too much effort to take care of myself. I never followed up with my OBGYN and let the infection that followed go untreated too long. Not only did I almost lose my life, but the scarring on my fallopian tubes made it virtually impossible for me to conceive again.

Patty wasn't wrong to ask me about my motives.

"They're special kids," I finally answered her. "I never really thought of it that way, Patty." I angled my body to face her. "I'll never stop wanting a baby of my own. And it's not impossible, though I know it's not likely," I hurried to add before she could question me on my grasp of reality. "But the girls definitely figure into it. They're a package deal, and I can't have Hunter without getting them too."

I bit the inside of my cheeks before blowing out a frustrated breath and finishing my thought. The one that truly weighed the most on my mind. "If anything, Patty, they scare the hell out of me. How the fuck am I ever going to measure up to their mother? Amy's easy; she's too young to really remember her, and she just wants a mommy. But Elizabeth and Meg… they know what they're missing, and I'm far too much of a mess to live up to their expectations."

"Jesus, Amber," Patty exhaled a frustrated sigh. "You are the biggest badass that I know. You are blissfully ignorant of just how tough you are. You took on your asshole ex when most women would have run for the hills and been thankful to get out with their lives and maybe most of their clothes. You have stayed in that house just to prove a point, even though sometimes I think you'd be much better off selling it and moving on. You've made your point, Amber. You've nothing left to prove to yourself, and you certainly have nothing left to prove to the cunt you used to be married to."

"I'm glad you haven't given up on children of your own," Patty continued. "As long as you don't lose sight of how much of a long shot it is. I can't really say much about Meg. I don't think I heard her utter a full sentence in the time I was there, but I can see the way Elizabeth watches you. She's certainly being cautious, but she likes you, Amber, and I bet you're going to have a fantastic impact on her life if things progress."

I didn't question for a second the sincerity of her words, and it made my heart swell with joy. "God, I hope you're right. I don't know the first thing about being a mom."

"Well, lucky for you, you don't have to be one right away. You're already starting by being their friend, and the rest of it will just fall into place. You're a natural teacher and you love kids, so just roll with that and everything else will be fine."

I turned to look at the passing scenery. We were nearing the outskirts of Denver now, and even the familiar places that I'd seen just a few days ago seemed somehow foreign. With each passing road sign, I felt more guilty that I'd wasted Patty's time. Despite knowing I should keep my options open and at least interview for the job, I knew I wasn't going to accept it if it was offered.

Patty broke the silence just before we turned onto my road. "So, what do you think, rent it or sell it outright?"

"Huh?" I mumbled, snapping out of the cycle of questions I kept asking myself.

"What you want is to see if this thing with Hunter is the real deal, right?"

"Yes," I drawled out, insinuating she should elaborate on her question.

"You can't do that from here or jumping back and forth between Denver and Homer Pass. I'm not going to push you to interview for a job you don't want. And honestly, if you don't want it, I don't want you there either. You're one of, if not my best friend, but that doesn't mean I'd accept less from you as an employee. So, if you've decided to be with Hunter, should we rent out your house or put it up for sale?"

I paused for a moment, but the safe answer was obvious. "I think it would be best to rent it, that way I've got something to fall back on if things don't work out in the great white west."

We both laughed at my description. I loved the people but doubt I'd ever fully embrace neck-high snowstorms. "Okay," Patty said, all business. "Let's look and see what needs to be done to get it ready for renters. I bet I can have it rented by the end of the week if we really try."

"That soon?" I asked, not really believing that my modest home would be that attractive.

"Absolutely. It's a beautiful home in a great neighborhood, and rentals are at a premium. I could probably draw things out and get you an obscene amount of money, but I know you'd rather it be quick."

"I think quick is best. I can't afford to wait."

Patty nodded. "Then let's get to work, and with a little sweat and elbow grease we can have everything ready to go and get you back to having mountain man monkey sex by Thursday night."

# 26

# Bombs Away

## Hunter

I leaned back in my chair with a satisfied sigh. In two days, I'd brought the inn to full staff. Well, as close to full staff as I could afford. I watched as two of Elizabeth's friends virtually skipped out of the dining room where I had been holding the interviews. They were nowhere near as mature as my daughter, but few sixteen-year-olds were. They could handle bussing tables and the minimal waitressing we needed at breakfast. At least I could have them for a couple of years until graduation. Somehow, I felt more confident in the future now. I had Amber to thank for that.

My phone buzzed with the notification that the lobby door had opened, and I almost ignored it because of my departing interviewees but remembered they were heading back to the residence to see Elizabeth. I pushed back from the chair and grabbed my coffee before heading down the hall to the front desk.

Rounding the corner, I stopped dead in my tracks. Standing behind the counter rummaging around the desk was someone I hadn't laid eyes on in over three years and hadn't spoken to in nearly ten. "Poking around where you have no business again, brother?" I didn't mask the vitriol in my tone.

"Is that any way to greet me after all this time?"

"Pfft," I hissed out, failing to come up with a more inspired response. "Obviously, you haven't changed. Get the hell out from behind there. This is my business and none of yours." I crossed behind the counter, setting my half-full mug of coffee down with enough force to slosh the liquid inside over the rim. I wouldn't be a bit surprised if we came to blows. I was still pissed he had the nerve to show up at Jenn's funeral. At least Janine had scared him off before I made a fool of him then. Or myself.

"Temper, temper, little brother," he said as he slithered out from

behind where he didn't belong. It also put three feet of counter space between us at chest height. If he thought that was a safe enough distance, I'd
be happy to prove him wrong. "I came here to talk. There's no reason this
animosity has to continue between us. I only want my share of the family
fortune. Fair is fair."

"You have your trust fund disbursement. You have the mine and the
land that goes with it. That's more than Janine and I have. I'd say you have
more than *your* share."

"Ah, you have always lacked vision. The family has more than the trust
fund and the mine. This inn is the crown jewel."

"You have the mine; the three of us have the trust fund, but this inn is
mine. And someday, it will belong to my daughters. You have absolutely
no claim to it."

He cut me off before I could continue to tell him to fuck off and never
come sniffing around me or my girls again. "That's where you're wrong,
Hunt. I am part of the trust, and the trust holds the mortgage you took
out to renovate the inn. Your name might be on the deed, but the trust
holds a lien on the property. Therefore, I have quite a substantial claim to
it, and as you're eight months behind on your payments, I think it's well
past time to foreclose."

My jaw clenched. I could feel my molars grinding. It was a miracle I
didn't crack one with the amount of tension between them. "I pay my
mortgage annually. After the season."

"Yes, you do. Unfortunately for you, your contract with the Trust calls
for monthly payments. I'm not surprised you never discussed this with
me, but as you didn't, I can only assume you're trying to defraud the Trust.
I was very disappointed that our sister is in on this sham as well. Then
again, it's what makes it possible for me to take you to court and force you
to either pay in full by February first or The Trust takes ownership. As
both you and Janine have disqualified yourselves as responsible trustees,
the judge has seen fit to grant me temporary sole control." He pulled an
envelope from inside his jacket and dropped it with a thunk in front of
me. "It's all there. Take your time and read it thoroughly."

"Bullshit." I spat out, looking down at the offending stationery with
such hate I'm surprised it didn't incinerate in a cloud of smoke and fire.
"No judge is going to do that without giving Janine and me the opportunity to respond."

"Nope. Sorry, baby brother, you had the opportunity. You both were
notified, and didn't show up for the hearing. Given your lack of compli-

ance, the judge granted my request."

"We were never served. I certainly wasn't, and Janine never would have ignored something like that or not told me about it."

"It's all there in black and white. You don't have to take my word for it. I doubt you would anyway," he said, motioning toward the envelope in front of me. "You have two months to pay off the mortgage or this inn is mine. Of course, if you want to be smart and have something left other than bad memories for your girls, we could discuss a buyout. I have a partner with deep pockets and big visions for Homer Pass."

I didn't really give two shits what sort of harebrained scheme he'd dreamed up this time, but curiosity got the best of me on the off chance that he might actually have found some legal loophole to screw me with. "Oh, please do share this vision with me."

"Let's just say that with the land from the mining claim and this hotel we have the basis for a very exclusive ski resort. My partner has the connections to get the land leases and waivers to cut trails, so this whole town will be one magnificent base lodge."

I couldn't hold my jaw shut. But words wouldn't come out. There was such a rush of thoughts I couldn't choose which one to run with first. He was delusional; that was for certain. It would take a lot more than this inn and the old mine to form the basis of a ski resort. He'd have to convince three-quarters of the town to sell, and I doubted more than one or two would be persuaded by money to pack up and leave. And no one I knew would want to spend a single second anywhere near what Henry was planning to turn this place into. "That will never happen. You know this town well enough to know the people here would never go for that."

"You'd be quite surprised at the reception I've received. Seems the people here like money just as much as I do." He turned and headed for the door. "I'll be around for a few days. My contact information is in the documents just in case you see reason and want to avoid a messy foreclosure."

The door shut behind him before I could hurl any more insults in his direction. I'm not sure how long I stared at the envelope before opening it. The temptation to throw it into the trash and forget about it was strong, almost as strong as the urge to set it on fire. But while Henry had more than his fair share of crazy schemes and half-baked ideas, I couldn't chance that this time he'd actually found a way to get what he wanted. He was just devious and self-centered enough to do something like this.

Knowing I needed a cooler head nearby so I didn't do anything stupid,

I pulled out my phone and made a call. It picked up on the second ring. "We need to talk as soon as you can get to the inn."

"Well, hello to you too, big brother. I'm doing great, thanks for asking."

"This is no time for joking, Janine. Henry just reappeared and dumped a pile of papers in front of me, claiming he was foreclosing on the inn on behalf of the trust."

"Fuck," she shouted so loudly I could have heard her without the phone. "That little…"

"Yeah, I know. How is he even related to us? But we can figure that out later. I need you to come help me read through this. Because if I do it alone, I'm afraid I might do something I'll regret."

"I'm on my way."

I walked back behind the desk and picked up the envelope. It was beyond my ability to understand how things had come to this. What had I ever done to Henry to make him act this way? What had Janine done? When I was a kid, I thought he hung the moon and stars until one day he just decided to hate me. I didn't think I'd ever understand why.

# 27

# *Circle the Wagons*

## *Hunter*

Less than ten minutes later, Janine came bursting through the main door. "Let me see it," she barked, reaching out toward me to take it even though she was still over twenty feet away.

"Hold on," I cautioned in my best calming tone. One I was taught to use with accident victims to help keep them from having panic attacks. "I thought I was the one who was supposed to be going berserk."

She let out a breath and inhaled again, settling herself. "I'm sorry, you're right. How about you pour me a cup of coffee, and we can sit down in the library and go over this?"

"Okay," I smiled. "Go get yourself settled and light a fire, and I'll get Snow to watch the front desk, so we're not disturbed."

"Good." She made her way down the hall toward the library, pulling her jacket off on the way. "Cream and three sugars," she called after me.

"Like I don't fuckin' know that after nearly forty years." Fuck. Why did she always do that, and why did it always piss me off? It's like that's exactly what she was trying to do.

"Closer to thirty," she snapped back, the irritation in her voice clearly evident.

I might be guilty of advancing her age just to irritate her too. She was thirty-four, so technically she was right. Perhaps instigation was a family trait.

A few minutes later I returned to the library, with her coffee in hand, and passed her the envelope before dropping next to her on one of the big leather sofas.

We read the document through, muttering curses as we went. Once we finished reading, she took a sip of her coffee and leaned back on the sofa. "He's accused us both of fraud and, while I'm not entirely certain, it sounds like he's trying to claim the entire trust for himself." She took another drink and shook her head. "He can't do that. We've done nothing wrong."

"It looks to me like he can, and he has, and it seems the court has agreed with him without even bothering to hear our side." I couldn't hold my temper any longer and pounded my fist into the arm of the sofa. "I'm going to fucking kill him."

"While I'd be more than happy to help you, neither of us is actually going to murder our brother. We can't go to prison; our children need their only parent."

Janine was right; my girls needed me, and the twins needed her. If what he said was true and he had someone lined up to bankroll the project, it would move forward whether he was involved if their partnership agreement included access to the trust money. "No, we're not, but we better find a way to fight this because I can't think of any way to pay the past-due amount in the next two months even if the inn is sold out every night."

She leaned forward, setting her mug on the coffee table, and picked up the court document. "Where's the original loan agreement we had the lawyer put together? I don't remember a specific schedule for repayment. Maybe it's perfectly fine that you pay annually."

I ran my hand through my hair, tugging at the roots just to distract myself from the anger building inside me. "Jenn was always the one to handle that sort of thing. There's a fireproof vault in the office. It's probably in there, but I'll be damned if I know where the key is."

Janine glanced in my direction and rolled her eyes. She didn't have to say it. I knew I was a shit businessman, but most of my bills were paid on time and I had a general concept of how much was in the checking account at any moment. Nowhere near enough to pay two-hundred-fifty thousand dollars that's for damn sure. "Well, start in Jenn's old jewelry box. That's where I keep my safe key, and if not, call a locksmith first thing tomorrow morning. If you're not obligated to make monthly payments, we can get this judgment tossed."

"And if I am supposed to make monthly payments?"

"We'll figure something out. I'm not going to let you lose this inn. Especially to our selfish, egocentric asshole of an older brother."

I forced a weak smile onto my lips. Not that I expected anything less from her, but she could have easily let me swing in the wind on my own with this issue. I was the one not living up to my agreement. I was the one losing the inn. We sat there in silence while she flipped through the pages until she dropped it back onto the coffee table with a huff and put it back into the envelope it came in. "Hey. What's this?" she asked, pulling three more sheets out I hadn't noticed before.

I watched as her eyes scanned the document, narrowing with each second that passed. "That deceitful little fucking son of a badger."

"What?" I asked, trying hard not to laugh at my sister's choice of descriptors for our brother. He was all those things, of course, though not literally the son of a badger.

"No wonder neither of us knew we needed to be in court. That shit-stain had papers served at Mom and Dad's cabin. I suppose it is still the legal address for the trust, but he knows damn well neither of us goes near the place regularly since they passed. And we've got no reason to check the mailbox either."

"Maybe that will be enough to get a judge to at least stay the order. And if we can delay it for a couple of months, then I can be caught up on the past due as long as the weather holds."

"It's worth a shot," she said, dropping the papers back on the table and patting my knee. "We'll get through this. Find the original document, and I'll call the lawyer in the morning." She stood and slipped on her jacket. "I've got to get home to the twins."

I rose and pulled her into a hug. "Thanks for coming by. I appreciate it."

"Always. Now it really is just you and me in this family because I don't care if I ever see that bastard again."

# 28

# Reconciliation

## Hunter

After Janine left, I brought our empty mugs to the kitchen, slipped into the office and dropped the envelope on the desk along with a foot-high pile of bills I needed to get to. I promised myself I'd do it after I dropped the girls off at school tomorrow morning. I wouldn't likely have time after tomorrow night as the weekend guests would start arriving around four and we'd probably have thirty for dinner.

I was just about to go back to my bedroom and dig through my closet to find Jenn's jewelry box when Snow shouted for me from the front desk. I hurried out because I didn't think it could be guest-related. She knew better than to bellow at me in front of customers. We might be a family business, but we were professional. Most of the time.

"What is it, Elizabeth?" I called, pushing through the kitchen doors.

"I've got a surprise guest for you. Come quick," she answered. By the tone of her voice, I assumed it was a pleasant surprise, and my mind immediately went to Amber coming back early. Even if I hadn't been expecting it to be Amber, I never would have guessed who was waiting for me when I reached the front desk.

"Auntie Janet's here," Snow said, hugging the woman who was the mirror image of her mother.

"I've missed you girls so much," Janet said, kissing Snow on the cheek. "Why don't you go let your sisters know I'm here? I've got something I need to talk to your dad about before we catch up, okay?"

"Okay. Don't keep her long, Dad," Snow warned, turning to leave. "Amy will never get to bed tonight if we don't give her a little while to get over the excitement."

I gave my daughter a crisp salute, which earned me her patented eye roll. Something I was getting all too used to seeing before turning to meet Janet's stare. The last time we'd seen each other hadn't ended well. She had outright blamed me for her wife's death. I was in no mood for a repeat of that drama, especially after everything else that had happened today. I knew better than most the way grief could cloud one's judgment, but there was a limit to my understanding, and I was way past that line.

Once Elizabeth was out of earshot, we both spoke at once, our words colliding in an indiscernible din.

Janet nodded toward me to proceed, but she'd obviously come here to say something, and she seemed calm and much more like the kind, sensitive woman I used to know. Given my current state of mind, I felt it was probably going to go better for both of us if I let her have her say. "Please, Janet, go ahead."

She forced a smile and took a deep breath. "I owe you an apology, Hunter. Actually," she added with a humorless laugh, "I owe you much more than just an apology. The last time I saw you, I was a raging lunatic. I had no right to treat you that way when you've always been the best big brother I've never had. I was distraught. I realize that's no excuse. I'm embarrassed by my behavior, and I completely understand if you never want to see me again."

"Never once have I consciously thought you were to blame for Jenn's death." Janet continued. "I knew you'd trade places with her in a heartbeat if you could, and I don't know where my words came from. I was hurt, and I guess I felt like everybody else should hurt too. It was the most despicable thing I've ever said or done. Please know there's not a day that goes by that I don't relive that moment and regret it with all my heart. I know you can never see me the same way, but I'm begging you to give me a chance. You... those girls," she added, swallowing back a sob. "You're the only family I have. Please let me be a part of their lives."

Well, fuck. What the hell was I supposed to do about that? I stepped toward her and wrapped my arms around her, pulling her into my chest. It was so much like holding Jenn that instinctively I kissed her head and rubbed her back like I used to do when Jenn was having a moment. Her body wracked with sobs, and all I could think of doing was to continue to hold her and give her the chance to let all her emotions free.

When she regained control, I stepped back from the embrace and handed her a couple of tissues from the box behind the reception desk. She wiped the tears from her face and blew her nose in a most unladylike manner that I couldn't help but laugh.

"It's been a long time since I've heard you laugh like that, Hunter. It sounds good. Real good."

"Well, it's a rather recent development," I admitted, Amber's face, her smile, flashing through my thoughts.

The corners of her mouth turned up ever so slightly. "Don't tell me the stoic, self-sacrificing Hunter might actually be taking a chance with a new woman?"

I was stunned that she would jump to that conclusion and more than uncomfortable admitting that she was right. Amber was definitely the reason for my improved mood. But there was still a part of me that didn't think it was right. Survivor's guilt is what I think it's called. "There is. But that doesn't mean I'm forgetting Jenn," I blurted out because of an unexplainable urge to defend myself.

Her eyes were still wet with tears, but her smile grew just slightly. "Oh, Hunter. It's okay. We both know Jenn wanted you to be happy. It's been three years. It's time to move on. No one will think you have forgotten her. Just because you've found someone new, doesn't mean you didn't love Jenn. I know she would want you to move on. Find someone to love. Just like when the day comes when I find someone new, it doesn't diminish the love I feel for Madison. I'm happy for you, Hunter. I hope it turns out to be the real thing."

All I could do was shrug and feign interest in the grain of the wood floorboards. "It's very new, but, yeah, I hope so too."

"Are the girls okay with it? Elizabeth must be giving you a hard time."

Despite my mood, I couldn't help but laugh at that assumption. "Quite the opposite, they love her. Elizabeth put her in room 108 when the inn was virtually vacant and has taken it upon herself to give me dating advice. Amy thinks she's hung the moon and the stars because she plays Barbies with her and reads her bedtime stories. I am no longer necessary. A pleasant addition, if I sit quietly on the bed too, but Amber is definitely the main attraction."

"Oh, Hunter. I'm truly sorry but also not. Amy wants a mom so badly. God knows, Janine and I tried, but she never let any of us near enough to try. Amber?" she looked to me for confirmation, and I nodded. "Amber must be pretty special to get past her defenses."

"I think so."

"How about Meg? What does she think?"

"If you find out, let me know," I said, lifting my shoulders. "She rarely says much about anything, but she seemed to gravitate toward her at

Thanksgiving dinner, so that's a ringing endorsement from her, I suppose."

"Amber joined you for Thanksgiving? It must really be serious."

I snorted, unable to control my thoughts about how crazy this story truly was. "Mm, it's serious, I guess, but I only met her the day before. It's a long story, but that's going to have to wait. I've got to get started on dinner for the girls. Would you like to join us?"

Tears filled her eyes again, but this time it wasn't with sadness and regret. "Does this mean you forgive me?"

"There's nothing to forgive, Janet. I know what it's like to be lost in grief. How you don't feel quite human, and you say and do things you end up regretting. I try not to be a hypocrite. Let's let the past stay in the past."

"Thank you," she murmured on a shaky breath.

I stepped closer, pulling her into a hug. "You're family, Janet. You'll always be family. No matter what." I felt the tension in her body ease. Frankly, I was relieved too. It was one less burden to lug around.

# 29

# Not What I Expected

## *Amber*

Pulling my rental car into the parking lot across from the inn, I couldn't help but smile. I peeked up at the second-floor window and couldn't wait to get back to my room. The snow was still piled high outside the building, and the banks on the side of the road were well over my head. I couldn't imagine how it was going to be in January if it was already this arctic-like before winter had officially started.

Somehow, that thought didn't give me shivers the way it would have in the past. In fact, I was rather looking forward to cold, snowy days drinking hot chocolate with the girls and cuddling up in front of the fire with a certain hunky lumberjack-type innkeeper. And maybe a little mountain man monkey sex.

The snow squeaked beneath my boots as I walked up the stairs leading to the main lobby of the inn. I was lugging a massive suitcase behind me, filled with enough clothes to last me a couple of weeks. This time I was prepared to stay.

As soon as I opened the door, I was met with the same warmth that I had been the first day in the midst of that blizzard. Hunter had told me last night on the phone he'd hired several new people, but I wasn't expecting anyone behind the front desk when I walked in. If anyone, I thought Elizabeth would be there, but it was someone I'd never met.

I froze.

I swore I was seeing a ghost because the woman staring back at me was a carbon copy of the woman in the photos behind her. How the hell was she standing there when she had been dead for three years?

She looked up from the computer screen and smiled. "Welcome to the Snowflake Inn. Are you checking in?"

I did my best to form words, but they only came out as a croak. My heart was pounding in my chest so hard all I could hear was the blood rushing in my ears. "I, ah, no, I, I'm already, ah…" I'm sure I sounded like a raving lunatic, but I was either seeing things and trying to carry on a conversation with an apparition, or someone had been lying to me, and the girls' mother was very much alive.

"Amber. You're back!" Elizabeth's excited greeting snapped me out of my stupor. She ran down the hall and nearly tackled me in a hug. "Dad said you weren't coming back until tomorrow."

"I wanted to surprise you," I said, sneaking a peek at the woman who had now moved out from behind the desk and was approaching us. I don't know if Elizabeth was surprised, but I certainly was. I'm sure my expression gave away my confusion as the woman raised a curious brow before a wave of understanding washed over her face. She uttered a soft laugh before smiling.

"Amber, I'm the girls' aunt, Janet," she said, holding out her hand. I shook it, slightly relieved, but still apprehensive about how she would receive someone who might be a large part of her nieces' lives. "You probably thought you were seeing a spirit." I nodded with a laugh. "Everybody always said we looked like twins. We didn't used to get confused as much because my hair was always dyed some outrageous color. I guess I finally grew up and left it natural." She let out a nervous laugh. "Sorry, I sometimes babble in awkward situations. The girls have told me so much about you. I feel like we've known each other for years."

"Don't worry," I laughed. "I yammer on too. It's nice to meet you. But I wish at least one of them had warned me how much you looked alike." I narrowed my brow and looked straight at Elizabeth. "Hunter told me last night on the phone that you'd come back to town, but I didn't realize you'd be working here."

"I'm not, really. Just helping now and then," she said.

"I took the day off from school because Dad and Aunt Janine have been meeting with the lawyer all day," Elizabeth added. "Aunt Janet didn't want me to be all alone."

"Oh," I said. My stomach knotted. "About the thing with your Uncle Henry?"

"Yeah," she said. Her jaw clenched and forehead creased. A part of me wanted to laugh because she looked so much like her father at that moment. "Asshole," she grumbled.

Hunter had given me only the briefest explanation about what was happening, and I hoped he'd give me more details now that I was back.

Not that I wanted to intrude on his business, but if I was going to commit to him and move my life to Homer Pass, I needed to know what I was getting into. "I should get my stuff up to my room. At least I assume it's still my room?" I said, looking at Elizabeth.

Her blue eyes nearly disappeared into her skull. "As if I would give it to anyone else," she said, grabbing my suitcase and wheeling it toward the minuscule elevator hidden down the hall toward the library. "At least you came prepared this time." Her grin was wide, and she had the same mischievous twinkle in her eye as her father.

She pressed the call button and tapped her foot impatiently. As soon as the door slid open, she shoved the suitcase in, reached inside, I assumed she hit the button for the second floor and jogged back in our direction. Then she bolted up the grand staircase two steps at a time.

I looked at Janet. Janet looked back at me with an arched brow. Moments later, Elizabeth came walking slowly back down the stairs. We both watched as she came back and stood in front of us.

"Why on earth didn't you just ride the elevator?" Janet asked. "Was that some sort of new fitness routine?"

"I'm not riding that thing," Elizabeth replied as if it might have been the stupidest question ever asked. "It's so small two people can't stand shoulder to shoulder in it. And if claustrophobia doesn't get you, the sounds it makes, God. It scares the sh… snot out of me," she said, avoiding inappropriate language just as her father appeared.

"There's nothing wrong with it. It passes inspection every year," Hunter said in a tone that led me to believe he was not in a joking mood. There were dark circles underneath his eyes, and his hair stuck out at odd angles, like he'd been tugging at it all day.

"Hi," I said, wondering if my surprise early arrival was actually a welcome one.

His focus shifted to me, and his expression shifted. "Hi," he said. The corners of his mouth twitched like he was trying to smile. "I must really be out of it. I didn't even notice you standing there." He stepped toward me and pulled me into a hug. "It's good to have you back. I didn't expect you until tomorrow."

"I got everything done, so I came back early. I hope that's okay." He was tense, and the way he held me lacked the usual undercurrent of passion. I hoped it was just because of everything that he was struggling with at the moment, but my insecurities wouldn't let me completely believe he wasn't all that happy to have me back.

"It's more than okay," he said. A small smile finally forced its way onto his face.

I exhaled in relief.

"Yeah," Elizabeth added. "Maybe you can help improve his mood. He's been a real pain since you left Monday night."

Janet cleared her throat. "I'm going to head out and let you all catch up on recent events." She hugged Elizabeth and did the same to Hunter. "It was really nice to meet you, Amber. I hope we have time to get to know each other better soon." She hugged me as well, which took me a second to return because I hadn't expected it.

"I hope so too," I said, meaning it with all my heart. If anyone had cause not to want me here, it was her. And I felt like she had accepted me as well.

Hunter and Elizabeth said their goodbyes, and Janet walked out the front door.

"Janine's in the family room, and the girls should be home from school soon. They should already be here, but Leo picked them up, so they probably tricked him into going to the Bighorn for an ice cream soda first. If you want to get your stuff up…" Hunter paused, looking behind me. "Where are your things? Aren't you staying?"

His concerned, disappointed look melted my heart. Before I could reassure him, Elizabeth answered without a hint of empathy. "Jeez, Dad. Get with it. I already brought her things up. That's why we were complaining about that hazard of an antique elevator," she said with an impatient huff. "Don't worry, judging by the weight of the thing, she's set until April." She smiled and gave me another hug. "It's really good to have you back." She turned and headed down the hallway. "I'll be in my room if you need me."

Hunter watched her disappear through the door, shaking his head. "I'd be lost without her, but I could really do without the sass."

"You *would* be lost without her," I said, wrapping my arms around his waist. "And I think you secretly like the sass. It keeps you on your toes."

He leaned in and pressed a soft kiss against my lips. "I have more than enough to keep my toes in shape without her attitude." His smile let me know he wasn't truly upset with her.

"I can tell. You want to talk about it?"

"I've been talking about it all damn day," he groaned. "Let's go out back. I might as well tell you all about it. I don't think I'm going to get any grumpier than I already am."

I rose on my toes and gave him a kiss. "I bet I can think of a few things to improve your mood."

"Mm," he hummed, a hint of warmth returning to his eyes. "I'm going to hold you to that. But right now we should probably go back and talk with Janine. Then, we have eighteen reservations for dinner to serve. After that, I'm all yours, and I don't want to think about this inn or anything else other than showing you just how much I missed you."

I smiled, kissing him again. "Now that's a plan I can definitely get behind."

**A**mber!" Janine shouted, getting up out of the armchair and pulling me into a solid embrace. "I'm so glad you're back. How did the interview go?"

"Christ," Hunter groaned, raking his fingers through his hair. Which only added to its already tousled appearance. "I'm such a jackass. I'm sorry, Amber. I'm so caught up in my own shit I didn't even think to ask."

I shook my head. "Don't worry about it. I completely understand. I forgot to mention it too when you told me Henry had appeared out of the blue." I hesitated to share I hadn't even gone to the interview. If things were really uncertain here, I might have to call Patty and see if the job was still available. I might have to move Hunter and the girls to Denver and not me to Homer Pass. "You both look like you've been through the wringer. How did the meeting with the lawyer go? And what actually is happening?"

Janine and Hunter shared a look, which I could only assume was to determine who was going to talk and what they were going to share. "You might as well sit down and get comfortable," Janine said finally. "This is going to take a while."

I settled onto the couch with Hunter. Janine returned to the armchair.

"The bottom line is that our brother is a selfish, self-centered asshole," Hunter said with an edge to his voice that made the hair on my arm stand on end.

"That's true, but this time he's found a way to actually make that a problem," Janine added. "Remember, I told you the remodeling of the inn got sped up because Jenn was pregnant?"

"Yeah," I said, knowing there was more to the story.

"Well, before then, Hunter and Jenn took their time with fixing this place up, using just the trust fund disbursement to fund repairs and what Hunter had saved up before paying off the tax liability."

"Janine," Hunter said, his tone carrying an obvious warning.

She either didn't hear it or didn't care. "Hunter, if Amber is thinking about taking that teaching job and moving here, then she deserves to know the facts."

"I didn't say she didn't. But we don't need to drop all of our problems in her lap. She's got her own things to worry about."

"I don't think you guys are dumping anything in my lap," I said, placing my hand on his knee in what I hoped would be a reassuring gesture. I turned so he could meet my gaze. "But I don't want you to think you have to share something you don't want to."

Hunter exhaled a long, frustrated breath. "Fine." He inhaled and exhaled once more before continuing. "We weren't making progress quickly enough because we couldn't afford to do the big things like the dining room. And the inn couldn't bring in enough money to sustain itself without finishing the upgrades."

"That makes sense," I said, just to let him know I was following along.

"I was young. There was a lot more liability than equity in the property, and I didn't have real estate development experience. I got turned down and laughed out of every bank I went to for a mortgage. I almost gave up. I felt like I was a failure. I was letting," he paused and looked at me, swallowing, "everyone down."

"You weren't a failure," I said, meeting his stare. "And I'm sure Jenn didn't think so." I placed my palm on his face and ran my thumb gently over his cheek. "It's okay to say her name, Hunter. I know she was a big part of your life. You have three beautiful girls together. If I can't accept that. I don't deserve you."

His deep brown eyes searched mine, looking for the truth. He raised his hand to grasp mine and gave it a squeeze. "Thanks." I could hear the gratitude, and perhaps a bit of relief, in his voice. We sat there in silence for a moment.

"Josh offered to help him, but Hunter has never been able to share this place with anyone. Especially since Jenn died."

"That's because it's not mine to share. It's Jenn's," Hunter snapped at Janine. "It will always be hers." He pulled away from me and rested his head in his hands.

Janine and I shared a look of concern. She pressed her lips together, hissing air between them. "In the end it was Josh's suggestion that he get a mortgage through the trust," Janine continued. "We talked to our lawyer and to the firm that manages the trust fund, and they put together a mortgage that would let Hunter and Jenn finish the inn. The three of us have equal voting rights, so when I endorsed it, we didn't even have to involve Henry in the approval process. Neither of us knew where he was, even if we had wanted to."

"Okay," I said. "That makes sense, but how is he able to cause problems for you now if everything was certified and legal?"

"Jenn was always very conservative with the finances," Hunter said. "We finished the first three floors, but she didn't want to empty our bank account by finishing the fourth floor. She figured it would be good to have that extra cushion just in case. Of course, she was right because we had to build this addition as the family grew, and then we had three terrible winters in a row. My disbursement always went directly to the mortgage, but we had to pull out of the mortgage money to pay the mortgage. I was working for Josh half the time just so we could put food on the table."

"Still, the mortgage got paid, right?" I asked.

"It did. But instead of making monthly payments, Hunter paid it all on March first, the day we get our annual payment. If it had been a good winter, he paid out of the inn's profits. If not, he dipped into what was left of the remodeling fund. I never cared, and until two days ago I didn't think it mattered. But when our lawyer reviewed the mortgage agreement, it stipulated that payments be made monthly."

"Shit," I said. What else could I say?

"That's how he gets to do this," Hunter said. "We are all recipients of the trust, but we are also trustees and, as such, have an ethical responsibility to manage the funds in the best interest of the trust, not the recipients. Henry's claim is that Janine and I colluded to benefit me at the expense of the trust. And because the deceitful little fucker got in front of a judge without us to explain, the judge issued a temporary ruling giving him control of the trust."

"Because I am technically eight months behind on the mortgage payments, he is calling the loan. I either have to pay it off in full or the trust takes ownership and will sell it to the highest bidder to recover the money."

"What about your voting rights?" I asked.

"The judge took them away," Janine answered. "That's what Hunter means by taking control. The judge believed we were trying to defraud the trust and therefore disqualified as trustees."

"It doesn't sound like your lawyer gave you much hope about challenging this," I said, looking between them.

Hunter's jaw flexed, and his hands balled into fists. "He didn't," Hunter grunted.

"That's not true. He said we should win because we weren't hiding anything. Hunter had been paying this way for the life of the loan. It took Henry sixteen years to figure it out, and most importantly, two out of three of us were okay with it."

"But?" I asked because there had to be a but if Hunter was still so stressed after the meeting.

"But," Hunter picked up where Janine left off. "Because Henry got in front of the judge first and convinced them to rule in his favor, the judge may be inclined to stick with their original ruling. We also know that Henry isn't smart enough to come up with this on his own. Whoever he has for investors must have convinced him to take this path to get control, and once they have control, they probably have the connections to push this through whether we have a case or not."

"We'll figure something out," Janine said. She sank back in her chair.

"We will," Hunter agreed. "I'm not giving up. There's no way I'm letting Henry ruin what I've worked so hard to build. I have to keep Jenn's dream alive if for no other reason than her girls deserve it."

"They do," I agreed. "And I'll do whatever I can to help."

He pulled me into his body. "All I need you to do is what we talked about before you went back to Denver. It means so much to me you want to help, but the inn is mine and the girls to worry about. I have to draw that line, Amber. I hope you understand."

Those words stung, and logically I knew they shouldn't. I had basically just met Hunter, and although things were moving at warp speed, I couldn't expect to be immediately involved in deciding things about his business. I didn't want to, even if he asked, which he clearly wasn't. All I had meant was that I'd be there to support him however he wanted. It seemed like he felt I was butting in to his stuff.

I sat up so that I could face him. "I understand, Hunter. All I was saying is that I'm willing to do what you want me to do. You're the boss."

A roguish smile lit up his face, which immediately eased my anxiety. "I do like the sound of that," he said, not even trying to hide his double meaning. "I apologize. I'm tired and stressed, and I know all you're trying to do is to be there for me. That means so much. It really does. As long as we understand what the boundaries are, I'll take all the help I can get. Especially from you."

I still felt a twinge of uneasiness, but when he leaned forward and pulled me into a kiss, everything except how much I cared for this man disappeared. Janine cleared her throat, breaking his spell over me, followed seconds later by Meg and Amy bursting through the back door.

I was quickly mauled by an overly excited Amy. Even the normally reserved Meg rushed over to give me a hug and tell me how happy she was that I was back. The unconditional acceptance from these girls overwhelmed me. Any uncertainty I felt was quickly forgotten.

That evening, Hunter's hard work staffing the inn while I was back in Denver was on full display. Janine was busy training three of Elizabeth's friends on waiting tables in the dining room. It was a perfect night for it. There were thirty guests for dinner and spread out over two and a half hours gave each of the girls an opportunity to learn firsthand without the overwhelming chaos of a full dinner service. That would be tomorrow night.

Hector from the Bighorn Diner agreed to sell Hunter two menu options for Friday and Saturday nights, which would take some of the menu planning challenges off Hunter's plate. I loved Hunter's cooking and working with him in the kitchen but couldn't deny I was looking forward to having Hector's loaded mac and cheese regularly.

Hunter had even lured four workers away from one of the Breckenridge resorts for the housekeeping staff. The only training they were going to require was where to find what they needed to service the rooms. Elizabeth and Meg were happy to give up that part of their responsibilities. There was still a lot to do, but everyone seemed to be in a much better frame of mind than last weekend. Even with the legal issues hanging over Hunter's head.

Amy clung to me like a barnacle on a ship's hull from the moment she came through the door from school. Hunter convinced me it would be more help to stay with the girls than to work with him in the kitchen. I couldn't complain about spending the evening with Meg and Amy in the residence in front of a roaring fire, drinking hot cocoa and binge-watching classic Christmas movies on the TV.

When Hunter joined us after the dinner rush, smelling of fresh-baked rolls, apple pie and his balsam fir body wash, it took all the self-control I had not to jump him on the spot. We carried her to bed together, and I read her a story before she drifted off to sleep. We went back and snuggled on the sofa. We stared into the fire, talked about the girls' week at school, how the new employees were working out and enjoyed each other's company. I had the strongest feeling of being part of a family for the first time in my life.

After the breakfast service the next morning, Elizabeth trained me how to manage the front desk, take reservations and process payments. I was hoping to learn enough about it to give the poor kid a break. A sixteen-year-old shouldn't have to spend every weekend working. She deserved time to be a kid, and if I could give her just a bit of that, then I would consider it a victory.

After an hour, she declared me a natural and ready to be on my own. She hustled out the door with her friends to hang out in town before I had a chance to protest. I wouldn't have anyway, and I knew Hunter was in the kitchen if I got myself into a pickle.

Hunter hadn't shared what he was going to do to deal with the lawsuit, or if he had any idea who his brother's mystery partner was. I knew things would slow down on Sunday afternoon, and we'd hopefully find the time to talk about it then. The weather report had another major storm heading our way mid-week, which meant a full house next weekend too. Maybe with the surprise of early-season business, he could make a payment on his mortgage and avoid the conflict.

The creak of the heavy oak door swinging open along with a cold gust of wind signaled the arrival of another guest. It was too early for the skiers to be back from the mountain. Elizabeth shared before she left, we had one new reservation for the evening that hadn't seemed ski related.

I looked up from the computer screen, where I was searching each tab to find out what information it held, to see the family entering the lobby. My smile froze halfway on my face, and a lead weight cratered in my stomach, nearly bringing up my lunch.

"Send your bellman out to collect our luggage along with your valet to park the …" The detached, pretentious sound of a familiar voice cut off when he met my gaze. "Amber? What… a surprise." Lance paused. A self-satisfied smile passed over his thin lips. "Failed at teaching. Apparently, failed at real estate, so now you're giving hospitality a try? Shame you chose a property that won't be in business much longer. I guess it's just another thing you'll fail at. Just like our marriage."

My hand cramped at the tightness of the grip I held on to the countertop. The desire to throw something heavy at the asshole's head was real, but I resisted the urge for no other reason than the toddler that stood at his side. "Lance, what an unpleasant surprise. Homer Pass doesn't seem nearly pretentious enough for you."

A smile that could only be described as a sneer spread across his face. "Really, Amber, still so bitter and envious after all this time. You should just move on. I certainly have."

A very unladylike snort escaped despite my best efforts to contain my emotions. "Oh, you moved on with your little trollop long before you had the integrity to admit it."

His jaw flexed, and the color rose on his face. One thing my ex-husband couldn't tolerate was being challenged, especially when it pointed out anything less than perfection in himself. He didn't like to admit he had been unfaithful. It didn't mix well with his self-image. "As much as I'd enjoy reimagining our past based on your delusions, we have a reservation, and you, apparently, have a job to do."

It fucking killed me he was right. I had practically forced Snow to go out this afternoon. Now I wished I hadn't, but at least I wouldn't be surprised to see them in the dining room later. I pasted on a smile and pulled up the registration screen, thanking the gods that I got it right the first time and didn't have to endure the embarrassment of fucking up in front of the douchebag. "I'm surprised you're staying here. Don't you want to be closer to your new house in Breckenridge?"

The corner of his mouth hooked up. "We do, but I have a dinner meeting with a business partner here this evening, and as this building, along with quite a bit of the mountain, will be mine, I thought I'd take a firsthand look." He paused and made a show of looking around the lobby, shaking his head and tsk - tsking as he did.

"What a shame," Lance said, without the slightest hint of sincerity. "This old dump saw its best days a hundred and twenty-five years ago. I had hoped to save it, but it will have to come down. Of course, the lodgings were always going to be on the mountainside, but I had hoped we could repurpose this as a welcome center of sorts. A pity. Come spring, this will all be nothing more than a pile of rubble."

There was no way I was going to stomach him staying here. I would empty my bank account and hand it to Hunter first if he needed the money that badly. Unfortunately, before I had the chance to tell him to go get fucked, Hunter's deep baritone intervened. "Oh, I wouldn't bet a penny on that happening." I jumped. I hadn't heard him come up behind me. And damn if the icy feeling in my spine that appeared at the same time Lance did didn't just melt a little at his presence.

"Hm," Lance mused, "you must be Hunter, Henry's delusional little brother who manages this…hotel?" he paused, drawing out hotel as if he was doing the word an injustice to describe this wonderful inn.

I felt Hunter tense behind me, and I couldn't help but wonder when Lance had become so bitter and reckless. He was always a sarcastic, self-absorbed prick, even if it had taken me years to realize it. But I told myself it was because he kept it hidden so well, but he was being downright confrontational this afternoon, and it appeared he had a death wish because Hunter had him beat by at least six inches in height and a good fifty pounds in muscle. I knew Lance would press charges if Hunter pounced, but he'd always had some hint of self-preservation. He would be a pile of pulp if Hunter snapped, and he seemed determined to push Hunter over the edge.

"Well, I *am* Hunter, but no one has ever accused me of being delusional before. I'm curious if you'd be willing to share what makes you think I've lost touch with reality."

"Why don't you join Henry and me for dinner tonight, and we can explain how on February 1st you and your family will have to find another place to live." His condescending tone had me looking for heavy items to throw at him again. "Henry told me he'd delivered the documents himself. So perhaps you're illiterate too."

A part of me wanted to sink into the floor, but a bigger part wanted to come out swinging. I ran off into the night when I'd discovered Lance fucking his secretary. He never knew I'd lost our child. He never knew we'd had a child to lose. I'd been young. I'd been foolish, and I'd just wanted it all to go away. I didn't have the will to fight. But I did now. And it felt good. But before I could pluck up the courage and tell Lance to fuck off, Hunter continued.

"And just where might this enlightening dinner be?"

"We will be eating here, of course; there's no other choice in this godforsaken town. There's a reservation for two, but if you're going to join us, I'm sure you still have at least enough authority to change it to three. Have room service sent for my wife and daughter, and as I said to your front desk staff here; I'll need a bellman for our luggage, and I don't know where your valet is at but, really, it's no wonder you're failing if you can't even keep your front of house staff at their stations."

A deep rolling chuckle escaped Hunter's mouth that was completely incongruous with the circumstances. His body pressed into mine as he leaned over to look at the computer screen. He wrapped his arms around me, reaching for the keyboard. The warmth that spread through my body was completely at odds with the present situation, but damn it felt good. I had never ever felt this way with Lance.

Hunter placed his hand over mine, and with a click of the mouse, Lance's reservation, which I had pulled up, disappeared from the screen. "Well, to start with, we have neither a bellman nor a valet. We assume humans are somewhat capable of taking care of their own luggage and cars. You are obviously less than human and require such assistance. Which means you would be at a significant disadvantage were you to stay here." The sneer on Hunter's face was even more ominous than the one on Lance's. I had never seen this side of Hunter before.

"Fortunately for you, there is no reservation here. And we are full for the weekend, so you won't have to suffer through such a challenge. I'm truly sorry for the mix-up. Perhaps there is something available in Breckenridge. As for dinner, we require 24 hours' notice for dining room reservations for non-guests." He stood straight, and I immediately missed his contact.

"That's preposterous," he shouted, banging his fist on the desk. "Henry made the reservations. I sat right there and listened to him as he did it. He is the owner, so no matter what you might want, what he says goes. I demand you call him this instant."

"I'm not sure what tales Henry has told you, but he has absolutely zero interest in, or control of, this property and only a limited temporary ability to transact business on behalf of the trust. If you wish to purchase a dried-up silver mine, then he's your man; other than that, you're shit out of luck."

Hunter stepped out from behind the counter, stepping next to Lance, emphasizing their difference in size. "Consider that, when you meet my brother for dinner, wherever you meet him for dinner. Just know it won't be here. Of course, there's a small chance things could change on February first. But again, not a bet I would make if I were you." Hunter leaned forward so that they were nose to nose.

"Now leave before I call the sheriff and have you arrested for trespassing," he said before stepping back behind the counter and picking up the phone. I nearly melted on the spot as Hunter wrapped a possessive arm around my waist. "This inn is still mine, and I won't tolerate anyone disrespecting me or my family. You are not welcome here."

Lance looked back at the mousy little home wrecker and his daughter standing next to him, then back at Hunter. I could almost hear his molars grinding. "Let's go. We've wasted too much time on these lowlife mountain hicks." He turned and looked me up and down before scrunching his face like he'd just gotten a whiff of rotting sewage. "God knows what I was thinking." He turned and stormed out of the inn while I stood there in silence. My words escaped me again. But I couldn't agree with him more. God knows what I ever saw in him.

We stood there in silence for a moment before Hunter cleared his throat. "Call me if you ever get another asshole like that. You shouldn't have to deal with the likes of him."

"That was nothing. I've seen him much worse," I laughed so hard tears streamed from my eyes. "Sadly, from the sounds of it, it won't be the last we see of him," I croaked out between guffaws.

"You know him?"

I lost the battle of holding back the nervous laughter and full-on exploded in hilarity.

"Amber, what in the name of God is so funny?"

Finally, I pulled myself back together and swallowed hard. "Lance is my ex-husband, and the woman he was with is now his wife but was then the secretary I found him fucking on his desk. Apparently, she could give him the children he thought I never could."

Before I could continue, the lobby door opened again, ushering in a furious-looking Elizabeth with two friends in tow.

"What's the matter, Snow?" Hunter asked quickly, walking toward an even more pissed off-looking teenager after his use of her nickname.

"Who's the asshole that almost ran us over pulling out of the driveway? Did you piss off another customer because they asked for an extra set of towels?"

That comment made it even harder to bring my laughter under control. Elizabeth had the teen snark down to a science, and she had half her teen left to go. I felt bad for Hunter. He had his work cut out for him. "I do not, nor have I ever denied our guests towels," Hunter said indignantly.

"That particular asshole thought he had a reservation, but he didn't. He didn't take the news well."

"What do you mean he didn't have a reservation? I took one this morning for our last two rooms. Was that Mister Tabor, adjoining rooms? I remember because we had a cancellation yesterday, and I was psyched that the two rooms we had were together. He seemed a little stuffy, but we need the…"

Hunter waved his hand, cutting her rant off mid-sentence. "He was an asshole. He's a business associate of your uncle, who was the one you spoke to when you took the reservation, by the way. I bet he didn't share that with you, did he? Mr. Tabor thinks he's going to buy this inn out from under us. And he was extremely distrespectful toward Amber."

I watched Elizabeth's expression shift from annoyance to fury, and I struggled to figure out what Hunter had said to upset her. I was really surprised when her head whipped momentarily toward the door and the recently departed non-guest and ex-husband and then back to me. "Oh, hell no." She walked past her father and wrapped her arms around my waist. "No one gets to disrespect my family." She let me go, not giving me a chance to answer. "Slide over. I need to put him on the blacklist right now."

"Well, to start, he's her cheating ex-husband." Hunter responded for me, and I didn't miss the hint of amusement at his daughter's reaction in his voice.

"No!" She froze over the keyboard, eyes wide and searching my face for the hint of a lie.

"Yes," I nodded. "Don't even ask what I ever saw in him. He was certainly good at hiding who he really was, until he wasn't."

"Everybody makes mistakes, Amber," Elizabeth added with more understanding than most people four times her age. "We can be kinda blind when we want something else to be true. It's not easy to admit when we're wrong."

Our conversation was thankfully interrupted by the phone ringing at the front desk. Switching seamlessly from the relationship expert to the front desk manager, Elizabeth answered the phone. "Thank you for calling the Snowflake Inn. How may I direct your call?" She listened for a moment, and then her gaze seemed to focus on something far off in the distance. I was about to ask her what was wrong when she snapped back into focus. "I'm so sorry; we are booked solid until after the first of the year. Goodbye."

She set the receiver down, and a smile filled her face.

"What's that smile about?" Hunter asked, beating me to the question.

"Just your ex's wife trying to pull one over on us," Elizabeth answered.

"How on earth could you know that?" I asked.

"Just a hunch," she said with a shrug.

I didn't miss the quick glance in her father's direction but didn't have a clue what passed between them. I'd seen her do the same thing a few times before right before she knew something she had no way of knowing. A shiver ran up my back, making the hair on my neck stand on end. I was going to have to ask her about her hunches one of these days.

# 30

# *Ready, Not Ready*

## *Hunter*

Amber and I talked a lot over the weekend, and I could tell that somehow she felt responsible, at least in part, for the looming deadline that meant the survival of The Snowflake Inn. She wasn't. It was just one of those inexplicable coincidences that her ex-husband was the business partner my brother had chosen to try to fuck me and the girls over with. It truly is a small world sometimes. But in the end, this was my problem and my responsibility to find a solution to.

I was drawn to Amber, and I knew in my mind that I loved her, but it was far too early to say those words. With Jenn's memory still looming large and the fight I was waging to keep her legacy alive, I didn't think I should feel this way. I certainly wasn't ready to admit it. Especially not to myself.

The bottom line was that she needed to understand that when it came to the inn, I could never allow her to be more involved than she already was. I couldn't let her replace Jenn. I wouldn't do it to her, and I wouldn't do it to our girls. They needed to remember their mother, and they needed to know that I did too. No matter how perfect Amber was, she couldn't replace Jenn in their hearts. Amber could be a welcome addition but never replace Jenn, and if that wasn't enough for her, then I would have to move on. It would suck, but I've been doing hard things all my life, especially for the last three years.

I poured myself a cup of coffee and made my way into the family room, looking forward to an hour of peace and quiet before I had to get the girls up and get ready for school. I had just left Amber sound asleep in her room. It killed me to slip away in the wee hours before dawn like we were doing something wrong, but I didn't want the girls knowing. Knowing what, I wasn't quite sure. I didn't want to think about Snow knowing anything about the sexual side of relationships, but that wouldn't last much longer. I didn't want them thinking I could leave their mother behind with someone I'd only known for just a couple of weeks, and I also didn't want to put pressure on Amber to have to fit into a family when she was just getting to know me.

"Why don't you just let Amber move her stuff down here and stay in your room?"

"Jesus, Snow," I jerked, spilling half of my scalding hot coffee on my hand. "What the hell are you doing up so early? You don't have to get ready for school for another hour."

"You're never going to stop calling me that, are you?"

I could see a smile of resignation fill her face as my eyes adjusted to the dim light. "Probably not. You're always going to be your mother and my little snowflake. It doesn't matter if you're sixteen or sixty." I closed the distance, shaking the coffee drips off my hand, and bent over and kissed her before sinking down on the sofa next to her. "Answer my question. What's got you up so early, bad dreams?"

"I had to get up early because it's the only way I could catch you red-handed. I knew I could never get you to admit it otherwise."

"Admit what?" Play dumb; that's what it says to do in the dad handbook, isn't it?

"Dad," she whined out like I was the insolent child. "We all know you've been sneaking up to sleep with Amber. You're not fooling anyone. Even Amy knows."

"What do you mean, 'Amy knows'?"

"Well, she just thinks you guys like to cuddle, but she knows you're not sleeping in your bed since Amber has been here."

"That's not true."

"It is, Dad. At least most nights, anyway. Don't treat me like I'm stupid. I don't lie to you; please don't lie to me. We've been through too much for that."

It truly bothered me sometimes how grown-up she was. How she'd had to grow up too soon just so our family could survive. I hated that I'd put that much responsibility on her, robbing her of her childhood. The least I could do was be honest with her. "You're right. I apologize. I guess I was just trying to protect you, but that was wrong. You don't need protection from this. Do you think I should stop?"

"God, Dad," she groaned, sounding so much like her mother when I frustrated her it was scary. "No, I don't think you should stop. I think you should ask Amber if she wants to move down to your room. She's part of this family, so she should certainly feel like we've welcomed her in and not kept at arm's length like she's some kind of dirty little secret. She deserves better than that." A wry smile crept onto her lips.

"What's that smile for?"

"I think Amy wants her down here so she can creep into your room in the middle of the night and snuggle between the two of you. So maybe you shouldn't have her move down if you still want some private time."

"My private time is definitely not a conversation I want to be having with my sixteen-year-old daughter."

"Well, it's not a conversation your sixteen-year-old daughter wants to be having with you either, but here we are having the conversation. And if you really love her, and I think you do. Ask her. If she agrees, then we could really use that room. We're sold out every weekend until the end of January, and that room could earn us at least a thousand a week. We need that money to pay the mortgage. We can't let Uncle Henry steal the inn from us, Dad, we can't."

"He won't, and you let me worry about that. You shouldn't have to."

"Well, I'll always worry, whether you think I should or not. We both know that we need the money, and maybe you could ask Josh to start on the fourth floor? Maybe he could let us pay in the spring."

"Please don't worry about this. I'll figure something out." I could feel my jaw clenching. I was such a failure. My teenage daughter was worrying over the family business when all she should have been worrying about was whether she was ready for her algebra test. Is there no one I can keep safe?

"So, you'll ask her and call Josh?"

"I'll think about it." That was all I could promise her. "But all your mother's things are still in the closet. I doubt she's going to want to."

"Stop at Benson's Hardware and pick up some packing boxes. I'll pack everything up when I get home from school today."

I turned to look at her, and the hair on my arms stood on end. She looked so much like her mother. "That's my responsibility, and I'm not…" I swallowed, trying to clear the emotion from my throat. "I'm not ready."

She slid over and wrapped her arms around my shoulder and pressed a kiss to my cheek. "I know, Dad. But it's time. It's long past time, and I am okay with doing it. Honestly, I want to do it." She pressed another kiss to my cheek and gave me one last squeeze before pushing herself up off the couch. "I'll be sure to save a couple of things for us to remember her by. She'll always be our mom, Dad. But it's time we all started living and loving again. I'm going to get in the shower. If you make breakfast, I'll get Meg and Amy ready for school."

My little girl was so grown-up. "It's a deal."

"Blueberry pancakes, please," she asked over her shoulder as she sauntered down the hall with the swagger of someone who felt like she'd accomplished a major goal.

All I could do was shake my head and agree. The trouble was that I wasn't ready. I might never be ready.

<h1 style="text-align:center">31</h1>

<h1 style="text-align:center">Commitment?</h1>

Amber

It had been a busy day. Elizabeth had asked me to cover the front desk for her that afternoon because she had some cleanup to do in the residence. I wasn't sure what she was talking about because she had the neatest room I'd ever seen for a teenager. In fact, I'd be mortified if she saw how messy my room was at my house.

I closed the book I had been reading and debated uncurling myself from the chair and climbing into bed. I'd gotten used to having Hunter with me every night and couldn't deny how much I enjoyed it. It was so much more than just earth-shattering sex.

There was a soft rap at my door, and my heart rate sped up ever so slightly. Obviously, it was Hunter. I'd been expecting him, but as time wore on, I thought maybe he'd had a change of heart. He'd said he'd be right up when I'd finished reading Amy her nightly story. And yet, more than an hour had passed. I wouldn't have blamed him if he'd decided it was best to end whatever this was between us before it got more complicated.

He disregarded it when I suggested it, but I couldn't help feeling that Lance's involvement in this scheme had something to do with me. Even if it was strictly a coincidence to start with. Even if he wasn't dense enough to miss the possessive way Hunter held me at the end of our confrontation. Even if this started as business, he would make it personal the moment he got a whiff that I was connected to the inn.

The last thing I wanted to do was make a bad situation worse. Elizabeth had interrupted with an unequivocal "no" when I suggested it might be best if I made myself scarce and returned to Denver. More than once, I'd heard Lance brag about the underhanded way he did things when he felt cause for a vendetta. If I were gone, then perhaps Hunter would have a fighting chance.

Making me think he might agree with me was his silence. He nodded in agreement with Elizabeth but didn't say so himself.

I opened the door, and all the doubts I had and all my resolve to do the right thing and leave melted away. My big, sexy innkeeper stood there with a tray of sweets and a pot of tea. How was a girl to refuse?

"I'm sorry it took so long. I was on the phone with Janine."

"That's okay. You had a lot to talk about."

"We did. I just wish it were more productive. It seems like whoever Henry got for a lawyer did a really solid job of finding every way to screw us over. If there was a loophole, they found it and closed it up tight as soon as they were done exploiting it."

"That sounds like the Tabor Group. They don't care who they hurt. If they want something, they get it."

"It looks like the only way to save the inn is to somehow come up with enough to pay off the mortgage completely before the deadline."

"You mean the whole thing? Not just the past due amount?"

He nodded silently as he poured our tea. "I could try to refinance with a bank, but what happens when I run into the same cash flow issues in the summer and early fall? It's a risk I don't want to take."

"How much do you need?" I asked, a spark of an idea forming in the back of my mind.

"A lot," was his vague reply. I considered pressing him for specifics. I needed a better idea if I was going to help, but I let it go. When he was ready to tell me, he would. I had to remind myself that we'd only known each other for days, not years.

"Whenever you want to talk about anything, I'm happy to help. Who knows, maybe lightning will strike and I could come up with a potential solution."

"Thank you. I appreciate that. I don't want to burden you with my problems when you've got plenty of your own to manage."

I laughed. "I think I owe you just a little help too. You certainly took on my problems when you didn't need to. I don't know where I would have been if you, Leo, and Janine hadn't stepped up to help me." We had settled into the chairs by the windows, and I leaned forward and took his hands, pressing a kiss to each one. "Let's help each other. I can carry burdens that aren't my own too."

On an exhale, he flopped back in the chair. "I know you can," he agreed, but he left it at that, leaving the 'but I'm going to do it on my own' unsaid.

We sat in silence for a while, quietly drinking our tea. I snagged two tarts he had brought because they looked far too delicious to ignore. Besides, sweets and tea are among the best antidotes to anxiety I know.

"Snow seems to think you should move downstairs into my room." He said, snapping me out of the plans to help him I was tossing around in my mind.

I couldn't tell from his tone whether this was just a statement of fact or if he had an opinion about it. "Does she?" I asked, hoping to urge him to express one, but he didn't take the bait. Finally, I gave up and asked outright. I wasn't in the mood for guessing games. "And what do you think?"

"Seems like a lot of pressure to put on you after only a couple of weeks. It's hard enough to get to know one other person, but to add three additional kids from six to thirteen, that's a hard ask. Don't you think?"

"There's truth to that," I agreed. "But that's part of dating someone with a family. If you're not up to dealing with it, waiting isn't likely to make it any easier." I paused for a moment, mustering up the courage to ask the riskiest question. "What do you want, Hunter? Do you think we're moving too fast, and you want to pump the brakes?"

Hunter met my gaze with an unreadable expression, and my gut twisted with anxiety. Please don't say yes. Please, please, please, don't say yes. I don't think I could stand the rejection. "I can't deny that the rational, cautious part of my brain tells me we're moving too fast. That this train we're on is going to derail in spectacular fashion once we hit a curve. But the other part of me, the biggest part of me, can't imagine not having you in my life. You're a very special person, Amber, and I can't deny how strongly I feel about you. You are smart, funny, and so fucking beautiful, but most of all you have the most loving heart I've ever known."

I could feel my chest squeeze with excitement, relief and just so much love for this man. He slid off his chair and knelt before me. Taking my hand in his, he kissed my hand and then held it like a lifeline to a drowning man. "I'm scared, not a hundred percent sure I'm ready, but I want to try to make this work. So yes, I'd like you to move down with me. With us. There might be sometimes when I'm not ready to share what I still see as Jenn's, but I promise to try as long as you promise to be patient with me."

Trails of moisture ambled down my cheeks, and I swear they weren't tears, but I'm a filthy liar. There was just so much love in my heart it spilled out all over this man's honesty and vulnerability. "I promise to be patient with you. Can you be patient with me, because I have plenty to sort out too?"

"Of course. Maybe we can help each other through it all."

My throat was too clogged with emotion to speak. All I could do was nod and smile. He eased up on his knees, leaning forward. His hand slid behind my neck, and he pulled me slowly forward. When his lips crashed against mine; it was over. I was his, body, mind and soul.

His fingers quickly worked open the buttons of my flannel pajama top. Apparently, flannel was the key element. I'd never heard of a plaid kink, but I wasn't complaining. He pushed the top over my shoulders, and I let it fall behind me onto the chair. His large hands cupped my breasts, kneading them gently, his thumbs brushing over my sensitive nipples. They rose immediately into eraser-hard points.

His tongue snaked out and traced the outline of my areola before he sucked it into his mouth. His teeth softly clamped around the tip, and a hiss turned into a moan as pain turned into pleasure. My fingers snaked through his thick, wavy hair as I pressed him to my chest.

"I fucking love your tits, Amber," he said. His voice was husky with desire. This was as close to dirty-talk as he'd ever come, and damn if I wasn't turned on because of it. Our lovemaking was passionate and intimate, but I wondered if I could get him into a place that was just a bit more feral. I was certainly going to try.

"They're yours, Hunter. All of me is yours."

"Fuck," he groaned. "Mine. You're all mine."

"Yes," I hissed. Placing a kiss on top of his head and pressed him closer against me. "Tell me what you want, Hunter. Tell me what to do. I'll do anything you want."

"Anything?" he asked. The desperate longing was unmistakable in his words.

"Anything," I confirmed.

He knelt in front of me, staring into my eyes, and I almost wanted to laugh. It was like he glitched because so many ideas flooded his brain at the same time. Fuck if that didn't make me wet.

"Stand up," I said, pulling him to his feet as I did the same. I made quick work of his fly and tugged his trousers to the floor. My hand wrapped around his stiffening cock and stroked it from base to tip.

Reflexively, his hips moved with the pace of my hand. It was as if his body couldn't help wanting to fuck me. Whatever part of me it could. There was only one thing I wanted then.

I dropped to my knees in front of him and took his cock in my hand. My tongue laved the base of his shaft, and I slowly ran it all the way to the tip. I circled it slowly before closing my lips around the bulbous head and inching my way back down his rigid length. It had been a long, long time since I'd been this eager to please a man this way. My lack of practice showed as I coughed and gagged several times before I could take him completely, the head lodging in the back of my throat as my nose pressed against his solid abdomen.

My efforts were rewarded with a string of expletives I'd never heard from Hunter before. Only his perfect thickness filling my mouth kept a smile from engulfing my face. Encouraged by the undeniable pleasure I was giving him, I worked my mouth up and down, quickening my pace and sucking harder as I did.

My left hand slid beneath the elastic waist of my pajama bottoms, finding my slick pussy. I moaned around his cock as I traced my seam with two fingers, finishing at my clit. I was swollen and so ready as I slowly rubbed circles around the sensitive nub, working in rhythm with the pace that my right hand stroked his shaft.

His hands twisted through my hair, cupping the back of my head and guiding me at the tempo he needed. I was completely lost in lust. I couldn't ever remember feeling this far gone to carnality before. "Jesus. Fuck," he groaned. His body shoving his steely rod in and out of my mouth. "Such a good girl," he panted. "Take that cock. Yes. Yes. Yes."

My fingers sped over my clit, and I could feel my orgasm building all the way from the top of my head to the tips of my toes. I had to stop because there was no way I could focus on two things at once, and, in that moment, I needed Hunter's release much more than I did my own. I cupped his balls with my now-free hand, and his grip tightened on my hair until it was just shy of painful.

Suddenly, he pulled back, making me feel empty at the lack of dick in my mouth. "Fuck, Amber. You've got to stop, or I'm going to come."

I smiled up at him from my knees and resumed working his cock with my hands. "That is exactly what I intend to do," I said before leaning forward and taking him back into my mouth.

Once again he pulled away, and I knew the look I was giving him was a full-on pout. Why wasn't he giving me what I wanted? I had never wanted to swallow before. I had done it to make my partner happy, but it was a sacrifice. Tonight, in my mind, it was an absolute imperative that I take every last drop of what Hunter could give me.

"Please, Amber. I want this to last. I need to make you come too."

I stood up, realizing that maybe being on my knees so long was not something my body was used to or particularly enthusiastic about. I don't know what came over me, but I was especially sassy. "You mean to tell me that a big, muscular man like you doesn't have the stamina to go more than one round?"

I knew instantly that my attitude had hit its mark. Just one brow arched, and I'd known him long enough to realize that was a challenge. His dark brown eyes burned not only with lust but with the intention to show me just how much stamina he had.

Winner, winner, chicken dinner.

His hands slipped under my arms, and he pulled me to my feet. "Amber Scott, that sounds very much like a challenge. Are you sure you're up for that?"

Ooh, he full named me. If he knew my middle name, Lynn, I bet he would have used that too. "Hunter Holmes," two can play that game, "I am up for absolutely anything you can think of tonight." I might regret that if the heat in his eyes were any indication, but that regret was for tomorrow when I couldn't walk. That's if I was a very lucky girl.

Several unintelligible sounds escaped his throat, and I'm uncertain if he meant to form words or not. He didn't.

Before I grasped what was happening, my pajama bottoms were at my ankles and Hunter had lifted me over his shoulder and deposited me on my bed in virtually the same motion. I whooped in surprise as my ass bounced on the mattress and he rolled me over onto my stomach.

A thwack sounded as the palm of his hand made solid contact with my ass.

I squealed in surprise. "Ow. That stings," I said, stating the obvious complaint. Before I could continue, he pressed a kiss to the affected spot and then massaged the still-tingling skin, turning the instant of pain into a deeper sense of pleasure. He spread me wide with both hands, opening me to his inspection.

I should have felt exposed. I normally would have felt vulnerable being stretched open, exposing my taint and pussy like that. Somehow with Hunter it was different. I was most certainly vulnerable, but instead of wanting to pull away and protect myself, the anticipation of what he was going to do next was almost more than I could bear. The guttural sounds emanating from his chest certainly enhanced my arousal.

The next thing I knew, his tongue was circling my forbidden entrance. No one had ever done that to me before, and it was immensely more pleasurable than I ever could have imagined. I sent a silent prayer of thanks to

Eros or whatever god had allowed me the good fortune to have showered before he arrived, or I would have had a whole new level of self-consciousness to overcome.

Before I could obsess over the new experience, his mouth moved lower, and I raised my hips without a conscious thought to grant him better access. His tongue played at my opening, circling, darting in and out. He was fucking me with his tongue and, if the noises he was making were any indication, enjoying himself very much. "Oh my fuck," I moaned.

"Jesus, Amber," he growled. "You are the most delicious thing I've ever tasted."

His mouth continued to devour my pussy, and then his thumb pressed against my puckered hole. My body went rigid. I wasn't an anal virgin, but it had been a long time. Long before Lance since I'd been comfortable enough to allow someone access there.

"Do you trust me, Amber?"

"Yes," I breathed, knowing it was the absolute truth.

"Then relax and let me give you everything."

It was so easy. Almost too easy to do as Hunter asked. I exhaled slowly and let the tension in my body go. Slowly his digit pressed inside, and an "oooh" escaped on a low sigh I could feel in my chest. He continued to work his thumb in and out, in and out of my ass. And with each stroke, I could feel the delight build in my core. His thighs pressed against mine, spreading me open. His free hand gripped my hip and guided me to my knees. The thick head of his cock pressed into my opening, and then all I could do was see stars as he filled me completely.

I rocked my hips to meet his thrusts. I was so fucking turned on I was scared I was too wet. That he wouldn't get the friction he needed. "Fuck, baby. It's so good," I murmured. "Is it good for you?" I asked, unable to ignore my insecurities completely.

"So good. So good," he moaned in answer. I could tell he was struggling to speak. His hand gripped my hip as he picked up the pace. His thumb continued to work my ass, and I felt so completely full. The sound of our bodies made as we collided together ramped my excitement even higher. His cock hit that special spot inside me at the perfect angle and at the perfect pace. My breath quickened, and like a tidal wave crashing onto the shore, my body exploded in orgasm.

His movement became erratic, and I felt his shaft pulse as he followed me with a release of his own.

We collapsed in a pile of panting, sweating flesh. I was in a state of bliss I couldn't remember ever experiencing before. The evidence of our efforts I felt pooling between my legs, and a feeling of pride washed over me. I was soaked between my legs. He must have come in gallons for me to be this wet. We were going to have to change the bed before we could ever sleep in it; it was so bad.

After a few moments of bliss, Hunter rolled off onto his side and gently stroked my hair. "That was something else," he said. "I've never experienced anything like it." All I could do was groan in agreement. My body was still too spent to move. It was without a doubt the most intense orgasm I'd ever had. After a moment or two of silence, he added, "I don't have to ask if you enjoyed it. The bed is soaked. Have you ever squirted that hard before?"

I turned to my side and met his gaze. "What do you mean I squirted? That's not a thing."

He chuckled, and it was like his whole body smiled. "Look down at the bed, Amber. I came more than I think I ever have, but it's certainly not me that's responsible for soaking the bedding."

I looked down to see a circle of sheets that was at least four feet in diameter looking like they'd just come out of a washing machine without the aid of the spin cycle. "Oh my God," I squeaked. "I did that?"

He laughed and then pressed a kiss to my lips. "You did, but I'm not willing to give God any of the credit for this."

# 32

# *Crazy Ideas*
## *Amber*

It had been a week since I had moved downstairs and into Hunter's room, which I guess was our room now. Things had gone well, although Amy had tried to establish a claim to the center of our bed. Hunter had tried to have a talk with her with no success. It wasn't until I tried it she seemed to accept that she should only do it for 'emergencies'. Two nights without a three AM visit and I've got my fingers crossed it works. I didn't have the heart to tell him his way hadn't worked. He still doesn't know I talked to her, and I guess it's best it stays that way.

It had been nearly two weeks since Hunter's brother dropped the lawsuit in his lap and even though he was still hesitant to share a lot about it with me, between what he did and what Janine told me they weren't much closer to a resolution. Their lawyer had filed a countersuit and requested an injunction to stay the February first deadline, but the hearing wasn't until the middle of January, and Hunter and Janine were advised to prepare for little to no success with either the injunction or the counter suit. Time was running out, and we were no closer to a solution.

The longer things went on, the testier Hunter became. Christmas was just a little over two weeks away, and it wasn't shaping up to be a very merry one at all.

Hunter had taken Amy for a routine check-up, and Elizabeth and Meg were at after-school activities. I was perched in my new usual spot behind the reception desk, reviewing the curriculum and lesson plans, preparing to start my new temporary position after the Christmas break. I was truly excited to get back into teaching. There was certainly a possibility it could be permanent starting next year depending on how much the school liked me. And of course, how much I liked them. I was planning a life in Homer Pass now. And a smile spread across my face at the thought when my phone dinged, notifying me of an incoming text.

I assumed it was Hunter giving me an update on when to expect them home or asking about dinner, but I was met with a text from an unknown number.

> Unknown: I know you're trying to rent the house. I told you that you couldn't handle it. I should let you rot in your own spiteful behavior. After what you did, you certainly deserve it, but I always liked the place, and so did Gina. We have very happy memories of fucking in every, and I mean every room. So, I'll write you a check for 500k, which is more than half of what we, no, what I paid for it. You already got the other half in the divorce. It's more than what you deserve. You have 24 hours to decide. L

How dare he! What I did? Had he really forgotten that I was the one who had found him balls deep in someone that wasn't me and not the other way around?

I kicked myself for not blocking his number instead of deleting it because then I wouldn't have been tempted to fire back a thousand different hateful responses. We had paid close to a million for it over ten years ago, and I knew the market had gone up some. Plus, we'd put money into the home, remodeling the kitchen, and the landscaping. Sure, I owed a lot on the mortgage, but if I sold it, I could probably clear over five-hundred thousand. It would really put pressure on things to work out with Hunter, but maybe, just maybe, it would be enough that Hunter could combine it with what he and Janine could contribute and pay off the debt.

I deleted the text. He could go fuck himself while he waited for a reply. I blocked the number and opened my contacts. There was one person I could trust who knew what they were talking about and would give me their honest opinion whether I'd lost my mind.

Patty picked up on the second ring, which surprised me because her schedule was usually so packed I'd end up leaving a voicemail and waiting days for a reply.

"Hey, girlfriend," her infectious enthusiasm came across the airwaves. "Please tell me you're not going to be one of those clients who call ten times a day to see if I've had any success."

"That's not why I'm calling, but seeing that you mentioned it. Have you had any success?"

She laughed. "It's only been listed for rent for two days."

"You know I'm joking."

"I do, but I know you're anxious, so I'll tell you we've already had ten inquiries. I haven't had time to vet any of them, but with that much interest, I'm even more confident we'll have tenants for the first of the year."

"That's great news," I said, meaning it but hoping she wouldn't get upset if I changed the rules.

"But?"

"Who said there's a but?"

"Well, you called for a reason, and we talked for hours two days ago, so I doubt this is just a call to catch up." I could hear the amusement in her voice. "I love you, girl, but if it's not about the house, what's up? Has your dream romance come to an untimely end and you need me to pick up wine and ice cream?"

"Don't even think that," I shrieked, my stomach twisting in knots just at the thought. "Honestly, it is about the house. I was wondering…" I hesitated, nervous about what her reaction might be.

"I don't read minds, honey. You're going to have to say it."

"Um," I swallowed and took a deep breath before pushing the question past my lips at warp speed. "How much do you think I should list the house for if I wanted to sell it?"

"Oh, honey," she sighed like the long-suffering friend she was. "We talked about this. That's an awfully risky move to make for someone you've just met, and the tax hit would be massive if you didn't put it back into another property right away." She hesitated for a moment, probably to give me the chance to interrupt with all my usual excuses about how she was wrong this time, but I just waited because I knew she'd have more to say. "Renting it is the safest thing for you. We agreed on that. What changed your mind?"

I took a deep breath and gave her all the details. Everything I knew about the lawsuit and the likelihood that they'd lose the inn. How horrible I'd feel if I just sat by and watched them lose everything. How my fucking ex was involved and even if giving Hunter money might not be the wisest choice, screwing my ex out of something he wanted made it pretty close to worth every penny.

"Fucking Lance," was the first thing she said when I stopped to breathe.

"Exactly," I said.

"Can't he just go get another mortgage? He's doing well, and he's got to have some equity in the property with all the improvements they made."

"He is doing well, but that's because there's a lot of snow this year. The ski season makes or breaks his business, and that's kind of why he's behind on the mortgage. He pays it after the ski season and then just tries to survive until snow flies again."

"But the mountains are beautiful in summer too. Doesn't he market to that population as well? I mean, hiking is great, but not everybody who hikes is about breaking their back sleeping in a tent and eating soupy, salty dehydrated mush for dinner. I like a nice walk in the woods as much as the next girl. Especially if there's a hunky mountain man to service my needs. There's nothing like an orgasm with a view, but at the end of the hike, I want a hot bath with bubbles, somebody else doing the cooking and a comfy bed to pass out in."

"You're right, and I don't know if he's tried, but right now is not the time for that discussion. He needs to either win in court or pay off the mortgage by February first."

"How much does he need?"

"I don't know. He won't tell me exactly because he doesn't want me to worry. My guess is between two and three million. All I know for sure is that he's behind by two-hundred-fifty thousand."

"That's probably a good guess given how long he's had the property and the annual payment. And how much do you owe on yours?"

I had to stop and think. I hadn't taken a proper look at the mortgage statement in a while because I knew it would be years before I could pay it off. "Somewhere around four-hundred-fifty thousand. I can text you the exact amount if you need it."

"No, that's close enough." She was quiet for a moment, and I twisted the hem of the Snowflake Inn polo I was wearing. "If you want to sell, and I have to say I don't think you should, you should probably be able to walk away with close to two million after commission and fees. Maybe if we get lucky, two and a half, but that's not likely, and I don't see any way that you could have cash in hand by February first. There's just not enough time. Washington Park is a desirable area, but the holidays are not the best time to sell, especially quickly."

I was floored that she felt she could get that much for my home. To walk away with that amount, it would mean it would have to sell for close to three million. I was thinking about a million four-hundred or five-hundred thousand at the most. But the realization that I wouldn't get the money in time to help made my eyes sting. I should have known it, which only goes to show what a shit realtor I was. "I can't believe I could get that much, but I guess I should have known that. Thanks for being here for me, Patty. You really are a good friend."

"Always, babe. Just like you've been there for me." I couldn't think of a time when I had, but it was nice of her to say. "I'll think about it and let you know if I come up with anything."

"Thanks again, Patty."

"Of course."

We said our goodbyes, and I returned to looking at the school papers but had to put them down. I just couldn't focus. I needed to help Hunter and the girls. I just couldn't come up with a way to do it.

An hour later, I was making dinner in the kitchen when my phone vibrated in my pocket. I was going to be upset if Hunter left it until fifteen minutes before he was due home to tell me he was going to be late for dinner. I pulled the phone out, putting down the big wooden spoon I'd been using to stir the stew to find Patty's name staring back at me.

Patty: Thought of something brilliant, even if I say so myself. I'll be at the inn by ten tomorrow morning. Make sure Hunter and Janine are ready for their white knight to come riding into town or her trusty steed. Actually, given the amount of snow you have, maybe I should use a snowmobile and not a horse.

I laughed out loud and tapped out a reply just as I heard Hunter and Amy come through the back door.

Me: Will do but can you give me a hint?

Patty: Nope. U have to wait but it'll be great. Ha! Look at me the poet.

I groaned. She's such a nut sometimes, but I loved her to pieces.

Me: CU tomorrow drive safe

Patty: -thumbs up emoji-

"What's up?" Hunter asked, walking into the kitchen. "I heard you laughing when I came through the door and then groan. Are you cracking under the pressure of having dinner ready for five?"

"Excuse me?" I raised my voice, feigning offense. "You've seen me under much more pressure than that right here in this kitchen, or are you so old and addled that you can't remember that far back? Because if you are…" my idle threat was interrupted by a burly innkeeper planting a wet kiss on my lips and pulling me into a bone-crushing hug.

Pulling back from the embrace, he looked down at me, and his deep brown eyes were filled with so much affection I wanted nothing more than to drag him right to the bedroom. Unfortunately, that wouldn't do. There was a meal to finish and three kiddos who didn't need that kind of education.

He pressed a kiss on my forehead before stepping back. "Dinner smells delicious, and I'm famished."

"It's just beef stew and rolls. Nothing special."

"It's very special. First, because you made it, and second, because I didn't," he added with a laugh. "Seriously though, what had you laughing before?"

I worried my bottom lip. I wanted to wait and tell him that Patty was coming up tomorrow morning specifically with an idea she thought could save the inn. I was afraid that if I didn't have time to ease him into the idea, he'd say no before he even heard it. He still wasn't open to hearing my suggestions. I doubted he'd be open to hearing Patty's, who was practically a complete stranger to him.

"Just something Patty texted."

"Okay," he said, turning to walk out of the kitchen. "How long before dinner?"

I took a quick peek at the oven timer. "Ten minutes until the rolls are out of the oven."

"Perfect. I'll tell the girls to get ready."

I just nodded, too concerned about how I was going to tell Hunter he had a business meeting tomorrow morning that I had arranged. I could deal with his anger; I just needed him to calm down enough to sit down and listen to what Patty had to say. She'd bend over backwards to help me, but she wouldn't waste her time driving all the way up here if she didn't think it was important, meaning something that could actually work.

Me: I need your advice and I need you to be at a meeting here at the inn tomorrow morning at ten.

Janine: OK and huh????????

Me: My friend Patty has some kind of plan to solve the mortgage problem. She'll be here at ten tomorrow to tell us about it. But I need to know how and when to tell Hunter. You know how he feels about it's his problem to solve.

Janine: OMG. He's such a stubborn ass sometimes ;−). Don't tell him. I'll tell him. You haven't experienced him in full Grizzly mode yet, and I need to be there to support you. Just tell him I'm coming by at nine-forty-five and he needs to be there.

Me: Won't he wonder why you didn't tell him yourself?

Janine: Probably not. Jenn and I used to do this all the time. He's just going to assume we've fallen into the same pattern.

Janine: I kind of like it.

Me: me too.

# 33

# Deception and Consequences

## Amber

I didn't enjoy deceiving Hunter. It wasn't the type of relationship I wanted to be in, but I also trusted Janine's judgment. He hadn't questioned me when I told him Janine was coming by and he needed to be here. Maybe he just assumed that she was as evasive as he was when it came to what was going on with the inn. Quite the opposite. If it weren't for her, I'd be practically in the dark and even more ill at ease than I was about its future as well as my own.

As it happened, Janine walked through the door only moments before Patty was supposed to arrive. "I'm so sorry, Amber. Carly was late, and I couldn't afford to leave our part-timer in the store without her there, especially this close to Christmas."

"Don't worry," I said. "Patty's not here yet."

No sooner had those words left my mouth than my best friend burst through the front door. With her wild red hair flowing behind her, wearing a sleek black pantsuit and a sharp-looking burgundy messenger bag slung over her shoulder, she looked like a freaking superhero of business flying in to save the day. "Good morning, ladies," she said, greeting us with so much confidence I couldn't begin to comprehend how she managed it. "Where's your handsome mountain man?"

"He's back in the residence," I said, looking at Janine with a *what the fuck do we do now* screaming loudly unsaid.

"I'm sorry, Patty, I just got here and we haven't told Hunter about this yet," Janine said. "Amber, why don't you take Patty to the office and let her get settled? I'll go soften the ground with Hunter. We'll join you in a few minutes."

I gave Patty a hug and led her back towards the office, which was just off the kitchen and dining room. We stopped on the way to grab coffee and then settled in, waiting for them to arrive.

"So, what's the big surprise?" I asked as much to fill the silence as out of curiosity.

Patty gave me her best impish smile. "You're just going to have to wait…"

"You've got to be fucking kidding me, J. You ambushed me. You and Amber both," Hunter bellowed from the family room, cutting her off.

I cringed in my seat, and Patty lifted a sculptured brow in my direction. "Janine was late, and you were early. Didn't exactly work out like I planned."

"I should say not. From what you said, I knew he wasn't going to be an easy sale, but I hope he at least can calm down enough to listen to what I have to propose," Patty said, though it struck me as much as a question as a statement.

I hoped so too, but I'd never heard him that angry before, so I wasn't so sure. The good news was that he wasn't still yelling, so maybe Janine was correct in assuming she could tame the bear. My fingers were crossed.

We sat there silently, both trying to pick up the conversation happening just around the corner. The best I could get was a word here and there, and from the expression on Patty's face, she wasn't having any better luck than I was.

Ten minutes later, a very pissed-off looking Hunter walked in, followed closely by his equally perturbed-looking sister. He dropped into the desk chair, arms crossed, and jaw so tightly clenched he'd likely chip a tooth. Worst of all, he didn't look at me once. Not even a quick glance in my direction. A shiver ran down my spine as a flashback of similar icy receptions flooded my mind.

"Well, now that we've managed our tantrums, I, for one, would love to hear what you have come up with to address our problem," Janine said to Patty, meeting her eyes with a warm smile completely at odds with her expression moments ago.

Patty lifted a questioning brow, but Janine just continued to smile at her and nodded.

"Okay," Patty started on an exhale. "Yesterday afternoon, Amber called me to ask about listing her home in Washington Park, which is one of the hottest and most exclusive neighborhoods in Denver. She's been in that home for over ten years, so she's amassed quite a bit of equity. Unfortunately, the only way to access that is to sell, and that could take more time than you all have, and while I wasn't given the exact figure, you need. I can tell you that the low end of that profit would be close to two million dollars. Can you at least share with Amber and me if that would be sufficient to clear the mortgage?"

"It doesn't fucking matter. I won't let Amber…" Hunter started.

Janine cut him off. "I told you not to pull that shit, Hunter. If you can't at least give them the courtesy of an answer, I will. That would be close, and I believe Hunter and I could fill in the gap if you're accurate in that amount." Janine said. Her all-business attitude was not one that I'd seen before. I was impressed. She gave off a definite bad boss bitch vibe that appeared to even influence Hunter.

"But honestly, Amber," Janine continued. "I have to agree with Hunter. How can we let you do this for us? We love you, and I already think of you as my sister, but it's only been a few weeks. What happens if something changes? It's not the kind of money we'd ever be able to pay back quickly."

"I know it's a lot of money. Honestly, I didn't have a clue my house was worth that much. But now that I do, I can't think of it going to a better cause. You helped me when I was no one but a stranger dumped in the lobby of your inn, frozen stiff and scared. Ironically, if I'd realized what I was sitting on, I wouldn't have been half as scared, but that's not the point; you helped me when I'd felt I was at the very bottom. Now, please let me help you. We can have a lawyer write it up as a loan. I don't expect to be an owner or treated any differently. I just want to help my family. Because that's the way I see you. I know how you feel, Hunter. I do." And it wasn't until that moment that he met my gaze. The fury I saw there took my breath away. Nothing I was saying was getting through.

I swallowed hard and continued. "I want to help because I can. Isn't that exactly what you told me, Janine?"

She breathed out a chuckle. "No fair using my own words against me."

I forced a weak smile in her direction. At least I felt love from someone in the room.

"Anyway, it's a moot point, isn't it Patty? You said it wouldn't be likely you could close the sale in time even if you found a buyer to pay the price we need," Janine said.

"I did. There's a solution for that, but I'd like to tell you about another possibility I've come up with that doesn't involve Amber having to sell."

Hunter opened his mouth, but Janine cut in before he could speak. "I'd

love to hear that. If we can find a solution that doesn't involve Amber
risking everything she has for us, I'm all ears."

"Stating the obvious, you're aware that Tabor Group Properties is the
backing behind Henry's scheme and they plan on bulldozing this town and
creating a resort for the billionaire boys," Patty began. "That's their MO
— buy up property, push out the locals and create something only the one
percent can enjoy. The company I work for, The Brown Group, is also
in property management and development, but we operate on a different
model. We seek a place just like this inn. Places with charm and a value to
the community and help them build something bigger than they could on
their own."

"Amber hasn't shared a lot with me, but from what she says, this inn
lives and dies with the ski season. I think you're missing an enormous
opportunity in the summer and shoulder seasons. This area is a paradise
for hikers and outdoor enthusiasts. And a lot of them like to hike just fine,
but they want a soft bed and good food, not a mosquito-infested tent and
freeze-dried whatever for dinner. The development side of our business
would be interested in investing in this inn and helping you market it more
effectively so that your rooms are near capacity year-round." Patty finished
looking between Hunter and Janine.

"Great, so I save my inn from one set of thieves only to hand it willingly over to another. This is my inn, Goddamnit, my dream, my dead
wife's dream and my children's future. I'm not signing it over to a bunch
of money-grubbing city boys who will take away what little control I have
the first chance they get." The tension was radiating from Hunter. His fists
were balled so tight that every muscle and sinew on his arms looked like
they were ready to snap like an over-tightened guitar string. His nostrils
flared, and for the first time I had to consider if he might actually be
capable of violence. He certainly looked ready to tear down the world just
to spite it.

Patty continued unfazed, completely calm and professional. "I appreciate your concern, Hunter. But that's not the way they operate. They act
as angel investors. Yes, they provide guidance, but you remain in control.
All decisions remain yours and yours alone. They also don't want to be
involved forever. They provide the financing much the same as any other
mortgage. It is based on profits to some extent, but they don't foreclose.
If things don't work out the way both parties want, then they help you
find alternative financing and move on. Based on what I see, you'll more
than double your business and be free and clear of any outside interfer-

ence before Elizabeth graduates from college."

"So, what? They just tuck a check under my pillow like the fucking tooth fairy?" He stood, the chair crashing back against the wall with a loud crack. "I may have been born and raised here in the mountains. I might not wear suits and ties like your usual clients, but I graduated summa cum laude from UC Boulder with a master's in business. I know a takeover when I see it, no matter how pretty a bow you put on it." He turned to walk out the door, but Janine stood and blocked his exit. He flinched, but he never lifted a finger to move her out of the way. He might be furious, but he was still a gentleman, and just a smidge of the tension I was holding in my shoulders relaxed.

"Sit back down, big brother. We're nowhere near done with this meeting and won't be until you take it seriously enough to listen to what Patty is proposing."

"This is my inn, Janine. And I'm not losing it to some investment scheme."

"Everybody in this room knows it's your fucking inn, Hunter," she snapped back, for the first time showing just a hint of frustration with her brother. "And I'm the trustee of the fund that holds the mortgage to this inn and, as such, I have the fiduciary responsibility to see that loan repaid, and the trust remain intact. We both know that what Henry is trying to pull will obliterate The Trust and leave our children with nothing. Neither of us wants that. While I believe we will eventually prevail in court. I am not convinced that the judge who issued this initial ruling isn't in the pocket of the Tabor Group. I'm not willing to risk winning too late to save this place. Once they level it to the ground, it won't matter if we get the trust back in our control."

"I would kill anyone who tries to take this place down," Hunter ground out between clenched teeth. There wasn't any doubt in my mind he meant it.

"I believe at this point you might actually be stupid enough to try," Janine said. But I can't let you ruin your daughters' lives that way either. So how about you sit down, pull your head out of your ass and listen, really listen, not just sit there and glare at her. You aren't a cartoon character, Hunter, you don't have ray beam eyes that can melt your enemies. And while I'm at it, you'd do well to remember that everyone in this room is a friend, not an enemy, but if you keep acting this way, I'm not sure how long that's going to be true." She pressed her hands to his shoulders and rose so that they were nose to nose. "Now, sit the fuck down," she gave him a gentle shove so that he fell back into the chair. "And start using that MBA you just bragged about so maybe somebody here might believe you actually have it."

He glared at his sister, and I couldn't help but admire the way she returned his stare with one equally intimidating. She didn't flinch, and I was sitting there quietly, quivering in my chair. At that point, I wanted to be anywhere but this room. I was filled with guilt for bringing my best friend into this conflict, but Patty was sitting there patiently, seemingly unfazed by the tension in the room.

After what seemed like hours, Hunter turned toward Patty and spoke. "I'm sorry, go ahead." He didn't sound sorry to me, but I was going to take this as a win. "How does this partnership, as you call it, work?"

Patty cleared her throat and took a sip of coffee before continuing. "I've spoken with the development team, and they've agreed to come here to meet you on Monday morning. They understand how busy you are, so a trip to Denver would be impractical. Of course, it will also give them an opportunity to become more familiar with the property. As a side note, one of the partners was a guest here last winter and fell in love with the place."

Hunter nodded, and his lips twitched in what possibly, maybe, could be an attempt at a smile. Winning.

"The details of the partnership are yours to negotiate. Each one is different based on needs and goals. But the basics are that the agreement forms an LLC. Shares would be divided so that you always maintain majority control and each interested party has a stake. In your case, I imagine you need The Trust to be included, and you could also give the girls shares as well if you wanted. The development's stake is usually about thirty percent, and their profit comes from the dividends on the shares. Over time, you buy back the shares and keep more of the profits. As I said before, most investments last from five to ten years. If you're as successful as I think you should be, you'll be back to sole owner in five or six years and maybe at that point you and Amber can choose to put her money to work for the business when she eventually sells the house in Denver."

I could see the wheels turning behind Janine's eyes as she relaxed into her chair. She met my gaze and smiled, nodding at me. My chest burned, and I felt a brief glimmer of hope, like we might actually be okay.

"I don't mean to be blunt," Janine said, leaning forward in her chair.

"Please do, I wouldn't want it any other way," Patty responded, offering Janine a polite smile.

"Why are you trying to help us? I know this is a business deal for you, but I sense there's more to it than that."

"Darn, and I thought I was maintaining my professional mask so well." Patty laughed and steepled her hands under her chin. "You're right, it is a business deal, and one I believe in. I wouldn't have put my reputation on the line with the partners if I didn't. But Amber is one of my dearest friends, and I will do anything and everything I can to help her. She wants to help you, and that's all I need to know. There's something special about this place. I felt it the moment I walked through the door the day I came to pick her up."

"Amber can attest that I'm a city girl through and through. I'm usually only interested in modern luxury hotels with ocean views. Ones that serve drinks with cute little umbrellas in them by a pool. But there's something special here even I can appreciate. And last but certainly not least, I hate Lance with an intensity only surpassed by my friend here, and any opportunity I have to fuck with him I will. He doesn't care who he hurts to get what he wants. He'll ruin this lovely little town, and I'll be damned if I'll stand by and watch it all burn without trying to stop it."

Janine's smile lit up the room. Apparently, Patty had nailed the answer. Janine stood and held out her hand. "We have a deal. Set up the meeting for Monday. Let me know what time and I'll have our lawyer here as well. Let them know the urgency of our situation, please. I don't want a lot of dicking around."

My smile matched Janine's, and the tightness that had been in my chest for days released so I could finally take a full breath. Maybe I'd actually helped. But my moment of euphoria came to a crashing halt when Hunter stood and spoke. "No. Damn it. I'm not interested. You are not going to steamroll me on this, sis; you know how I feel." He turned toward me next. "You know how I feel too, Amber. We've talked about this. More than once. I set my boundaries, and you've trampled them with no regard for me or my daughters. This is not what I want or need from a relationship."

My mouth fell open, and I felt as if my chest had just been cleaved open with a rusty ax. Maybe I was stupid to fall in love so fast, but I'd opened my heart to this man and his family. The first time I'd loved anyone in years. And it sure felt like I'd just been cast aside when the only thing I'd done was try to help the people I loved. Wasn't that the right thing to do?

"I'm sorry you came all this way for nothing, Patty. They should have known better." Without another word, Hunter turned and stormed out of the office. And quite possibly out of my life.

# 34

# Fuming

## Hunter

Ifumed out of the office feeling like everyone I loved had betrayed
me. Janine and Amber both knew my boundaries and apparently didn't give a damn about me enough to respect them. Janine,
obviously, I couldn't get rid of, but Amber was another story altogether.
Despite knowing better, I'd let her into my heart and, yes, I loved her.
But how she repaid that love was unacceptable. I told her flat out that the
inn was off limits. It was a part of me that had to remain separate from
whatever we had, and not only had she trampled all over that line, she'd
brought her fucking friend in to boot.

Janine I was stuck with, but Amber, she was optional. And even as that
thought crossed mind, I knew it wouldn't be that simple. In a matter of
weeks, she'd taken up residence in my heart, and it would hurt like hell to
lose her. Not only would I have to get over her myself, not something I
could do quickly, and I knew that all too well. But my girls would be hurt
too. How could I have been so irresponsible as to have allowed her into
this family? Amy was going to be devastated, and Snow would be pissed
that she had lost another woman she trusted.

My head was spinning so fast I didn't know what to think. I could
picture that feelings wheel in the therapist's office I took Meg and Elizabeth to after Jenn died. All the fucking red and orange emotions whirling
around inside me all at once. Violated. Furious. Hurt. Deceived. Anxious.
Confused. Bitter. Betrayed. Lonely. Disrespected. Foolish. Afraid. It was
like a roulette wheel with that damned little ball bouncing in and out, setting off another emotion before I'd processed anything.

I grabbed my keys off the table and slammed the door behind me. I
couldn't even stay in my own home. I knew if I did, I'd say something
I'd regret. It might be over with Amber, but I wouldn't be cruel. I needed

time to sort things out. This is why I didn't want to be in a relationship, because I never had any practice at them. Jenn was the only woman I'd ever been with.

I pulled the door of the truck shut with enough force to shake the whole damn thing. "Fuck," I screamed at the top of my lungs, drawing it out until my throat was raw and couldn't handle the strain. I jammed the key into the ignition and turned it so hard that I might have bent the key. I felt like a spring coiled so tight it would explode in all directions and slammed my fist repeatedly against the dash until pain shot up my arm.

I exhaled and flopped against the headrest. Exhaling again, I put my truck in drive and sped out of the inn parking lot. With no real thought, I headed out of town on the road toward Breckenridge. My mind raced with everything that had happened over the past few weeks, and I couldn't grasp where or why everything had gone so wrong.

Before I realized it, I'd passed the spot Leo told me he'd crashed into Amber, putting most of this shit show in motion. It took some effort, but I pushed aside the irrational fury I had toward Leo for being so fucking careless as to hit her in the first place. If he hadn't, my life would have been a hell of a lot less complicated than it was now. I wouldn't feel like I was being torn to pieces feeling unfaithful to Jenn and not wanting to give up on a woman who now holds my entire heart in her palm.

The forest and mountains blurred as I continued to drive. Where I was going, I didn't have a clue. Eventually, I'd have to turn around in order to pick up the girls from school. They were the only reason I had to go back. If it weren't for them, I could abandon it all. Pretend it never happened and disappear into the wilderness, never to be seen or heard from again. A coward's way out. I wasn't a coward, never had been, but right now it held a definite appeal.

Eventually, I found myself driving through the streets of Breckenridge, taking in the fancy lodges and retail spaces. Watching tourists flock from one spot to the next, huddled in their designer outfits. A fucking waste of money. I hadn't been skiing in years, but a nondescript black bib, an old wool sweater and maybe a shell that doubled as a raincoat if the wind was up or the temperature down worked just fine. I was there to ski, not to pose for a social media reel. Maybe that was my problem. If I were a little more conscious of the image of the inn, maybe I'd attract more guests and wouldn't have to sweat whether I could make it one more year.

Now that I'd had time to digest it, some of what Patty said made sense. We could do a better job of marketing the inn. There was still no way I was going into business with anyone, supposed 'angel' or not, but if I talk-ed to Snow about it I bet she would have some ideas about social media and Janet's degree was in marketing so maybe she could contribute too. I couldn't ask too much of her, though. She had her own troubles to get through.

I pulled my truck into a filling station and grabbed a cup of coffee be-fore turning back toward Homer Pass. I would have to rely on winning the legal battle. It was my only option to do this on my own. I'd talk to Amber when I got back to the inn. I owed her an apology for losing my shit. I could let her know I still wanted her, but this part of me wasn't available. If that wasn't good enough, I'd just have to accept it and move on. If it were and she could be satisfied with what I was willing to give her, then maybe we could make this work.

I made it to the Homer Pass School just in time to get the girls, only to watch as the stream of children that exited the building when the bell sounded did not include them.

I waited at the curb for five minutes after the last child left, growing more anxious and pissed off by the second. When I realized I hadn't seen Janine's kids exit either, I dug my phone out of the center console where I'd stashed it. It wasn't out of the question that Janine had picked them all up, but we usually discussed it first. When I powered up the phone, I found a text from my sister.

> Janine: Picked the girls up from school early. I couldn't let Amber leave without giving her a chance to say goodbye. Don't think the discussion is over.

I loved my sister, but the discussion was over.

A knot formed in the center of my chest that made me want to puke. Apparently, the discussion wasn't the only thing that was over. If Amber needed to say goodbye, that meant she was heading back to Denver.

I didn't want her to go. I just needed her to understand my boundaries. I put the truck into drive and sped back toward the inn. With any luck, I could catch her before she left. I had the feeling that if I didn't, she wouldn't be coming back. The more I had time to calm down and think about it, that was a possibility I didn't want to become a reality.

# 35

# Tears

## Amber

As soon as I heard the door slam, I knew it was over. There was no coming back from this, and the tears I had been valiantly trying to hold back finally gushed out. I was immediately wrapped up in two sets of arms. One old friend and one new, and I was equally thankful for both of them because I didn't think one person would be enough to hold me together. I thought finding Lance had broken me, but this was a whole new level of being shattered.

"It's okay, honey. Let it all out," Patty whispered as she stroked my hair.

"The minute I see him, I am going to rip him a new one so big he'll never be able to sit down again. That fucking fool," Janine growled, and as badly as Hunter had hurt me, I felt sorry for him, because there was no doubt in my mind she was serious.

We sat for a moment. The only sounds were my sobbing, and I couldn't seem to bring it under control.

"Set up the meeting for Monday," Janine told Patty, speaking over my shoulder. "He'll be here if I have to chain him to that chair and beat him to a bloody pulp."

Patty snorted as she continued to comfort me. "I can't do that, Janine. As much as I want to help and believe in what I just proposed, if I show up here on Monday and the partners see the same Hunter I just witnessed, the meeting will be over before it starts. And in my experience, there won't be a second chance. They're professionals, but they also make their decisions based on gut feeling and personalities, and if they don't believe Hunter is fully committed, they'll walk away without a second thought."

Janine let out a heavy sigh. "I'm sorry. You're right. I had no right to put you in that kind of position. I'm just so damn desperate." She pulled back from our hug with another sigh. "Can you at least give me a couple of days to bring him around before you tell them we're not interested?"

"That I can easily do," Patty agreed. "Do you honestly think you can change his mind?"

Janine shook her head, and her lips tipped up in an ironic smile. "I can be very persuasive, and while we're both Holmes with a stubborn streak a mile wide, Hunter loves those girls and sooner or later he will see this is his best way to ensure their future. I only hope he figures it out quickly."

"We all do," Patty agreed.

I needed to pull myself together and get my things. With any luck, I could be packed and gone before Hunter came back. I hated to leave without saying goodbye to the girls. I was going to miss them so much, but it couldn't be helped. I couldn't face Hunter, not after the things he said. If he really thought I didn't understand the place Jenn would always hold in his heart, he didn't know me at all. I was willing to accept that his past belonged to her, but if he couldn't give me all of him here and now, this would never work. I took a deep breath and pulled myself away from Patty.

Before I could stand, Janine's phone rang, and I was more than angry at myself for hoping it was Hunter saying that he'd changed his mind and he was sorry.

"Hi honey," Janine said, confirming how stupid I'd been to hope it was Hunter. "What's wrong? You don't usually call me instead of your dad?"

The urge to butt into the call, because it was obviously one of the girls, was strong, but I reminded myself I wasn't welcome to cross that boundary, as Hunter termed it. Not anymore. "Patty, could you help me pack up my things?" I asked her as I stood to leave and give Janine privacy, but she held up a finger to keep me in place.

"You did?" Janine continued, her brow furrowed with concern. "Of course, I'll come and pick you and your sisters up." Her hand covered her mouth, and I watched as moisture collected at the corners of her eyes. "That's okay, Snow. Don't worry. I won't let Amber leave before you get here to say goodbye. I'll be there in ten minutes. I'll call the office to let them know I'm picking you up."

She ended the call, and I couldn't help the stunned stare I shot in her direction. "The girls want to come say goodbye. I hope you don't mind. I couldn't tell them no. Snow was pretty upset."

Had Hunter already texted her and let her know I was leaving? That took care of any hope I had that he'd change his mind. "I don't mind at all. I didn't want to leave without talking to them, but I have to leave before Hunter comes back if I can."

"I'll be quick. I promise." She nodded.

"I can't believe Hunter would text her at school and tell her I was leaving. I know he was angry, but he never struck me as that heartless."

A tear escaped from Janine's eye, and she thumbed it away quickly. "You're right. He's not, and he didn't." She paused for a moment with a quick glance in Patty's direction before a decisive look crossed her worried face. "Snow said she 'saw' you leaving and knew that she had to get here as soon as she could. She snuck into the bathroom with her phone, not wanting to waste time trying to explain the unexplainable to her teacher." She reached out and placed a hand on my arm. "I know it sounds crazy, but her mother was the same way, and her grandmother before that. The Howard women all seem to just know things sometimes. Elizabeth can probably explain it to you if you're interested. Lord knows I've tried to understand it but can't."

Patty gave me a quick glance, and I to her, but as strange as it sounded, I believed her. There were a lot of things in this world I couldn't explain. What's one more to add to the list?

The girls came charging into Hunter's room just as Patty and I finished stuffing the last of three trash bags full of my things. The three of them wrapped themselves around my waist and talked over each other in a kind of chaos of emotions that was both heartbreaking and heartwarming at the same time.

I sat down on the side of the bed to get closer to eye level with them all. "I'm really sorry, girls. I'm going to miss you all so much."

"Please don't go, Amber," Amy said through trembling lips and tear-stained cheeks that nearly ripped what little that was left of my heart out of my chest. "I'll make Daddy say he's sorry, and he won't do it again. Whatever it was. I promise."

Patty caught my eye, and she dragged two of the bags toward the door, mouthing that she'd meet me outside whenever I was ready. I nodded, which was the most I could manage. I had to work hard to keep my voice clear. Now that the girls were here, it was so much harder than I thought it would be.

"I know you'd try, Amy, but I'm not sure this is something we could get over with a sorry." Her sobs grew deeper, and I pulled her as close to my chest as I could without suffocating her. "I'm really going to miss reading you bedtime stories." As soon as the words left my mouth, I knew I'd made a huge mistake. This wasn't about me; it was about them. Amy's deepened sobs only confirmed how large my fuck-up was.

"How will I get to sleeeeep?" Amy wailed. The words she said were interrupted with sobs and sniffles, breaking another piece of my shattered heart.

"Oh, baby, the same way you did before I came. Your daddy will read to you, just like before."

"I'm mad at Daddy. I don't want him to read to me. I want you," she cried into my now snot and tear-stained shoulder. I stroked her hair and kissed the top of her head.

"I know. I know," I murmured into her silky golden locks as she calmed. "You can call me anytime you miss me and want to talk, okay? Elizabeth has my number, but you have to ask Daddy first."

"Really?"

"Really."

"But what if he says no?"

"Then you'll have to wait until he says yes. Daddy's the boss, and he loves you more than anything in this world. He always wants what's best for you."

"Is that why you're going?" Meg asked so softly I barely heard her. "He loves us more than he loves you? Are we the reason you have to go?"

I shifted Amy onto one hip and pulled Meg into a hug. "That's not true. Never think for a minute that you guys are responsible for this. What happened, the reasons, is between me and your dad. They're adult things and things you guys don't need to worry about for a long time yet. I love your dad, but sometimes grown-ups need more than love. And the way your dad loves you, that's different. There is nothing your dad wouldn't do to protect you and keep you safe, and that will never change. There's nothing you can do that will ever make your dad love you less. I'll tell you a secret. The way your dad loves you is one reason I love your dad."

"So, you still love him?" Elizabeth asked, deep furrows lining her fore-head. "Even after what he said, and how stupid he was?"

"Elizabeth, your dad isn't stupid, and I don't know what you think he said, but yes, I love him. Just like I love all of you, and it doesn't matter that I won't be here anymore because I always will."

"I don't think he said anything, Amber. I saw it. You and Aunt Janine and your friend Patty were trying to show him how he could save the inn, and he was too stubborn to listen to you. And right before he stormed out of the office like a two-year-old having a tantrum, he got angry and turned on you. He said, 'This is not what I want or need from a relationship', didn't he?"

My jaw dropped. If that wasn't exactly what he said, it was close enough. Close enough that they stung every bit as much hearing them from her mouth as they did from his.

"I know things sometimes, Amber. I can't explain it, but I do. Sometimes I hear my mom talking to me, though I'm not as sure about that because it's usually when I'm sad and need cheering up. But right in the middle of math class, I saw my dad hurt you and say stupid things he didn't really mean, and I knew you were leaving. So yes, my dad is stupid sometimes, and this is one of those times because you're the best thing that's happened to him since he met my mom."

A tear rolled down my cheek. I just couldn't hold back anymore. I needed to go. I didn't want to leave these girls, but there was no way I was strong enough to face Hunter. Especially if he was still in a foul mood. "I'm sorry, girls. Patty's waiting for me, and I have to go." I hugged Amy and kissed the top of her head and repeated the process with Meg and then moved on to Elizabeth and did the same, not knowing how she would respond. She surprised me by hugging me the hardest of all and kissing my cheek.

"I hope this isn't goodbye forever, and if it isn't, it would really mean a lot to me if you'd call me Snow."

I looked into her eyes but couldn't focus through the tears in mine. All I could do was nod. I wrapped all three in one last hug and then grabbed the last bag and rushed for the car. I couldn't turn around and look at them because if I did, I'd never find the strength to go.

# 36

# Facing the Firing Squad

## Hunter

Pulling into the circular drive at the front of the inn, I took the steps two at a time. Amber's rental was still in the lot out front, so maybe I wasn't too late. I burst through the door, a man on a mission.

"The prodigal son returns," Janet commented from behind the reception desk.

"Where's Amber?" I asked, ignoring that Janet's presence behind the desk was not a good sign. There was no reason for her to be there other than Snow being so pissed at me she was refusing to work.

Janet made a show of looking at her watch before answering. "My guess is halfway back to Denver by now." Her brow lifted in a way that reminded me of the look I got from her sister when I asked a question I should have known better than to ask.

"What are you doing here?" I asked, not wanting to continue the Amber discussion and hoping for some insight about what I would walk into with my girls.

"You're welcome. I'm happy to help," she answered, her sarcasm a pretty fair indication that Janine had brought her up to speed on this morning's shitshow.

"Thank you," I said grudgingly even though I was glad she was here to help. She struggled to be at the inn because it reminded her of Jenn. Welcome to my life. Every. Fucking. Day. "I do appreciate the help, but I'd appreciate a little less of the attitude. I've had quite enough for one day."

"Oh, you're nowhere near done with attitude, former brother-in-law of mine. You have three furious, broken-hearted females sitting on the couch in your living room. My guess is you're in for days if not weeks of attitude. And the way I heard it, you deserve every ounce of sass you get."

I bit the inside of my cheek to keep myself from saying what I wanted to say. If I lost my shit now, I'd have to go back outside and walk around the inn a dozen times before I was calm enough to face my daughters. They could say whatever they wanted within reason, but I didn't need this from Janet. "I suppose I have my sister to thank for updating you on today's drama."

"Nope, Snow called and told me all about it. Told me she wasn't up to working today and could I please come and cover the desk. From the sounds of it, you told Amber to mind her own business and, if she couldn't do it, she should leave. I don't blame her a bit for going. I might have even broken a few things on the way out the door just to spite your arrogant ass."

"Janine had no right to tell Snow what happened today, certainly not a warped version of it."

"Your sister didn't say a word to Snow. And neither did Amber before you jump to another delusion."

"Well, Snow found out about it somehow."

"She did, and I'm sure she'll tell you how if she decides to speak to you at all."

I was sure that was going to be the way of things. My oldest was already adept at the silent treatment. I could deal with whatever my girls had to say, or not, but I was done talking about this with Janet. I expected her to understand. The one person who could empathize with my grief, but I guess not. "Seriously, Janet, thanks for helping, but we don't have any arrivals tonight and only a handful of guests for dinner. If you've got something else you need to do, you can head out. I can manage it from here."

"No offense, Hunter, but I think you'd better focus on your girls tonight. I've got the desk, and Hector will be here in about thirty minutes to handle dinner as soon as he's done at the diner. They need to understand, and honestly, I think maybe you could use some time to reflect on things yourself."

"What the hell do you mean by that?"

"Stop blaming my sister for your unhappiness."

"Oh, for the love of…," I could hear my voice raise enough that I'm sure the girls could hear me out back, but I was just too far gone to care. "Stop with the bullshit, Janet. I have never blamed Jenn for anything. It's my fault. It's always been my fault, and it's always going to be my fault. I blame myself, and there's not a fucking thing I can do to change it. Your sister is in the fucking ground because of me. It should be the other way around."

I could feel the muscles in my neck straining, and my temples were throbbing. I was so done with this bullshit. What the hell was with everyone today getting into my business and telling me how I was fucking up my life? "I do my best every day to make it up to her. To give the girls the best I can. To keep this inn alive, to keep her dream alive."

"Jenn's gone, Hunter." I could tell she was fighting hard to hold back tears and losing the battle. She exhaled slowly before she continued. "As hard as it is for both of us, she's gone. And I pray every night to whoever or whatever is listening that she's happy and in a better place. You have to live your life, Hunter. You have a right to happiness, and you've got to stop using her as an excuse not to go after it. I wish I'd listened to her better when we had her. She had a gift. The same one my mother and grandmother had. And now Snow has it too. She knew she was going to die young, and she told anyone who'd listen to make sure you didn't die with her. The girls deserve all of you, Hunter. Amber deserved all of you. Not just the little part of you that you allow not to be stuck in that grave with her. If you want to keep her dream alive. Live. It's the only way. Live every day like the gift that it is."

She walked around from behind the counter and hugged me and kissed my cheek. Anger still coursed through every vein and fired on every nerve in my body, but there were no more words. I've felt dead since the day she died, and it's been a battle every fucking day to stay just alive enough to be there for my daughters. Except for the past few weeks after Amber arrived. Now death called again. At least it was familiar.

"Go be with your girls, Hunter," she said, taking hold of my shoulders and giving them a gentle shake to emphasize her words. "Live. Show my sister you loved her by living and loving like she would have done if she could have. It's something I have to learn to do as well. Maybe we can help each other figure it out along the way, huh?"

Exhaling with a bob of my head, I gave her a quick hug. "If I haven't figured it out by now, I'm not liking our chances," I said with a humorless laugh. "Thanks, though. We can try. I'm so done with being pissed at the world."

"I know," she said, patting my shoulder affectionately. "Me too."

Walking away in silence, Janet's words echoed in my head like a coyote's howl through a canyon. I stopped in the kitchen and poured myself a cup of coffee. One sip confirmed it was the same pot I'd brewed this morning.

I could have dumped it down the sink and brewed a new one, but drinking this would be an excellent punishment. Just nowhere near what I deserved.

"Ugh," I groaned, taking another sip of the bitter liquid. After dumping the rest of the coffee into the sink, I took my time making another pot. Honestly, with the way my stomach was roiling, it was the last thing I wanted. The truth was, I wasn't ready to face my girls. It was a chickenshit thing to do, but that was me, feathers and all.

When I walked from the kitchen into the living room, I was surprised to find a fire roaring in the fireplace. Snow had never started a fire before, and it was something I didn't want them doing on their own. Tonight was not the night to mention it. They were all huddled together on the couch. Snow in the middle with Meg's head on her left shoulder and Amy's on her right. I stood there just looking at them and couldn't figure out what in the world I'd ever done that earned me such a precious gift as the three of them. Was I really guarding myself so closely that I was depriving them of the father they deserved? They deserved the absolute best.

"Hello girls," I said as I walked toward the couch. I wasn't completely surprised that Snow and Meg didn't respond, but Amy was always happy to see me. As I walked around to face them, a dagger went through the center of my heart. Their blank stares into the fire were rimmed with red, swollen eyes, and tears trailed down their cheeks. I had done this. Even I couldn't deny that this was all my fault.

With a heavy sigh, I sat down on the coffee table in front of them, but they all continued to stare right past me into the fire. Not one so much as spared me a glance. I sat for another moment or two, but the silence was eating me alive.

"I guess we've all had a pretty bad day, huh?" Silence. Silence, like I didn't even exist.

"Can we at least talk about it? We've always been able to talk about what bothers us."

Silence still reigned supreme until Amy finally broke down and looked in my direction. Her tiny brows were drawn together, and her eyes would have burned a hole straight through me if she could. Her bottom lip quivered, and then her words twisted the dagger in my heart even deeper. "Why, Daddy, why? Why did you have to be mean to Amber and make her run away?"

What in the ever-lovin' fuck was I supposed to say to that? So of course I went for the standard parental avoidance method. "I'm going to miss Amber too, but what happened is grown-up stuff…"

"Liar," she screamed, pushing back the blanket they were cuddled under, and standing with her little fists balled so tight I wasn't entirely sure she wasn't going to take a shot at my jaw. I would have deserved it. "If you were going to miss her, you wouldn't have been mean. You would have said you're sorry, and she'd still be here. But you didn't, and I hate you." She turned and ran toward her room.

"Amy…" I called after her.

"I hate you. I don't ever want to talk to you again," she yelled as she disappeared down the hallway.

I started to get up to go after her.

"Don't," Snow's sharp command stopped me from getting to my feet. "She's angry, and she doesn't want to talk to you. If you go after her now, it will only make things worse."

She moved to get up. "I'll go check on her," Meg offered, stepping past me without making eye contact. "I don't want to talk to him either."

Once Meg left, Snow finally lifted her head and looked me directly in the eyes. The silent treatment was easier to take. She looked so much like her mother. And nothing good ever came after I saw the same creased brow, narrow eyes and set jaw on her mother.

"How could you do that to someone who you love? How could you say those things to someone who loves you and was trying to help you? I don't understand, Dad. It's a side of you I've never seen before, and I saw you when you were at your worst after Mom died. You were angry at the world and ready to burn it to the ground, but you never treated the ones you loved, the ones that love you, like that."

Her words were hitting far too close to home, and coupled with the talking to Janet had just given me, I was on defense. I didn't want to be. I wanted to make things right by my daughters, but I couldn't seem to help myself. "I don't know what your aunt or Amber told you…"

"Stop it, Dad," she shouted. "Nobody told me anything. I saw it all. Every word you said. It was like I was right there in the office with you."

I wanted to dismiss this as foolishness. To think that it was just a way she could put a guilt trip on me for something she obviously was very upset about but I couldn't. Her mother had a way of knowing things there was no reasonable way to know, and I'd seen Snow do the same thing since she was a little girl. Even more so recently. Still, my rational brain couldn't concede what my eyes had seen. Stupidly, I went with the rational approach. "I don't know how because you were in school."

"Jesus, Dad." She said with perhaps the most intense eye roll I'd ever seen her manage, and she was world class with the eye roll thing. I ignored her language because I knew it would get worse, and today just wasn't the day. "You know Mom could sense things sometimes. Like the time when I stepped on a nail working with you on the third floor. She ran into the room about two seconds after it happened. That was a pretty quick response from someone who'd been a mile away at the grocery store, don't you think?"

"Coincidence. She was worried anytime you were with me because she knew I was a shit father."

"Aargh," she bellowed, her face turning a dangerous shade of beetroot red. "Stop being an ass. You know it was more than a mother's intuition. She knew she was going to die, and even though she didn't want to burden a thirteen-year-old, she knew she didn't have a choice. For months before she died, she kept telling me I had to make sure you kept living." Tears rolled down her face in waves. She did a remarkable job of keeping her voice strong despite the tremor beneath. "I'm sorry I've done such a shit job, Dad. I keep trying, but I don't know what the hell to do."

Liquid streamed down my face. Snow was such a special young woman, and I felt even more like shit that she'd had to bear this burden because of me. I moved to pull her into the hug I knew she desperately needed.

"Don't," she stopped me for the second time tonight. "I love you, but I'm still too damn mad at you." She wiped the tears from her face with such force that I could tell she was just as close to raging at the world as I was. She held my gaze so I could see her conviction. "I have the same gift Mom had. I've thought so for a while. I get feelings about things. Sometimes it's like someone's whispering in my ear, giving me a hint about what's going to happen. But today was totally different. I never believed Mom when she told me that her grandmother could actually 'see' things, not just 'sense' them. But, holy crap, Dad, it's real. Right in the middle of algebra, I zoned out, and I was sitting in that meeting with you. That's how I know what happened."

Panic crashed into me, and all I wanted to do was hide. I was physically there, and I didn't even know what had happened. Why the words I said came out of my mouth. I was embarrassed because I couldn't fix what was wrong. Frustrated for the same reason and exhausted from all the responsibility that sat on my shoulders.

I was standing there in front of my daughter. My precious Snowflake, and what she saw she didn't like. I needed her to appreciate what I was trying to do. I needed her to understand me. "Then you know everything

I did and said was for you and your sisters. To keep your mother's dream alive. I could never disrespect your mother by letting someone else interfere with her dream."

"Men," she huffed, sounding remarkably like her mother. "A part of her will always live on in this inn, but it was only a small part of her dream. She dreamed of us being a happy family. Even after she was gone. Especially after she was gone. That was the most important part of her dream. You're a wonderful dad, and I've never thought for a minute you didn't love us and did your best for us. But all of us know you're not happy because you're trying so hard to do what you think she wants; you end up doing the opposite because there's none of you in it."

Apparently, my teenage daughter was the adult in the room tonight. My chest was tight with guilt and sorrow, knowing that she should never have been in this position. My selfishness and stupidity had brought us to this point. I still didn't have a fucking clue how to fix it.

"What do you think I need to do?" Her quizzical stare communicated I might lack sincerity. "I want to know what you think, Snow. I'm not going to promise I'll do it, but I'll listen to what you think."

"How about we start with you apologizing to Amber and we can move on from there."

That was not at all the answer I was expecting. I thought she'd be on me about refinancing, but this woman we'd known for less than a month was at the apex of the get Dad's head out of his ass to do list. "Really? Why is apologizing to someone we've barely just met the first thing you thought of?"

With the long-suffering attitude my daughter had perfected, she droned out her reply. "Because she's the one, Dad. You need to apologize and make it a good one if you want any chance at her taking your grumpy ass back."

Ignoring the grumpy part because that was at least partially true, I focused on the more important part. "What do you mean 'she's the one'?"

"Because I've seen her before. Before she ever crossed our threshold." Her eyes darted down to her lap, deciding whether to add the next part. "And because Mom told me she was."

Knowing things wasn't new to me. I'd heard it many times with Jenn, but this was a bit more than that. "Mom told you?"

She nodded. "I hear her sometimes. Usually, it's like a whisper of wind, and I can't say for sure if I'm just thinking it or maybe wishing it. But the day Leo dropped her off, when I checked Amber in, I heard her as clearly as if she was standing right next to me. 'Give her room 108' is what she said. It's why I gave it to Amber. She promised I'd know, and I did. The way you guys were looking at each other didn't hurt either. I was too young to notice if you ever looked at Mom like that, but I bet you did. She's the one, Dad. And I don't know if we can do it without her, but none of us really wants to try. She loves you. She loves all of us. And she deserves to be your one and only. I know you loved Mom. Mom loved you too, which is why she wants you to be happy now. She wants all of us to be happy. But you can't be happy, none of us can, until you join us here and stop holding on to back there."

"So, all I need to do is apologize and you will talk to me again?"

"Nope." There was enough mischief in the small smile that touched her lips to make me believe she might have already started to forgive me. "You need to show her you can give her all your heart. There's enough room for all of us there. Even Mom's memory."

I told her I'd try to, and I would. I just didn't know if I could. One thing I knew was that I couldn't do it without cleaning up a few loose ends. The sun had long set, so it would have to wait until tomorrow, but once I dropped the girls off for school in the morning, I had some questions that needed answering.

# 37

# *Visiting Hours*

## *Hunter*

My tires crunched over the icy coldness of the snow beneath my truck as I pulled into the parking lot. A bright blue sky dotted with wispy white clouds met my gaze as I looked up to the heavens. It was a beautiful, cold, early winter day. December twelfth. Jenn's birthday. Or what would have been her fortieth. She only made it to thirty-six.

Early on, I came here often after dropping the girls off at school. It seemed to keep me sane. At least that's what I told myself. I'm sure there were those around town who thought the opposite. Out here alone, talking to myself, staring at a stone. Just another poor soul who had one too many terrible things tossed at him. Overwhelmed and swept away in the stormy seas of life.

My boots squeaked atop the frigid crystals of snow covering the drive. Somehow, this path always seemed to be plowed where the others in this place were not. My lips pressed into a thin lined, sad smile. Somehow, I suspected Leo was behind that. I might not always show it. Who was I kidding? I never showed it, but I appreciated what he and others did to keep me afloat. I would have drowned in an ocean of despair if not for him and Janine. And my girls. Always my girls.

Out here in the open, the wind had blown away most of the precious powder dumped on Homer Pass since the day before Thanksgiving. There were only a few inches of hard, crusty snow meeting my knees as I sank down in front of the stone.

Jennifer Marie Howard-Holmes
Loving Wife and Mother
December 12, 1984–August 6, 2021

I set down the small balsam wreath the girls and I had bought at the base of the stone. The cold and the steady breeze already had my eyes watering and nose leaking like an old Ford. It had nothing to do with the hurricane of emotions spinning in my chest.

That's my story and I'm sticking to it.

"Hey." I swallowed; my voice thick with emotion, barely better than it had been three years ago when my world fell apart. When all our worlds collapsed. "It's been a while, but it's been pretty hectic." I couldn't hold back a wry chuckle. "Of course, you already know that if you can hear me talking right now, so I don't know why I even bother speaking. I guess it's more for me than you, but you'd tell me that figures because I always had a selfish side."

"You told me you were teasing me when you said that, but I know the truth in it. I could be selfish, and honestly, Jenn, I guess that's why I came to see you today. The girls probably would have liked to help me deliver the wreath, but I needed to talk to you alone." I must have been losing my mind. My heart raced. I wasn't wearing gloves, and it was freaking five de-grees out, and my palms were sweaty, so of course I avoided why I came, and slipped into my usual routine.

"The girls are doing good. Snow is running the inn like she was born for it." Steam rose in front of me as I huffed out a laugh. "Of course, she was born for it. She was born there, so why wouldn't she be? I'd be lost without her, and I know that's too much responsibility to put on a kid, but I think she'd never forgive me if I tried to take it away from her. She's so much like you. Not just her blonde hair and blue eyes but her take no shit attitude. God. I could really use you now. Lord knows, I don't know what to do with her half the time." A shiver rattled my spine, and I used the sleeve of my coat to clear the mucus leaking down my face. I didn't even have to close my eyes to see the head shake and sigh from Jenn would have given me if I'd done that in front of her. "We were actually sold-out Black Friday weekend. And of course, I hadn't hired seasonal help yet. She was a rock star babe. You'd be so proud."

"Meg's Meg. Quiet as ever, and just goes with the flow. I don't know if she purposely tries not to get noticed, but she's so observant, never misses a thing. When she does speak, you better listen. And Amy, well, I really wish you were around for her because I'm afraid that you're only pictures and stories to her. She was so young when we lost you, and I so want her to know her mom."

"Christ, they all look like you, Jenn. Even if I wanted to forget, how could I with three mini versions of you staring back at me every day? Snow, with her dogged determination; Meg, with her quiet strength; and Amy, with a heart that's so full of love and joy you can't help but smile when you're in her presence. All I can see is you and wonder if I had anything to do with making them at all. I guess they'll all thank you someday for that."

My freaking eyes were leaking, and when I opened my mouth to continue talking, only a croaking noise escaped around the colossal lump in my throat. I inhaled a giant snotty sniff and wiped my nose with the back of my sleeve. Again. "Yeah, I know. Such a guy." I could hear her in my head. Her soft voice filled with laughter and happiness whenever I did something like a caveman.

A gust of wind washed over me, kicking up a swirl of icy snow crystals like a mini winter tornado. A shiver ran through my body that had nothing to do with the temperature. And I swore I could hear a voice. Jenn's voice.

*Stop it, Hunter.*

"What?"

*You know 'what'. You didn't come here to apologize to me or to feel sorry for yourself. Tell me why you came, babe. Don't be scared.*

"I'm not scared."

*Mm, hmm. You always beat around the bush when talking about the hard things.*

I let out a long, slow breath. Fog billowed where the oxygen escaped my lungs and mixed with the frosty air in the lonely cemetery. "I've met someone. I swore I never would. You were it for me, Jenny. My forever love. Even though you told me I needed to if anything bad happened to you. Shit… Why do I feel so awful about it?"

*Because you've got this fucked-up notion in your head that it's cheating on me, and you're an honorable man and would never do that to me. To anyone. But I've got a newsflash for you, my love. I'm gone. I didn't want to be, but I am, and it's been over three years now. It's time, baby. It's time.*

All I could do was shake my head as tears continued to stream down my frozen cheeks. A part of me was ready, but there was still a part that was afraid to move on.

*Tell me about Amber.*

"How do you know her name?"

I swear I can hear her laugh whispering through the trees. *Stop avoiding the question.*

"Well, Leo plowed her into a snowbank and then brought her to the inn the afternoon before Thanksgiving."

*I know all that, silly. Tell me how you feel; why did you show up here today instead of just yelling at me from wherever you happen to be when you need my advice?*

"Because you never answer me there. The only place I ever seem to hear you is here."

*I'm always with you, Hunter, and always will be, but get back to Amber. Tell me.*

"The girls seem to like her. Snow actually set her up in our room. She's never done that before. She told me last night that you were the one who told her to do it. Really? And oh God, Jenn, Amy just adores her, but that's probably because she spent an hour with that little cherub playing Barbies and reads to her every night before bed. The poor kid is starving for attention, and I know I don't give her enough. It's just so hard without you. Trying to keep the inn afloat. Making sure their homework is done. Bringing in a little more money by staying with the fire department. Even though every damn time I hear the alert tones, it takes me back to you. I can't hear that fucking tone without your broken body flashing in front of my eyes. Damn it Jenn. Why did you leave me?"

A sob escaped me, and I swore I wouldn't let it happen this time. I swore I wouldn't break down. I swore I wouldn't blame her again for something that wasn't her fault. If anything, it was my fault. I should have gone to the bakery to pick up that cake. Not her. Another sob, deeper, more consuming, than the first, wracked my body. "I'm sorry, Jenn. I'm so, so sorry you're not here to watch them grow. I promise I'll never let them forget you. I know Snow never will, but Amy… she was so young."

I raked my fingers through my hair before scrubbing the tears from my eyes with the heels of my hands. Inhaling an icy breath, I let go of the truth I was trying to hide, even from myself.

"I think I love her, Jenn. And I feel horrible because it's supposed to be you and me raising our daughters. I feel like I'm betraying you. Cheating on you. Replacing you and being disloyal to our daughters all at the same time. And worst of all, I think I fucked it all up beyond repair. I said some stupid things yesterday. I have this wall with your name on it. I won't let anyone pass. Tell me I shouldn't take it down. That I'm doing the right thing by trying to do this on my own."

*Hunter Holmes, you listen to me and listen to me good. We were blessed with three lovely daughters and a son. My biggest regret is that you never got to meet him because I know you deserved a little bit more testosterone in your life. I was your first love, and you were mine, and nothing will ever change that. But you can't keep that from letting yourself love again. I would never deny you that. You deserve that, and our daughters deserve to feel a mother's love and not love from beyond the veil. They'll always have my love, but Amber has love to give them too. Love to give you, and you all deserve that. Take down the wall, Hunter. Take it down.*

"But…"

*No buts. Stop using my death as an excuse to pretend you're the one that died that day. You need to move on. To live and to love. Not only for our daughters but for you because you are one of the good ones, Hunter Holmes. You're far from perfect, but you are a good man, and I can tell you this. Amber needs you just as much as you need her. She's nearly lost all hope of finding love. Of finding someone she can trust with her heart. You're the one who can show her that. That's why she was sent here. That's why she's willing to give you and the girls everything she has. And don't think for a second I'm talking about the money. That's only a symbol of her heart, which is much more valuable. She needs you every bit as much as you and the girls need her.*

"What if it's too late? What if I can't figure out how to take down the wall? She went back to Denver after I wouldn't let her help bail out the inn. Told her it was my problem to solve. The inn was mine, and someday the girls. And she should respect our boundaries."

*Oh God, Hunter, sometimes you really are so dense. Would you have said that to me?*

"Of course not. The inn was yours more than anyone's. I love Amber, but she's got to understand that the inn represents you, and if I let her past that boundary, that's a betrayal I could never do to you."

*You're not listening, Hunter. Please stop and hear what I'm trying to tell you. I'm gone, and nothing on earth is mine anymore. The girls are part of my legacy, but the dead have no claim to the living. Amber will always know where the boundaries lie, but she's a kind, loving woman and unless you let her all the way in; and that means letting her save the inn if she can for you and the girls, then you don't deserve her. Fix this, Hunter. Find a way to let her in. I've never known you to be a quitter. Don't start now. Don't let her push you away just because she's scared. Sometimes being a gentleman means not taking no for an answer.*

"What do you mean by that?"

*You'll figure that out. You always do, but your first step has to be to let me go. I love you, Hunter, then and now. I always will and I'll always watch over you and the girls, but it's time to let me go. This grave is too small for all of us. Go back to the world of the living. And I mean all the way back. Take care, my love, and I know someday we will meet again. Amber too.*

Another stiff breeze raked ice chips across my cheeks and took my breath away.

"I'll try, Jenn, but you have to help me."

I listened. The wind rustled the pines in the distance, and I could hear the snow falling from their bows. "Jenn?"

I waited. I prayed to hear her again, but she was gone. This was the only place I ever heard her, and I knew I was crazy. I talked to her all the time, but when I kneeled in front of her headstone, she always answered. I could hear her voice as if she were standing next to me, but she was gone, and I shivered at the thought that she might not come back. What the hell did she mean, Amber needed us too?

I didn't know how long I'd been staring at the slab of black granite marking her grave, hoping to hear her speak to me again. Eventually, the cold took over my body, and I knew it was time to go. It wouldn't do our girls any good if I kneeled here in front of their mother's grave and froze to death. I brought two fingers to my lips and then traced the letters carved into the stone, commemorating a life cut way too short. A body six feet under frozen dirt, stolen from a family that loved and missed her every single day. But she was right. If we didn't go on living, then we dishonored her memory, and none of us wanted that. "Okay, baby. You're right. It's time, and I'll do my best. It's time to live and love again. Time to stop trying to do everything on my own."

*You can do it, Hunter. I have faith in you. I always will.*

It was just a whisper on the breeze. But I knew it was her, and that's all I needed to move on.

It was also time to tell the girls about the unborn child buried with their mother. The little brother they never got the chance to meet. A secret I've kept buried inside for too long. We never got around to discussing his name other than to agree that it would not begin with an H. William came to me, a faint murmur in my ear. No doubt that was right. I would make arrangements for the stonemason today, though I knew it would have to wait until spring. I'd let the girls decide on a verse to have inscribed for both of them.

Pushing myself up, I made my way back to the truck. I opened the door and hoisted myself into the cab. With a groan, I sank back into the seat. I blew on my fingers to warm them before scrubbing them over my stubbled face and dragging them back through my hair.

My mind was calmer now. Fixing things with Amber seemed to be the first thing I needed to do, but I didn't know where to start. Before I could sit there and lose myself in thought even longer, my phone dinged with an incoming text.

Janine: Meet me at the Bighorn in 5. You can buy me lunch as a start to earning my forgiveness.

I hesitated for a moment. I had more than just Amber's forgiveness to earn. Janine's, the girls'. Patty's too if I was being honest with myself. I didn't think I was quite ready, but I had to start somewhere. It might as well be with my sister. And at least there was less chance of things going south if we were in public.

Me: K

# 38

# Coming to Terms

## Hunter

I walked into the Bighorn a few minutes later. Janine was already seated in a corner booth. She waved me over with a half-smile hinting at her lips. I took that as a positive sign and maybe more acceptance than I deserved.

"Here," she said, pushing a steaming cup of coffee toward me. "That should help you thaw out a bit."

"Thanks." I wrapped my still stiffly frozen hands around the mug.

"Did you have a good talk with Jenn?" she asked. I looked up and met a carbon copy of my own eyes. "Something told me you'd go there today. I saw your truck in the lot when I was looking for you. I didn't want to disturb you there."

"Oh, yeah?" I shook my head. I didn't know what it was with all the women in my life having some kind of sixth sense. "And what do you need to find me for, Janine? Now is not the time or place to talk about what happened yesterday."

I could just make out the shrug of her shoulders beneath her heavy oversized sweater. "Nothing, really. And I'm not going to say a word about yesterday. Yet. I just figured that your conscience would drive you there to talk to her."

"Don't be ridiculous," I scoffed, because there was no way I was letting my little sister know just how fucking crazy I truly was. She needed me to be strong and not some nut job who visited his dead wife's grave, hoping for advice.

"Really? Because I know you well, big brother. Women around here have been throwing themselves at you for ages, hoping that you were ready to move on. Some of them didn't even care; they've even been will-ing to pity fuck you just to get you out of the funk you've been in for the last three years."

I ground my teeth at the thought of that. "I've lost my wife, and my daughters have lost their mother. Jenn was the love of my life. You don't just move on like it didn't exist. And I certainly wasn't interested in a pity fuck. How pathetic is that?"

She reached across the table, prying my hands off the mug and folding them into hers. "I know you don't just move on, Hunter. And you're too good of a man to accept anything less than something genuine. Which is why I knew I'd find you there. Amber's genuine. And real. And you love her, but you'll never be able to love her completely until you let go of Jenn."

"I don't think I can ever let go of Jenn." My stomach twisted at the words because I thought maybe I already had.

"Hunter, I know you will never stop loving her. You will never forget her. She's the mother of your daughters. But it's time to let go. You deserve to live your life, and Amber deserves to have all of your heart."

"My daughters have my heart." I sat a little taller, bristling at Janine. I was tired of hearing the same damn thing from everyone. Maybe I needed to take it to heart.

"You know what I mean. There's a love that we give to our children and there's the love that we give to our partners. Amber deserves all of that. Nothing held back for a ghost. You know damn well Jenn wouldn't want that. That's why she not only told you, but told Snow. Please believe I'm not trying to lay a guilt trip on you. I'm not. But the only reason she ever said a thing to that kid is because she knew you'd try to hold on to something you could never hold again. She knew you were a good man and would always listen to your daughters, even if you shut everyone else out. Including me."

I grunted because I didn't want to agree with her. I knew she was right, but there was no way I was ready to admit it. From the look that was in my sister's eyes, she knew exactly what I was thinking and, honestly, it pissed me off. Damn women psychics.

"Come on, grumpy. Let's give Emma our order. I'm famished, and I think we both might be in a little better mood with some food in our stomachs."

Shaking my head, I turned and flagged down everyone's favorite waitress. "Fine. I suppose I'm paying?"

"Damn straight," Janine laughed. "Now let's talk about Patty's proposal."

Janine and I discussed yesterday's meeting over lunch at the diner. This time I truly listened. I was still leery of letting someone else into the business, but if I didn't, there was a very good chance I wouldn't have a business to keep anyone out of. I would negotiate as best I could, but the deal had potential. With help from the investors, I could finally finish the fourth floor, and apparently, Janine had talked with Patty while Amber was saying her goodbyes, and we could even look at expanding, adding a new wing with modern rooms and a pool and spa. That would broaden our potential appeal. No matter how hard I worked, I doubted I could do that on my own.

Once we were done with lunch, I knew I had two phone calls to Denver to make. I made the first one on the way back to the inn. A meeting was set with the Brown Group at the inn on Monday morning. The second I needed to think about a little more, and I wanted the girls' input before I dug myself an even deeper hole. I knew I needed Amber's forgiveness, and I needed to show her I was ready and willing to give her all of my heart. To give her everything she deserved and more.

I was met by Janet behind the desk again. "Is Snow still on strike?" I said, trying for a lighter tone than yesterday.

"Not exactly. I offered because I was going stir crazy in the tiny apartment I'm renting while I'm waiting for estimates on the rebuild. Spring can't come soon enough."

"Are you talking to Josh? He's the best around."

"I know. He's at the top of the list, but the insurance company demands three estimates, so now I have to act like I'm interested with two other contractors. I don't enjoy deceiving people."

"I know what you mean, but it's part of the game. I'm sure they're used to estimate roulette." She nodded as I walked past but stopped. "Hey, Janet?"

"Mm?" She looked up from the computer screen to meet my gaze.

"Would you be interested in doing the marketing for the inn? I couldn't pay you much, at least not right now, but we need a better social media presence, and we have to do something, anything, to market this place when there's no snow on the ground."

A bright smile filled her face. "I'd love to. Can I add it's about damn time?"

"Good and you can because it is," I returned her smile, and it felt good. It felt like just a little bit of weight had been lifted from my shoulders. "Give it some thought, and we can maybe talk about it next week? I've got a couple of pressing issues to fix before I can give you my full attention."

"You got it, Bro," and it was good to hear the humor in her voice. Neither of us had been good company recently. I turned and walked down the hall to the addition. "Hey, Hunter," she called after me.

"Yeah?"

"I'm glad you've decided to come back. You're right; the marketing can wait a few days. Go make the good choices. I'm proud of you."

"Thanks," I answered. Time to make my girls proud, and I needed their help to do it.

I walked into the living room to silence. Meg was curled up in a chair reading. The only light in the room was the glow from her screen and the colored lights from our tree. A tree that Amber had helped me and the girls put up the Sunday after Thanksgiving. There was Christmas music playing, hot chocolate and Christmas cookies being consumed, and laughter. So much laughter and love. It was nothing like the somber process it had been for the past three years. I should have paid more attention to the signs.

There were presents under there for a woman that I missed terribly, and I'd have to remove unless I wanted another revolt Christmas morning if she didn't come back. This needed to work.

Meg cocooned in a chair wasn't a surprise, but the absence of my other two daughters was. Amy usually took care of the silence with her constant chatter, and Snow was normally somewhere near her sisters. "Where are your sisters?" She didn't even flinch. It was possible she didn't hear me; she often gets lost in her stories, but it was just as likely I was still on the silent treatment plan. Yesterday I accepted it, but no more. They might be mad at me, but they would not ignore me. "Meg," I barked, and this time she jumped so she couldn't pretend she couldn't hear me. "Answer me. Where are your sisters?"

Slowly, her gaze lifted from the screen of her e-reader and met mine. She was giving the stink eye her best effort, but that just wasn't who she was. I, on the other hand, was adept. She caved. "Amy's in her room, and Snow is delivering towels or something to a room on the third floor."

"Thank you." I smiled, letting her know I wasn't the grumpy guy she'd been seeing recently. "Finish up the chapter you're on. When Snow comes back down, we're going to have a family meeting. I'll get Amy."

"I'll get her, Dad. She's still pretty angry at you." She uncoiled from the chair and wrapped her arms around my waist. "I think she might be more stubborn than Snow. We're in big trouble."

"If you're right, we are," I laughed in agreement. "Should I make cocoa?"

My only answer was a thumbs up raised over her head as she walked away.

I returned with a tray of hot cocoa and cookies. Bribing my kids with sugar was not beneath my dignity, not when I was in this deep with all three of them. Amy wouldn't even take the drink, keeping her arms folded tightly across her chest. "Don't you want your cocoa, Peanut?" I asked, hoping my special name for her would soften her mood.

All I received in return was a "Hmph".

Tough crowd.

I sat on the edge of the chair across from them and leaned forward, taking a sip of the hot chocolate, giving myself a minute to collect my thoughts and maybe to give the sweets time to take effect on my daughters. "There are some things I need to do. And I need your help to do it."

"You need to say sorry to Amber. I won't help until you do that, and Snow and Meg won't either. Will we?" Amy said, looking toward her sisters for support.

Snow cocked a challenging brow in my direction, and Meg looked between Amy and me, not sure what to do. Helping me apologize was exactly what I wanted them to do, but I needed to know why this was so important to Amy. I knew she adored her, but something told me there was more to it, and I needed to understand. I owed that to both Amy and Amber to understand their connection.

"Why is that so important to you, Amy?"

She stared at me just as defiant as ever.

"I'm going to apologize. That's what I need your help with, but I need to know why this means so much to you, so you know I'm sorry too."

Slowly, I watched her features relax. Her eyebrows shifted back over her eyes. Her shoulders drooped to normal position, and her folded arms left her chest, one reaching for the cocoa waiting for her on the table. I held back the smile that was itching to emerge on my face. The last thing I wanted to do was seem smug and end up back where we started. And I still wanted an answer to my question. "Please, Peanut. I promise I won't be angry."

"William told me she's going to be my mommy. Amber plays Barbies and reads me stories and smells good and gives really good hugs. Snow tries but she should be a kid and not worry about being my mommy and I've always wanted a mommy and I really like Amber, we all do, and I thought Amber would be a really good mommy and then you were mean to her and she ran away and I don't understand why William would lie to me because he never has before and if Amber stays away, she can't be my mommy so you have to apologize so she can come back and be my mommy. That's why."

I wasn't surprised at her reasoning, though there was a whole hell of a lot to digest when she finally came up for air. It all made sense, but I couldn't figure out who this William was. I knew most of the kids in her first-grade class, and there wasn't a William to be had. "Amber is certainly all those things, and I'm going to do everything I can to show her how sorry I am." A smile spread across her face that was so big it seemed like she was smiling with her whole body. "But, baby, who is William? You probably shouldn't be talking about family stuff with your friends at school."

The smile faded from her face, followed by a look of confusion. She looked at me like I'd grown a second head, and it had pink hair with purple highlights. "William's not a friend from school, Daddy. He's my brother. He was in Mommy's belly when she died, so we never got to meet him, but he lives with her in heaven, and he talks to me. Especially when I'm sad or afraid. Sometimes Mommy talks to me, but William says she's so busy with you and Snow that he has to help. He looks out for Meg too, but he says she doesn't really talk back. That's why he usually talks to me."

My heart dropped to the pit of my stomach. I couldn't write this off as the overactive imagination of a six-year-old. Not when I'd spent my morning talking with her mother. But no one knew about my son. A son I'd named William just this morning. And yet here was Amy talking about him like an old friend. Apparently, at least two of my daughters had inherited a gift from their mother that I couldn't fully comprehend. I was more than just a little freaked out.

Needing a second opinion, I turned to the only one in the room I knew who could fully understand what Amy had just claimed. When I looked at Snow, she was staring at an unidentified horizon. Slowly a smile tipped up at the edge of her lips, and she returned my stare and nodded.

"How long have you been talking with William?" Snow asked.

Amy shrugged. "Whenever I miss Mommy, he comes. Does he talk to you too?"

Snow shook her head, and I didn't miss Amy's shoulder straightening just a little in pride. Meg looked totally lost, and I could empathize with her confusion.

I took a deep steadying breath and hoped with everything I had Jenn was here by my side. She should have been here physically, but at least she could be here in spirit. "Amy, sweetheart, what you just told us is true. Mommy was pregnant when she died, and it was a baby boy." I swallowed twice, drawing on every ounce of composure I could muster to get myself through this. "She was actually on her way to pick up a cake for the party we were going to have that night to make the big announcement to everyone."

I broke. A sob reverberated through my body, and I was immediately enveloped in six loving arms and a sea of blonde wavy hair. After a moment, I was able to compose myself and continue. "I didn't tell you girls because losing your mother was more than enough grief to manage. And I'm so proud of all of you for how you were able to move on. It's not a simple thing to do. Especially when you're all so young."

"But why wait until now?" Meg asked, always the one to try to understand every angle.

I shook my head. "I should have told you before, but I was trying to protect you. And maybe I wasn't ready to talk about it myself." I exhaled and continued. "I visited your mom today and put the wreath you got her by the marker. I promise I'll take you to visit her later, but today I just needed to visit by myself."

"It's okay, Daddy," Amy said, hugging me tighter. "We understand. Sometimes you just have to have grown-up time."

"Thanks, Amy. It really means a lot to me you understand." I forced a smile and kissed the top of her head. "Your mom and I had never discussed a name for your brother but today, when I was there I decided we should call him William," I heard one of the girls inhale sharply, "so I guess I got that right, huh, Amy?" Her little blonde head bobbed in agreement.

"He's buried there with your mom, and I was thinking that we should add his name to the stone. What do you guys think?" I didn't have to wait to hear that they all agreed. "I was also thinking that we should put something special on the stone... a verse or something." I looked down at them to confirm they were on board. "I'd like it if the three of you could come up with it. This is something that should have meaning for all of us."

We sat quietly for a moment, and I was just about to add that they could take their time. They didn't have to decide until spring, when Meg broke the silence. "Gone from our lives too soon but forever alive in our hearts."

Snow wrapped her in a hug before I had a chance to. "That's so perfect, Meg," Snow spoke against her cheek.

Amy crawled across my lap and joined her sisters' embrace. "Yeah, Meg. The bestest."

I rubbed the tears away that were staining my face and leaned over to take a drink of my now tepid hot chocolate.

We took some time to get our emotions in check, and when I felt we'd had enough, I cleared my throat, preparing to discuss the most pressing matter; what to do about getting Amber back.

"Thanks, you guys. I'm so proud of all of you."

"Thanks, Dad," they said in unison.

"But what are you going to do to get Amber back?" Meg asked.

"Yeah, Dad. You've got to get her back," Amy added.

"Do you have any ideas?" Snow chimed in, cutting to the heart of the matter.

"I do," I said, "but this affects all of you too, so I want to make sure everyone is okay with what I have in mind."

# 39

# *I Am Not Okay*

## *Amber*

It had been four days. Ninety-four hours to be exact since The Snowflake Inn disappeared from Patty's rearview mirror. Ninety-seven hours since Hunter broke my heart. But who's counting?

It took Hunter thirty-two hours before he called. I think he called to apologize, but I didn't answer. I didn't listen to the voicemail he left. I haven't answered any of his calls since. I stopped counting at sixty-seven. Nor did I look at, read or respond to the dozens of texts he sent in addition to the phone calls. Who's counting?

Not me, that's who.

As soon as I got through the door of my house, I dumped the trash bags full of my things in the corner of my bedroom, peeled off my clothes and took a long hot bath. Once the water turned to ice and my feet looked like dehydrated fruit, I forced myself out of the tub and into a comfy pair of gray sweatpants and a light blue henley. I have not bathed or changed my clothes since. Why should I?

Don't answer that.

If you answered I would expect you to ignore the smorgasbord of stains that were on the above-mentioned sweats and henley. There were numerous dark brown splotches from Triple Chocolate Fudge Brownie ice cream, several red-orange remnants from a combination of SpaghettiOs and canned ravioli, a sticky substance, likely from an exceptionally delicious quart of General Tso's Chicken, and an enormous maroon stain on my right thigh where I spilled the merlot I was resting there when Patty startled me. She actually let herself in without knocking. Honestly, there was a slight possibility she did knock because I was very focused on torturing myself with an endless loop of Hallmark Christmas romances.

Okay, maybe I needed to change. Maybe I needed to take a shower. Maybe my heart was so broken I'd never be able to function again. Maybe I needed to answer my phone that was vibrating on the coffee table in front of me, ricocheting off empty takeout containers and dirty dishes. Maybe I was just the tiniest, itty-bitty bit drunk and not thinking entirely straight. Maybe I was spiraling.

Maybe.

If I had answered the phone, I would have had to talk to Hunter. I would have had to listen to the apology I knew he was going to give me. I would have had to listen to the girls I loved so much beg me to come back because he's devious like that, and he would have known I could never deny them. Even if I could tell *him* no. And it was doubtful I could do that either.

I loved him. I missed him. I just couldn't trust him. Not in the usual, he's off screwing other women, way. That would have been easy to walk away from because I've been there and done that. And experience was the key to success. No, I couldn't trust that I would ever have all of his heart.

Of course, there would always be a place in his heart for Jenn, and I wouldn't have loved him like I did if I thought he could just forget she ever existed. But I needed him to give all of himself to me in the here and now. It would be impossible to live wondering what I could or couldn't say about the inn. There was no way I could stand by and watch him struggle and not be able to help. I couldn't. I wouldn't. It was hard as hell, but I would have all of him or none at all. I wouldn't settle for less than I deserved. Making that mistake again was just not an option.

Looking around, I took in the stark white walls, sprinkled with the pretentious art Lance forced on us. The white furniture was his choice as well. Nothing in this house was me. I couldn't afford to redecorate, but now that I knew how much this place was worth, maybe I could sell and buy something further out of the city. If I did that, I could have a nice place and still have money left over to make the place mine. It's something I would need to think about seriously after the holidays.

The more I thought about it, I realized that teaching is what I most wanted to do. I couldn't hold back a groan as I realized I was going to have to call the Homer Pass Board of Education and let them know I wouldn't be taking the position after all. It killed me I had to let them down. Seeing the girls in the halls or lunchroom every day wasn't in my future like I thought. Just one more good thing I lost. One more good thing I never got to experience at all.

I looked around the room again, noting the lack of holiday decorations. I had trimmed a tree with Hunter, and that's the one I wanted to look at. Christmas was nine days away, and I couldn't have cared less. One of the few reasons I had for enjoying the winter was gone. I wasn't in the mood for shopping, but I would have to get something for Patty. That should probably be nice because she'd been here every day to bring supplies and make sure I was still upright and not completely hidden from the world under my duvet.

Nope, no hiding. I was very high-functioning; I put my big-girl panties on every day, got out of bed and plopped right down on the couch. Tortured myself with holiday rom-coms and then flopped back into bed every night. Actually, that's a lie. Oh, I did all those things except the big-girl panties. Nope. I wasn't wearing any panties at all. I was going commando, freestyle, easy-breezy, free-balling, not that I had balls to go free, but, you know, it's not something to be taken literally.

No bra either. My girls were unconstrained. I'd have regular old bouncing betties if I took a brisk walk. No chance of that. Exercise could be hazardous to your health.

Hunter would lose his mind if he found me braless. Anytime he discovered me that way, it wasn't long before we were naked. I didn't even have to try to seduce him. All I had to do was set the girls free. Maybe give the ole nips a tweak, so they'd stand at attention and he'd notice quicker. But if my boobs were unbound, I was never far away from sexy fun times. God, I missed sexy fun times.

Mountain man monkey sex was the best.

Well, maybe with how stained and stinky the outer wrapping was now, he wouldn't want to get close enough to find out.

I really should have showered and changed. It was nearly four PM. Tomorrow. That was a plan. Goals are good. My goal for tomorrow was to take a shower and change my clothes. I had a plan. I couldn't wait to tell Patty. She would be so happy for me.

As if thinking about her brought her to life, she walked through my front door carrying two large grocery bags and a box of wine. I assumed the bags contained the necessities, like ice cream and easy-to-prepare pasta. We'd switched to box wine yesterday because the bottles from the previous days. were threatening to overflow from my recycling container. She was late. I'd run out of wine two hours ago, and I was losing my buzz. I wasn't complaining. I knew what side my butter was breaded on. I'd have been a total wreck without my bestie.

"Oh God," she groaned, wrinkling up her face like she'd just downed a glass of sour milk. Which reminded me I hoped she'd picked some up because I forgot the gallon I had on the counter last night, and when I went to pour it on my cereal this morning, it came out in the consistency of cottage cheese. Dry cereal sucks.

Dropping my supplies onto the dining room table, she turned to face me. She fisted her hands on her hips and spread her legs. I giggled a little because I pictured her in one of those cute little hats. You know, the ones with the dimples on top and the wide brims. The kind drill sergeants and park rangers wore. Maybe I could go visit a national park. I had free time.

"Amber, I love you. You don't deserve all the horrible things that have happened to you. But this has to stop. I'm done enabling you."

"What are you talking about?" I couldn't understand what had her upset. She was smiling when she walked in. She was definitely not a friendly mister park ranger, sir. She was a sergeant. Did I need to salute?

"Honey, you reek." She closed the space between us and tugged me out of my safe, comfy little cocoon on the couch.

Definitely a sergeant.

"It's not even five o'clock and you're already buzzed. You've been wearing the same clothes since Thursday afternoon, and it's Monday. You're going to shower, and I'm going to open some windows. I don't care that it's twenty degrees outside; the air in here is toxic. Living in a haze of BO and old takeout is just not healthy."

I just stood there staring at her, trying to process what she was saying.

Checking her watch, she let out a huff. "Okay. We've got time," she said. She gave my arm a tug and dragged me toward my bedroom. Geez, give a girl a chance to get her bearings.

We walked down the hall, through my bedroom, and into my ensuite. Patty turned on the shower. Once I was up and walking, I felt a little woozy. I held onto the vanity for a moment because, for some reason, my bathroom floor was rocking like a small boat in heavy seas.

"Okay. Up with the arms," she said, tugging the top over my head and dropping it on the floor. She yanked down my sweats, and I couldn't help thinking that I wished Hunter were here to do this. It would be a lot more fun. He wouldn't sound as upset as she did.

Wait.

I had a plan. I was supposed to do this tomorrow. What would I do tomorrow if I did it now?

"Step up," she said, which interrupted my happy daydream about my hunky innkeeper and plans. Nope. Not my innkeeper. "Now the other foot, Amber. Come on, work with me here." I was totally naked. I didn't think I'd ever been naked in front of her before. I'd liked to be naked with Hunter. Sexy fun times, yay!

She guided me into the shower, making sure I didn't trip over the little edge at the bottom of the door that kept the water from leaking out. That was such a good idea. It would be dangerous to have water all over the tile floor. I could have slipped and hit my head and got an owie.

"Are you okay to wash yourself, or do you need me to help?"

"I can do it," I said. Of course, I could do it. I was a big-girl with big-girl panties. I thought I should probably put some on once I got dressed again. But no bra. Bras suck. "You can go put the groceries away. I don't want the ice cream to melt. There's nothing worse than soupy Chunky Monkey. No soupy Chunky Monkey for me." Oh, God, monkeys. I miss Hunter. I miss Hunter and our marvelous mountain man monkey sex.

I was showered. Not shaved, because in my condition it could have been lethal. I was dressed, with underwear, and somewhat more sober, sitting at my kitchen counter with a steaming mug of hot coffee in front of me. I gripped it with both hands and took a long sip. The aroma alone made me feel just a little bit more in touch with reality.

Reality sucked.

I croaked out a thank you, and Patty slid onto the stool beside me. "How was your day?" I asked as much to keep her from lecturing me and reminding me of my misery as out of genuine curiosity. If I focused on her life for a little while, it meant I forgot about mine.

"Great actually. An important business deal is really coming together. You're showered and dressed in something clean. All in all, I'd say my day was a great success."

"Awesome," I said and nothing more. A good friend would have asked for details about the business deal because… Well because that's what good friends do. I was a shit friend, too mired in her own sorrows to really care.

"Aren't you going to ask about the deal?"

See. Shit. Friend. She had to prompt me to ask about her deal. "Tell me about your deal, Patty. I bet it's really interesting." I said, dripping with as much fake enthusiasm as I could muster, along with pasting an equally fake smile on my face. It must have been a funny smile too because she snorted coffee through her nose and had a choking fit.

"Well," she started, after she cleaned up the mess and refilled her mug.

"I went with the partners to visit this cute inn in this beautiful mountain town. You'll have to check it out. It's called The Snowflake Inn."

My jaw dropped, and I set my coffee down, suddenly much more sober. "Janine got Hunter to change his mind?" I really needed to take lessons from that girl on how to move immovable objects. It might come in handy one day.

"She did. Or something did. Not only was he civil and attentive, but he was completely engaged. It was supposed to be maybe an hour-long meeting. Just a meet and greet so the partners could see the property. We were there for five hours and negotiated the whole thing. Color me shocked, but it was like Hunter had had some kind of epiphany."

My heart swelled. I was so happy for him. Happy that the girls would keep their inn. Keep their mom's dream alive. It really sucked that I couldn't be a part of it, but that just wasn't meant to be. "I'm so happy to hear that, Patty. I truly am."

"I know, honey. I can see it in your eyes." She placed her hand over mine and gave it a squeeze. "Hunter told me he's been trying to get ahold of you. Said he's called and sent texts."

She squeezed my hand again, which made me look up at her. Her head tilted to the side. "You haven't even read them or listened to the voice-mails, have you.?"

I shook my head. "You know I haven't, and I told you he called."

"You made it sound like he'd called once or twice. He said it's been more than a hundred times. He really wants a chance to make things right with you, Amber. Don't you think you should at least give him a chance to apologize?" She let go of my hand and sat back in the chair, folding her arms over her chest. "You said you loved him. It seems like it would be the right thing to do. I'm not saying you have to go back to him, but neither of you deserve to have it end like this."

I hated that she was right, but I just couldn't bring myself to do it. I knew the moment I heard his voice I'd cave. I'd go running back only to find out I still didn't have access to all of him. All I could do was shrug. We'd been over this before. "I don't think he's called a hundred times. I only counted sixty-seven." I didn't say I stopped counting after that.

She was about to respond when her phone rang. Frankly, I was happy to be off the hot seat.

"This is Patty. You're here? Excellent. We'll be right out." She ended the call, looking at me with an impish smile. "Come on," she said, trying to pull me out of my chair.

She was being awfully pushy, but I was ready and wasn't about to be pushed. Or pulled. "You did NOT give Hunter my address."

"Of course not," she laughed.

"Then why is he out in front of my house and why are you trying to aid and abet his attempts to apologize?" I didn't find her laughter funny.

"He's not out in front of your house, and the only thing I'm aiding is getting you your car back. It's Leo who is out front. Now get up. Get your shoes on so the man can get your car into your driveway and get home before midnight."

"It's not Hunter?" I hated how much that disappointed me.

"I told you, it's Leo," she said, a hint of annoyance in her tone. "Now come on. He's helping you out. Let's not keep him waiting."

I followed her out of the kitchen and down the hall. I pulled on my boots, threw my coat on and stepped out onto my front stoop. Sure enough, Leo's flatbed was parked on the street in front of my house. Betsy was tied down to the bed, looking all shiny and new. The rental car I'd abandoned during my escape from the inn was strapped down behind it.

Once again he was my savior because the last thing I'd wanted to do was to have to sneak back to Homer Pass and recover either the rental or Betsy. I headed down my front walk to get a better look at her.

"There's my snow angel," Leo said, walking around the cab of the wrecker. "How are you, Amber?"

"Okay," I croaked out, and gave him a hug. "It's good to see you."

"It's good to see you too," he said. "But I don't believe for a minute that you're okay." He smiled and tossed the ever-present cigar nub into a snowbank. "Though I will say you look a damn sight cleaner and smell betterthan Patty told me to expect." He hunched over, laughing. I didn't think what he said was as funny as he did.

I shot an accusatory glare in my supposed best friend's direction. She smiled and stared back unapologetically with a lift of her shoulders. "I guess it's a good thing you decided to shower," she said.

Before I could fire back that I hadn't decided to do anything, Leo asked where I wanted the cars. He went about unloading them, pulling Betsy into my garage, and leaving the rental in the driveway. I'd have them come pick it up in the morning.

"All set," he said, handing me both sets of keys.

"Thank you so much, Leo. I really appreciate all that you've done for me. Especially after everything that's happened. I wouldn't have blamed you if you never wanted to talk to me again, let alone go out of your way to help me."

"Don't talk nonsense, child," he said as he wrapped his hands around mine. "I don't know what Hunter did, but that doesn't change the fact that me and a whole bunch of other folk in Homer Pass care about you. We miss you. And you're welcome to come visit anytime. Don't forget that, okay?"

He patted my hand and walked toward his truck as I rasped out a weak "okay" around all the feelings balled up in my throat. I had expected him to try to convince me to give Hunter another chance. Oddly enough, I was disappointed he hadn't.

He reached up and took the handle next to the cab door and turned back to face me. "When you're ready, you might think about letting Hunter tell you how he cares and misses you too." He pulled himself up into the cab. "Just a thought," he added, and shut the door before I could respond.

Patty and I stood there and watched him drive away. His words echoed around in my mind long after the rumble of the diesel engine faded into the distance.

Once we were back inside, I spent a few minutes cleaning the dirty dishes and trash out of my living room. I was not ready to give up my couch cocoon, but I had to admit a clean cocoon was a good cocoon.

It was just after six when my stomach growled with such ferocity that we both laughed until we cried. Patty ordered us food from Antonio's, one of the best Italian restaurants west of the Mississippi as far as I was concerned. The only trouble was they didn't deliver.

"You know, Amber, Leo might have had a point," she said.

"A point about what?"

"Calling Hunter. At least listen to what he has to say. It can't hurt."

"It can't hurt? It nearly killed me to say goodbye to the girls. My legs were shaking so much I looked like a newborn colt when I left. If I had to stop on the way out, I might not have been able to start again. Momentum was my savior, Patty. If you hadn't been driving, I probably would have had a panic attack on the way. And this time I really would have driven off the side of the mountain. Tumbling down into the ravine in a fiery ball of twisted metal. Dead. Splat. Gone. I'm too young to die, Patty. Too young."

She just shook her head and laughed at me. Laughed. At. Me. She said that I'd gone round the bend, lost the plot and hopped on the express train to crazy town. I ask you, was that any way for a friend to talk with a friend?

She shared more of the details about the meeting. I figured she was just trying to bait me into wanting to give Hunter the second chance he deserved. I was just too scared. I couldn't survive another broken heart. I couldn't. I wasn't doing so well as it was.

Patty was just getting up to go get the food when the phone rang. I thought at first it was hers because she answered it, but upon further inspection it was mine. Why was she answering my phone?

"Hi. No. This is Patty. Yes. I think it went very well too. I was going to call tomorrow morning and let you know the documents should be ready by Monday. I'll email them to your lawyer as soon as I have them. I promise. I know you've got a full house until after New Year's, so it shouldn't be a problem to do the signing at the inn." She laughed, and it hurt knowing that he was probably laughing too. I loved his laugh. I missed his laugh.

"Well, it might take a little longer than normal, but don't worry; you'll have the cash in hand before the deadline. You won't lose the inn on a technicality. Henry and the douche canoe are going to be very disappointed."

She smiled and winked at me as if I wasn't dying inside. I should be there to kiss him. To give him a hug and join in the celebration with Janine and the girls. At least somebody was going to have something to celebrate for the holidays.

She slipped her coat off the back of the chair and grabbed her purse. Was she planning on taking my phone with her while she went to pick up our dinner? Was she planning to keep talking to the love of my life while I sat there wallowing in grief? Maybe she *was* the shit friend.

"Yes, she's here. Hold on a minute and I'll put her on."

I started shaking my head with such vehemence I saw stars. Did she have memory problems? We'd gone over this several times in the last hour. I couldn't trust myself talking to him. "No," I mouthed to her while she waved the phone in front of my face.

"Yes," she hissed back, shaking it harder.

She could hiss all she wanted to, but I was not going to lose that verbal tug of war. Certainly not to a snake.

"No," I said again, turning to walk away. She grabbed my arm before I could manage it and forced the phone into my hand.

"Talk to him," she whisper-yelled. "You owe it to yourself, and you owe it to him." She picked the box of wine off the counter. "If you don't, I won't come back with the food, and I'm taking the wine with me. Do this, or you're on your own for the rest of this ordeal. I love you, and it's time for some tough love."

She *was* the shit friend. I was the good friend, and this was all the proof I needed to prove it. A good friend would never threaten to withhold wine or lasagna from a woman in crisis. But what's a girl to do, crisis or not? I must have alcohol and pasta because it just wouldn't be worth living without them.

"Hello?" I mumbled.

"Amber?" His deep voice was music to my ears. God, I missed him so. "I didn't think you were going to pick up the phone."

"What would make you think that?" Feigning ignorance, yeah that was a plan that was certain to succeed.

His deep laugh came over the phone almost as addictive as it was in person. "Maybe because you haven't answered the last hundred times I called."

"Oh, that." I was out of sassy responses. I just wanted to crawl into the phone and get zapped by whatever technology these smartphones used all the way to Homer Pass and jump into his arms. But I couldn't do that. I had to stay strong. I couldn't risk this. Even for him. Especially for him.

"Why, Amber? Why couldn't you at least listen to what I had to say? I'm so sorry. I was an ass and a fool. I miss you. The girls miss you."

Oh, no, no, no. Not going to happen. I couldn't allow him to bring them into the equation. I was done for if I allowed it. "Don't do that, Hunter. This is about us. I love those girls like they were my own." Tears streamed down my face. I thought I'd cried myself out because by Sunday no more tears would fall. Apparently, twenty-four hours was more than enough time to rehydrate the tear ducts.

"You're right. That was a desperate move by a desperate man. I won't do that again. Just tell me what I have to do to make this right. I'll do anything, Amber. Even this deal with Patty means nothing without you here to share it."

"It means you get to keep the inn. It means you don't have to murder your brother. I would say that's something. I think it is quite a lot of something."

We talked for a long time. We talked about the big things and the little things, and even though I couldn't bring myself to trust that he could let me in all the way; it felt good to talk with him. I could hear the girls in the background, and I yearned to talk to them too. I couldn't do it, though. I didn't want any of them to think there was a chance that I could go back into their lives unless I was sure there was.

Maybe in time we could be friends. I could drive up in the summer, and we could all go for ice cream sodas at the diner. I'm sure there were other things to do there, but all I knew of Homer Pass was snowbanks, Janine's store, the Bighorn and the inn. I wanted to be a part of that community, but it sure didn't look like that was my lot.

Hunter was a good man, and all this proved to me the longer we talked was that I still had trust issues. He seemed to have conquered his demons, but mine were still poking their pitchforks into my side, filling me with doubt. I couldn't dump this on him. I couldn't dump this on the girls. He seemed willing to try. I just knew that as long as the inn was his priority, I'd always wonder if I truly held all of him or if there was still a part that held Jenn alive in his heart trying to keep her dream alive.

Patty came back with the food and smiled when she saw me still on the phone. "Still Hunter?" she mouthed, and I nodded. She disappeared into the kitchen, and I assumed she was putting our food in the oven to stay warm. It smelled delicious, and my stomach started making noises again in agreement.

She made herself scarce, but I knew she was here. And I knew that there was nothing left to say that could change my mind. I had to figure my own shit out. Then maybe, just maybe, I could take a chance for love. I just couldn't make Hunter wait for something that would probably never change.

"So, what do you say, Amber? Are you willing to give us, I'm sorry, I mean, are you willing to give me a second chance?"

The damn tears were back, and I struggled to speak.

"Amber?"

"I'm sorry," I squawked out. "I… I don't know. I'm not ready." I swallowed again and took a deep breath, getting myself ready to do the absolute hardest thing I'd ever done in my life.

"Please, Amber. If I were there, I'd be down on my knees begging you. I'm begging you. Just one more chance."

Fuck. Fuck. Fuck. Fuckity. Fuck. Fuck. And there went almost every ounce of resolve. Almost. "Give me some time. You want to be ready for me, but I've got shit to figure out too. It's not fair if I do this too soon and end up running away again. It's the best I can promise." I'm such a chicken.

There was a long silence. I checked the phone to make sure the call hadn't dropped. Finally, there was a garbled sound on the other end, and I heard Hunter clearing his throat. "If that's the best you can do, then it is all I can ask."

There was another long pause, and I could tell that he was struggling to hold it together just as hard as I was. The best thing to do was to end this. Not just the call but the relationship. But I was emotionally exhausted, and I couldn't find the strength to do it. Well, the strength to walk away. I could end the call.

"I need to go, Hunter. Patty came back with the food a while ago, and I'm famished." It was a lame excuse, but it was also true. I was famished, but I didn't think I could swallow even a sip of water and keep it down right now.

"Okay. I'm sorry I didn't realize you hadn't eaten. Thanks for talking to me."

"It was good. I'm glad we did."

"Me too. Goodbye, Amber. I miss you."

"I miss you too. Goodbye, Hunter." I pressed the button and ended the call. "I love you. So much," I murmured through a sob that shook me to the core. Arms wrapped around me as Patty pulled me into her chest. I cried until I ran out of tears. Patty didn't say a word. She didn't need to. She just held me tight so I wouldn't slip away.

# 40

# An Unwelcome Encounter

## Amber

Since my call with Hunter, I'd steadily pulled myself back to functional. I'd stopped day drinking, showered every day, wore clean clothes every day, wore underwear every day, not always a bra because, yeah, they still sucked. Sometimes I even wore my big-girl panties.

I'd mustered the determination to get a Christmas tree. Just a week before Christmas, the selection was limited, and I'd ended up with a Charlie Brown special. Despite my best efforts, I did not manage the results that those cartoon kiddos had, but it was a tree, and there were lights and ornaments, and there were gifts under it. I didn't bother with any other decorations; not even a wreath on the front door. The only points I'd be receiving for effort would be from that meager tree.

I tapped into a home equity line of credit I'd forgotten I'd set up so I had enough money to get through a couple of months until I could figure things out. Patty and I talked about it. A lot. And I was going to put the house on the market after the first of the year. There were so many terrible memories associated with the place I needed to stop torturing myself just to make a point. Especially one I'd already made. I'd done it. I stood up to Lance and won.

I hadn't had much good happen lately, so I latched on to the one bright spot, which was that my house was worth over three times what I thought it was. For the first time since my divorce, I wasn't consumed by worry about my finances. It was the Friday before Christmas. I stopped at the bank to sign some paperwork for the loan, certifying the reappraisal, and met Patty for lunch at the Sixteenth Street Mall. The place was a hive of activity this close to the holiday, and though crowds usually made me uncomfortable; I latched onto some of that energy. I was happy. Almost.

After doing a bit of Christmas shopping, and finding absolutely the most perfect gift for Snow, I ducked into a little cafe for a cup of tea and a sweet. Tapping into the good vibes I felt, I plucked up the courage to call the Homer Pass Board of Education and let them know I couldn't accept the position.

It killed me because it felt like cutting the last tie to Homer Pass and any hope of a life with Hunter. Except the superintendent refused to accept my decision. It was the most bizarre conversation I'd ever had.

She told me she understood the predicament I was in, but also knew that things sometimes changed in situations like mine. Orientation was on the third of January, she informed me, and the students returned the following Monday. Only if I didn't show up for orientation, would she consider my decision final.

She must have been desperate for someone to take the job.

Next, I called my mother to let her know I was going to book a last-minute flight and come to Florida for Christmas. And that's when things shifted from bizarre to Twilight Zone weird.

I wanted to see my mom, but I'd be lying if I said that was my only reason. The thought of being alone so close to Hunter was dangerous. I had to limit my temptation to give in and drive to Homer Pass on Christmas Day. Orlando would be a safe distance to discourage such a disastrous decision.

Except she told me not to come. She said that Walter was surprising her with a trip and they wouldn't be there. They never went anywhere. Ever.

What the fuck, Mom? For ten years she's asked, and when I finally said yes, she said no?

I slipped on my coat and picked up my packages, making my way out of the cafe. The mall was even busier than before, and I had to dodge and weave my way through the crowd. The fact that I was still trying to sort out the peculiar conversations with both the superintendent and my mother probably contributed to my not watching where I was going. When I turned down a side street toward the parking lot, I slammed into a man equally distracted. Half of my packages went flying to the ground.

"Jesus. Fucking. Christ." He barked. "Watch where you're fucking going, you stupid…"

"Stupid what?" I screamed back. "Why don't you watch where you're going, you arrogant ass." I froze before I could continue my verbal barrage.

Lance stared back at me, his face crimson with rage. "Unbelievable. For five years I was able to avoid you, and in the last month you're fucking everywhere. What a fucking nightmare."

"Trust me, asshole, I feel exactly the same way." I threw my shoulders back and looked him directly in the eye, not backing down from him. He always hated that we were the same height.

"Shouldn't you be up in that little hick town, screwing your flannel-clad bumpkin?"

"Where I am or what I do is none of your fucking business." I did not want to get into it with him, but I would not back down. Not this time. Besides, I would have had to turn my back on him to pick up my things, and based on his expression, he probably would have stabbed me if I had.

"See, that's where you're wrong, Amber. Right now, that shithole of an inn is my business. And you know what? That's all your fault. I would probably have walked away from that deal. It's far too messy with the trust and who controls it. Or not. But as soon as I saw what that guy, Hunter is it, meant to you, well, what a perfect opportunity to make you pay for what you did to me by hurting the ones you love."

There was so much to process, but I grappled onto the one thing that made the most sense. "What I did to you?" I screeched. I'm sure people were staring at us, but I couldn't have cared less. "What did I ever do to you? You're the one who fucked somebody while we were still married. You weren't the one who was treated like what they wanted didn't mean shit. You were the vindictive one. You have a new wife and the children you always wanted. Move on with your life and let me move on with mine."

"You know damn well what you did, Amber."

All I could do was stare blankly back at him. He'd lost his mind. It was all I could think of. His inability to take responsibility for his own actions forced him to come up with some fantasy reason of why it was all my fault. I could see the frustration steaming off of him at my lack of under-standing.

"You're a murderer, Amber. There's no other way to put it. I wonder what Hunter would think of you if he knew. I'm sure you'd never have the courage to tell him. You never had the integrity to tell me."

My mouth fell open, but I couldn't make a sound. I couldn't for the life of me understand what the fuck he was talking about.

The sneer that filled his face told me he'd achieved exactly what he was hoping for. "You murdered our child. Yes, I had an affair, but that didn't give you the right to abort our child. How could you do that, Amber?

How could you kill an innocent child, no matter what I did to you? That's why I…" His words faltered. There was so much hurt and anger spilling out of him even I couldn't deny he believed every word he was saying. He swallowed, and tears streamed down his face. "That's why I'll never stop tormenting you."

We stood staring at each other. I did my best to collect my thoughts. For the first time in years, I saw the smallest glimpse of the man I once loved. Not the heartless thug he'd turned into but someone who had genuine emotions. "When did you find out I was pregnant? How did you know?"

"So, you admit it. You admit you were pregnant and got rid of our child just to spite me."

"Answer my question, Lance, and I'll answer yours."

"I already know the answer. I don't need your lies."

"No. You. Don't. You don't know anything at all if you think for one second I would ever have given up a child I so desperately wanted. No matter who the father was."

Lance stared at me, and I stared back. I could do this all day. He needed his answers more than I needed mine.

"That night in the office. Once I'd put myself back together. I followed you as you ran out of the building. You knew our marriage was over long before that night. You never fit into my world. You always thought you were too good, too principled."

"I was ready to tell you we could divorce. I would have bought you a home in a nice middle-class part of town. Somewhere you'd be comfortable. But good old Herb grabbed me and kept me from getting to you before you drove off."

"I was about to fire him when he shoved a positive pregnancy test in my hand. Said you'd dropped it when you were running out. Explained you'd come to the office that night with big news and wanted it to be a surprise. Then the old fucker punched me in the face, breaking my nose. The bastard quit on the spot, depriving me of the satisfaction of firing his wrinkled old ass."

I gasped. That kind old man had defended me. It cost him his job, and I never knew. I never had a chance to thank him.

"I wanted to tell you I knew," Lance continued. "I wanted to provide for you and our child. Our marriage was over; we both knew that. We didn't love each other, probably never did, but I didn't hate you. Not until after I realized what you did."

He ran his hand over his face and then dragged it back through his receding hairline. "My father convinced me to starve you out. Make you realize our child would be better off with me. With the advantages that my family could offer it, advantages that you never could provide. You knew how much I wanted a family. You knew I would care for my child. So, I waited, and I watched. You never said a word, and eventually I realized what you did because you obviously weren't pregnant anymore."

"I hired a private investigator." Lance continued with his story. I was furious with him. And yet a part of me knew that, as fucked up as it was, he was devastated by what he thought I'd done. "He found records of your prescription for misoprostol. I did my research. I know it's a drug used for medically induced abortion. So don't even bother trying to deny it. I have the proof. I know what you did. I just don't know why?"

"You fucking fool." I couldn't hold back the inappropriate laughter spilling out of my mouth. "I had a miscarriage. The prescription was used after it happened to clear out the tissue that was left behind in my uterus. Maybe you need to do more thorough research. And guess what, Lance. You 'starving me out', as you call it, contributed to that miscarriage, so you're every bit as responsible as I am."

I held up a hand to keep him from interrupting me. "Not only did the loss of that baby devastate me more than your infidelity, but I was under such stress I fell into clinical depression. I was so depressed that I couldn't get out of bed most days. I didn't take care of myself. I didn't go to the doctor for follow-up appointments and nearly died from an infection because of what was left behind inside me after the miscarriage."

"You nearly killed me, Lance, and worse than that, because of that infection I have virtually no chance of ever having a baby. Go away, Lance. Leave me alone. Leave Hunter and his daughters alone. You will never, ever do anything worse to me than you already have. You can't torment me anymore."

I stood there for a moment and glared at him. All the guilt. All the loss. All the shit I spent months in therapy to process and feel halfway whole again inundated me, and it took every ounce of resolve and strength I had to stand there. But I did.

And as I did, I watched as the outrage drained from his face. In fact, he was now ghostly pale. Tears continued to flow from his eyes. "You were a decent man once. At least I think you were," I said, stooping down to collect my bags. "Maybe you should listen to your instincts about Henry."

"I, ah, I," Lance stammered.

"Goodbye, Lance. It's a shame you never bothered to get to know me. If you had, you never would have believed the lies you told yourself about me." I pushed past him, packages in hand, and headed for my car. I hated that my good day had been intruded on by that ass, but at least now I understood why he was the way he was. I guess I was wrong. I had needed his answers just as much as he had needed mine.

# 41

# Signing

## Amber

I thought a lot about my confrontation with Lance as I drove home that afternoon. I talked more about it with Patty that evening. She was still unforgiving about how he had treated me over the years. So was I, but for the first time since that night at Tabor Tower, I saw some hint of a human being underneath his armor of hate.

His animosity toward me was at least understandable given what he believed I'd done. Obviously, I hadn't, and I believed it would have been my choice to make if I had. Still, on some level, I could understand his reaction. I'd never agree with it, but now that I understood it, I might someday forgive him for it. Though that really depended on what he did now that he knew the truth.

Keeping my pregnancy from him had never completely felt right to me. It's something I'd worked through in therapy. I remember in one session my therapist had asked me if sending him my medical records from the miscarriage would help ease my conscience. I had dismissed it as preposterous at the time, but now it felt like the right thing to do. What he'd done was wrong. But maybe I'd been wrong too.

The moment I'd dropped the envelope at the post office, it felt like a weight had been lifted off my chest. The note I included said only, 'for your research'. As Christmas was only two days away, he wouldn't receive the records until after the holiday. I didn't know what his reaction would be, but at least he couldn't accuse me of trying to ruin his family time.

With one issue resolved, I focused back on what was bothering me most.

Had I thought about my call with Hunter? Every. Single. Day. Several times a day. Honestly, it was almost all I thought about. I kept doubting my decision. How could I build trust in someone if I didn't give them a chance to prove themselves? Was I making another mistake?

I tottered into the kitchen and poured myself a cup of coffee, then made my way to my usual spot on the sofa. Patty had started calling it my nest. She wasn't wrong. There were pillows, a couple of throws, and snacks within reach. Both sweet and salty, of course, because a girl can never be sure what kind of munchies will hit and when.

I'd weaned myself off of holiday romance movies in favor of true crime shows. They seemed much healthier for my psyche. Seeing a hot, swoon-worthy guy surrounded by mistletoe and Christmas cookies did not help me right now. On the other hand, guys murdering their wives so they could be with their mistresses sent an obvious message to me that men are evil and should be avoided at all costs.

Exactly what the doctor ordered.

When the episode on TV turned out to be one I'd already seen, twice, I picked up my e-reader and started a biography that had been on my to-read list for ages. I'd barely gotten through the first chapter when my phone rang. I was surprised to see Patty's name come up. She never called while she was working. Especially since I was mostly a functioning, clean human again.

"Hey, you. What are you doing calling in the middle of the day?"

"That's not very nice. Makes me feel you don't want to talk to me."

"You know that's not true. It's just that you're usually far too focused on making your millions during business hours."

"I see your point, but it's Monday. Christmas Eve is tomorrow, honey. Most of the office took the week off. It's only a handful of no-life, no-family losers like me left milling around," she laughed.

"So what's up?"

"I know this is last minute, but I've got some paperwork I'd like to have you sign."

"Paperwork?" I groaned. "What paperwork?"

"Didn't we decide to put your place on the market after the first?"

"We did, but it's not the first, and I just started a great book." I knew I should have just done it without question, but I was in my cocoon. "Can you bring it with you tomorrow night when you come for dinner?"

"Amber," her tone let me know she was not impressed by my procrastination. "First, it has to be notarized. Second, we want to be first to market, and I'm on vacation after today. You know that. If we wait, it won't be until after the first."

"Ugh. Fine," I griped. "I'll change and be there in an hour."

"Perfect. Make it forty-five minutes and where something nice. We can go out for an early dinner after."

"Why do I have to wear something nice?" I asked. My friend was acting suspiciously. I could have sworn she was a notary.

"Because. I want to go somewhere nice, and let's be honest, honey, the way things have been recently, there's a fifty-fifty chance you'd show up wearing leggings with holes in them and a stained t-shirt."

"Hey," I protested. "I've been much better the last few days."

"Yes, you have. And I'm your best friend and want to make sure you keep up the momentum. I gotta go. See you soon."

Before I could ask what she was really up to, she hung up. I had a passing thought that it might have something to do with Hunter. But there was no way he'd come into Denver. He had a full inn to take care of. If it was about him, at least I wouldn't have to be in the same room with him.

I shut off my e-reader and headed for my room. Tugging off the *hole-free* leggings I had been wearing, I slipped on a pair of black wool dress slacks. I looked in my closet for a sweater to pair with them. I had that gorgeous red cashmere Christmas sweater Janine had tucked into my bag. I pulled it off the shelf to find the note she'd written still attached.

> *We have a family tradition of dressing up on Christmas Eve. I'm hoping you'll have a chance to wear this with us.*
> *Love J.*

I thumbed the tear away that threatened to form at the corner of my eye and put it back on the shelf. I would wear it on Christmas Eve; it just wouldn't be while I was with them. I found a forest-green cable-knit V-neck that would look seasonal but not over the top and added a red and green scarf that matched the holiday vibe I was going for and tied it in place.

It took me just about twenty minutes to drive the nine miles downtown to Patty's office. It was easier to get a parking space than I had expected. I guessed she hadn't been wrong when she said most of the office was out for the holiday. I'd made it there in thirty-five minutes.

Ruth looked up from the reception desk and greeted me with a smile. "Hi, Amber. Patty's still in a meeting." Ruth got up from behind the desk and led me down the hall to one of the conference rooms. "She asked me to put you in here until she finishes up."

I'd known Ruth for years and could have easily waited for Patty in the reception area, passing the time with Ruth. I arched a brow as she opened the door and motioned me in. She smiled and shrugged. I stepped inside and picked the chair at the head of the conference table. I might as well chair my own meeting, I laughed at my joke.

I sat down and turned the chair to stare out at the wonderful view of the downtown the wall of windows in the room provided. As I fidgeted back and forth in the chair, I was brought back to the afternoon at Leo's garage and Amy spinning in circles, giggling as she waited for us to finish our business. I don't know why I did it. Maybe just to feel closer to a little girl I missed so much, but I pushed hard, spinning the expensive leather chair just like she had done with that squeaky old relic back in Leo's shop. I had just completed my third revolution when the door opened behind me. I turned, ready to ask Patty why she'd had me sequestered in here, but instead of Patty, Peter Brown walked through the door. As in Peter Brown, the owner and lead partner in the Brown Group. The child-like grin on my face disappeared in an instant, replaced by abject mortification.

"Amber, how nice to see you. Merry Christmas," he said, reaching out his hand to shake mine. His lips were pressed together, no doubt to stifle a laugh. "I'm glad you could keep yourself occupied while you were waiting."

"Um, hi," I stammered. "Um, Merry Christmas to you too." I stood and shook his hand, my body wobbling dizzily. "I, ah, I'm sorry. Ruth put me in here to wait for Patty. I'll just show myself back to the lobby and get out of your way."

His head tilted to the side like he was more confused than I was before a smile inched up at the corner of his mouth. "Patty will join us in just a moment. I felt bad that we were running a little long and didn't want you waiting on your own." He placed his hand on my shoulder, guiding me back into the chair. "Can I get you coffee or something?"

I started to decline. But anxiety was coming on, and my mouth was as dry as a desert. Embarrassment could do that to a girl. "Coffee would be great," I forced out with an arid tongue. "And maybe an explanation about what's going on."

He smiled and leaned forward, pressing a button on the communication hub in the center of the table. "Ruth, could you please bring in the refreshment service now?"

"Certainly, Mr. Brown."

"Didn't Patty tell you we had some paperwork to sign?" he asked.

"She did, but let's be honest, Mr. Brown…" he cut me off.

"It's Peter, please; we've known each other for years."

"We have," I agreed. "And I know a little about your business. I know Patty could handle the contract for selling my home. And my little home is at least a zero or two short of being worth your time."

"I'm hurt, Amber," he said sarcastically, clutching his chest and laughing. "We treat all our clients with the same professional respect."

I rolled my eyes in a move I knew Snow would be proud of. Damn, I missed that girl. Young woman, I corrected myself. Before I could push him for a better explanation, Ruth arrived with a cart of coffee, a tea caddy and a selection of delicious-looking pastries. I could hear Patty talking as she walked down the hall, and it sounded like she wasn't alone.

Peter took a mug from the cart and poured me a coffee.

"Cream or sugar?" He asked.

"No, thank you."

"She takes it black," a beautiful baritone added from just outside the door. An instant later, the owner of the voice that I heard in my dreams every night appeared at the threshold.

"Hunter," I gasped. It was a whisper, a prayer and an accusation as Patty met my gaze as she followed him into the conference room. She was followed by two men. One I recognized as one of her coworkers; the other I didn't know. "What's going on? Why are you here? I thought you had an inn full of guests you need to take care of."

"I do. If we get this done quickly, I might just be back in time to serve them dinner," Hunter said with a laugh. "Hector will be there if I'm not, but even if he wasn't, you are more important, Amber. You will always be more important."

His eyes met mine, and everything that I had planned to say got forgotten. I was so lost in those beautiful brown orbs.

"Let's get started, shall we?" Peter said.

"We're still waiting for…" Patty started.

"I'm coming," Janine said, walking in and closing the door behind her. "God, I'm so sorry. I totally lost track of time," she said, wrapping me in a hug. "I've missed you," she whispered before kissing my cheek. "It's been so long since I've had two hours to myself to shop in a store that didn't sell groceries, or that I didn't own, it was nearly impossible to pull myself away. I hope you weren't waiting for me too long."

"We just sat down," Hunter said, smiling at his sister. I didn't miss while he still looked like the weight of the world was on his shoulders, it seemed just a little bit lighter than the morning everything went to hell. "But let's get this done."

"Excellent," Peter began. Patty slid a folder in front of me as everyone else looked down at theirs. "I'll give a quick review just to confirm the details and give Amber a moment to bring herself up to speed. Feel free to stop me with any questions."

"Why am I here?" I blurted out, getting more anxious and confused by the second.

"I'm getting to that," Peter said. "I promise you'll understand very soon."

He smiled at me, hesitating before he continued. "We are here to sign the agreement forming Snowflake LLC. An investment in The Snowflake Inn and surrounding property to allow for the renovation and expansion of said property. This represents an initial cash investment of ten million dollars by The Brown group and investment of hospitality assets held by Mr. Hunter Holmes. The current mortgage held by the Holmes Family Trust will be discharged as soon as practicable but not later than twenty-one days after the deposit of funds into Snowflake LLC accounts. Mr. Hunter Holmes attests that no other liens are or can be claimed against said property."

"Why the hell am I here?" I leaned over and whispered in Janine's ear. She had sat down next to me.

She reached across and tapped the folder that I'd yet to open. "It's all in there," she smiled. "But I think he's about to tell you, regardless."

Peter was still talking. "Shares in Snowflake LLC will be distributed as follows. The Brown Group will hold thirty-four percent, Hunter Holmes eleven percent, Janine Holmes eleven percent, Elizabeth Janet Holmes eleven percent, Meghan Janine Holmes eleven percent, Amy Marie Holmes eleven percent, and Amber Scott eleven percent. Is everyone in agreement?"

My ears rang, and it felt like the room spun around me. I noticed everyone around the table nod and then turn to look at me. I couldn't understand why they were looking at me. I couldn't understand why I was in the room at all. The information Peter provided reverberated around in my head until one sound bite stood out: *Amber Scott, eleven percent.*

"Wait. What? Did you just say I have an eleven percent stake in the company?" I'm sure my voice was so high that there were dogs barking in Wyoming.

"He did," Hunter and Janine said together.

"Why am I listed as a shareholder?" I couldn't quite make it make sense.

"Because you are part of this family. At least I want you to be," Hunter said, his eyes now melting with heat. If he kept looking at me like that, my core was going to be melting too.

"Hunter. No." I murmured.

"Why don't we give them the room for a minute?" Patty said. Everyone got up and filed out of the conference room. Janine clutched my shoulder as she passed but didn't say a word.

The thought that Hunter was trying to buy my love passed through my mind. I quickly dismissed it. I refused to confuse a man like Hunter with a man like Lance. "But I'm not part of the family, Hunter," I said. "I still have things I have to figure out before we can even be together. *If* we can be together."

"I know. But I believe in my heart that you will be."

"Why? What would make you give up control of the inn? You've been so insistent that it was off limits. That you had a responsibility to Jenn."

"That's a fair question," he said. "I said those things, and it took me a while, but I realized I was wrong. The possibility of losing you opened my eyes. And a wise woman, whom I loved and respected, told me recently that the dead have no claim to the living. I've been pretending to be the one in that cemetery for far too long, Amber. Thank you for being the one who finally made me realize that. It might have taken me longer than it should have, but I know now. I just hope it's not too late."

This was such a change, and if he truly felt this way, my biggest fear, that I could never have all of him was gone. It still didn't change the fact that I had no claim to that property. I didn't want what wasn't mine. I didn't want what was rightfully Hunter and the girls' "It doesn't feel right."

"It is right. The girls agreed the moment I suggested it. Well, including Janine was actually Meg's idea because it made 'the math easier to math'. Don't tell her that's the reason though, okay?"

I couldn't help but laugh. "That's a secret I might need convincing to keep."

A smile spread across Hunter's face that was so beautiful it was like watching the sun rise over the ocean. There was more than a hint of mischief in it. "I can think of several things to try."

"I bet you can." Every nerve in my body was awake and paying attention to what he might suggest, but I still didn't understand. "I'm happy you've been able to break free of your chains, but that doesn't explain why you gave an ownership share to me."

"Because I want to help break your chains too. You want all of my heart. And you deserve all of my heart. I will always love Jenn and be thankful for the daughters we have, but that doesn't mean I don't love you completely. I mean that, and I think you can believe that too. But actions speak louder than words. The one thing that symbolized my ties to Jenn was the inn. I hope that by giving you an equal share, that proves you are more important to me than that heap of sticks and bricks could ever be."

He was right. If there was one thing that proved to me he was ready to give himself to me, it was that. "I don't know what to say. It's a lot to process."

"I understand. Take your time. You don't have to give me an answer today."

"But we're here for the signing. If I wait, won't it put getting the money in time in danger?"

"It might, but I don't want that to force your hand. We can redistribute the shares. There's one other thing you should know," he continued. "As the girls are minors, the agreement stipulates that you, Janine and I each act as conservators for one of the girls. I get Elizabeth, Janine has Meg, and you have Amy. So technically you'll outvote me after next year for a long time. You get to be my boss." He finished wiggling his eyebrows like the goof I knew he could be.

I smiled at him. I loved him more than I'd ever loved anyone in my life. This was just so much to wrap my mind around, and I felt like I had to make a life-altering decision, not just for myself, but for a family that I cared so much for. If I made the wrong decision. It wouldn't just ruin my life.

Hunter stood and came around the table to kneel in front of me. "I love you, Amber. I think I knew it from the first moment I saw you in the lobby trying to get your bearings. You felt like the world had bowled you over, not just Leo's plow. I want you in my life for the rest of my life. I've never been more certain of anything. Never," he repeated, and I got the sense that included Jenn. "But I couldn't live with myself if I thought for a second I had forced you into it."

He kissed my forehead and stood. He turned and opened the door. "Sorry. You all can come back in now."

Once everybody was seated, Hunter came back and stood by me with his hand on my shoulder. "I want to thank everyone for all that you've done to make this agreement happen. Amber needs some time to think about everything. Peter, when's our drop-dead date?"

"January second."

"Patty, can we have an alternative agreement written up without Amber as a shareholder by then?" he asked.

Patty nodded. "It might mean paying a few lawyers overtime, but it wouldn't be hard to do."

"Great," Hunter said. "Then, if it's okay with you, Peter, I suggest we take care of signing this agreement now. Amber can take her copy home and think it over. If she decides to sign, then Patty can take care of that with her, and we'll be set. If she decides not to sign, then Janine and I will come back on the second and sign the alternative."

"That works for me," Peter agreed. "Is that okay with you, Amber?"

I looked at Hunter. "Thank you." Then I turned to Peter. "That's fine with me. I appreciate everyone's understanding."

I watched as documents were passed around the table. Signatures were scrawled on appointed lines, and I noticed Janine and Hunter were signing their names twice. Of course. They had to sign for the girls as conservators; only my signature was missing over Amy's name.

I pulled out my copy and scanned the details one more time. There were still too many questions racing through my mind, but I knew I could be there for Amy. I grabbed a pen from the center of the table and signed my name above Amy's. "I can say yes to that," I said as I passed my copy to Hunter.

He took the document and looked down at my signature. A smile spread across his face. "I'm glad."

I signed the other three copies, and Patty collected them all. "Great. That takes care of everything for now," Patty said. She slid a copy across the table to me. "Read that over, and we can talk about it tomorrow night at dinner if you want."

I laughed, "You can count on it." Everyone else chuckled.

"Well, I have an inn full of hungry guests I have to get back to feed," Hunter said. "And if I don't hit any traffic, I just might make it in time."

He stood and started toward the door, hesitating when he stepped next to where I was sitting. "It was good to see you. The girls wanted to make sure I told you that you are still welcome for Christmas, and Elizabeth refused to reserve room 108 just in case."

"Hunter, I…"

"No pressure," he cut me off. "I just wanted you to know that's how we all feel." He leaned down and kissed me on the cheek. Without another word, he walked out the door.

"What he said," Janine hugged me and kissed my cheek as well. "I wish I could stay and talk, but if I don't hurry and catch him, Hunter will forget we're riding together, and it's a long uphill walk to Homer Pass." She walked a few steps and turned. "Don't forget to wear that sweater tomorrow night." Before I could reply, she hustled down the hall after Hunter.

# 42

# As Good As I Can Be

## Hunter

I speed-walked out of the meeting, down eight flights of stairs, through the lobby, down the block, and around the corner to where I'd parked my truck. Once I'd opened the door and climbed inside, I took my first conscious breath. It took every bit of resolve that I had to leave that meeting and not get down on my knees and beg Amber to sign the damn contract and come home.

I wanted her home, and in my heart, I knew her home was at The Snowflake Inn. Her home was with me and the girls.

I rested my head on the steering wheel. I kept asking myself if I'd done the right thing. Jenn's words echoed through my mind: "sometimes being a gentleman means not taking no for an answer." When we had the room to ourselves, my plan was to plead my case until Amber finally gave in and signed. More importantly, agreed to give me a second chance. But I couldn't do it. She hadn't shared a lot about her marriage to Lance, but from what little I knew about it, he'd never given what she thought or wanted much consideration. I would never be that man.

Keeping things light had been nearly impossible, but I knew if I was as intense as I sometimes was, she'd feel even more pressure to make a decision. It killed me to wait, but I had to. This had to be on her time, not mine.

A tap on the passenger window startled me out of my thoughts. I unlocked the door so Janine could get in.

"How are you doing?" she asked.

"As good as I can be. That was a lot harder than I expected."

"I know," she said, leaning over the console and giving me a hug. "And I'm so damn proud of you." She sat back in her seat and wiped a tear from her eye. "You did the right thing."

"Did I?" I asked. I wasn't sure about that.

"You did a lot of things right in there. Signed a deal that will keep the inn alive and well and in your family for a long, long time. Proved to everyone you love that you're ready to go on living. And did everything you could to show Amber how much you loved, respected and wanted her."

"I hope so."

"I know so," she said.

"I couldn't do it, though."

"Couldn't do what."

"I was ready to beg, plead and cajole Amber until she said yes," I said. "I went in there fully intending to take Jenn's advice and not take no for an answer."

"So why didn't you?" she asked. Her brow arched, and a knowing smirk on her mouth.

"Because in the middle of explaining the deal to Amber, I realized I hadn't understood what Jenn had meant. She was far too independent to suggest that I manipulate someone into giving me the answer I wanted. I think I knew that already when I chose not to bring the girls with us today. Amber would never deny the girls."

"What she meant was that I should never stop trying as long as there was hope. It's why I suggested the alternative agreement."

"That was a surprise," Janine said. "What made you think of that?"

"Because I knew Amber accepted that I'd included her to prove I would let her into every part of me. The thing she wanted most. But I also understood that Amber could see it as a way to trap her or maybe taking something that she didn't have a right to. I had to let her have a choice. A choice to do what she felt was the right thing."

Janine smiled and reached across and took my hand. "I'm even prouder of you now. You're pretty smart for a guy that claims to have no insight into relationships."

I shrugged. "I had a lot of help, and I owe you a lot of thanks." I started the truck. "But we'd better get going. I have an inn to run."

# 43

# A Quandary

## Amber

I remained seated as everyone except Patty filed out of the conference room. I had a powerful urge to run after Hunter and tell him yes. I had an equally powerful urge to pummel my best friend for springing a surprise attack on my fragile emotions. "What the actual fuck, Patty? You're supposed to be on my side."

"I am on your side," she said, moving to sit next to me. "I will always be on your side. Whatever you decide."

"Really? Bringing me down here under the false pretense that I had paperwork to sign doesn't really feel like being on my side. It feels like being on Hunter's side."

"It wasn't a false pretense. You did have paperwork to sign," she said with a smug smile that told me she knew I was right but was refusing to admit it.

"Paperwork for *my* house. Not other paperwork. This is other paperwork, Patty," I said, raising my voice and pounding the folder in front of me with my fingers. "Other. Paperwork." I enunciated each syllable to make my point.

"Six of one, half-dozen of another," she said, totally dismissing me with a shrug. "I might have stretched the truth just the teensiest bit, but needed to get you here and I didn't have the time to get into it with you. Would you have come if you had known Hunter was going to be here?"

"Of course not," I answered.

"Well then, I rest my case. You needed to hear what he had to say. You needed to understand what he did, and I think this was a much better option than him showing up on your doorstep with the girls," she finished, leaning back in her chair.

I grunted because I knew she was right. I could never have done something with the girls looking on that I knew hurt them. It was hard enough to do what I had to do without three sets of ice-blue eyes staring at me.

"What the hell am I supposed to do, Patty? I don't deserve an ownership stake in the inn. I want Hunter's love, not his money."

"This is about his heart, Amber. Don't you see that? This is him proving to you without a doubt that he wants you to be involved in every part of his life. The way I see it, it's the grandest gesture of all grand gestures."

"It is pretty grand," I agreed with a sigh that included more than just a little longing for the man that made it.

"What does your heart tell you to do, Amber?"

"Ha!" I fake laughed. "She can't be trusted. She chose Lance once. That's all the proof you need of her inability to make sane decisions."

"Honey," Patty said, shaking her head. "We all make mistakes. You're older and wiser and stronger than you were then. And we both know Lance couldn't hold a candle to Hunter."

"Maybe," I muttered, not completely convinced of her confidence in me.

"Do you love Hunter?"

Was she stupid? Did my best friend just lose her mind? "Of course."

"Do you think he loves you?"

"Why are you asking me such dumb questions?"

"Because you seem to need the dumb answers before you can figure out what you want to do," Patty said, leveling me with a challenging look.

"Fine," I huffed. "Yes, I love Hunter. Yes, I know he loves me. And before you ask, yes, I believe I have all of him, not just some of him."

"Then what is it that's still standing in your way?"

I couldn't answer that, no matter how hard I tried.

I skipped dinner with Patty after the signing. I needed to figure my stuff out, and I needed to do it on my own. At least try to before she came over to spend Christmas Eve with me.

I tossed and turned all night and finally gave up and got up at the ungodly hour of six-thirty.

I padded into the kitchen, made a pot of coffee and then dropped into my nest and watched the morning news. Another snowstorm was on the way tonight and forecast to continue into Christmas morning. Four to six inches here in Denver but more than a foot in the higher elevations. I smiled, thinking that was wonderful and wondered when the hell my brain had been swapped with someone else's. When had I ever been that happy about snow? But I knew the truth. I was happy for Hunter and the girls and what a good ski season could mean for their future. I couldn't help but remember how beautiful it was to watch the snow fall outside the big picture window in Hunter's family room. How I'd stood there drinking my hot cocoa and watched the girls sled down the hill. The smiles and the laughter. Damn it. I missed them.

I had the roast prepped and ready to put in the oven for dinner by noon. The house was clean. All my gifts were wrapped. I didn't even have a stray load of laundry to do. What I didn't have was anything for dessert. I might have been leaning heavily on sweet snacks for the past few days.

I took a quick peek at the clock, almost one. Patty wasn't coming until four, so I had plenty of time to run out and get something. The last-minute rush at the grocery store would be in full swing. It would be crazy busy.

No way. Not dealing with the crowds. I had all I needed to bake a batch of Christmas cookies, and baking might just help me forget the decision I was still trying to avoid and get a little into the Christmas spirit.

I put the last two baking sheets into the oven. Ten dozen cookies might be a bit of an overkill for two people. But who knows, we might be overrun with carolers tonight, and you must have cookies and cocoa for carolers. I'd never had carolers at this house before, but you gotta be prepared, right?

Baking had helped my mood, and I was proud I had pushed past my funk to do it. Yeah, my mind had wandered back to working with Hunter in the kitchen the day after Thanksgiving. How we had pulled together as a team and fed all those people. But that was a good memory, and that's what I wanted to have of my short time with Hunter and his family. Good memories.

Taking the last batch from the oven, I left them on the counter to cool while I filled the gigantic cookie jar that had once been my grandmother's. More good memories, me, my mom, and my grandmother baking for Christmas dinner. I might not have had a dad, but I had them. It was nice to focus on the good things I had and not the things I didn't. It was hard though, not to be very conscious of Hunter. The one thing I wanted most of all.

As I put the last of the cookies into the jar, I remembered how excited

Amy had been to help me decorate them one afternoon after school. She loved sprinkling the colored sugar on top, having only had frosted cookies before. I couldn't deny the small hope that whenever she saw sugar-decorated cookies, she would think of me and the brief time I was lucky enough to have her in my life.

I wiped a tear away. I refused to lapse into sadness. That was a good memory, and I was determined to focus on the good. Cookies stored, kitchen cleaned, I checked the time. It was just after two. I didn't have to put the roast in until a little after five. I trudged down the hall to wash up and change.

After a quick shower, I brushed out my hair and did my makeup. I went to my closet and found a red and green plaid wool skirt that fell just below my knees. I'd had the thing for six years and never worn it. I was thrilled that it still fit when I slipped it on. I'd never felt festive enough to wear it, and I couldn't understand why I felt tonight was the night, but I did. I pulled on my black high-heeled boots, zipping them up to my knees and, last but not least, I pulled Janine's red sweater over my head. Placing her note on my bureau. I checked myself in my full-length mirror and couldn't deny that I liked what I saw. I couldn't help feeling that it shouldn't be Patty I was dressing for tonight.

I made my way back to the living room and put on my Christmas playlist. I stood there and looked at my meager Christmas tree. All the gifts neatly wrapped underneath. Gifts that wouldn't be opened on Christmas Eve or Christmas morning. Who knew exactly when I would get to give them to three young ladies and their oh so handsome father. Was I making another mistake? I thought back to the last question Patty had asked. What was standing in my way?

The key turning in the front door deadbolt announced Patty's arrival. She was hours early but just in time. She looked up to see me standing there, and her eyes widened, and her lips slowly curved up into a smile. "Wow. Look at you."

"You like?"

"You look stunning, Amber." She set the shopping bag full of gifts she was carrying on the floor and crossed her arms. "It seems like there's something you might like to say."

I nodded. "You asked me a question I couldn't answer yesterday. I know now the answer was fear. But you know what, Patty? I don't think I'm afraid anymore."

# 44

# I'll Be Home for Christmas

## Hunter

That was a wonderful buffet, Hunter," Mrs. Small said as she made her way toward the library. "You and your family are doing such a wonderful job here."

"Thank you, Mrs. Small. We're doing our best," I said. The idea of a Christmas Eve buffet was something Amber and I had come up with one night as we lay in bed just talking. We'd wanted to do something special but also give us the opportunity to spend time with the family as well.

I had also set up an open reception in the library with desserts, coffee and tea for the guests to enjoy as they wanted. At least they weren't all forced to hibernate in their rooms this way. I had never expected it to be so popular. The last time I'd checked, I would have sworn every guest we had was in there, and they didn't look like they were planning on going back to their rooms any time soon. It was like one big family party. Except one of our family wasn't where she was supposed to be.

I shut the double French doors to the dining room and turned out the lights. I'd worry about the final cleanup later. I walked down the hall to the library intending to round up the girls, and the rest of my family and head back to the residence to do our usual celebration.

It was already nine o'clock and well past Amy's bedtime. I'd done the holidays enough times with kids to know they never went to bed on time on Christmas Eve, but I wanted to avoid her being up so late that she was a total trash puppy tomorrow.

This was the first year we'd ever had a full inn. The best year we'd had before this was ten rooms; this year it was all thirty-six. well thirty-five, room 108, was still empty. I had hoped Snow's insistence on leaving it vacant meant she'd had one of her 'feelings' about Amber coming back to us. The look on her face when I asked told me she hadn't.

In fact, all three girls had been very subdued the past couple of days. I knew they had hoped for better news from me after the signing. So had I. Today had been a nightmare because every time a door opened, I looked up hoping to see Amber walk through it. Now, I just hoped I could get through our family gift giving without breaking down. I was trying to stay positive, and I wasn't about to give up, until she told me I had to. Don't take no for an answer. I was going to keep trying. I just hoped I'd understood what Jenn meant.

We could have rented out twice as many rooms as we had. I needed to finish the fourth floor. That was first on the list once the funding from the Brown Group came through. I sent a silent thank you to Amber. Without her connection to Patty, none of this ever would have happened. If only I'd realized how grateful I should have been to her before, I wouldn't be fighting to hide the melancholy I was feeling now.

I walked into the library, and there was barely room to turn around. Hotel guests and locals mingled and talked. Almost everyone was dressed in holiday finery. There were a couple of people in ugly sweaters with twinkling lights on the front. Leo had been one of them until he left about fifteen minutes ago, complaining about broken-down plows and how he was the only reliable driver up here. I tried to convince him to wait, or he'd miss our gift exchange, but he wouldn't wait. The roads could have waited an hour. Especially where it wasn't even his time to plow.

Superintendent Miller was here, and I knew she'd been hoping to find that Amber had returned too. She was currently deep in conversation with Hector and Emma from the diner. I scanned the room and found Megan and Amy in a corner quietly entertaining themselves. As soon as I found Snow, I'd grab them and head back to the residence. The party in here would have to go on without us. This business was important, but if I'd learned one thing in the past few days, it was that family was the most important.

It took me a minute, but I spotted Snow by the fireplace talking pleasantly with Walter and Barbara. I wasn't looking forward to having to apologize to them later. To anyone who didn't know her, she would appear to be enjoying the conversation, but I could tell she was putting on a brave front. All my girls were missing Amber, every bit as much as I was. Something the couple said broke through her facade because a bright smile suddenly filled her face. She excused herself and weaved her way through the room and said something to her sisters, who got up and headed in my direction. I assumed they must have realized what I wanted, but when I went to ask them to grab their aunts and meet me in the residence, Snow spoke before I had a chance.

"We'll be right back, Dad. Could you check the coffee? I think it's running low."

"The coffee can wait. Don't you want to open your presents?" I asked, figuring that would be enough incentive to change their minds.

"We can't leave our guest unattended, Dad," Snow admonished me like I was the child.

"Yeah, Dad," Amy agreed.

There was something very wrong with my children. "Where are you going?" I asked, not trusting their willingness to wait even ten seconds to open gifts.

"We'll be right back, Dad," Megan answered. "We've got something to do."

"Like what?"

"It's a Christmas surprise, Dad," Snow said, rolling her eyes. "Don't be such a Grinch."

They hurried down the hall, whispering, and unfortunately there was enough background conversation in the library that I couldn't catch what they were saying.

"What are they up to?" Janine asked, sliding her arm around my shoulders.

"I don't know. Snow said it was some kind of surprise."

"Mm," she hummed. "Something then. I guess we'll find out," she laughed. "This was nice tonight. Not exactly our usual family celebration, but good all the same." She gave my arm a squeeze before stepping around to face me. "How are you doing?"

"Fine," I grumbled. We both knew it was a lie, but I didn't want to get into it.

"Really? Because I know you were hoping Amber would show up tonight."

"I've got to give her time," I said, knowing it was true. It didn't make it any easier. "There's always tomorrow."

"There is," she agreed. "Let's get some pie before it's all gone." She tugged me by the arm and led me to the dessert table. She was a won-derful sister. Pie would always cheer me up when something went wrong when we were kids.

## Amber

I was focused intently on Patty's taillights in front of me. We'd barely made it to Aspen Park before the snow got heavier. The higher up we drove, the harder the snow fell. It was beautiful. I just wished I could have enjoyed it more than trying so hard not to have a repeat per-formance of a month ago.

We were probably about fifteen miles from Homer Pass when she pulled into a scenic turnout. I took a full breath for the first time in an hour and uncoiled my fingers from their vice grip on the steering wheel.

Her car door opened, and she slid out, pulling her hood up over her head and making her way toward me. She was dressed more reasonably for this weather than I was, though at least this time I had multiple reason-able choices packed if I was forced into survival mode.

"It's a damn good thing you love him so much because I'd hate to be risking my life like this for a crush that will be gone next week."

"I'm sorry, Patty. I told you that you could have ridden with me." I wanted to get to Hunter and the girls tonight. Maybe I should have waited until tomorrow after the storm. One more questionable decision I'd dragged my best friend into. "Should we maybe wait here until the snow lets up a little? I don't want either of us to drive off the side of the moun-tain."

"Don't worry, honey. I've called in the cavalry."

Before I could ask her what she meant, familiar flashing yellow lights tinted the air, and a large orange truck pulled up in front of us. One of my newest, most favorite people hopped out of the cab. "Good evening, ladies," he said, wading through the snow toward us. "This is getting to be a habit, Amber. If you like to drive in the snow so much, I'm going to have to teach you to drive a plow." His body shook when he laughed, and, yeah, my mind when straight to Santa and bowls full of jelly.

"Thanks so much for coming to help us," Patty said. "You're welcome to teach me. That looks like a whole lot of fun."

"I could be convinced," he said with a wink. I could have been imagining it, but I would have sworn his cheeks got about five shades redder. "Okay, then." He took a breath and rubbed his hand over his face. "There's a whole bunch of people that will be happy to see you, so we better not dilly-dally any longer."

"A whole bunch?" I asked. "What do you mean by that?" I figured Hunter and the girls would hope I decided to sign and come back, but who else would be waiting for me?

Patty drew her brows together and scowled at him, which was very odd, and he gave her a sheepish look and a shrug. What was going on here?

"Let's go," Leo said. "The weather's not getting any better." Before I could ask either of them for an explanation, they both hustled back to their vehicles. "Follow me," he shouted, pulling himself up into the truck.

Driving the last few miles was much easier following Leo and his plow, and I breathed a sigh of relief when we pulled into the parking lot across from the inn. The walkway and steps looked freshly shoveled, and I was happy because my boots were made for style, not for snow. I wondered whether Leo had said something before he left. A part of me wanted this to be a surprise, but that wasn't important. The important thing was that I was here.

I stepped out of the car and looked up and The Snowflake Inn. Almost every window was lit, and it was like the old girl was glowing with life. The giant wreath on the front door, the garland wrapped on the railings on the porch and the lights from the Christmas tree Hunter and I had put up in the library shone through the window. It was a picture postcard, and if I hadn't been in such a hurry to get back with the people I loved, I would have fished out my phone to take some pictures for the new social media account.

I pulled as many of the bags of presents out of the back seat as I could carry. My clothes and the rest of my overspending would have to wait for later. I needed to see them, hug them, be with them as quickly as I could. As I walked up the stairs, I looked up to see three smiling faces standing at the top waiting to greet me.

"Welcome home, Amber," Elizabeth said, as she ran down the steps halfway to meet me.

"It's good to be home, Snow," I said cautiously, meeting her eyes as I used that name for the first time.

Her eyes watered, and her smile grew wider as she wrapped me in a hug. "You remembered," she whispered in my ear.

"Of course," I murmured back.

"Yeah, Amber, welcome home." Amy added, following right behind her sister.

"I'm so happy you're back," Meg said, her face stained with tears.

It absolutely melted my heart. I pulled all three of them into my chest and did my best not to topple back down the stairs, bringing all of us ass over teakettle into a snowbank. "God, I've missed you guys," I said. My bottom lip trembled as I fought back the overwhelming joy I was feeling. "Have you been out here long? Did Leo tell you I was on my way?"

"Leo knew?" Elizabeth asked. "Is that why he left?"

"I called him because the driving was getting terrible," Patty said, climbing up behind me. "Sorry, girls, Amber wanted to surprise you."

"But you knew," I said, looking at Elizabeth.

She nodded. "Only about five minutes ago. That's when we came out and cleaned off the steps."

"Does your dad know?" I doubted he did because I couldn't imagine him not being out here if he did.

"Nope," Amy answered. "This is going to be the bestest Christmas surprise for him ever." Her smile could have filled her face twice over.

"Then how about we go inside and give it to him?" I said and kissed her forehead. As much as I loved the girls, I wanted to see Hunter.

"There's a surprise for you too, Amber," Amy added.

"Amy!" Elizabeth said crossly.

I decided not to ask, but my curiosity was certainly piqued.

The moment we walked into the lobby, I could hear the din of conversation coming from the library. My heart swelled. He'd taken my suggestion and had a reception for the guests. I couldn't wait to see how it was going, but I didn't want my reunion with Hunter to be quite so public.

"Are those our presents?" Megan asked before I could tell them to go down and get their father.

"Mm hmm," I nodded. "I'll tell you a secret." I lowered my voice and bent to Amy's level. "There's even more in the car. I couldn't carry them all."

"Yay!" Amy and Megan shouted together.

"We have lots for you too," Amy assured me.

Apparently, the girls' shout was loud enough to be heard in the library, because when I looked up, Hunter was stepping into the hall with a brow arched, looking in our direction. "What's going on…" He stopped mid-sentence when his focus landed on me. "Amber," he breathed and moved swiftly in my direction.

I wanted to move to meet him halfway, but my feet were frozen in place. He was standing in front of me before I could move. His palm rested on my cheek. "You're here."

"I'm here," I answered. "And I plan on staying if you still want me?" His eyes were so dark with passion and want, it felt indecent to be just standing here with him in front of the girls.

"Always," he rasped, and then his lips were on mine. His mouth swallowed my gasp. My head tilted automatically to welcome him, and he didn't need asking twice. Our tongues tangled in a familiar dance. There was nothing awkward or timid about this kiss, and any thoughts that there might be a lingering distance between us were gone. My hands laced through his hair as I pulled him closer. It was sweet. It was passionate. It was salty from the tears streaming down my face. I never wanted this kiss to end.

A throat cleared behind me. "You guys maybe want to put a bookmark in that before it moves beyond what the girls should see?" Patty's special brand of sarcasm broke Hunter and me apart.

"Yeah, Dad, kissing is gross," Megan said.

"You keep right on thinking that, honey," Patty stepped in. "It's much safer that way. Then you don't have to take your life in your hands and drive up a mountain in a blizzard on Christmas Eve."

"Come on, Amber," Snow said. "Aunt Janine is in the library, and I know she wants to see you too."

"Yeah, and you're gonna be so surprised…" Amy started.

"Not if you tell her first," Megan cut in.

I looked at the three of them. They were definitely up to something, but I couldn't think what it could be. I hadn't known I was going to be here myself. "Before I go in, I want to give you your first present."

Amy jumped up and down, clapping her hands. I reached down into one of my shopping bags and pulled out a folder. Pulling out a copy of the contract forming Snowflake LLC. I looked first at Amy, then Megan, and finally focused on Snow. "Do you guys know what this is?" Amy shrugged, but Megan and Snow nodded. "Your dad did a very brave thing to show me how much he loved me, but it affects all of you too. I want to make sure that you're okay with what he did."

"We know Daddy loves you," Amy said, hugging my leg. "And I love you too."

"Aw," I said, bending down and lifting her into my arms. "I love all of you, but what Daddy did was a big deal. More than I ever could have expected."

"We know, Amber," Snow said, meeting my eye and silently communicating she knew exactly what I was referring to. "And we all wanted him to do it. It was a family decision and not one we made without thinking about all the possibilities."

"Okay." I eased Amy back onto her feet. And took a deep breath. "What this showed me was that I had all of Dad, not just little pieces. It helped me overcome a fear I've been hiding behind for a long time. One that kept me from loving your dad the way he deserved. Fear made me run away when things got hard, and one thing I want to prove to your dad is that I will not run away again. Even if things get really hard. I want you girls to know that too. I didn't want to sign this because I don't think I deserve it, but then I realized that if I did, then maybe that would show you all that I was committed to this family too."

I pulled a copy out of the folder and handed it to Hunter. "I signed these before I left. Patty and I delivered a copy to Peter Brown on our way here. Everything is set, and he promised there wouldn't be any delay in the funding."

Snow and Hunter collided trying to hug me, and we laughed as we found our way into an awkward embrace. Tears were flowing freely down our faces.

"Why are you guys crying?" Amy asked, thoroughly confused. "I thought everyone would be happy Amber's back."

"That's why we're crying, silly," Snow said, picking her up.

I pulled Megan to my side, and we all hugged together. We were a family.

# 45

# *Oh Holy Night*

## *Hunter*

I handed my copy of the contract to Snow and asked her to run it into the office.

"Here," Amber said, giving Snow the folder with her copy and Janine's. "They can all be together. Just like we're together." Snow gave Amber a hug and ran off with the documents.

While she did that, I helped Amber tuck the bags with her gifts behind the reception desk. There was no need to lug them into the library.

Snow returned quickly, and we walked down the hall to the library. I exchanged a quick look with the girls, who all returned knowing smiles. The moment we walked into the space, Janine spotted us and bolted in our direction.

"Amber," she shrieked. "Oh, thank God. I was so scared you weren't going to make it. I know how you hate driving in the snow."

Amber laughed, pulling Janine into a long embrace. "I might not have, if Leo hadn't come out to rescue me again." They held each other for a few moments before stepping back. "Was it really just the weather that had you worried about my arrival?"

"They all knew you would come back, honey. It was just a question of when. I didn't raise my daughter to runaway in fear."

I watched as Amber processed the source of the words that came from behind her. Recognition spread across her face, and she slowly turned, taking in the woman who spoke.

"Mom!" The shriek of joy from Amber's mouth was all the confirmation I needed to know that Patty and I had done the right thing. I met Patty's gaze, and we shared a smile. It had been Patty's idea to fly Amber's mother and stepdad out from Florida. Most of all, I wanted all of Amber's family here for Christmas, found family and natural too. Patty had agreed but thought it wouldn't be a bad plan to have her here just in case Amber needed additional convincing to overcome her fears.

"It's so good to see you, honey," her mother said, squeezing her tight. "I've missed you so much."

"I've missed you too, Mom. But why didn't you tell me you were coming? What was all that about Walter taking you away?"

"We wanted to surprise you. You sounded so stressed when we talked on Thanksgiving. Walter suggested we come for Christmas. We wanted you to have family around, and I know how you want to be independent. If I had told you then we were going to come, you would have just felt like you'd failed and not that we were doing something we wanted to do, not something we had to do."

"Thank you. I'm so glad you're here, but why come all the way up here? Why didn't you just come to the house in Denver?"

"You can thank Patty for that. I called her to let her know I was coming, and she told me everything that was going on with Hunter. I had a feeling that you would take the chance, and I didn't want to get in the way of your making that decision. One way or the other." Her mother kissed her cheek and stepped back from their hug. "Now go say hello to everyone else who is here to see you. Walter and I are staying until after the first of the year. We'll have plenty of time to catch up. I look forward to your showing me around this darling little town you now call home."

"Okay, Mom," Amber said. She thumbed away a tear from the corner of her eye and turned to greet Hector and Emma from the diner. She stopped and talked with the Smalls and a couple of other guests who had been here each weekend since Thanksgiving.

Superintendent Miller took her by the arm. "I'm so looking forward to seeing you on the third." The look the two of them exchanged was a look that held a secret I didn't understand.

"Me too," Amber replied, her eyes watering again. "Thank you for believing in me."

"Of course, darling. After all these years in education, I'm a pretty good judge of character. It wasn't hard for me to see that everything would work out in the end."

We spent another hour mingling with the guests and friends in the library. Everyone was exhausted by the time we were done with the reception. It was hard, but even the girls agreed it would be best to open gifts on Christmas Day.

Amber's parents and Patty headed up to their rooms. Everyone else headed home, and the girls willingly headed for bed. Amy was asleep before Amber finished the first page of her picture book. And maybe that was my favorite gift of the night. To see my daughter's peaceful expression as she slept and to watch Amber brush her bangs from her face before resting a kiss on her forehead.

All the lights were off in the family room except for the tree. A fire burned low in the hearth, bathing the room in a soft, ethereal glow. I sank down onto the sofa, exhaling a deep sigh. It had been a long day, but everything had worked out in the end. Amber was back. My girls were happy and safe. And I'd managed to not only keep the inn afloat but maybe even set it up for success neither Jenn nor I had ever dreamed possible.

"You must be exhausted," Amber said, and she sat down next to me. She wore that damn flannel nightgown I just couldn't resist. "You've had a long day, and I'm guessing we have breakfast for seventy to make in the morning."

I groaned. The clock on the mantel struck two just as I placed a kiss full of promises on Amber's lips. "I'm sure I will be, but right now, I'm so happy to have you home to worry about it."

"And I'm happy to be home," she said, returning the kiss. As our kiss deepened, she turned and straddled me. Her gown rucked up over her thighs as her body pressed onto mine.

"Fuck," I moaned through our kisses. I could feel the heat of her core through the worn gray sweats I'd thrown on. Whatever fatigue that had been creeping into my body was now forgotten.

"Mm," she hummed, reaching between us and stroking my cock through the fabric separating us. "Somebody seems very happy to see me." Her smile was loving but held the promise of something much naughtier. My hips raised to meet her touch, and she slipped her hand beneath the worn waistband, stroking her thumb under the sensitive head, spreading the pre-cum that had already formed, down my shaft. "Maybe we should turn off the lights on the tree and go to bed ourselves."

"To hell with the lights," I said and eased her off my lap before leading her down the hall to our room.

I had barely closed the door behind us when Amber pulled the nightgown over her head and laid down. Her eyes locked on mine as she spread herself for me. The corners of her mouth tipped up in a seductive smile as her hand slid between her legs. "Fuck me, Hunter. Claim me so that there will never be a doubt in my mind who I belong to. Fuck me like if you don't you'll die because that's exactly the way I feel. You're mine. Now and for the rest of our lives."

I heard the fabric give way as I ripped the t-shirt I was wearing over my head, and I nearly tripped stepping out of my sweats because there was just no way to get out of them, and into her, fast enough.

"You're mine," I growled as I pulled her hips to the edge of the bed. I lifted her legs to my chest and thrust inside her with a ferocity that had us both groaning in ecstasy. "And. I'm. Yours," I grunted in a staccato beat matching each thrust into her soaked pussy.

"Yes. Yes. Yes," she answered, echoing my rhythm.

Her perfect full tits bounced with each crash of our bodies. My hands reached out to cup them. My thumbs rubbed circles around her perfectly peaked buds. She reached between her legs and rubbed her clit. Her teeth sank into her bottom lip, biting back a moan as my cock slammed into that special spot inside her womb.

"Shit. Fuck. Shit," she cried out. "God, I'm going to come. Fuck. Hunter. Yes." Her back arched and stiffened before every muscle in her body spasmed as she came. I slowed my pace but fucked her through the orgasm until her she into the bed.

Her chest rose with a deep intake of breath before she exhaled and pulled herself up on the bed, laying her head on a pillow. Her hair fanned out beneath her, and the post-orgasmic glow on her cheeks was radiant. I didn't think I had ever seen anything more beautiful in my life. I eased onto the bed next to her and placed a chaste kiss on her lips.

As I lay down next to her, she chuckled. "I hope you don't think we're anywhere near done yet, Hunter Holmes." She pushed herself up onto her elbows and met my gaze. "We're claiming each other tonight. I wouldn't mind at all coming again, and you absolutely need to come." Her hand wrapped around my still-hard cock and stroked me as she continued to talk. "I want to feel you inside me tomorrow morning. I want to remember tonight all day. I want to fight to concentrate on anything except how fucking sexy you are while the girls open their presents; to sit at dinner next to you and still feel the slickness between my thighs and know it's all your doing. And then I want to crawl into bed tomorrow night and do this all over again. I know it's unreasonable, but I want this every night for the rest of our lives. I want to be close to you, Hunter. So close, it's like we're the same person."

Fuck. This woman. I was the luckiest man alive. I might not be the smartest, but I was intelligent enough to know I could never refuse her. Before I could move, she threw her leg over my hips, facing away from me, and guided my cock back inside her. She tipped her head back, allowing her wavy chestnut mane to fall between her shoulders. I had an unobstructed view of her sexy back. I couldn't resist running my fingers over her shoulders, down her ribcage to her perfectly proportioned waist, resting on her generous hips. I guided her pace as she rode my cock. She was so wet and tight I knew I wouldn't last long. Then, she leaned forward, pressing her hands to my shins, giving me a perfect view of her core. My dick was slick from her arousal, and her forbidden entrance gaped ever so slightly.

Her ass was so fucking perfect, and the way it rippled each time she came down on my shaft was enough to make me lose my mind. Without a thought, my hand came down on a cheek with a loud crack.

"Ooh," she squealed, but never missed a beat.

"You like that?" I asked.

She looked back over her shoulder and met my stare. Her pupils were blown wide like I'd never seen before. She bit her lip and nodded. "Mm hmm," she cooed.

I smacked the other cheek.

"Oh, fuck," she groaned

Her pace picked up, and I was getting closer by the second. I knew I couldn't hold out much longer. I wanted her to come again, but most of all I needed to look into her eyes when I came. I needed her to see that she had me. All of me.

I gripped her hips and gently pushed her off and onto her back. It was like she knew exactly what I was thinking, what I wanted, because it was precisely what she needed herself. I hovered over her and our mouths met. The kiss was languid but intense. Our tongues tangled in an erotic dance. A flawless balance of dominance and submission.

I slid inside her in one steady push, and we held perfectly still for a moment. Skin pressed to skin. Deep as I could physically be inside her. We were one. Slowly we rocked our hips in sync, grinding against each other in a way I knew would give her the most pleasure. Our pace quickened until I couldn't hold back anymore. My body stiffened, and I felt my orgasm build from the top of my head to the tips of my toes until I was throbbing my release deep inside her pussy.

In one of those rare confluences of perfection, she followed me over the edge. The quake of her body, more subtle this time, but perhaps, was even more intense because of it. Her ankles locked behind my back as she held me in place as I continued to empty myself into her. Her fingers raked through my hair before cupping my face.

Our gazes locked, and in that moment, as our orgasms faded from our bodies, it was as if I could see directly into her soul and she into mine. There was no turning back now. Neither of us could run and hide because the other simply wouldn't allow it.

I knew she felt exactly the same.

As the moment passed, she nuzzled into my body and, not for the first time, I noticed how perfectly she fit. Every curve molding together. Our pieces fit seamlessly. We were made for each other. I'm not sure how long we stayed like that, but slowly, we relaxed to the edge of blissful sleep.

We had served Christmas breakfast to over eighty family, friends, and guests of the inn. After a quick cleanup, we made our way back to the family room to open presents. My eyes stung with unshed emotion as I looked around. For the first time, the large open space felt small. But that was because it was overflowing with a family's love.

Janine and the twins shared the armchair I usually occupied while Amber's mother and stepdad took up residence at one end of the sofa. Patty was at the other end, laughing at something my cousin Leo was saying. God only knew what tall tale he was spinning for her benefit.

Meg sat crisscross in the recliner, silently taking everything in, like usual, and Snow was sorting through presents, ready to do her annual job as Santa's special elf and deliver them all. I wasn't a bit surprised that Amy had commandeered Amber the first second she could. They were sitting on the floor next to the tree and she was busy explaining each new bit of Barbie paraphernalia Santa had left her - a Barbie remote control SUV, the Dream Closet with about sixteen thousand outfits which had been supplemented by several Santas, namely Amber, Janine and Patty, because apparently my abilities were suspect. God only knew what more pink surprises awaited her wrapped under the tree.

When the chaos of presents was finally done, I was feeding another log onto the fire. Amber's mother stepped up and wrapped me in a hug. "Hunter, thank you so much for including us in your family's Christmas."

I smiled and looked over her shoulder to see Amber in the recliner with Meg, looking through the pile of books she'd gotten. Amber had convinced her it was okay to read something that wasn't on a screen. Amy was playing quietly at her feet, dressing and undressing several dolls in new outfits. I got the feeling Amy didn't trust I wouldn't say something stupid again and scare her away. I guess she figured she had the power to stop that from happening. She might be right.

To complete the trifecta, Snow was sitting on one of the arms holding the Reformation cashmere sweater Amber had given her like it was the most precious thing ever made. I had never been hip enough to buy the *right* brands. I nodded in their direction so her mother could see what I did. "I'd say my girls would tell you it's your family now too. How do you feel about being a grandma to three?"

She looked up at me with watery eyes and a slight tremor of her lips. "I say it's the best Christmas gift ever."

The irony of the successful start to the inn's season this year was that our family Christmas dinner was an intimate affair for sixty. While some of our guests were with family and others had chosen to get dinner at the ski area, most elected to come back to the inn to eat. More than one guest had commented that it felt like being home. We'd always had excellent reviews and more than a few repeat guests, but it wasn't until Amber arrived, anyone had ever told us that The Snowflake Inn felt like home. I could only explain it as her own special brand of magic. I guess our family was growing in more ways than one.

It was after eleven by the time the last of our guests had left the library, which was rapidly becoming a popular gathering place. I knew Amber had loved it when she first arrived here. I made a mental note to ask her what she thought we could do to improve it. Maybe a hot-drink bar with coffee, tea and hot chocolate. I couldn't help but laugh. A month ago I wouldn't have asked anyone's opinion about the inn. I might have *listened* to Snow or Janine. Maybe.

I closed up the library and walked back to our quarters. I shut off the lights on the tree and banked the fire in the hearth. I looked around the room. It wasn't exactly a mess, but it was definitely lived in. Unwrapped gifts were stuffed under the tree. I exhaled a satisfied sigh.

For the first time in three years, I was truly content. Truly whole. Christmas had come, and I didn't feel like something or someone was missing. A shiver rolled down my spine, followed by an overwhelming sense of peace. I thumbed a tear from my eye and sent a silent Merry Christmas to Jenn. I would always love her, but now I could move on in freedom. A manacle that I'd forged myself out of guilt and misguided loyalty was finally and truly broken.

A warm set of arms wrapped around my waist, and soft lips brushed against my cheek. "It's okay, Hunter. I feel her too. And I'll thank her every day for trusting me with you and the girls." Amber brushed another tear from my face. "I love you, Hunter. I know it's taken me too long to say that. I think I've known it from the first time I saw you in that apron, covered in holiday pies. I just haven't trusted myself enough to say it without fear. But I can now. And I do now. I love you, Hunter Holmes, and I'm never going to be scared of that again."

"I love you too, Amber." I kissed the top of her head and breathed in the contentment I felt with her next to me. "Welcome home."

# 46

# *Judgement Day*

## *Amber*

Isat in the back row of the small courtroom. Leo on my left and Snow on my right. Hunter hadn't wanted her here, but I convinced him she should be. We held each other's hands the entire time. We listened as the lawyers on both sides stated their cases.

Henry and Lance sat at one table and Hunter and Janine at the other. There were other people in the gallery. I assumed they were there waiting to be heard next. No one, it seemed, was here to support Henry and Lance, and I couldn't find it in my heart to feel bad for them. They both might have had their demons to deal with, but I was well past any sympathy for Lance. I assumed he had received the information I sent him but had heard nothing in return. I wasn't really surprised; he never could admit when he was wrong.

Anxiety roiled in my stomach like eels in a barrel. I didn't understand why this was so drawn out. Hunter and Janine had presented the judge with all the documentation. The mortgage had been paid in full. The Holmes family trust was intact.

Lance's lawyers started saying something about fraud, and the judge held up his hand. He sorted through the papers in front of him and looked at each table. "I've heard enough from you, counselor. And given you more than ample opportunity to convince me why the documents provided by the defendants don't speak for themselves."

The judge cleared his throat and looked directly at Henry. "From what I see in front of me." The judge said. "The only fraud is in the manner in which you have attempted to get ahold of assets that are not rightfully yours. While the contact information is technically correct, you hold a responsibility to provide complete information to the court. You knew well that your parents' cabin was only sporadically occupied by seasonal guests.

It had not served as the primary address of the Trust for over ten years since your father passed. The business addresses of The Snowflake Inn and the Homer Pass General Mercantile are well known to you, and you have visited them on multiple occasions."

The judge continued. "Any amount owed to the Trust that was in arrears has been brought current. In fact, the private mortgage issued to Hunter Holmes and The Snowflake Inn LLC has been paid in full well ahead of maturity. It could be argued that payment patterns throughout the life of the loan were consistent and acceptable to the other trustee and the Trust's fund management firm. As a trustee, you were notified annually for twelve years before you challenged this practice. It appears to this court that you are either incompetent and failed to notice this practice or chose to use the judicial system to litigate personal grievances you have with your siblings."

I didn't want to jump to conclusions, but it certainly seemed to me that the judge was not happy with Henry and things were going our way. Snow glanced at me, and the grin that spread from ear to ear told me she thought so too.

"Mr. Tabor. Your firm has a reputation for shrewd business dealings. And while there are those that do not appreciate your methods, I have never seen you join in partnership with such questionable company. I recommend you assess your continued involvement with this partner carefully."

"Due to the nuisance nature of this suit, the court hereby orders the plaintiff to reimburse the defendants for all related expenses incurred in the performance of their defense. The defendants will submit to this court within 30 business days a full accounting of the said expenses. The plaintiff will repay in full the amount approved by the court within 90 days of notification from the court," the judge finished, banging his gavel on the desk. "This court finds in favor of the defendants. This court is in recess."

Snow and I were out of our seats and hugging Hunter and Janine before the judge's gavel hit the bench. Out of the corner of my eye, I saw Henry turn to speak with my ex-husband, only for Lance to turn his back on him and walk out of the courtroom.

Henry looked after him for a moment and then stuffed a pile of papers into a messenger bag, which he slung over his shoulder before turning to follow Lance out of the room. He never looked even once in our direction.

"Henry," Janine called after him. He stopped and turned to meet her stare. He just stared back, not uttering a sound. "If you ever decide you're ready to come back to this family, I'll be ready to listen. But this is all up to you. You get to decide if you want to fix this. I'm done trying."

"She's right, Henry," Hunter added. "It's time for us to be a family again."

His lips pursed together, and I watched as he swallowed. With a shrug, he turned and left. I don't think I'd ever witnessed such despair.

After a brief wrap-up with their lawyer, we all left the courthouse with the intention of going out for a celebratory lunch. My desire to celebrate dropped substantially when a certain douche canoe locked us in his sights and strode toward us with a determined stride.

"Amber," Lance said with a nod. "Congratulations, as I told you before, I'm not surprised at the result. You were right. I should have listened to my instincts about Henry."

His tone was as close to polite as I'd heard from him in five years. "Thank you," I said, uncertainty clear in my tone.

"I wanted to thank you for sending me that information. Apparently, I should have listened to my instincts on other things as well. I regret how things ended up between us, and you're right. It's way past time to move on."

My mouth fell open. That was closer to an apology from him than I ever expected to get.

"I wanted to let you both know that The Tabor Group Properties no longer has any interest in development at Homer Pass." He reached into his suit jacket pocket and pulled out an envelope, handing it to Hunter. "Consider what's in the envelope my apology to both of you. I sincerely wish you the best of luck." He turned and walked down the steps, turning to look back at me when he reached the bottom. "Goodbye, Amber," he said and turned and walked briskly across the courtyard.

I stood there in stunned silence, watching Lance disappear down the street. My mind was still trying to process what had just happened.

"Well, I'll be damned," Hunter said, which brought my attention back to the people I was with.

"What is it?" Snow asked.

Hunter was holding several pieces of paper. "Well, one is the deed to the Holmes mine and property. The other is the power of attorney for Henry's interest in the Trust. It looks like Henry gave everything he had over to the partnership with Lance."

"Oh, Hunter," Janine said, her eyes watering with emotion. "What did we ever do that would make him risk everything to do this?"

"I don't know, sis," Hunter said. I slid my arm around his waist and leaned close to him to offer whatever comfort I could. "I just don't know." He exhaled a heavy sigh. "At least he'll still get his trust allowance, but it sure looks like you and I control all the family assets."

"I guess so," she agreed. "We've got some decisions to make, but I want to use it to support our friends and neighbors in Holmer Pass. What do you think?"

"That sounds like the best idea ever," Snow said, giving her a hug. "Instead of turning Homer Pass into a playground for the rich, maybe we can make it a place for regular people to come and be with their families. You know, camping, mini-golf, stuff like that."

"I'm so proud of you, Snow," Hunter said. "How about we talk about that over lunch? I'm hungry, and I'd like to sit down and spend some time with my family."

# Epilog

# A New Season

## Hunter

Istood out front looking up at the inn and couldn't keep the smile from my face. Less than a year ago, when I stood in this spot, all I ever saw was a ton of responsibility and unaccomplished tasks. Now I saw hope and just how good life could be once you decide to live.

Janet's marketing had worked so well that we were nearly as busy this summer as we had been last winter. And with the record amount of snowfall, we had our best ski season ever. Things had fallen in line so fast that we went from hanging on by a very frayed thread to flush with more capital than we had time or ideas to use.

Amber's presence at the inn was undeniable the moment she crossed the threshold. Now after nine months, it was a truly tangible thing. The huge front porch of the inn, which I had nearly torn off years ago, was now a highlight. Wicker furniture with comfortable cushions filled the space. She had added window boxes along the railings, and flowerpots hung from the frieze beam. It was visual confirmation that The Snowflake Inn was alive and well in every season, not just the winter.

Amber had enlisted Meg's help with the flower project, and my middle child bloomed at the opportunity. Amber had wormed her way past Meg's quiet exterior wall and discovered a creative side I never knew existed. It was just one of many examples of how Amber had enriched all our lives.

My two girls in question were sitting side by side in wicker rockers enjoying the pleasant environment created by the fruits of their labor. Meg was still lost to the world, her nose in an e-reader. Amber was doing what she did best, making people feel at home, actively chatting with a couple dressed in hiking gear.

The local mountain club had just completed a link trail that led from our parking lot to a trail junction a half-mile away, joining to a system of trails in the Pike National Forest. Our guests loved it. And it's just one of many things I never would have imagined before Amber came into my life.

I looked down at the tray of drinks I was holding in my hands. Evidence of our first attempt at community investment. Janine's assistant at the Mercantile, Carly, had always wanted to open a bookstore and cafe. With help from the Trust, Homer's Passing Fancy opened three weeks ago and has been a tremendous success.

Inn guests receive a discount at Passing Fancy, and we now have an option for rooms that do not include breakfast to encourage guests to experience The Bighorn Diner too. With the increased tourist presence in the town, the Moose Jaw Tavern has started featuring live music on Fridays and Saturdays. Not all the locals are excited about the changes to our sleepy little town, but almost everyone has benefited from the growth over the past nine months.

The renovations on the fourth floor were nearly complete. Josh had convinced me to add a pair of elevators to the project. It was over thirty-thousand dollars that hadn't been in my original budget, but with how good the season was and the fact that the most consistent complaint, really the only complaint we ever heard, was how scary our elevator was. It was nearly one hundred years old. Elizabeth refused to ride it, putting the housekeeping cart on and pressing the button before jumping off and walking up the stairs. It was a worthwhile investment just for the reduction of teenage sass.

Amber finally allowed our guests to get on with their hike as I made my way up the steps onto the porch. I leaned down and placed a PG-rated kiss on her lips. I wanted to give her a little more, but Meg was still sitting right next to her. "Was my beautiful fiancé talking our guests' ears off again?" That's right, I made it official when we escaped for some 'couple time' on Memorial Day weekend. We planned on getting married on Thanksgiving Eve. The one-year anniversary of the day we all began living again.

"I was not talking anyone's ear off," she laughed, grabbing her extra-large black iced coffee from the tray I was holding. "I was simply making our guests feel welcome and answering their questions about the trails available."

"It's a good thing you brought drinks, Dad," Meg chirped in without lifting her eyes from the screen. "Keeps you from spending a lot of time in the doghouse."

It was wonderful that Amber had helped Meg come out of her shell, but the added sass that came with that transformation, I could do without. Sometimes. "Oh, yeah? Maybe I should just give this caffeine-free caramel macchiato to someone who shows a little more appreciation for their father?"

"If I didn't love and appreciate you, I wouldn't warn you when you were treading on thin ice," she replied with a grin, finally looking up from the screen. Her hand thrust out with fingers flexing, begging for the sweet concoction I'd brought her.

"Nice try," I laughed, handing her the drink. "Enjoying your last week of school vacation?" The question applied to both my women. Amber had been hired permanently as the middle-school English Language Arts teacher. We were in a small town, so kindergarten through eighth grade were all in the same building with the high school only a hundred yards away on the other side of the athletic fields.

Amber wouldn't have Meg for another year. And Snow complained because she'd never have a chance to be in her class. I enjoyed knowing Amber would never be far from all three of my girls. I think they liked the idea too.

"Don't remind me, Dad," Meg groaned.

But Amber smiled with her usual enthusiasm. "I can't wait. It will be nice to be back in a classroom that's truly mine, teaching a subject I love. Getting plowed into a snowbank turned out to be the best thing that's ever happened to me. Because it led me here to you."

## *Amber*

I looked out the window of the second-floor room we were using for the bridal party to get ready for the ceremony. The large tent that would hold our reception stood like a citadel atop the rolling slope that led down to the river behind The Snowflake Inn. Unlike a year ago, the sky was a mix of sun and clouds, not the blizzard conditions that led to this day. The clouds were dark and producing flurries, which only seemed right. I actually wanted some snow, and not just because it meant business for the inn.

We'd taken a risk with the tent for our reception. I'd suggested our dining room. It was the only space large enough in Homer Pass, but Hunter didn't want me to feel odd because that's where he'd married Jenn. He said I deserved my special day with no shadows from the past. I loved him for thinking of me that way, but I forced him to agree that if the weather turned bad, the dining room would be plan B.

The ceremony would be in the lobby with just family and close friends, but the town and our hotel guests were all invited to the reception. It was going to be big. The inn was sold out for the weekend, and there hadn't even been a decent snowfall yet. Things had changed so much in a year. We had one special guest. I had been sure to invite the Smalls to the ceremony; it just seemed right that the family that had thought Hunter and I were married two days after we met should be here to see it become a reality.

Janine had just left after helping me with my hair and makeup. My chestnut mane had been put up in a chignon bun with tendrils hanging down to frame my face. I was still wrapped in one of the inn's fluffy white robes. Just like the one I had fallen in love with my first night here. The one I was wearing the night when I held Hunter against my chest and told him everything would be alright. I smiled at the memory of how wonderful his head felt against my bare breast. It still did.

I spied the white gown hanging on the back of the door. I hadn't intended to go with a fancy wedding dress, but the girls had convinced me it was necessary. They wanted to see me 'like a real bride', as Amy had put it. They helped me pick it out, and it was perfect. It was me, and I smiled because Snow had encouraged me to go with the strapless gown that highlighted my 'perfect boobies', one of the features she knew her dad loved about me. God, it kind of freaked me out I was about to have a seventeen-year-old stepdaughter that could talk to me about things like that.

The ceremony was an hour away, and I should put the dress on, but I was waiting as long as I could. Patty wasn't back yet to help me. But that was just an excuse. I was scared to put it on too soon because of the roiling nausea in my stomach. It had nothing to do with nerves about marrying Hunter. I'd never been more certain I was doing the right thing in my life.

A belch that felt a little too solid had me sprinting into the bathroom just in time to take another turn driving the porcelain bus. I had just finished emptying the contents of my stomach when Patty returned, dropping a brown paper bag on the vanity and kneeling to gently rub my back.

"Oh, honey. I'm so sorry you're going through this on your big day."

I pressed a smile to my lips as I stood and went to the sink to rinse my mouth out. I wasn't going to thank her with barf breath. "Thanks," I said. "I didn't think you were going to make it back in time."

She laughed. "Well, you're the one who insisted I drive all the way to Breckenridge because you didn't want to risk someone seeing me buying these at the IGA three minutes away."

I couldn't help but roll my eyes. Snow must be rubbing off on me. "You know how small towns are by now. I couldn't risk someone saying something to Hunter before I did."

"You don't even know what there is to say yet."

"That's my point. If someone said something…" I didn't want to finish that thought. I reached into the bag and pulled out a package and ripped it open. It had been years, but there was no way I was going to forget how it worked. "Here goes nothing."

Twenty minutes later, I was staring down at three identical white sticks. All with two pick lines staring back at me. "Looks pretty conclusive to me," Patty said, wrapping her arm around my now wedding gown clad shoulders. "Don't you think?"

I nodded, biting my bottom lip. The impossible, or at least highly improbable, had happened.

I was pregnant.

Patty rushed to dab a leak from the corner of my eye before it could ruin my makeup. "Should I tell him first? What if he doesn't want another child? We never even talked about this because we didn't think it was possible."

Before she could answer me, three girls and their aunt burst into the room with all the excitement and chatter one would expect on a day like today. I quickly tossed the evidence back into the paper bag and tucked it into the corner out of sight, hoping that they wouldn't notice.

Janine looked at me from head to toe and fought back tears. "Oh, Amber," she sighed. "Hunter is going to lose his mind."

"Is that a good thing?" I asked, trying to lighten the moment. My tummy was twisting again, but this time it was the jitters, not morning sickness. I was just minutes away from marrying Hunter. How could that be?

"It's a very good thing," she said, pulling me into a hug.

"You look beautiful, Momma," Amy said, her eyes wide and grinning from ear to ear. Not long after I returned on Christmas Eve, the girls asked if they could call me Momma. Jenn would always be Mom, but I couldn't just be Amber. We had to find a mop to clean up the tears of joy

I shed.

"Thank you, Amy. You look beautiful too. So grown-up." The girls were part of the wedding too. Amy was the flower girl, Snow and Meg joined Janine as bride's maids and Patty was my maid of honor. Maybe it was overkill. The wedding party nearly equaled the size of the guest list, but I couldn't imagine leaving any of them out. Josh and Leo were standing up with Hunter.

"I hope I look this pretty when I get married," Meg added.

I hugged her close. "You'll be even more beautiful because it will be your special day."

"Are you ready? Walter's already waiting at the top of the stairs," Janine asked. I had an idea, and I was debating asking the girls what they thought. I still didn't know how Hunter would react. Maybe I should tell him before the ceremony, just in case he was upset and thought I'd tricked him.

I didn't know what to do.

The only one who hadn't commented on my dress was Snow, and she was the one who picked it out. I hoped she hadn't changed her mind and thought the dress was too revealing. "What do you think, Snow? Do I look ready?"

I turned to face her. I wanted her honest opinion. It was as if she were looking straight through me. "Snow?" Slowly her eyes went back into focus, and she smiled. The next moment she wrapped her arms around me in a bone-crushing hug.

"Yes, you look ready," she whispered in my ear. "You should definitely do it. He's going to be over the moon." Her words took me by surprise, and I struggled to catch up and understand her meaning. She stepped back and placed her hand on my belly. "Boy," she mouthed silently, nodding her head.

She had seen it. My eyes widened, and my mouth hung open. She nodded again, smiling like a loon.

"What is it? What's wrong?" Janine asked.

And before I could form words to answer, Snow cut in. "It's a secret, Auntie Janine, but Momma is going to tell you real soon. Won't you, Momma?" Just to be a little bit bratty, she put extra emphasis on Momma.

Logic told me it wasn't real, that I couldn't trust it, but experience is the greatest teacher. Snow could see things the rest of us couldn't. I grabbed a tissue and dabbed the corners of my eyes. "Nothing is wrong." I smiled. "In fact, everything is perfect."

Moments later, I was walking down the grand stairway into the lobby holding my stepfather's arm. When we turned at the base of the stairs and as soon as I saw Hunter, my breath caught in my throat. He was so handsome. I was the luckiest girl in the world, and in just a few moments he would officially be mine. And the look in his eyes told me he felt exactly the same way.

Superintendent Miller was also a justice of the peace, and she performed our ceremony. She gave a lovely message talking about Hunter as a boy and how she and I had grown close in my brief time at the school. We exchanged our vows, and I didn't bother to fight back tears listening to the heartfelt words he shared about his feelings toward me. Hunter declared his intent, and then she turned to me.

"Do you, Amber, take Hunter to be your lawfully wedded husband? To have and to hold, in sickness and in health, in good times and not so good times, for richer or poorer, keeping yourself unto him for as long as you both shall live?"

As subtly as I could manage, I slipped my left hand behind my back, and Snow slipped the little white plastic device into my palm. My heart was pounding so loudly in my chest that I was sure that the guests at the reception could hear it outside. Slowly, I brought my hand around and placed it over Hunter's. And with confidence I wasn't entirely convinced I possessed, I spoke the most important words of my life. "We do."

I could hear Janine gasp behind me. There were murmurs from the others who were gathered around to watch our union, but Hunter's brow creased, and his head tilted to the side as he tried to process my words. Gradually he noticed that I had placed something in his hand.

He stared at it blankly for…one. Two. Three. Four. Realization washed over his expression. "We?" His voice was an octave higher than I'd ever heard it before.

I bit my bottom lip and nodded. "We."

In an instant, I was off my feet, being swung in circles. His mouth crashed into mine, and I could taste his salty tears mixing with mine. He sat me back on my feet to the sound of laughter and applause. We were pressed together in the biggest and best group hug ever.

Somewhere over the din of congratulations and sobs of joy I could hear Superintendent Miller. "I now pronounce you husband and wife." I heard the laughter in her voice. "Hunter, I'd tell you, you may kiss the bride, but you never were very good at waiting for instructions."

We danced and talked and laughed the afternoon away with our friends and family, especially the family I've found. Word spread quickly about the additional reason for our celebration. By some miracle, sparkling cider had been found to toast to our lives together. It certainly hadn't been pre-planned. I suspected Tom had made a special trip to the IGA and cleared off its shelves. Ah, the benefits of a small town. It didn't matter that he'd closed for the afternoon for our special occasion.

I had asked him about closing on the traditionally busy day before Thanksgiving. All he did was shrug his shoulder and smile. "Everyone in town is going to be celebrating with you at the inn. Who's going to be shopping? And if they aren't bright enough to plan ahead, they can have Spam. Everyone around here has a can or two in the cupboard. You know, for when we get a four-foot snowstorm. No one in their right mind drives in one of those. God knows it ain't safe to drive when Leo's out with his damn plow."

He was correct. I hadn't been in my right mind then. But everything was so right now. I knew we'd have our troubles, but there was a voice inside that said we'd find a way. Because love always finds a way.

Afternoon bled into evening, and our guests made their way home or up to their rooms in the inn behind us. Leaving us with hugs, kisses and wishes for a happy life together. Hunter and I stood by an open flap in the tent looking out over the beautiful view of the mountains beyond. The moon peeked out from between the clouds just as a squall blotted out the view. The girls rushed out along with the twins and danced in the snow with squeals of unbridled joy. Before I knew it, Hunter and I joined them, and then Janine, Patty, Janet, Leo and Josh followed. Even my mother and Walter couldn't resist. Me and my family dancing in the snow. What a dif-ference a year makes. What a difference finding love in all its forms makes.

I love winter. The purple skies after a storm that's wrapped the world in a cozy blanket of white. The brisk winds that wash over you and make you feel alive. Every time I see a snowflake, I know I'm home.

*-The End-*

# Acknowledgements

There are so many people without whom this book would not have become a reality. First and foremost, my family, friends and the handful of coworkers who know my secret second identity. Special thanks to my mom, who promises she skips the spicy scenes. I can't afford that much therapy. Sarah, I'm so grateful for all those times when we spent more time talking about this book than my caseload.

Thanks to the wonderful community of authors I have met both online and in person over the past few years. From aspiring newbies, like me, to best-selling champs, you have all been so gracious and giving of time and honest advice.

To my outstanding beta readers, especially Katie, Marissa, Kim, Isabella, and Jenny, who all pointed out the hard truths when I needed it, but also encouraged me and kept me motivated to finish this marathon.

For the understanding and patience of my cover designer, Lynn, who took my vague ideas and made them a reality, and for your patience, when I got a little picky, thank you. And to my vastly underpaid editor, thank you for making me look good!

And last, but by no means least, a very special thank you to N.H. Every time I wrote Snow, I saw your face. Your infectious enthusiasm, incredible resilience despite a mountain of challenges to climb over, and, most of all, your steadfast belief in the power of love to heal everything. I love your sass and eye rolls. I appreciate your patience when translating from teen to English. And the next time the mean girls get to you, remember they've never inspired a character in a book and you have!

Thank you. Thank you. Thank you. I could never have done this without all of you, and I am eternally grateful.

# About the Author

## Bryn Byrnes

Bryn began writing, not to be a professional writer, but to work through all the complex emotions felt during the 9 to 5 work as a mental health counselor. Who'd have guessed that it would come out as a steamy contemporary romance?

Fortunate to travel the world, Bryn's roots lie along New England's rocky coast where he can frequently be found walking his writing partner, Beau, a six-year-old golden retriever. Inspiration for Bryn's stories comes from watching and listening to all the fascinating people encountered along the way.

When not chained to the keyboard, Bryn is active on Facebook and Instagram. We'd love to hear from you there or contact us directly through his website https://www.brynbyrnes.com/